**Peter May** was born and raised in Scotland. He was an award-winning journalist at the age of twenty-one and a published novelist at twenty-six. When his first book was adapted as a major drama series for the BBC, he quit journalism and during the high-octane fifteen years that followed, became one of Scotland's most successful television dramatists. He created three prime-time drama series, presided over two of the highest-rated serials in his homeland as script editor and producer, and worked on more than 1,000 episodes of ratings-topping drama before deciding to leave television to return to his first love, writing novels.

His passion for detailed research for his books has taken him behind the closed doors of the Chinese Police force, to the kitchen of a three-star Michelin chef, and down the Paris catacombs; he has worked as an online private detective, was inducted as a Chevalier of the Grand Order of Gaillac wines and earned honorary membership of the Chinese Crime Writers' Association.

He has won several literature awards in France and received the USA's Barry Award for *The Blackhouse*, the first in his internationally bestselling Lewis Trilogy, and the ITV Crime Thriller Awards Book Club Best Read for *Entry Island*.

He now lives in south-west France with his wife, writer Janice Hally.

BY PETER MAY

## The Enzo Files

*Extraordinary People*
*The Critic*
*Blacklight Blue*
*Freeze Frame*
*Blowback*
*Cast Iron*

## The China Thrillers

*The Firemaker*
*The Fourth Sacrifice*
*The Killing Room*
*Snakehead*
*The Runner*
*Chinese Whispers*
*The Ghost Marriage: A China Novella*

## The Lewis Trilogy

*The Blackhouse*
*The Lewis Man*
*The Chessmen*

## Standalone Novels

*Entry Island*
*Runaway*
*Coffin Road*

## Non-fiction

*Hebrides* with David Wilson

# PETER MAY

# CHINESE WHISPERS

includes the exclusive China novella

## THE GHOST MARRIAGE

riverrun

First published in Great Britain in 2004 by Coronet Books
This paperback edition published in 2017 by

riverrun

Quercus Editions Ltd
Carmelite House
50 Victoria Embankment
London EC4Y 0DZ

An Hachette UK company

A CIP catalogue record for this book is available
from the British Library

ISBN 978 1 78429 534 9
EBOOK ISBN 978 1 78206 554 8

10 9 8

Typeset by CC Book Production
Printed and bound in Great Britain by Clays Ltd, Elcograf S.p.A.

For Tom and Lesley

He that hath eyes to see and ears to hear may convince himself that no mortal can keep a secret. If his lips are silent, he chatters with his fingertips, betrayal oozes out of him at every pore.

Sigmund Freud, 1905
('Fragment of an Analysis of a Case of Hysteria')
By permission of Paterson-Marsh Ltd, London

# SUNDAY

# PROLOGUE

*She sits in the lobby watching the Western women drift by, heady strands of exotic scent lingering in their wake. They mask their age with dyed blonde hair and painted faces, drape themselves in haute couture and walk with style on heels that would kill. Skin as pale as ivory, eyes green or blue or hazel. Startling. Bizarre. They have everything she aspires to: money, men, carelessness with a freedom they take for granted. But it is an aspiration she will never realise. For she will never see tomorrow.*

*She catches a glimpse of her reflection. So much light and glass, polished steel and shining marble. She is everywhere she looks. And, by contrast, she is shocked by her plainness. It is only too apparent to her, even beneath the veil of make-up; the slash of red on her lips; the eyes she has tried to make seem a little less slanted; the curl she has attempted to tong into limp black hair. She feels dowdy, ugly.*

*She becomes aware, then, of a man leaning against the desk at Reception undressing her with his eyes, anxious to catch hers so that she knows what is in his mind. He is not ashamed of his lust and it makes her uncomfortable. She has good legs, long and slender. Her skirt is short to make the most of them. But she uncrosses them now, and presses her knees firmly together. She knows what it is he wants, and she knows it is not her.*

*A voice speaks her name. Close by. Soft, gentle. She turns, startled by its intimacy, and he is smiling down at her. He is older than she imagined, but his hair is full and dark and he is not unattractive. And there is something reassuring about his being Chinese, too. She jumps to her feet, drawing full lips back over white teeth in her brightest smile. He will be no ticket to a better life, but neither will he make false promises, and he will know the value of the money he puts in her hand when it is all over. So simple. The undulating melody of her cellphone bringing his response to her two-line ad in the Beijing paper. A price agreed, a rendezvous arranged. She glances over her shoulder as he sweeps her towards the revolving door, and sees the disappointment in the eyes of the Westerner at Reception. Unfulfilled fantasies. And she feels the power of denial.*

*She is shocked by the cold of this late fall night, lulled into a false sense of warmth by the extravagant heating of the foreigners' hotel. The municipal government has only just turned on the city's heating system, a week later than usual to save money. She pulls her leather jacket more tightly around herself and slips her arm through his, hoping it will be warmer in his car.*

*But if he has a car, it is nowhere nearby. They walk east on Jianguomenwai for a long time, late-night traffic dwindling on the boulevard, the occasional bikers drifting past them like ghosts in the dark of the cycle lane. All the time he talks to her, like he has known her for years. About some new restaurant in Chongwen district, a hat he bought in Wangfujing. He is easy company, but she wishes they would reach his car soon. The digital display on the clock on the far corner of Dongdoqiao Road, above the Beijing Yan Bao Auto BMW franchise, shows a quarter past midnight. It flashes alternately* a temperature reading of minus two. The lights go out in Sammie's Café, which claims to be the place in Beijing where East eats West. The last burger-chomping patrons have long gone, probably on the last subway train at eleven-forty. The gates of the Beijing Subway are drawn now and padlocked, the ticket hall beyond brooding in silent darkness. The sidewalk is deserted here, shutters drawn on supermarket windows, a news-stand battened down for the night. Gold characters on red hoardings reflect light from distant street lamps. Xiushuimarket. Silk Street. A gaping black hole leading to a narrow alleyway where stallholders closed up for the night hours ago.

To her surprise, they turn into the tiny market street, and are swallowed up immediately by its darkness. She hesitates, but his grip on her arm only tightens, and her surprise turns to alarm. She wants to know where they are going. Where is his car? He has no car, he tells her, and he cannot take her home. Here they will not be disturbed. She protests. It is too cold. He promises to keep her warm. And perhaps another hundred yuan . . .

She is slightly mollified, and reluctantly allows him to lead her deeper into the alley. Here, in the day, thousands of people clamour and haggle for bargains, stallholders shouting and spitting and throwing the dregs of cold green tea across the flagstones. She has been here many times, but never seen it like this. Cold, deserted, shuttered up. Above the stalls, on the east side, the lights of apartment buildings seem to plunge the alley into even deeper gloom. On the west side, three-storey luxury apartment blocks lie empty, as yet unsold. She glances back. The lights of the boulevard seem a long way away. Up ahead, the street lamps lining the road outside the US Embassy Visa Office seem feeble, devoured by the night.

*Her eyes are adapting now. She can make out signs for silk carpets, fresh water pearls, 'cloisonné', seal carving. She wishes she were somewhere else, fulfilling the fantasies of the man at the reception desk, perhaps. In some warm hotel room.*

*They are almost at the far end of the alley when he propels her into an opening, and she feels the freezing cold of metal gates pressing up against her back. She feels his breath on her neck, lips grazing her skin, and she tenses for the inevitable. It never gets any easier. But he steps back and says she should relax. He takes a pack of Russian cheroots from his coat pocket and his lighter flares briefly in the dark. She fumbles in her purse for her cigarettes and he lights one for her. She is still shivering from the cold, but less scared now. He leans against the wall, talking about the demolition in the north of the city and the new apartment blocks they are building there. He blows smoke into the air and watches it drift past a banner forbidding smoking. He asks her where she lives, and if she has a day-job. And she tells him about the antiques stall at Panjiayuan, and about her mother, and has no inkling of the contempt he has for her. She thinks his smile reflects his interest. She thinks his eyes are kind.*

*She finishes her cigarette and he tosses his cheroot into the darkness. Embers scatter as it hits the ground. He steps closer, a hand slipping into the warmth beneath her jacket, his hand searching for small breasts pushed up into fullness by the Wonderbra sent by God for Chinese women. Hot breath on her face. She can smell the bitter smoke of his cheroot. His hand lingers only briefly at her breast before gliding up to her neck, fingers softly encircling it as he finds her lips with his and she chokes back her repugnance. Only, she has no breath. And she cannot speak. And for a moment she wonders what has happened* to her, before realising that his fingers have turned to steel and are crushing her windpipe. She struggles to free herself, but he is far too strong. His face is still close to hers, watching as she fights for a life that is fading so quickly. His eyes are wide and full of something she has never seen before. She cannot believe she will die like this. Not here. Not now. Lights flash in her eyes, and the fight in her starts to ebb. Too fast. Too easy. All too easy. Then darkness descends like a warm cloud. And she is gone. To a place she has never dreamed of.

Her slight frame has become a dead weight in his arms, surprisingly heavy in lifelessness, as he lowers her to the ground, arranging her carefully on the paving stones. He glances quickly each way down the alley, and can hear the guard stamping his feet just beyond the far end of the market street, where embassyland stretches off into silent darkness. There is a frisson for him, knowing that there is someone so close. So oblivious. It somehow emphasises his superiority. Crouching beside her, he looks at the dead girl on the ground and runs fingertips lightly over the features of her face. She is still warm. Blood still oxygenated. There is a tiny smile on his lips as he draws the knife from beneath his coat.

# MONDAY

# CHAPTER ONE

## I

She woke with a start, heart pounding, consciousness holding on to the distant echo of the cry which had invaded her dreams. Dreams which hardly ever took her far from the surface, lingering always in the shallows where light and hearing were only a breath away. She sat upright, drawing that breath now, eyes quickly forming shapes from shadows, broken light from the street cut in small pieces by the branches of trees. She never drew the curtains. That way she could see fast, without blinding herself with sudden light.

There it was again, tiny and muffled, and unaccountably devastating in its effect. Nature had surprised her with this sensitivity, tuned to detect the smallest sound, even in sleep, triggering the fight or flight response that had her awake and alert in seconds. There was a third cry, and then a fourth, followed by a long grizzle and a series of sobs, and her alarm subsided into a weary acceptance that she would have to get out of bed. She glanced at the clock display on the bedside cabinet and saw that it was a little after five. Chances were she would not get back to sleep.

She slipped quickly from the bed and lifted her dressing gown from the back of a chair, shivering as she pulled it on and hugged it around herself. The heating would not come on again for another hour, and she still could not get used to the fact that she had no control over it. As she opened the door, she glanced back at the bed and the shape of Li Yan curled up in the foetal position, sheets and blankets pulled tightly around him, the soft, regular purr of his breathing filling the room. And she wondered why Nature did not endow fathers with the same sensitivity.

Li Jon Campbell lay on his back. Somehow he had managed to kick himself free of the quilt and had been wakened by the cold. And now that he was awake, he would discover that he was hungry. Margaret lowered the side of the cot and lifted her son into her arms, scooping up the quilt and wrapping it around him. In another month they would celebrate his first birthday. He was already a big boy. Ugly, Margaret told Li, like his father. Thick, black hair and beautiful slanting almond eyes, he looked like any other Chinese baby. And Margaret might have doubted that there was anything of her in him except for the strangest, startling blue pupils that met hers every time he looked at her. It was odd that it should have been her eyes that she had most obviously given him. She had read that the blue-eye gene was the weakest, and that within a few hundred years would be bred out of the human race entirely. Li Jon was doing his best to redress the balance.

She cuddled and whispered to him as she carried him through to the kitchen to prepare a bottle. She had been too weak after the Caesarian to breastfeed. His crying subsided, and he contented himself with grabbing her nose and holding on to it as if his life depended on it. She pulled herself free as she took him into the sitting room and dropped into a soft chair where she could cradle him and push the rubber teat between his lips. He chewed and sucked hungrily, and Margaret took the moment, as she always did, to find a small island of peace in the shifting sea of her unsettled world.

Not that she ever consciously analysed her position these days. She had long ago stopped doing that. It was not a deliberate decision. More a process of elimination. Her whole life was focused now on her baby, to the exclusion of almost everything else. She could not afford to dwell on her semi-legal status, living unauthorised in the official apartment provided by the Beijing Municipal Police for the father of her child. She survived from visa extension to visa extension without daring to think what she would do if ever her application was refused. She had no real income of her own, except for the money they gave her for occasional lectures at the University of Public Security. She had not wielded her pathologist's knife in almost a year. She was, in fact, no one she would recognise. She would pass herself in the street without noticing. She was less than a shadow of her former self. She was a ghost.

Li Jon was asleep by the time she laid him back in his cot, making sure he was well wrapped and warm. But now she had lost all her own heat, and hurried back to bed, dropping her gown on the chair and slipping between sheets which had also grown cold. She shivered and slid across the bed to the heat radiating from Li Yan's back and buttocks and thighs, and felt his skin burning against hers. He grunted, and she felt the reflex of his muscles as he tried to move away from this source of cold. She tucked in tight and held on.

'What are you doing?' he mumbled sleepily.

'Oh, so you're not dead,' she whispered, and her voice seemed inordinately loud in the dark. 'Or deaf. Or *completely* insensitive.'

'What?' And he half turned towards her, still drowsy and heavy-eyed, clinging to the last vestiges of what had been a deep, dark slumber.

She slid a cold hand across his thigh and found, to her surprise, a full erection. 'What the hell were you dreaming?' she demanded.

He became aware of her cold, and his heat, and felt a warm flood of arousal fill his belly. 'I dreamed I was making love to you,' he said.

'Yeah, right.'

He flipped over so that he was facing her. 'It's been a while.'

'It has,' she acknowledged. She squeezed him and smiled. 'But I see that everything's still in good working order.'

'Maybe we should give it a run out, just to be sure.'

'Maybe we should. It might generate a little more warmth than the central heating.'

'Just a little more . . .' He nuzzled against the cold skin of her neck and felt her shiver as he breathed on her. She felt him grow harder as he dragged his lips across her breast to find a nipple, puckered and hard with cold and arousal. He flicked at it with his tongue and then bit until she moaned, and he ran a hand over her belly in search of the soft blonde hair between her legs. He felt the long, vertical weal of her scar, still ugly and livid. No cosmetic bikini-cut, this. And he knew that she was still self-conscious about it. He moved up to find her lips and the warmth of her mouth, flipping over again to lie between her open legs, and then, half crouching, let her guide him inside her. He felt a shudder running through her whole body, like the deepest sigh, and his cellphone began playing Beethoven's *Ode to Joy*.

'In the name of the sky,' he hissed into the darkness, and immediately felt her go limp beneath him. It was a long time since she had asked him not to answer a call, a final acceptance of the way the dice had fallen. For both of them. And for the briefest of moments, he was tempted himself to let his answering service pick it up. But Margaret was already turning away, the spell broken, the moment lost. He snatched the phone from the bedside cabinet.

'*Wei?*'

Margaret listened bleakly as he had a quickfire exchange in *putonghua* Chinese. A bizarre four-toned cadence that she had never made any real attempt to learn. And yet she knew it was a language her son would speak, and she did not want there to be any part of him she could not understand. Of course, she would teach him English. She would speak to him always in English. But she also knew from her years with Li that there would always be that something Chinese about him that would remain just out of reach.

Li hung up and dropped the phone on the table, rolling on to his back and staring silently at the ceiling. There was a lengthy silence. Their passion had not been spent, but it was gone. Finally he said, 'There's been another one.'

She felt her stomach flip over. 'Another mutilation?' He nodded and she ached for him. She knew how much they troubled him, these killings. It was always worse with a serial killer. The longer you took to catch him, the more people died. In this case young women. Young, fresh-faced prostitutes trying to eke a living in this new, money-driven China. Every new killing was like an accusation of failure. Li's failure. And eventually the guilt would get to him, and he would start to feel responsible for every death. Like he had killed them himself. Like now.

## II

Zhengyi Road was empty as he cycled north in the dark beneath the trees, dry leaves crunching under his tyres. Up ahead, in the brightly lit East Changan Avenue, the first traffic of the day was already cruising the boulevard: buses packed with pale, sleepy faces, taking workers to factories across town; trucks on the first stretch of long journeys on new roads, carrying the industrial produce of the north to the rice fields of the south; office workers in private cars getting in ahead of the rush hour. Where once the cycle lanes would have been choked with early morning commuters, only a few hardy souls now braved the cold on their bicycles. Car ownership was soaring. Public transport had improved beyond recognition – new buses, a new underground line, a light rail system. The bicycle, once the most common mode of transport in Beijing, was rapidly disappearing. An outmoded transport.

At least, that was what the municipal government thought. They had issued an edict to every police station demanding a response time to all incidents of just twelve minutes, an edict well nigh impossible to achieve given the gridlock that seized up the city's road system for most of the day. Some stations had brought in motor scooters, but the municipal authority had refused to license them. And, almost as an afterthought, had also denied officers permission to attend incidents on bicycles. A return to the bike would be a retrograde step, they said. This was the *new* China. And so police cars sat in traffic jams, and average response times remained thirty minutes or longer.

Li had a healthy disregard for edicts. If it was quicker by bike, he took his bike, as he had done for nearly twenty years. As Section Chief he always had a vehicle at his disposal, but he still preferred to cycle to and from work and get motorised only when required. And no one was about to tell the head of Beijing's serious crime squad that he could not ride his bike if he wanted to. This morning, however, as an icy wind blew down Changan Avenue from the west and cut clean through his quilted jacket, he might have preferred to have been sitting behind the wheel of a warm Santana. But that wasn't something he would ever have admitted. Even to himself.

He tucked his head down and pedalled east into the heart of the upmarket Jianguomen district of the city, a flyover carrying him across the Second Ring Road, past a towering blue-lit section of restored city wall. He could see the floodlights illuminating the new City Hall building just to the south. The roar of traffic and exhaust fumes rose up to greet him from below. He quite consciously avoided the thought of the scene that awaited him. They had told him she was the fourth. And with the previous three, whatever his experience and imagination had prepared him for, it had not been enough.

Half a dozen police vehicles were pulled up on the sidewalk at the entrance to the Silk Street Market, engines idling, exhaust fumes rising into the cold morning air. There was a forensics van from Pau Jü Hutong, and Li recognised Pathologist Wang's car parked up beside the body bus from the morgue. It must have broken all speed limits on empty roads to get there before Li, all the way from the new pathology facility out on the north-west perimeter, near the Badaling Expressway. Another planning coup by the municipal government. By the time a detective got there and back, it could take him the best part of a day to attend an autopsy.

The police activity had attracted a large crowd: local residents, curious commuters on their way to work. Numbers had already swelled to over a hundred and were still growing. Not even subzero temperatures could diminish the eternal curiosity of the Chinese. Two dozen uniformed police officers made sure they stayed behind the black and yellow crime scene tape that whipped and hummed in the wind. Li saw the red digital display on the clock tower flash up a temperature of minus six centigrade. He held up his maroon Public Security ID and pushed his bike through the onlookers. A cold-looking officer with a pinched red face saluted and lifted the tape to let him through. Two hundred metres up the alley, Li could see the photographer's lights illuminating the spot where the body had been found. A bunch of detectives and forensics officers stood around it, stamping to keep warm. As Li approached, someone spotted him coming, and they moved aside to let him through, opening up like the curtain on a stage to reveal a scene that looked as if it had been set for maximum theatrical effect.

Wang Xing was crouched beside the body, making a careful examination, latexed fingers already sticky with blood. He turned his face towards Li, pale and bloodless, like a mask from a Peking Opera, and for once had nothing to say.

The girl lay on her back, head turned towards her left shoulder, revealing a seven-inch gash across her throat. Blood had pooled around her head like a ghastly halo. Her face had been so savagely slashed it would be almost impossible to make a visual identification. Her black leather jacket lay open, revealing a white, blood-spattered blouse beneath it. The top few buttons of the blouse had been undone, but it did not otherwise appear to have been disturbed. The girl's arms lay by her side, palms up. Her left leg extended in a line with her body, her right leg was bent at the hip and the knee. Her skirt had been cut open and pulled away to expose the abdomen which had been hacked open from the breastbone to the pubes. The intestines had been drawn out and dragged over the right shoulder, one two-foot piece completely detached and placed between the body and the left arm. What struck Li, apart from an extreme sense of shock, was the impression that this body had been very carefully laid out, as if by some grotesque design. There was something bizarrely unnatural about it. He turned away as he felt his stomach lurch and wished that he still smoked. As if reading his mind, someone held out an open pack. He looked up to see Detective Wu's grim face, jaw chewing manically on the ubiquitous gum. Li waved him aside and stepped out of the circle of light. The image of the dead girl was burned by the photographer's lights on to his retinas and he could not get rid of it. She could only have been nineteen or twenty. Just a child. He felt Wu's presence at his shoulder, breathing smoke into the light. 'Who found her?'

Wu spoke softly, as if to speak normally might disturb the dead. Li was surprised. Wu did not usually show such sensitivity. 'Shift worker on his bike, taking what he thought was a short cut home.'

Li frowned. 'He didn't know they'd fenced off the road at the other end?'

Wu shrugged. 'Apparently not, Chief. He almost ran over her. You can see his tyre tracks in the blood. They've taken him to hospital suffering from shock.'

'Did you get a statement?'

'Detective Zhao's gone with him.' He took a drag on his cigarette. 'We also spoke to the PLA guard at the embassy end. He was on duty all night.'

Li looked back up the alley. It could only have been a hundred metres. Maybe less. 'And?'

'Heard nothing.'

Li shook his head. Still the girl was there. Every time he blinked. Every time he closed his eyes. He took a deep breath. 'Do we know who she is?'

'Found her ID card in her purse, along with a couple of hundred yuan. Her name's Guo Huan. She's eighteen years old. Lives in Dongcheng District, not that far from Section One.' He carefully removed an evidence bag from his pocket and held it up to the light for Li to see. 'We also found this . . .' Trapped between the sheets of clear plastic was what looked like a cutting from a newspaper or magazine. Li took it and held it to catch the spill-off light from the photographer's lamps, and saw that it was a two-line ad from the personal columns of one of Beijing's what's-on magazines. *Cute Chinese Girl looks for Mr Right. I am slim, well-educated and work in antiques. Please send me e-mail. Or telephone.* Thinly disguised code for a prostitute seeking customers. There was an e-mail address and a cellphone number. Wu blew smoke through his nostrils like dragonfire. 'He's making a fool of us, this guy, Chief. We've got to get him.'

'We've got to get him,' Li snapped, 'not because he's making a fool of us, but because he's killing young girls.' He turned back towards the body as Pathologist Wang stepped away from it, peeling off his bloody gloves and dropping them in a plastic sack. As was his habit, he had an unlit cigarette clamped between his lips. He bent towards the flame of Wu's proffered lighter, and as he took the first drag Li saw that his hand was trembling.

Characteristically Wang would make some smart quip, or literary allusion, after examining a body at a crime scene. His way of coping. But this morning, 'Shit,' was all he said.

Li braced himself. 'You want to tell me about it?'

'I never saw anything like it,' Wang said, and there was a tremor, too, in his voice. 'And I've seen some shit, Chief, you know that.'

'We all have.'

Wang's dark eyes burned with a curious intensity. 'This guy's insane. A twenty-four-carat maniac.' He stabbed at his mouth with his cigarette and drew on it fiercely. 'A similar pattern to the others. Strangled. I can't tell till autopsy if she was dead when he cut her throat. Unconscious certainly, and lying on the ground. He would have been kneeling on her right side, cutting from left to right so that the blood from the left carotid artery would flow away from him. The facial stuff . . .' He shook his head and took another pull at his cigarette. 'She was dead when he did that. And the internal stuff.' He looked at Li very directly. 'She's a mess in there. From what I can see, it's not just the womb he's taken this time. There's a kidney gone as well.'

'Organ theft?' Wu asked.

The pathologist shook his head. 'Not a chance. Not in these conditions. And it wasn't surgically removed. Both the uterus and the kidney were hacked out. He may have some anatomical knowledge, but he's certainly no doctor. He's a butcher.'

'Maybe literally,' Li said.

'Maybe,' Wang agreed. 'But even a butcher would use a knife with more care. This was uncontrolled. Frenzied.'

'How sure are you it is the same killer?' Li asked.

'Completely,' Wang said, reversing his usual reticence to commit himself to anything. He fished in his jacket pocket and pulled out a clear plastic evidence bag. He held it up to the light, and Li saw the half-inch remains of a brown Russian cheroot. 'If we get as good a DNA sample off this as we got off the others, we'll know for certain.'

### III

The sun sneaked and glanced and angled its way off windows in high-rise apartments and office blocks as it lifted off the eastern horizon and beamed directly along the east–west boulevards of the Beijing grid system. As it rose, it coloured the sky blue. A painfully clear sky, free from pollution or mist, dipping to pale orange and yellow along its eastern fringe. A silvery sliver of moon was caught falling in the west behind the purple-hued mountains. Li's breath billowed and wreathed around his head as he pedalled slowly north, weaving through the traffic along Chaoyangmen Nanxiao Da Jie.

Everywhere the building work went on, rising up behind green-clad scaffolding from the rubble of the old city. Cranes stalked the skies overhead, the roar of diggers and pneumatic drills already filling the early morning air. Most of the street stalls he had cycled past for years were gone; the hawkers peddling hot buns and sweet potatoes from sparking braziers, the old lady feeding taxi drivers from her big tureen of soup, the *jian bing* sellers. New pavements had been laid, new trees planted. And all along Dongzhimen, east of Section One, new apartment blocks lined the street where just a year before squads of men equipped only with hammers had begun knocking down the walls of the old *siheyuan* courtyards which had characterised Beijing for centuries. It was cleaner, fresher, and there was no doubt that life for ordinary Beijingers was improving faster than it had done in five thousand years. But, still, Li missed the old city. He was unsettled by change.

So it was comforting for him to know that Mei Yuan was still at the corner of Dongzhimen where she had sold *jian bing* from her bicycle stall for years. During the demolition and construction work she had been forced to move to the opposite corner of the Dongzhimen-Chaoyangmen intersection. And then she had faced opposition to her return from the owners of a new restaurant built on her old corner. It was a lavish affair, with large picture windows and red-tiled canopies sweeping out over the sidewalk, brand-new red lanterns dancing in the breeze. Street hawkers, they told her, had no place here now. Besides, she was putting off their customers. She would have to find somewhere else to sell her peasant pancakes. Li had paid them a quiet visit. Over a beer, which the owner had been only too anxious to serve him, Li had pointed out that Mei Yuan had a licence to sell *jian bing* wherever she wanted. And since the officers of Section One of the Criminal Investigation Department of the Beijing Municipal Police, just across the road, liked to get their *jian bing* from Mei Yuan – on that particular corner – the restaurant might like to reconsider its attitude to the *jian bing* seller. It did.

Li saw steam rising from the tin-roofed glass cover that sat over the hotplate and the pancake mix and bowls of sauces and spices that surrounded it. An elderly couple were paying Mei Yuan for their pancakes as Li cycled up and leaned his bicycle against the wall of the restaurant. He watched them bite hungrily into their hot savoury packages as they headed off along Ghost Street, where thousands of lanterns swayed among the trees and the city's new generation of rich kids would have spent the night eating and drinking in restaurants and cafés until just a few hours ago. Mei Yuan turned a round, red face in his direction and grinned. 'Have you eaten?' she asked. The traditional Beijing greeting.

'Yes, I have eaten,' he replied. The traditional response. If you had eaten and were not hungry, then all was well.

'Good,' she said. 'A *jian bing*?'

'Of course.'

She poured creamy mix on to the hotplate and scraped it round into a perfect pancake. 'You're early this morning.'

'A call-out.'

She detected something in his voice and threw him a quick glance. But she said nothing. She knew that if he wanted to talk about it he would. She broke an egg and smeared it over the pancake, sprinkling it with seeds before flipping it over to paint it with savoury and spicy sauces. Her fingers were red raw with the cold.

Li watched her as she worked; hair tucked up in a bun beneath her white cap, quilted blue jacket over jogpants, sweatshirt and trainers. Her white cotton coat hung open, several sizes too small. She made a poor living from her pancakes, augmented only by the money Li and Margaret paid her to baby-sit for Li Jon. Both Li and Mei Yuan had lost people close to them during the Cultural Revolution. He, his mother. She, her son. Now one was a surrogate for the other. There wasn't anything Li wouldn't have done for the old lady. Or she for him.

Her demeanour never changed. Her smooth round face was remarkably unlined, crinkling only when she smiled, which was often. Whatever misery she had suffered in her life she kept to herself. And there had been plenty. Wrenched from a university education and forced to work like a peasant in the fields. A baby lost. A husband long gone.

'What are you reading?' he asked, and he pulled out the book she had tucked down behind her saddle.

'A wonderful story,' she said. 'A triumph of humanity over ignorance.'

'*To Kill A Mockingbird*,' he read from the title in English.

'The writer is completely inside the little girl's head,' Mei Yuan said, and Li could see from her face that she was transported to some place on the other side of the world she would never see. Her escape from a life that offered little else. 'She must have been in that place herself, to write it like that.'

She put a square of deep-fried whipped eggwhite on top of the pancake, broke it in four and deftly folded it into a brown paper bag which she handed to Li. He dropped some notes in her tin and took a bite. It tasted wonderful. Spicy, savoury, hot. He could not imagine a life that did not start each day with a *jian bing*. 'I have a riddle for you,' he said.

'I hope it's harder than the last one.'

He threw her a look. 'Two coal miners,' he said. 'One is the father of the other's son. How is this possible?' She tossed her head back and laughed. A deliciously infectious laugh that had him smiling too, albeit ruefully. 'What?' he said. 'What?' A group of passing cyclists turned to stare at them, wondering what was so amusing.

'You're not serious?'

'Is it really so easy? I mean, I spent ages trying to work out if maybe one was the father, and the other the stepfather . . .'

'Oh, Li Yan, you didn't!' Her smile was full of mock pity. 'It's obvious that they're husband and wife.'

'Well, yes it is,' Li said. 'I just didn't see it immediately, that's all.' He had found a website on the internet which specialised in riddles. But none of them were in the same class as the ones Mei Yuan dreamed up for him.

'I have one for you,' she said.

'I thought you might.' He wolfed down another mouthful of steaming pancake and waited in trepidation.

She watched him chewing for a moment, reflecting on the problem she was about to set him. 'Two deaf mutes are planting rice in a paddy field, far from their village in Hunan Province,' she said. 'It takes them an hour to make their way from one end of the paddy to the other. They have just finished lunch. One has the food, the other the drink. By sign language, they agree to meet again and share their food and drink when they have finished planting the field. They each have to plant another ten rows. When he has finished his work, the man with the food can't see his friend anywhere, he waits for a while, and then, thinking his friend has gone back to the village, he eats the food himself. The next morning, he wakes up to find the other man shaking him, signing furiously, and accusing him of abandoning him and keeping his food to himself. But the man with the food says he only ate it because the other one went off with the drink and abandoned him. The man with the drink insists he was there all along! They are both telling the truth. How can this be?'

Li groaned. 'Mei Yuan, I give you two lines. You give me a novel. Too much detail.'

'Ah,' Mei Yuan grinned. 'It is in the detail that you will find the devil.'

Li waved his hand dismissively. 'I'm not even going to think about it right now.'

'You have more important things to think about?'

His face darkened, as if a cloud had cast its shadow on him. He closed his eyes, and still the image of the girl was there. 'Yes,' he said. 'I have.'

And she knew she had crossed a line into dangerous territory. She made light of it. 'Maybe by tonight you will have had time to think.'

'Tonight?' Li frowned.

'Before you go to the Great Hall of the People. I have never been in the Great Hall of the People. If I were not baby-sitting, I would have gone to see you there myself.'

'The Great Hall of the People,' Li muttered. He had forgotten that it was tonight. How could he have forgotten? He would, after all, be centre stage. He cringed again with embarrassment at the thought of it. The Public Security Ministry was anxious to improve the image of the police, and with increasing coverage of crime by the media, Li had become one of the most high profile senior officers in the public eye. He was still young – under forty – tall, powerfully built and, if not exactly handsome, then striking in his looks. He had been considered perfect for the propaganda posters. And some PR person in the Minister's office had dreamed up the idea of a People's Award for Crime Fighting, to be presented in the full glare of publicity at the Great Hall of the People. Li's objections had been dismissed out of hand. Summoned to the office of the city's Police Commissioner, it had been made clear to him that this was not a matter in which he had any choice. When news of it leaked out, it had led to some good-humoured mickey-taking by some of his junior officers at Section One. But he had also become aware of jealousy among more senior officers at police headquarters downtown where he knew he had enemies. His spirits dipped.

'I have other riddles to solve today, Mei Yuan. Why don't you try yours on Margaret?'

'Hah!' Mei Yuan grunted. 'She is always too quick. She is smarter than you.'

Li tossed his paper wrapping in the bin. 'Thanks for the vote of confidence.' He mounted his bike.

'You are welcome. Maybe I will ask her, when I see her at the park.'

Li wheeled down off the sidewalk on to the road. 'She won't be there for *tai chi* today, Mei Yuan. She has to go to the visa office to get her extension application in.'

'She still has to do that?' Mei Yuan raised an eyebrow. 'Don't you have *any* influence?'

Li snorted. 'You know the authorities frown on our relationship, Mei Yuan. Pin-up policeman living in sin with foreign devil. Doesn't exactly fit the image of the poster campaign It's only tolerated because everyone pretends it doesn't exist. Besides, the Entry-Exit Police are a law unto themselves.' He pushed off into the road to the accompaniment of a symphony of horns and called back over his shoulder, 'See you tonight.'

## IV

The new visa office was opposite the Dongzhimen Bridge on the Second Ring Road. It was too far for Margaret to cycle with Li Jon strapped into the baby seat in front of her handlebars. Life had been simpler when the visa office was located in its original crumbling grey brick building on the east side of the Forbidden City, five minutes from the apartment. Now its replacement, in a twin-towered monstrosity of stone, glass and steel, was a twenty-five-minute taxi ride on a good traffic day.

Her taxi parked up beneath the flyover, and the driver settled down, meter still running, to read his *Beijing Youth Daily* while Margaret struggled to get the baby buggy out of the trunk. She was not in the best of humours by the time she had negotiated four lanes of traffic and a revolving glass door that wouldn't revolve. And since the counters were on the first floor, there was also the escalator to contend with, which was never easy with the buggy.

The concourse was busy this morning, queues forming at all the counters, raised voices echoing off marble floors and walls. Margaret queued for ten minutes to get her application form, and then made her way to the line of desks to sit down and fill it in. Li Jon was not being co-operative. He had been fed and changed before she left, but something was troubling him, and he had been fractious and prone to complaining all morning. Much as she loved him, she found his periods of unaccountable bad temper difficult to cope with. She was sure that one day she would be able to have an intelligent conversation with him and ask him what was wrong. But until then it was a guessing game. Colic, teething, stomach-ache, hunger, dirty diaper. Any one of any number of things. She gritted her teeth and filled out her form.

There was an unusually large number of people queuing at the foreign counter today and she had to wait nearly twenty minutes before she was seen, acutely aware of the meter in her taxi clocking up every second of it. A frosty young woman in a neatly pressed black police uniform, hair scraped back severely from a pockmarked face, demanded Margaret's passport. She gave it lengthy scrutiny, before turning her attention to Margaret's application for a six-month visa extension. Margaret waited impatiently, Li Jon still griping in the buggy beside her. Finally the girl turned the form back towards Margaret and stabbed it with her pen. 'No,' she said sharply. 'You fill in address here.'

Margaret scowled. 'I filled in my address.' But her heart was pounding. The address she had given was her official address in the staff apartment block at the University of Public Security – an apartment she had not occupied for nearly a year.

'No,' the visa cop barked again. 'You fill in wrong place.'

Margaret looked at the form again and saw that in her hurry she had accidentally filled in the space allocated for a previous address. 'Shit,' she muttered under her breath. She started to score it out and write it in the correct space. But the visa cop pulled the form out from under her pen and started to tear it up.

'No, no, no. You fill out new form.'

Margaret glared at her, barely able to contain her anger or the caustic comment fighting for expression on the tip of her tongue. New China was still bedevilled by the bureaucracy of Old China, and its bureaucrats were just as intransigent. 'Could you give me another form, then, please?' she said through clenched teeth.

'Forms at that counter,' the visa cop said, pointing to the far end of the concourse where Margaret had queued earlier. 'Next.' And the next in line tried to push past. A tall, fat, balding American in a business suit.

But Margaret stood her ground. 'No, wait a minute! I queued for a form. I filled it out. You tore it up. I want you to give me another form and I'll fill it out right here.' She looked at the line of unsympathetic faces behind her. 'And these people can wait.'

But the visa cop just shook her head and pushed Margaret's passport back at her. 'No form here,' she said.

'Chrissake, lady, go get a form,' the fat American said. 'Face it. You're in China.'

As if sensing her tension, Li Jon started to cry. Margaret felt her blood pressure soar. She grabbed the handles of the buggy, spun it around and wheeled it off across the concourse. She hated having to admit defeat. It was another fifteen minutes before she found herself back at the application counter pushing her freshly filled-out form across it at the frozen-faced visa cop, who gave no indication that she had any recollection of their previous encounter.

'Passport,' she said, and Margaret almost threw it at her. Having examined it only fifteen minutes earlier, she proceeded to examine it again in great detail as if for the first time. Then she looked at the form, scrutinising it carefully, section by section. Margaret stood watching her impassively as she entered details into a computer terminal behind the counter. Then she stamped the form several times and pushed a receipt back across the counter, along with the passport. 'Visa over there,' she said, pointing to a young man in uniform sitting further down the same counter. All the people who had been in the line behind Margaret at the visa application desk now stood in the line ahead of her at the visa issuing desk.

Margaret leaned over the counter and said, 'Chicken feet.'

The visa cop looked at her in surprise. 'I am sorry?'

'Someone told me once they were good for the complexion. You should give them a try.' And she wheeled the still wailing Li Jon down to the visa issuing desk. It was petty, childish even, but it made Margaret feel just a tiny bit better.

But as she stood in the queue at the visa issuing desk, she saw Miss Chicken Feet with the bad complexion walk along behind the counter and whisper something in the ear of the issuing officer. The young man looked up and ran his eyes quickly down the line. They rested briefly on Margaret, and then he nodded and turned back to his computer terminal. The girl went back to her desk. Margaret began to worry. When she finally got to the head of the queue, the officer didn't even look at her. He took her receipt and her passport, and his keyboard chattered as he entered data into his computer. He took a thin sheet of official paper from a tray, scribbled on it, and then stamped it with red ink and pushed it across the counter at Margaret. 'Come back in two days for passport,' he said.

'What?' Margaret couldn't believe it.

'Two days,' said the officer. 'Next.'

'I've never had to leave my passport before,' Margaret said.

The officer met her eye for the first time. He was coldly impassive. 'You want visa, you come back in two days. Okay?' And he was already taking the passport from the next in line.

Margaret knew she was beaten. She glanced along the counter and caught Miss Chicken Feet smirking.

## V

Smoke rose from cigarettes, and steam from thermos mugs of green tea. The detectives of Section One sat around the meeting room wrapped in coats and wearing hats. Some even wore gloves. The heating had broken down again.

One wall was covered with photographs taken at four crime scenes. Four young women strangled and savagely mutilated. Each one worse than the last. Sunshine slanted across the wall, bringing cold light to a very dark place. The mood in the room was sombre as they listened to Detective Wu outlining the details of the latest killing. Li watched him pensively. Wu was one of the Section's senior detectives now, but he was still in love with his image. He always had a piece of gum in his mouth and a pair of sunglasses in his breast pocket that he would whip out one-handed and clamp on his face at the first blink of sunshine. Since the sun was shining today he was wearing them pushed back on his forehead. He had been proudly sporting a growth on his upper lip for years, and was considerably chastened when his daughter had brought home a school essay in which she had written of her father, 'He is growing a moustache.' To his credit, he told the story against himself. His own personal uniform consisted of baseball boots, faded denims and a short leather jacket, and he grew his hair just long enough to comb over the thinning patch on top. He had been divorced for nearly five years.

He held up a photograph of the chewed-up remains of a brown Russian cheroot still in its evidence bag. 'It's like a calling card,' he told the room. 'He leaves one of these at every scene. It's no accident. He knows we'll find them. It's like he's saying, here's my DNA. You got my code, but you'll never get my number. The bastard's playing games with us.'

'Why would he do that?' The question came from one of the youngest detectives in the Section. Sang Chunlin was tall and wore dark trousers, black shoes and a black jacket. He, too, had a penchant for American-style shades. His thick black hair, cut short side and back, was long on top and swept back in a quiff. The other detectives called him Elvis.

'If we knew why he did any of it, Elvis, we might be halfway to nailing him,' Wu said.

'Well, whatever motivates him it's not sexual.' This from Detective Zhao. 'He didn't have sex with any of them, did he? There's been no trace of semen found at any of the scenes.'

'We don't know that in this case,' Wu said. 'At least, not until we get the reports back from the autopsy and the lab. But, anyway, who knows how he gets his kicks? He takes bits of them away with him.'

Qian came quietly into the room at the back and slipped into a seat. It was unusual for him to be late. But Li knew there would be a good reason. He nodded a silent acknowledgement to his deputy. Qian was several years older than Li. Steady, reliable, the Section plodder. Li had persuaded his superiors at headquarters that Qian should be given the deputy's job, so that Li could hand him most of the responsibility for running the Section. Qian would be good at that, he had told them. And it would free Li up to take a more active role in leading investigations. And he had been right. It was a partnership that worked well.

The rest of the detectives were now actively engaged in a debate about motivation, a topic of discussion which, until recently, would have been anathema. Traditional Chinese police work was based on the painfully meticulous collection of evidence, leading to culprit and conviction. Only then would motivation become apparent. Unlike the West, where detectives considered motive the starting point of an investigation. But like everything else in China, this too was changing. And Li had been personally instrumental in altering the working practices of Section One.

While he still believed there was value in large group meetings attended by all the detectives, talking through the evidence, discussing the case in the minutest detail, the time it took was no longer a luxury they could afford. The crime rate was soaring as unemployment grew, and it was impossible to keep track of the floating population of itinerant workers moving from city to city. They had to find ways of dealing with crime more quickly and efficiently. They had embraced technology, installing their own Chinese Automated Fingerprint Identification System, CAFIS, at the forensics headquarters at Pau Jü Hutong. Portable computers the size of a briefcase were available to take out on the job. Fingerprints could be taken at any remote location and sent back by landline or cellphone for computer comparison. They had developed software called AutoCAD which could produce scale 3-D computerised re-creations of crime scenes from photographs and a single measurement. They now had access to a computerised ballistics database for the whole of China. And some of the most sophisticated laboratory analysis equipment available had been installed at the new pathology centre in the north of the city. But it was at the sharp end – the working practices of investigating detectives – that reform was most required, and Li had instituted a system of spreading the workload by delegating only two detectives to each case.

It was working well. But this case was different. He needed more men on the job. Each pairing still had its own workload, but every detective in the Section had now been drafted in to work in some capacity on what was in danger of turning into the worst case of serial murder since the People's Republic came into being in 1949.

Li looked again at the photographs on the wall. A grotesque catalogue of inhuman behaviour. And he couldn't help but wonder about motivation. There was something very cold and controlled about all these killings. Pathologist Wang had described the latest attack as *frenzied*, and yet the killer had taken the time to arrange a piece of intestine beside the body, and carefully laid the remaining entrails across the girl's shoulder. In the previous case, he had taken the contents of the girl's purse and arranged them on the ground around her feet. It was bizarre behaviour.

All the victims were prostitutes. They had all been murdered within the same square mile of the city's Jianguomen district, an area where a large population of foreign embassy staff and five-star tourist hotels attracted a slightly higher class of call girl. All had been strangled, although this was not always the cause of death. All had been killed on a weekend. The first victim, twenty-three-year-old Shen Danhua, had been discovered in a quiet cul-de-sac behind the Friendship Store off Jianguomenwai Avenue. Her face and head were so swollen and distorted from strangulation that identification by relatives had been a problem. She had been stabbed thirty-nine times.

There was a gap of three weeks between the first and second murders. The second was found on a building site behind the China World Trade Center by labourers arriving for the early shift. Li looked at the photographs on the wall. They had pinned up a portrait picture of each of the girls to remind them that these were people, not just victims. It was only too easy to become desensitised, to start seeing corpses as dead meat rather than human beings. The second victim, Wang Jia, had been an exceptionally pretty girl. In the photograph her parents had given them, she was smiling radiantly at the photographer. It was a smile that haunted them all, a reminder of their failure. She had been strangled, and then had her throat slashed twice, left to right, one cut severing both carotid arteries, the windpipe, gullet and spinal cord. Her killer had cut open the abdomen from a centre point beneath the ribs, down the right side and under the pelvis to the left of the stomach, and then stabbed at her private parts with the tip of his knife. The pathologist concluded that the attack had been savage and violent.

Just eight days later, the third murder shook the Section

to its core. The victim, Lin Leman, was slightly older, nearly thirty, found in an alleyway behind stalls where Russian traders sold furs in Ritan Road. Like the others, she had been strangled and had her throat dissevered. But for the first time, the murderer had removed trophies. The entire abdomen had been laid open, the intestines severed from their mesenteric attachments and placed by the victim's shoulder. The uterus, the upper portion of the vagina and the posterior two-thirds of the bladder had been removed entirely, and no trace of them could be found in the vicinity of the crime scene. The only conclusion they could draw was that the killer had taken them away with him.

To compound the bizarre nature of the killing, they had found items from her purse laid on the ground around her feet. A comb, a pack of cigarettes, a lighter, a torn envelope bearing a date stamp from just a few days before. Pathologist Wang had expressed the opinion that these items had not arrived there randomly or by chance. It was his belief that the murderer had gone through her purse and deliberately arranged the items he had found there at the feet of the corpse. But he could not offer up any explanation.

Nor could any of them understand why the killer left the unsmoked end of a Russian cheroot close by each body. Clearly he had smoked the cheroots before committing the murders. To linger for a smoke afterwards would have been to invite discovery. But he must have known that the police would find the butts. And, if he was a man of any education, that DNA could be recovered from traces of saliva. It was like leaving a signature, an artist's autograph on his work, so that there would be no room for doubt in identifying the author.

The detectives had moved their discussion from motive to modus operandi. Wu was clear on their killer's MO. 'He chokes them until they are unconscious,' he said. 'Then he lays them on the ground, on their back, and kneels on their right side. He leans across the body and cuts the throat from left to right. Look at the pics . . .' He waved his hand toward the gallery of horrors on the wall. 'You can see the blood always pools around the left side of the head, never down the front of the body, which it would if they'd still been standing. In some cases the spatter pattern on the ground shows that the blood spurted out from the left carotid artery. The victim was still alive after strangulation, the blood still under pressure.' He paused briefly to light a cigarette. 'The point is, he makes sure he gets as little blood on himself as possible. Then, once they're dead, he starts cutting them open.'

Li spoke for the first time. 'The trouble with all this is, we know what he does and how he does it. But we haven't the first idea why, or who. We need some kind of picture in our minds of this man. A profile, some way of narrowing down who we're looking for. Is he educated, is he a professional man? What age is he, is he married? Does he have sexual or psychological problems? He only kills at weekends. Does that mean his job, or a family commitment, makes it impossible for him to do it during the week?' He remembered his Uncle Yifu's counsel. *The answer always lies in the detail*. And Mei Yuan's words came back to him from earlier that morning. *It is in the detail that you will find the devil.*

'He's clever,' Li went on. 'All these girls advertised in the personal columns of magazines. They all gave e-mail addresses and cellphone numbers. But he never e-mailed them. We would have found those e-mails on the girls' computers, and that might have led us back to him. He knew that. And he knew we could check mobile phone records. That's why the only calls we can't account for were made from public phones. He's one step ahead of us at every stage.'

They did not have a single witness. Li was certain that the killer had not chosen Jianguomen by chance. It was an area of four- and five-star hotels, restaurants, bars. It had a transient population of embassy workers and tourists. The murderer most probably met his victims in hotel lobbies where people were coming and going all the time. The girls would feel safe meeting him in a public place, and no one would think twice about a couple making a rendezvous and heading out for the night. Afterwards, their faces were so disfigured, either because of being choked or, in the case of the latest victim, brutally slashed, that by the time police had obtained photographs and got them circulating round the hotels, the chances were that anyone who saw them together had already checked out and moved on.

'We're still running DNA checks on all known sex offenders,' Zhao said. And he shrugged. 'Nothing yet, though.'

A slow, laborious, time-consuming process, that Li was certain would lead them nowhere. But it had to be done.

'Can I read you something?'

They all looked around in surprise. Qian sat selfconsciously clutching a book that he had taken from his bag. Li saw several coloured strips of paper marking various pages in it.

'I swear by my ancestors I never knew you could read,' Wu said, and the room erupted in laughter. 'You been taking literacy lessons, boss?'

But Qian did not smile. There was something odd in his manner, and he was pale, as if all the blood had been drained from his face. The laughter quickly subsided, and the faces of dead girls looked down on them reproachfully.

'On you go, Qian,' Li said.

Qian started flipping through the pages to his first marker. 'I just wondered if this might seem familiar,' he said. He found his place and started reading. Smoke rose from cigarettes in absolute silence.

'There were twenty-two stab wounds to the trunk. The left lung was penetrated in five places, and the right lung in two places, but the lungs were otherwise perfectly healthy. The heart was rather fatty, and was penetrated in one place, but there was otherwise nothing in the heart to cause death, although there was some blood in the pericardium. The liver was healthy, but was penetrated in five places, the spleen was perfectly healthy, and was penetrated in two places; both the kidneys were perfectly healthy; the stomach was also perfectly healthy, but was penetrated in six places; the intestines were

healthy, and so were all the other organs. The lower portion of the body was penetrated in one place, the wound
being three inches in length and one in depth. There was
a deal of blood between the legs, which were separated.
Death was due to haemorrhage and loss of blood.'

In silence, Qian flicked through the pages to his next marker
and began reading again.

'Her throat had been cut from left to right, two distinct
cuts being on left side, the windpipe, gullet and spinal
cord being cut through; a bruise apparently of a thumb
being on right lower jaw, also one on left cheek; the
abdomen had been cut open from centre of bottom of
ribs along right side, under pelvis to left of the stomach,
there the wound was jagged; the omentum or coating
of the stomach, was also cut in several places, and two
small stabs on private parts; apparently done with a
strong bladed knife; supposed to have been done by some
left-handed person; death being almost instantaneous.'

Someone muttered 'shit' under his breath, like the sound of
a pin dropping. And they all heard it. Pages rustled, and Qian
moved on to a third passage.

'Examination of the body showed that the throat was severed deeply, incision jagged. Removed from, but attached
to body, and placed above right shoulder, were a flap

of the wall of belly, the whole of the small intestines and attachments. Two other portions of wall of belly and "Pubes" were placed above left shoulder in a large quantity of blood. The following parts were missing: – part of belly wall including navel; the womb, the upper part of vagina and greater part of bladder.'

'In the name of the sky,' Wu said. 'These sound like pathology reports on the first three murders.'

Li was on his feet. 'What the hell are you reading from?'

Qian slowly closed the book. 'Detective Wu is right,' he said. 'They are extracts from police and pathology reports. From nearly one hundred and twenty years ago.'

Every eye in the room was on him, every detective struggling to make sense of what he was saying.

'I read a review yesterday of a book published for the first time in China. Even from the review I was struck by certain similarities. So I went out first thing this morning and bought it. And it became clear to me very quickly that I was looking at something more than coincidence.' He held the book up. '*The Murders of Jack the Ripper*,' he said. 'The world's first documented serial killer. He may have murdered as many as seven women in the streets of London, England, in the fall of 1888. And someone is replicating those murders in exact detail, right here in Beijing, one hundred and fifteen years on.'

Li felt the hairs rise up on the back of his neck.

# CHAPTER TWO

## I

The perfume of the post-mortem was a haunting scent. Usually it took Li hours to get the smell of it from his nostrils. Blood and decay, the smell of rotting food from the stomach, the stink of faeces from an open intestine, the almost sweet whiff of burning bone as the oscillating saw cut through the skull. Today he barely noticed. The mutilated corpse of Guo Huan lay on the autopsy table, empty of all her vital organs, chest prised open, the last of her body fluids slowly trickling away along the drainage channels and into a collecting bucket. It was cold enough in the autopsy room for his breath to cloud in front of him, but the chill that reached into his bones had nothing to do with the temperature.

When he and Wu arrived, Pathologist Wang had finished with the body and was breadloafing the brain. It was routine stuff. He had already examined the organs the killer had left him. Shortly he would start dictating his notes, and his assistants would reassemble the body as best they could, stitch it up with coarse twine and deliver it to the morgue for cold storage. There was no doubt about the cause of death.

Li looked at the young girl's horribly slashed features. Her nose was almost completely severed. 'Can't you do anything about the face?' he asked.

Wang looked up and raised an eyebrow. 'Why?'

'She'll have to be formally identified.' He could not imagine how it must feel for a parent to look upon their own child in such a state. He did not want to imagine it.

'Not a lot,' Wang said, and he turned to slice through another half-inch section of brain.

Li had discarded his quilted jacket, and since they had arrived late had not donned the regulation protective clothing. He wore, instead, a long, heavy coat that he kept in the office. It dropped well below his knee. He had left the collar turned up against the cold. It had big pockets. He lifted the flap of one and took out Qian's book. 'Before you dictate your notes,' he said to Wang, 'I'd like to read you something.'

Wang glanced up, mildly curious. This was a departure, even for Li. 'Something literary, perhaps?' he asked. 'Something from your uncle's collection.'

'Even older than that,' Li said. He opened the book at a page he had folded over, and started to read.

'The throat was cut across to the extent of about six or seven inches. A superficial cut commenced about an inch and a half below the lobe and about two-and-a-half inches below and behind the left ear and extended across the throat to about three inches below the lobe of the right ear. The big muscle of the throat was divided through on the left side. The large vessels on the left side of the neck were severed. The larynx was severed below the vocal cord. All the deep structures were severed to the bone, the knife marking intervertebral cartilages.'

He looked up and found Wang watching him, open mouthed. Wu said, 'You'll catch flies.'

Wang snapped his mouth shut. 'You had someone eavesdropping my autopsy,' he said.

'Wait,' Li held up a finger and started reading again.

'The skin was retracted through the whole of the cut in the abdomen, but the vessels were not clotted. Nor had there been any appreciable bleeding from the vessel. I draw the conclusion that the cut was made after death, and there would not be much blood on the murderer. The cut was made by someone on the right side of the body, kneeling below the middle of the body. The intestines had been detached to a large extent from the mesentery. About two feet of the colon was cut away. The sigmoid flexure was invaginated into the rectum very tightly.'

He looked up. 'I'm going to skip a bit here.' And then he continued,

'The peritoneal lining was cut through on the left side and the left kidney carefully taken out and removed. The left renal artery was cut through. I should say that someone who knew the position of the kidney must have done it. The lining membrane over the uterus was cut through. The womb was cut through horizontally, leaving a stump of three-quarters of an inch. The rest of the womb had been taken away with some of the ligaments. The vagina and cervix of the womb was uninjured.'

He closed the book. 'Is that about how it was? What you found during autopsy?'

'What the fuck is this, Chief?' Wang almost never swore. It made it all the more shocking when he did. 'Did you have someone else look at the body before me?'

Li waggled the book. 'This autopsy was carried out by an English physician called Doctor Frederick Gordon Brown. I just read you excerpts from a deposition he gave to an inquest into the murder of a forty-six-year-old prostitute called Catharine Eddowes in London in 1888.'

Wang shook his head in disbelief. 'That's not possible.'

'Jack the Ripper,' Wu said. 'You probably never heard of him. But somebody has, and he's copycatting his killings.'

Wang looked thoughtful for a moment. 'Oh, yes, I've heard of him,' he said finally. 'I attended a talk on the Ripper by an expert on the subject.' He shook his head as if to try to clear it of some fog. 'I never made the connection, though. It's funny how detail escapes you.' He looked at Li in wonder. 'And yet I always had the strangest sense of *déjà vu* about these girls. Of course, he never went into quite that much detail.'

'Who?' Li asked.

'I can't remember his name,' Wang said. 'He was some retired English detective who'd written a book about it. He came over from England with a delegation of judges and lawyers for a week-long series of seminars which was supposed to foster an understanding of the English legal system.'

'When was this?'

'About two years ago?'

Li frowned. 'I don't remember that.'

Wu said, 'I think maybe you were in the States then, Chief.'

Li looked down at the book he was holding in his hands. 'Was his name Thomas Dowman, this retired English detective?'

Wang shrugged. 'Could have been.'

'Then this is his book.' Li dropped it on the table. 'Translated into Chinese.' Wu picked it up and started riffling through the pages, hungry for more detail. Li said to Wang, 'In it he describes the discovery of the third victim as having been found with the contents of her pockets arranged on the ground around her feet.'

Wang closed his eyes. There were thoughts occurring to him that were almost too awful to contemplate. He said, 'Something I remember very vividly from that talk.' Li waited for him to go on. But it was some moments before he could bring himself to speak. 'It gets worse.'

'What do you mean?'

'The mutilation,' Wang said. 'His next victim.' He looked at the girl on the table. 'After this one. You wouldn't want to read about what he did to her, never mind see it.' He looked very directly at Li. 'You've got to catch this killer, Section Chief, before he does it again.'

Li felt the almost unbearable burden of responsibility pressing down on him. Where did they begin? He had not one single concrete lead to go on.

Wang said, 'Your English pathologist was only partially right, though.'

Li looked at him. 'What do you mean?'

'What was it he said? *There would not be much blood on the murderer?* Okay, so most of the mutilation took place after death. But you can't hack someone about like that, remove a kidney and a uterus and not get blood on yourself. Quite a lot of it.'

Li said, 'So unless he lives alone, someone must know who he is. Because he's coming home covered in blood.'

Wang inclined his head in acknowledgement.


## II

In the car park, Li sat behind the wheel of his Santana and opened up the laptop on his knees. He plugged in his cellphone and got it to dial him into the police database from its memory. On the passenger side, Wu was still flicking backwards and forwards through Dowman's book on the Ripper. He stopped suddenly and looked at Li. 'You know, what I don't understand is why anyone would cover up for someone doing stuff like this.'

Li shrugged and tapped the relevant details into vacant fields. 'The history of serial killers is full of loved ones turning a blind eye. Wives, lovers, mothers. More denial than cover-up. Even when confronted with all the evidence, they don't want to admit it, even to themselves.' He hit the return key, and several moments later a screen flashed up with Guo Huan's particulars. A file and a photograph of every resident in Beijing was accessible from the database. Guo Huan had lived with her mother and grandfather. Her father was dead. Her photograph was on the top right corner of the screen. A black and white picture, of not particularly good quality. Li could not tell how good a likeness it might be. But it was better than nothing. He took a note of the address, then shut down the computer and called Qian. When he got through he asked, 'Has Guo's family been told yet?'

'The community police sent someone out to break the news a short time ago,' Qian told him.

'Okay. Wu and I are going to visit the mother. Meantime, pull the kid's photograph from the database and get it circulating in the lobbies of every hotel in Jianguomen. I'll see if we can't get something better from the family. Someone, somewhere saw her with the killer. We need to find that someone. We need a witness.' He hung up and turned the key in the ignition.

Traffic was unusually light, and they cruised east on the Third Ring Road past row after row of new multistorey apartment blocks, shopping malls, and official buildings clad in stone, aping the classical style of traditional European architecture. The sun was low in the sky and blinded Li as he turned south on Andingmenwei Da Jie. Wu still had his head buried in the book. 'It's amazing, Chief. It's like he's making a carbon copy. The Ripper only killed on weekends, and all the murders were within the same square mile of the Whitechapel district of London. All the victims were prostitutes. They were all strangled and then had their throats cut. And then the mutilation.' He shook his head. 'It's strange, though . . .'

Li glanced across at him. 'What is?'

'Catharine Eddowes wasn't the Ripper's fourth victim. You know, like Guo Huan. He killed someone else earlier that night. Someone they called *Long Liz*. Elizabeth Stride.' The English name felt odd on his tongue. 'He strangled her, cut her throat, but that was it. Seems they figured he was interrupted before he could hack her up. So he went off in search of someone else and found Eddowes.' He looked at Li. 'You don't think maybe there was another murder last night, someone we haven't found yet?'

Li's heart sank. It wasn't something he really wanted to think about. 'If there was another victim, she's bound to turn up sooner or later,' he said. 'With a bit of luck, maybe our man didn't think an interrupted job was worth copying. Let's hope so.' A thought occurred to him. 'How long has that book been on the shelves, Wu?'

Wu shrugged. 'Don't know.' He flipped to the front of the book. 'First published in China this year. So it could have been out there for months.'

'Except that Qian said he read a review in the paper yesterday. You don't review a book that's been out for months. Find out when it was released.' Wu made a note, and Li said, 'How many women did the Ripper kill in the end?'

Wu shook his head. 'They don't seem to know for sure. At least five. Maybe as many as eight.'

'So if our man sticks to the script, we could be looking at another four murders.'

Wu nodded grimly. 'Worse than that though, Chief. The Ripper was never caught.'

Guo Huan had lived with her mother in a tiny two-roomed house occupying one side of a *siheyuan* courtyard close to the Confucian Temple at Yonghegong. A broken-down gate led from a dilapidated *hutong* alleyway into a narrow, covered passage cluttered by two old armchairs, a smashed-up television set, the rusting carcass of a long-dead bicycle and, at the far end, a neatly stacked row of coal briquettes. The grey-tile roofs of the four ancient Beijing dwellings overhung the courtyard. Moss and weeds grew in the cracks and the courtyard itself was nearly filled by a large scholar tree which had shed most of its leaves. Birds hung in cages from its branches, squawking and screaming at Li and Wu as they ducked in out of the passageway and crunched dry leaves underfoot. The whole area was due for demolition within the next six months.

Sunlight slanted obliquely across the courtyard to shine through the smudged, filthy windows of the Guo house. Li knocked several times and got no response. He shaded his eyes from the light to peer inside, but there appeared to be no one there.

'What do you want?'

Li and Wu turned at the sound of a woman's harsh voice,

her tongue rolling itself around a very distinctive Beijing *r*. She wore a dark woollen hat, an old blue Mao jacket over a long pinafore, and woollen leggings under thin cotton trousers, and stood in the doorway of the tiny apartment on the opposite side of the courtyard.

'Public Security,' Li said. 'We're looking for Mrs Guo.'

'Do you people never talk to one another?' she asked, her voice heavy with contempt. 'There was one of your people here looking for her an hour ago.' She looked the two detectives up and down. 'And *he* had a uniform.'

'Do you know where she is?' Wu asked.

'She's not here.'

'Yes, we can see that.' Wu controlled his impatience. 'Do you know where we can find her?'

'Panjiayuan. She and that girl of hers sell antiques down there.' She snorted. '*Antiques!* Hah. Junk, more like. What do you want her for?'

'None of your business,' Li said.

As they made their way out into the *hutong*, they heard her shout after them, 'And you can stick your public security up your arse!'

Wu and Li exchanged glances that turned into involuntary smiles. Li shook his head. 'Whatever happened to public respect for the police?' he asked.

The Panjiayuan Market did its business behind low grey walls in the treelined Panjiayuan Lu, just west of the East Third Ring Road. A vast covered area of stalls played host to the

Sunday fleamarket, but lay empty during the week. A fruit and vegetable market did brisk business in an open cobbled area at the west end of the compound. Stalls selling traditional paintings and antiques were sandwiched between the two, washed by dull sunlight filtered through a plastic roof. In a cul-de-sac opposite the main gate, a trishaw driver sprawled sleeping in the back of his own tricycle under a candy-striped canopy as Li and Wu drove in. A banner was strung across a wall just inside the gates. *Gather all the treasure and make friends in the world.* Which Li took to be a euphemism for *Collect all your junk and sell it to the tourists.* Some of the older buildings that lined the outer wall of the market had been restored to their original splendour, and several traditional Chinese shopping streets had been constructed within, in the shadow of the twenty-storey apartment blocks that grew like weeds here in this south-east corner of the city. Empty shop units, empty apartments, populated only by the ghosts of the people whose homes had been razed to make way for them. Building, it seemed, was outstripping demand.

Li and Wu wandered between stalls peddling paintings and wall-hangings, watched by suspicious, dark-eyed vendors nursing glass jars of green tea or sitting around fold-up tables playing cards. It was clear the two men were neither tourists nor casual Chinese. Which could only mean one other thing. At the far end of one of the aisles, a group of tourists was gathered around a table watching an artist at work, carefully crafting a pen and ink scene of ancient China. Next to him a group of men and women, wrapped up warm against the cold, was playing *Great Wall* on a rusted metal table. Li interrupted them, flipping open his ID. 'I'm looking for Mrs Guo. She sells antiques.' One of them nodded towards the far aisle, but none of them spoke.

'Chatty types,' Wu muttered to Li as they passed a big-bellied shiny Buddha on a plinth. A wooden pig rose up on its hind legs snorting its derision, and a line of bronze warriors gazed upon them impassively. They turned into the aisle at the end and it stretched ahead of them in gloomy half-darkness for sixty or seventy metres. There were stalls and tiny shop units and tables groaning with junk: teapots and door-knockers; small figurines in armour; inlaid wooden boxes; wristwatches displaying Mao heads that nodded away the seconds. Behind glass, shelves of traditional chinaware, ornate wooden carvings. Two teenage girls sat beside a table of polished gramophone horns. 'Looka, looka,' one of them said, not yet savvy enough to recognise police out of uniform.

Wu said curtly, 'Mrs Guo.'

The other one nodded towards a shop unit two doors along. 'Police there,' she said conspiratorially.

'Thanks for the warning,' Li said.

There were three people squeezed around a wooden table in the tiny, cluttered shop unit. A woman with long dark hair who looked in her middle forties, a very old man in a wide-brimmed hat drowned by a heavy coat two sizes too big for him, and a young uniformed community police officer. The shelves were lined with blue-ink china vases, and the ceiling was hung with dozens of bells on chains. The young policeman looked up with what seemed like relief when Li and Wu arrived. The old man stared into some unseen place with glazed eyes, and a large, clear drip of mucus hung from the end of his nose. The woman's eyes were red, her cheeks blotched and tearstained. Li saw something like hope in her eyes when she looked up at them, as if she thought that somehow they might have come to say it had all been a terrible mistake, and that Guo Huan was really alive and well. He ached for her, and the false hope she was conjuring out of the depths of her despair. He said, 'I'm Section Chief Li Yan, Mrs Guo. Detective Wu and I are investigating your daughter's death.' And whatever hope she might have fostered, he knew he had just stolen away.

He saw her face go bleak. 'The uniform says she was murdered,' she said.

'I'm afraid so.'

'Found her up Silk Street Market,' the uniform said. 'Isn't that right?' He looked to Li for confirmation, not remotely awed by the presence of superior ranks. 'Hacked to pieces apparently.'

The girl's mother gasped her distress and tears blurred her eyes.

Li glared at him. 'I think you can go now, officer.'

'That's alright, Chief. They said I should stay down here and offer support. It's part of the job in the community branch.'

The mother turned to Li. 'What was she doing in a place like that at night, alone with a man?'

'Well, you should know,' the uniform said, wearing his disapproval like a badge.

Li turned to Wu. 'Get him out of here.'

Wu grabbed the uniform by the arm and yanked him out of his seat. 'Hey!' the officer protested. But Wu had him out of the door and into the alley before he could give further voice to his indignation.

Mrs Guo looked at Li in consternation, her cheeks shining with silent tears. 'What did he mean?'

Li shook his head and sat down where the uniform had been. '*He* doesn't know what he means,' Li said. 'These community police are just messenger boys. They don't know anything.' Outside in the alley, they heard raised voices, and the sound of something breaking. Li glanced at the old man. He hadn't moved since they came in. 'Is he alright?'

A dead look fell across the mother's face. 'Who knows? He's my father. He's been like that since he had his stroke ten years ago. And what does the State do for him? Nothing. I have to pay for all his medical care. I have to nurse him at home. Me and Huan, with one bedroom among the three of us. That's why she had to work nights. We needed the money.'

'Where did she work?'

She shrugged. 'Different places. Bar work mostly. She said there was always casual work in Bar Street up in Sanlitun.' Her face crumpled in consternation. 'Is it true? Was she really . . . cut up?'

Li nodded. There was no way he could conceal it from her. She would have to identify the body. 'I'm afraid so.' And he wondered if Guo Huan's mother really believed that she was working in bars in Sanlitun all those nights she went off on her own. But, then, if her daughter was bringing in good money, perhaps she didn't want to know any different.

Wu reappeared and stood in the doorway. He nodded to Li almost imperceptibly. Li said, 'Did she ever tell you she was meeting anyone? Ever mention a name, a rendezvous?'

The mother held her hands out helplessly. 'We didn't talk much,' she said. 'About anything. She left school four years ago, and we've been working in the shop here together every day since.' She glanced at her father. 'With him.' She paused, dealing with some painful private memory. 'We ran out of things to talk about a long time ago.'

Li nodded and allowed her a little space before he said, 'Mrs Guo, I'd like your permission for a team of forensics people to go into your house and go through all your daughter's things.'

Her mother sat upright suddenly, as if offended by the idea. 'I don't think I'd like that. What difference does it make now anyway? She's dead.'

Li said patiently, 'She might have known her killer, Mrs Guo, in which case we might find some clue to his identity among her things.' He paused. 'She wasn't his first victim. We want to stop him from doing it again.'

Mrs Guo sank back into her despair and nodded desolately. 'I suppose.'

'And if you have a recent photograph of her, that would be very helpful.'

She reached into a cupboard and pulled out a cardboard shoebox tied with pink ribbon. She placed it carefully on the table, undid the ribbon and lifted the lid. It was full

of photographs. 'I always meant to put them in an album.'
She looked around her shop. 'I sit about here all day and do
nothing. The more time you have, the more time you waste.'
She started taking out pictures and laying them in front of her.

They didn't appear to be in any date order, as if they had
been taken in and out of the box often. There were family
groups, taken in happier times, a man on Mrs Guo's arm
whom Li took to be her husband. There were pictures of a little
girl smiling toothily at the camera, cheap prints on which the
colours were faded now. Guo Huan in school uniform – a blue
tracksuit and yellow baseball cap. Guo Huan with short hair,
Guo Huan with long hair. All appeared to have been taken
several years earlier. Her mother fingered every photograph
with a kind of reverence, each with its own memory, every one
with its own baggage. And then she pulled out a strip of four
photographs of a much older Guo Huan. She handed it to Li.
'These were taken a month or two ago. In one of those booths.'

Li examined them closely. The smile was self-conscious, and
each photograph in the sequence was almost identical. She
had shoulder-length hair, and a pretty face all made-up for the
occasion. Having seen her in Silk Street and at the morgue,
Li would still never have recognised her. She had a freshness
about her, an absence of cynicism, the anticipation of youth
for a life ahead. A life that would never be. 'May I take these?'
he asked. 'I promise to return them.' The mother nodded and
he handed the strip to Wu. 'And I'm sorry to ask, Mrs Guo, but
we will need you to make a formal identification of the body.'

A look of panic flitted across her face. 'Oh, no, I couldn't.'

'Is there someone else, then?'

She thought for a moment, and then her face collapsed into resignation as she shook her head. 'When do you want me?'

'I'll have a car come and pick you up in the next hour.' Li glanced at the old man. 'Will he be alright?'

'I'll have someone watch him,' she said. And Li saw her lower lip start to tremble as she tried to hold back the tears. But they came anyway, big and silent, making wet tracks down her cheeks. 'They only let you have one child.' She took a deep breath. 'And I'm too old to start again.' She looked at her father, and Li was sure it was resentment he saw in her eyes. 'He's all I have left.'

As they made their way back through the gloom of the antiques alley, Wu said to Li, 'That goddamned community cop was determined he wasn't leaving. Actually put up a struggle. Bust a vase.'

'Put in a complaint,' Li said.

Wu grunted. 'Not worth the paperwork, Chief.'

But if Wu was content to put it behind him, the community cop was not. He was waiting for them out front, lingering in agitation beneath a moongate leading to a neighbouring compound. He came chasing after them. 'Hey,' he said, catching Li's arm. 'Your detective assaulted me.' He barely had time to draw breath in surprise before Li wheeled around and pushed him hard up against the wall, his forearm against the officer's throat. The hapless policeman's hat went spinning away across the cobbles.

'You're lucky I don't break your neck,' Li hissed at him.

'I guess you were off the day they taught sensitivity at cop school.' He released him. 'Don't go near that woman again.'

The incident had lasted only seconds, but already a crowd was gathering. It was unheard of for a police officer to be handled like that, and those who had been witness to it were enjoying the moment. The officer straightened his coat and stooped, with as much dignity as he could muster, to retrieve his hat. 'You haven't heard the last of this,' he called after the two detectives. And then he turned and glared at the crowd. 'What the fuck are you looking at!'

The trishaw driver was still asleep under his candy-striped canopy as Li and Wu turned out of the main gate. Wu was chewing furiously on his gum. 'I don't know about you, Chief, but I'm starving.' He checked his watch. 'How about we stop somewhere for a bite of lunch.'

Li said, 'I'm never hungry after an autopsy.' He sighed. 'But I've got a lunch appointment at twelve, so I'm going to have to find an appetite from somewhere.'

Wu was not impressed. 'Lucky you. Who's buying you lunch?'

'An American polygraph expert from the Chinese Academy of Sciences. He's set up a demonstration this afternoon for a group of top Ministry of Public Security people.'

Wu was unimpressed. 'A polygraph demonstration?'

'No,' Li said. 'It's a new thing called MERMER.'

'Mermer?' Wu pulled a face. 'What the hell's a Mermer when it's at home?'

'Some kind of foolproof way of detecting guilty knowledge

in the brain,' Li said. 'At least, that's what they claim.' He cast a wry smile in Wu's direction. 'A good job your wife never had access to it.'

Wu laughed. 'If she had, we'd only have got divorced all the sooner.'

## III

The Mo Gu Huo Guo mushroom hotpot restaurant stood on a corner, in the shadow of the tall cylindrical tower of the Central Music Conservatory, just off Pufang Lu. Its speciality was mushrooms from Sichuan and Yunan Provinces. Margaret stood on the steps in the sunshine with Li Jon in her arms. The American polygraph expert had wanted to meet her. He had married a Chinese cop and thought that the two couples might have quite a lot in common. She watched as the Santana pulled up under the trees, a chill wind rustling stubborn leaves that refused to fall. As Li climbed out, Wu slipped into the driver's seat and drove off.

Margaret eyed the father of her child as he approached her across the broad curve of pavement, his shadow falling away to his right. He looked good in his long coat, tall and broad-shouldered, his black hair cropped in its distinctive flat-top crew cut. His pants were still sharply creased, although a little crinkled around the knee, and his white shirt was tucked tightly in at his impossibly narrow waist. Clothes hung beautifully on the Chinese frame, and Margaret marvelled at how she was still attracted to Li, even after all this time. Her stomach did a little flip, and she remembered how their passion had been frustrated by the call on his cellphone in the early hours of that morning. And she saw a weariness in his face that she recognised as owing more to what the call had led him to confront than to the simple interruption of his sleep.

He smiled and stooped to kiss her, and ran a hand through the black hair beginning to grow more thickly now on his son's head. 'Been waiting long?'

'Just arrived.'

'They're probably already here then. We'd better go in.'

He wasn't volunteering anything about his call-out this morning, and she knew better than to ask.

The restaurant was drum-shaped, like its taller neighbour, the Central Conservatory. It had dining halls on three floors, with private rooms around the outside on the second and third. A pretty waitress in a red jacket and skirt led them up a circular staircase and around a pillared corridor which skirted the second-floor dining room. The American and his wife were waiting for them in a private room about two-thirds of the way around. They stood up from a table with a large pot sunk into its centre, over a concealed gas ring. Steam rose from bubbling stock. The room was ablaze with sunlight, and Li and Margaret were dazzled by it, entering from the dark inner hall.

The polygrapher was tall and slim, a man in his forties with a head of thick, greying hair. He wore a baggy brown suit and checked shirt, with a tie loose at the neck. 'Yeh, blinding isn't it?' He grinned at them as they shaded their eyes. 'But, then, I always figure I look better when you can't see me.' He shook

Li's hand warmly. 'Good to see you again, Li Yan. You haven't met Chi Lyang, have you?'

'No.' Li shook hands with a slight, but attractive-looking Chinese woman in her mid-thirties. Her long black hair was drawn back in a ponytail. She wore jeans and sneakers and a white blouse. '*Ni hau*,' he said.

She smiled. 'Hi.'

The American turned to Margaret, extending his hand. 'And you must be Margaret. My name's Bill Hart. I have heard *so* much about you, Margaret.'

'All of it bad, no doubt.'

He shrugged a shoulder. 'Pretty much. But I figure, hell, with a reputation like that, you gotta be worth meeting.'

Margaret raised an eyebrow. 'I hope I won't disappoint you, then.'

He grinned. 'Don't you dare.' And he turned to his wife. 'This is Chi Lyang.'

Margaret shook hands with her. 'Don't believe everything you hear about me,' she said. 'Since I became a mother I've retired from hostilities.'

Lyang smiled, dark eyes sparkling. 'Well, since I became a wife, I've had to retire from the police. But I still like to indulge in a bit of hostility now and then.'

'And, boy, can she be hostile,' Hart said.

'We should get on just fine, then,' Margaret said.

Lyang cupped her hand under a sleepy Li Jon's chin and he squinted at her in the bright sunlight. 'He's beautiful,' she said.

'I hope you don't mind me bringing him. I couldn't find anyone to look after him at short notice.'

'If I'd known I'd have brought Ling with me. She's fifteen months.'

'It's Li Jon's first birthday next month.'

'Well, you'll have no shortage of things to talk about,' Hart said. He rattled off some Chinese at a waitress and she disappeared, returning quickly with a highchair for Li Jon.

They settled themselves around the table, and the red-jacketed serving girls brought in a large tray with plates bearing a variety of raw sliced mushrooms and placed it on a side table. Hart ordered beer, and another waitress brought a large, cooked black chicken in stock and tipped it carefully into the bubbling liquid in the centre of the table.

'You ever had black chicken before?' Hart asked Margaret. She shook her head. 'Just tastes like chicken, except it's black,' he said.

Lyang said, 'In traditional Chinese medicine, black chicken is used to treat female diseases.'

'And since I don't have any female diseases, obviously it works,' Hart said.

Margaret smiled. 'Hmmm,' she said. 'Sounds appetising.'

Li said to Lyang, 'You speak exceptionally good English.'

She inclined her head a little in acknowledgement. 'I was a translator at the Ministry of State Security. Russian and English. That was before I moved over to Public Security.'

'And if she hadn't become a cop, I'd never have met her,' Hart said.

'And if we'd never met, I'd still have been a cop,' she replied. There was no hint of rancour in her tone, but Margaret sensed some underlying tension. She knew only too well that the authorities would not allow a serving police officer to marry a foreign national. If you wanted to marry, you had to quit the force. She glanced at Li, but he was avoiding her eye.

'We met at a conference in Boston,' Hart said. 'Lyang was trained in polygraphy at the University of Public Security here in Beijing. She was on an exchange trip to see how the Americans do it.'

'And no doubt we Americans do it better,' Margaret said. 'We always do everything better, don't we?'

Hart smiled indulgently at her sarcasm. 'We do it differently. And we've had a lot more experience. The Chinese began using the polygraph just ten years ago, and it has only been employed in around eight thousand cases since then. Compare that to the States where we've been using lie detection for more than seventy years, and almost every government employee has to submit to a polygraph test to get his job. I think we know a little more about it.'

Margaret shrugged. 'What's to know? It's just a bunch of wires and sensors that read heart-rate, breathing, perspiration. The operator is the lie detector, not the machine. It's all psychology. Smoke and mirrors.'

Hart laughed infectiously. 'You're right, of course, Margaret. Which is why experience counts for so much.'

'Then how come you manage to get it wrong so often?'

'Margaret . . .' Li said, a hint of warning in his voice.

But Hart was unruffled. 'Relax, Li Yan, I'm enjoying this. It's good to do battle with someone who can make a good argument.' He turned back to Margaret. 'Actually, we have a pretty high success rate. Ninety per cent or higher.'

But Margaret was unimpressed. 'Not according to the OTA. You know what that is?'

'Sure. The Office of Technology Assessment. It's an arm of the US federal government that analyses and evaluates current technology.'

'Whose evaluation of the success rate of the polygraph is as low as fifty per cent. Hell, I can *guess* and be right half the time.'

Lyang was grinning. 'Still enjoying the argument, Bill?'

But Margaret wasn't finished. 'I read somewhere that between one and four million private citizens in the US submit to a polygraph every year. Even assuming you did have a ninety per cent success rate, that's a heck of a lot of people to be wrong about. People who might lose or fail to gain employment, people stigmatised as liars because of inaccurate polygraph tests. It's not science, Bill, it's voodoo.'

Hart's grin never faltered as he eyed Margaret with something approaching admiration. 'Jesus, Margaret, they were right about you. I'd love to get you in the chair and wire you up. Pin you down on my territory.'

'Okay,' Margaret said, to everyone's surprise.

'What, you mean you'd let me give you a polygraph test?'

'If you let me give you an autopsy.' The others roared with laughter. And Margaret broke into a smile for the first time.

'I reckon I'd find out a lot more about you in an hour and a half than you'd ever find out about me.'

Hart nodded, still smiling, acknowledging defeat. 'Okay,' he said. 'I give in. Let's eat.'

And the waitresses brought the mushrooms to the table and started cooking them in the stock with the chicken. Lyang showed Margaret how to mix up her own dip from three dishes of sesame paste, chilli and garlic, and dip the cooked pieces of mushroom in the mix before eating. Margaret was surprised at just how delicious the mushrooms were, each with its own distinctive flavour and texture. A waitress broke up the chicken in the pot and served portions of it into each of their individual bowls. It melted in the mouth.

'Actually,' Hart said, washing down mushroom with beer, 'I'm not in favour of using the polygraph on employees or job applicants. I regard it only as a useful tool in criminal interrogation. It is at its most effective when the suspect *believes* the machine will catch him in a lie. You'd be amazed at how often they just confess.' He spooned some of the stock into his bowl and drank it like soup. 'You know, the Chinese invented a pretty good method of lie detection about three thousand years ago.'

Li looked up surprised. 'We did?'

'Sure we did,' Lyang said. 'Works on the principle that if you are telling a lie you produce less saliva. So the ancient Chinese gave the suspect a mouthful of rice to chew, then told him to spit it out. If he was afraid of the test, because he was lying, he would suffer from dry mouth and the rice would stick to his tongue and the roof of his mouth. An innocent person, on the other hand, would be able to spit it out clean.'

Hart said, 'But the Indians had an even better one. They would put lampblack on the tail of a donkey and lead it into a dark room. Suspects were ordered to go into the room and pull the donkey's tail. They were told that it was a magic donkey and would be able to tell if the suspect was being truthful or not. When the suspects came out of the room their hands were examined. If they didn't have any lampblack on them they hadn't pulled the donkey's tail. Why? Obviously because they were scared of being found out. Guilty as charged.'

'Almost as scientific as the polygraph,' Margaret said.

'Well, if it's science that impresses you,' Lyang said, 'it's a pity you won't be at the MERMER demonstration this afternoon.'

Margaret looked at Li. 'And why am I not invited?'

Li said, 'Because it's a demonstration for top Ministry of Public Security people, Margaret. The Deputy Minister himself is going to be there.'

'We're trying to secure funding for further research,' Hart explained.

'Don't worry, I'm not invited either,' Lyang said. 'Husbands don't like their wives seeing them caught in a lie.'

Hart held his hands up. 'I am taking no part in this demonstration. I just set it up for Lynn.'

'Who's Lynn?' Li asked.

'Professor Lynn Pan. She's an American Chinese. She was a pupil of the system's inventor, Doctor Lawrence Farwell, back in the States. She came to live and work in China last year, sponsored by the Chinese Academy to develop a Chinese version of MERMER.'

'What exactly *is* Mermer?' Margaret asked, intrigued.

'It's an acronym,' Lyang said. 'It stands for Memory and Encoding Related Multifaceted Electroencephalographic Responses.'

'Sorry I asked,' Margaret said. 'What does it mean?'

Hart said, 'Electroencephalography is a non-invasive means of measuring electrical brain activity.'

Lyang waved her hand dismissively. She turned to Margaret. 'He's a scientist, he doesn't know anything about language. In layman's terms, they put sensors on your scalp and use a computer to measure your brain's electrical responses to certain stimuli. Might be something as simple as a photograph of your child. You recognise it, so your brain makes an entirely involuntary electrical response. Proof that you know this child. They show you a picture of someone else's child, you have no response. You don't know the kid.'

Hart said, 'It can be used to discover guilty knowledge in the brain of a criminal. They've done extensive testing in the States, using FBI and CIA personnel.' He smiled. 'Since you're so interested in percentages, Margaret, you'll be pleased to know it has proved one hundred per cent successful in all tests to date.'

'Sounds like it could put you guys out of business.'

'Oh, I doubt it,' Hart said. 'MERMER has very specific and narrow applications. It requires a lot of expensive equipment and meticulous preparation.' He glanced at his watch. 'Speaking of which, we don't want to be late.' He signalled the waitress for the check and a gaggle of girls rushed to get their jackets from the stand.

As they rose from the table, Lyang said, 'Are you busy this afternoon, Margaret?'

Margaret laughed. 'Lyang, these days I'm never busy.'

Lyang said, 'I'm going for a foot massage later. Why don't you join me?'

'A foot massage?' Margaret was incredulous. She had seen the signs for foot massage springing up all over the city. It was the latest fashion. But it seemed a little decadent.

'It's the most wonderful way of relaxing I know,' Lyang said.

'It's not so easy to relax with an eleven-month-old baby demanding your attention twenty-four hours a day.'

'That's what's so good about the place I use,' Lyang said. 'They have a crèche. You can forget baby for an hour and a half.' She smiled. 'Go on, treat yourself.'

'On you go,' Li said. 'And when you learn how it's done you can practise on me.'

Margaret gave him a look.

As a waitress handed Li his coat, Qian's book slipped from the pocket and fell to the floor.

Lyang stooped to pick it up and raised an eyebrow as she read the title. '*The Murders of Jack the Ripper.*'

Hart laughed. 'What's this? Becoming a student of unsolved murders, Li?'

Li smiled reluctantly. 'I hope not,' he said.

But Margaret was looking at him curiously. 'Jack the Ripper?'

Li sighed. There was no avoiding an explanation. 'I take it you know who he is?'

'Of course. The Ripper murders were probably the first

documented case of serial killings anywhere in the world.' She shrugged. 'I'm no expert on the subject, but there can't be many people who haven't heard the name Jack the Ripper. He's kind of like the bogeyman.'

Li nodded solemnly and turned to Hart. 'There's been a spate of particularly gruesome murders in the city during the last few weeks.' He glanced at Margaret. 'We think the killer's copycatting the Ripper murders.'

Margaret found her interest engaged. 'Who in Beijing would know enough of that kind of detail to be able to replicate them?'

Li held up the book. 'Someone who's read this.'

Margaret took the book and looked at the Chinese characters with frustration. She said, 'I wish I'd taken the trouble to learn to read Chinese.'

'It's only a translation,' Li said. 'You could probably get the English original on the internet.'

'Professional interest aroused?' Hart asked.

'Of course,' Margaret said. 'Wouldn't you have liked to wire up some of the suspects and bamboozle them with your parlour tricks?'

He grinned. 'Well, if you'd done the autopsies, Margaret, I'm sure you'd have provided me with ample ammunition to extract a confession.' He turned to Li. 'Maybe you should get Margaret working on this one, Li Yan.'

'I've retired,' Margaret said simply, and she lifted Li Jon from his chair and turned out of their private room into the gloom of the inner restaurant.

# CHAPTER THREE

## I

The Chinese Academy of Sciences was in a six-storey grey-tile building off Sanlihi Lu, facing west towards Yuyuantan Park, and flanked by the Ministry of Finance and the Chinese Institute of Seismology. Hart drew his car up on to the sidewalk and parked facing steps leading up to glass doors. A hanging white banner announced in bold characters that this was the *Presidium of Chinese Scholars*. A Chinese flag whipped and snapped in the wind and cast its shadow on the green-tile roof above the main entrance.

On the fifth floor, five of the most senior officers in the Ministry of Public Security sat around a large reception room, drinking green tea and smoking. Vertical blinds shielded the room from the sun as it swung westwards. One wall was taken up by a mural depicting a tranquil scene from an ancient Chinese garden. Everyone, with the exception of Li, was in uniform and he realised immediately that he was in breach of etiquette.

'I'll leave you to it. Good luck,' Hart said, and he ducked

out the door. What had been an animated conversation fell away into silence as the occupants of the room regarded the newcomer. Procurator General Meng Yongli sat stiffly, with his hat on the chair beside him. 'Punctual as always, Li,' he said, his tone rigid with disapproval.

'You might have taken the time to change into your uniform, Section Chief.' This from the Deputy Minister of Public Security, Wei Peng. He was a small, squat man with the demeanour of a frog, and he enjoyed exercising his power. 'We are here representing the Ministry today.'

'Give the man a break.' Beijing's Deputy Commissioner of Police, Cao Xu, was so relaxed he was almost liquid. His hat had been tossed on the low table in front of him, and he was slouched in his seat, with one leg up over the arm of it. He was a man who, at one time, had been destined for the top. A predecessor of Li's in the hotseat at Section One, he had looked set for the Commissioner's job when a past indiscretion had caught up with him and he was promoted sideways to deputy. His progress on the career ladder was at an end and so he had no need to toady to his superiors. It made him something of a loose cannon. He took a long pull at his cigarette. 'After all, the Section Chief is up to his eyes in murder, isn't that right, Chief?'

'And has our hero cracked the case yet?' Beijing Police Commissioner Zhu Gan's use of the word *hero* was laden with sarcasm. He was a tall, lean man with rimless glasses who viewed Li through them with patent dislike. He was not one of Li's champions, and had made clear to him on numerous occasions his distaste for the award ceremony scheduled for the Great Hall of the People that evening. In his view it was, he had told Li, a dangerous return to the cult of personality. Li might have agreed with him, had he been allowed. But in almost the same breath Commissioner Zhu had told him that since the edict had come from the Minister himself neither of them was in a position to raise objections.

'What developments, Li?' The slight build of the older man who sat sandwiched between the Procurator General and the Deputy Minister in no way reflected his status. As Director General of the Political Department, Yan Bo pulled plenty of clout. Li recognised him, but had not had any previous dealings with him.

Li looked at the faces expectantly awaiting his response. He did not feel that this was the occasion to share with them the news that their killer was modelling himself on Jack the Ripper. Nor did he feel like explaining that the reason for his failure to change into uniform was that he had been un-avoidably detained by lunch. 'I've just come from an interview with the dead girl's mother,' he said. Which was not entirely untrue. But he wondered if it would have passed Hart's poly-graph test.

'She's the fourth, isn't she?' said Deputy Cao taking another pull on his cigarette.

'That's right,' Li said. 'And probably the worst case of muti-lation I've seen. Not only did he hack her face to pieces, but he cut her open and made off with her uterus and her left kidney.' His words conjured images for them that they would, perhaps, have preferred not to envisage so soon after lunch, and they were greeted with silence. Li added, 'I could have done without being here at all this afternoon.'

Commissioner Zhu said dismissively, 'I'm sure your team can manage without you for a few hours, Section Chief.'

The door from an inner office opened, and an attractive young woman in her early thirties emerged into the meeting room cradling an armful of folders. Her hair was cut short, spiky on top, and she wore a man's suit – Armani, Li thought – black pinstriped, over a white open-necked blouse. She had a radiant smile which she turned on the room. 'Gentlemen,' she said, 'I am so glad you could make it this afternoon. My name's Lynn Pan, and have I got a show for you.'

She looked Chinese, but everything else about her was American. Even her heavily accented Chinese. Li immediately sensed a rise in the testosterone level in the room. She had spoken only a couple of dozen words, but already she had these middle-aged senior officers from the Ministry eating out of her hand. They were on their feet in an instant.

She laid down her folders and went round each of them individually, shaking their hands, presenting them with her business card and her winning smile, receiving theirs in return. She arrived at Li last, and he wondered if he imagined that she held his hand just a little longer, that her gaze fixed his just a little more warmly. Her eyes were a rich, dark brown with a deep inner light, and they turned Li's stomach to mush.

'Gentlemen, please be seated.' They sat in their various chairs around the room, and she drew up an office chair on wheels and positioned herself so that she could see them all. She let her gaze wander around the assembled faces, and they almost held their breath waiting for her to speak. Finally she said, 'You know, there's one thing that every criminal takes with him from a crime scene. Can you think what that is?'

There was a moment's silence, then Li said, 'His memory of what happened.'

Professor Pan turned a brilliant smile on him. 'You're absolutely right, Section Chief Li.' He felt like the star pupil in the class, and the teacher had even remembered his name. 'It's like a video recording in his head, and there's nothing he can do to erase it.' She looked around the other faces. 'Usually we search a crime scene for traces of what a criminal has left behind. Fingerprints. DNA. Fibres. All useful in identifying the perpetrator. But what if we don't find anything? Well, if we have a suspect, we can always look inside his head. Because if he's guilty, the crime scene will have left an indelible print in his brain. Impossible, you might say.' She flashed her winning smile once again. 'Not any more. Because MERMER lets us do just that – look inside someone's mind and detect knowledge. Replay that video, read that indelible imprint.' She paused. 'We call it brain fingerprinting, and we have the technology.'

It had a nice ring to it, Li thought. Brain fingerprinting. It wasn't about collecting evidence left at the scene by the criminal, it was about reading the print the crime had left in the culprit's brain.

'Now, I don't want to get technical about it,' the professor said, 'because it's a highly complex piece of science. But the essence of it is this: if you are shown something that you recognise, there is a unique electrical response in your brain. It doesn't matter if you deny recognising that something or not. Your brain's response is always the same. You have absolutely no control over it. And you know what?' They all waited eagerly to know what. 'We can read that response. We attach sensors to your head, entirely non-invasive, and plug you into our computer, and we will know what you know and what you don't.' She waved her hand airily towards the ceiling. 'Which is as much good news for the innocent as it is bad news for the guilty. Because we can rule you out, just as certainly as we can rule you in.'

She stood up and clasped her hands and seemed for a moment transported to another place. She began walking slowly around the room as if addressing students in a lecture room. 'We call that unique electrical response a MERMER. It's an acronym. It doesn't work in Chinese, so there's no point in me trying to explain. It's just what we call it. I learned about MERMER from its inventor, who was my professor at university in the United States. Doctor Larry Farwell. A very smart man. Smart enough to recognise that I was smart enough to invest his time in. And now here I am, back in the land of my ancestors, developing a uniquely Chinese version of the process that could revolutionise criminal investigation in the People's Republic. In every test carried out to date it has proven one hundred per cent successful.' She spun around to face them, eyes wide. 'But I don't want you to take my word for it. I want to prove it to you. Because we need your support for the funding that will make this process available to every criminal investigation department in the country.'

It was a very slick and persuasive presentation, and she had been in the room for less than ten minutes. There wasn't one of the senior law enforcement officers present who didn't want to believe her.

'I'm going to demonstrate just how effective MERMER is by subjecting you to a test that I developed for work with my students,' she said. 'My assistant and a team of graduates will prepare you for it. You will be split into two groups of three. One group will be briefed on a specific criminal scenario, the other will not. I will be unaware which of you is in which group. But afterwards, when I test you, your brain will provide the answer for me. And I won't need to ask you a single question. All you will have to do is look at some photographic images on a computer screen while I monitor your brain's response. And the reason it's foolproof?' She held out open palms and smiled, as if it was simplicity itself. 'Your brain just can't lie.'

## II

Li sat on a stool at a science bench in a darkened room with Procurator General Meng and Commissioner Zhu. Blinds were drawn on the window, and the only light in the room was a desk lamp that focused their attention on a spread of grim photographs arranged on the benchtop. They were colour eight-by-tens of a particularly bloody crime scene. Most crime scenes now seemed all too depressingly familiar to Li. This was no different. Two women and a young man stripped naked and lying side by side by side at odd angles on the top of a makeshift bed. The covers were soaked red by their blood, the dark brown-red of long dried blood. It was smeared on their bodies, and their trunk wounds were gaping dark holes, like so many black beetles crawling over them. Li recognised them as knife wounds. There was a close-up of the male. The back of his head was missing, as if a bullet fired through the front of it had taken the back away as it exited. But he was lying face down, so it was impossible to see the entry wound.

The room had been shot from various angles. It appeared to be a bedroom. Drawers had been pulled out of chests, and contents strewn about the floor. There were curtains on the window, but one of them had been pulled free of its rail at one end, the hem of it clutched in the hands of one of the dead women.

Beyond the light, and flitting back and forth on the periphery of their vision, one of Lynn Pan's graduate students was laying more photographs in front of them.

'I want each of you to imagine that you are the murderer,' she was saying, 'and that this is the scene you have left behind you.' More photographs. 'This is the house. You can see it's a small dwelling in a suburban area of the town.' A row of featureless white-tile dwellings was shaded by a line of trees. 'You can see something lying in the drive. Something you took from the scene and dropped there.' She laid another photograph in front of them, and they saw that it was a white shirt, torn and bloody. She reached down behind the bench and lifted up a large, clear plastic evidence bag with the bloody white shirt sealed inside.

'Is this a real crime scene?' Procurator Meng asked, looking with distaste at the shirt. It was a long time since he had been actively involved in crime scene investigation. 'I mean, is that real?'

'Of course,' said the assistant. 'We wouldn't have the resources to mock up something like this.' She lifted another evidence bag on to the counter top. It contained a serrated hunting knife with a bone handle. 'And this is the weapon you used to commit the murders. You can handle it if you like.'

Li lifted the bag and removed the weapon carefully from inside. He ran the blade lightly across the flats of his fingers. It was still sharp. It was heavy, but nicely balanced. Not a cheap knife. A professional hunter's weapon. Two inches of the blade at the hilt was serrated. He looked up and found Commissioner Zhu watching him. 'Don't let it give you any ideas, Li,' he said.

Li smiled, flipped the knife over, and held it out to the Commissioner, handle first. Beijing's top cop took the proffered weapon and examined it carefully. Li watched him handle it with the confidence of one used to knives. 'You look like you were born with one of those in your hands, Commissioner Zhu.'

The Commissioner looked at him, surprised. 'Is it that obvious?'

Li shrugged. He wasn't sure what the Commissioner meant. 'You just seem comfortable with it, that's all.'

The Commissioner smiled. A rare sight that Li had seldom seen. 'It's been a long time,' he said. 'In Xinjiang Province, where I grew up, my father hunted deer in the forest. My earliest memories are of going hunting with him. Of course, we had no guns. We set traps, with salt as bait, and killed the animals by slitting their throats. My father taught me how to gut a deer in under ten minutes. We ate well.' All the time he was turning the knife over in his hands, examining it with what seemed to Li almost like fondness.

'I thought it was the antlers that deer were killed for in the north-east. Some superstition about their powers of healing.'

The older man looked up. 'It's Sichuan you come from, isn't it?' Li nodded. 'Pandas,' said the Commissioner. 'A protected species. You probably didn't do much hunting in Sichuan.'

'I've never much liked killing anything,' Li said. 'Even for the table.'

The Commissioner did not miss what he took to be an implied criticism. 'No doubt you'd rather other people did the dirty work,' he said.

'May I see it?' The Procurator General broke in, impatient with their fencing. Unlike the Commissioner, he handled it very gingerly, at arm's length, before laying it back on the bench.

The graduate placed some more photographs in front of them. 'This is the vehicle you used to get to the victims' house,' she said. It was a battered old blue Japanese car. Photographs of the interior showed smears of dried blood on the seats, the dash and the steering wheel. Another gave a close-up of the licence plate, revealing that the vehicle came from Nanchang, in Jiangxi Province.

'This is the town where you committed the murders,' the student said, spreading out photographs of what Li took to be the main square in Nanchang, a place he had never visited. There was a photograph of the Gan River running through what looked like an industrial city, largely redeveloped. It did not seem like a town you would find in the tourist guides. 'And these are the gloves you wore. They were found in the trunk of your car.' She placed a bloodstained pair of white cotton gloves on the benchtop, still in their evidence bag. 'You can take them out if you like.' But none of them took up the offer.

Li looked again at the photographs of the crime scene. It seemed unreal. Blood and death frozen in the frame of a photographer's camera, overlit by his floods, as if staged for investigation. There was nothing that resembled a living human being less than a corpse. He supposed it was that sense of unreality that protected you from the grim truth, that each of us was mortal and would one day pass this way, too.

The student had finished briefing them on their crime. She stood back. 'You can go through the photographs again if you like,' she said. 'Re-examine any of the exhibits.' But they had had enough of it. So she opened the blinds and the room flooded with afternoon sunshine. They blinked away the light, and their focus, and the spell was broken, returning them abruptly from Nanchang to Beijing.

The girl smiled nervously. She was not used to being in such exalted company and felt exposed now in the full blaze of sunlight. She said, 'Professor Pan will show you some photographic images on a computer screen. Some of these images will mean something to you. Some will not. Some will be relevant to the crime you have "committed", some will be irrelevant. Some will be familiar to you, although not relevant to the crime. Professor Pan will explain exactly what she requires of you when you go into the computer room.' Her eyes fixed on Li. 'You first, Section Chief.'

It was a square, featureless room without windows. A door led out into the hallway, and another through to a small lecture room. Cream-coloured walls looked as if they had not seen a paintbrush for some time. The floor was covered with grey carpet tiles. There were two large computer desks placed at right angles to each other in the centre of the room. The bigger of the desks had a large monitor attached to a computer mounted beneath it. A laptop was wired into both. They, in turn, were connected to another computer placed on the smaller desk. Cables spewed out of everything and were arranged in tidy coils on the floor. A single overhead lamp focused light on the two desks, leaving everything outside its circle of illumination sunk in gloom.

Lynn Pan carried her own inner light with her, and she seemed to glow as she showed Li into the room. He noticed the way that she was always touching him, a hand on his shoulder, or on his arm as she guided him to a seat at the smaller desk. She then sat on the edge of his desk looking directly down on him, her legs stretched out and crossed in front of her, her calf grazing his. It made Li feel slightly uncomfortable for the first time. But it was not a feeling that lasted long. She fixed him with her eyes and her smile, and he had that mush sensation in his stomach again.

'I hear it's a big day for you today,' she said, and he frowned, uncertain what she meant. 'The People's Award for Crime Fighting.' And his face immediately coloured with embarrassment. But if she noticed, she gave no indication of it. 'I would have loved to go,' she said. 'If I'd been invited. I've never been in the Great Hall.'

'Be my guest,' Li said.

'Wow! Invited by the recipient.'

Li searched her face and her tone for some hint of sarcasm, but found none. She had that openness and innocence about her that was common to almost every American he had ever met. Except for Margaret. Her cynicism and sense of irony marked her out as very different from most of her fellow countrymen.

'Hey, listen, if I can get out of here on time I'll be there.' Pan's smile was radiant. 'But I gotta process you guys first. Convince you I'm worth backing. Yeah?'

She stood up, suddenly businesslike, and lifted a primitive-looking headset from the desk. Wires trailed out of the back of it like a Chinese queue. It consisted of a broad blue headband made from some kind of stretchy material that fitted across the forehead and around the back of the head. Another band ran from front to back across the scalp, attached by velcro strips at both ends. Electrodes, each with their own little

sewn-in velcro pad, could be moved about on the inner surface of the bands. 'To optimise the placing of the electrodes,'
Pan explained. 'Everybody's head is different.' She spent some
time fitting the headset to Li's larger than average head, her
small breasts stretching her blouse just above his eyeline. He
tried not to let his eyes be drawn. But he could smell her perfume, feel her warmth, and there was something irresistibly
intimate about her hands moving across his scalp, touching
his face, his neck. Warm, soft skin against his.

She talked as she worked. 'When I've fixed this, I'm going
to give you a list of nine items. We call them *targets*, but that
won't mean anything to you right now. I'll explain in more
detail afterwards. Anyway, the list will describe things like a
knife, a landmark in your home town, your apartment block.
Afterwards, I'm going to show you a sequence of photographs
on your computer screen, and when you see a picture of any
one of those items on the *target* list, I want you to click the left-
hand button on the computer mouse.' She leaned across him
towards the desk to pull the mouse towards them. 'Take a look
at it. I don't know if you're familiar with computers or not.'

'Sure,' Li said. He placed his hand over the mouse. It was
divided in two at the finger-end, and each half could be clicked
down separately. 'The left-hand side for anything on the *target*
list.'

'And the right-hand side for everything else. So you click
once for every image you see.'

Li shrugged. 'Seems simple enough.' He smiled. 'So how do
you know what apartment building I live in?'

She grinned. 'We've done our homework, Mister Li.'

'If you'd wanted my address you only had to ask.'

'Perhaps, but I'm not sure your partner would have been too happy. She's an American, isn't she?'

Li raised an eyebrow. 'You *have* done your homework.'

'On all of you.' She stood back and smiled at him ruefully. 'Sorry to disappoint.'

She finished arranging his headgear, and then skipped around to the other desk and opened a beige folder with Li's name marked on the front of it. She leaned over to hand him his *target* list and sat down at her computer to prime it for the first test. Li looked at the list. As Pan had said it would, it described nine items: *a knife with a jewelled handle; the body of a man washed up on a beach; a woman's dress with blood on it; a pair of leather gloves; a red car with a missing front fender; your apartment building; the statue of Mao Zedong in front of the provincial government building in your home town; a photograph of a crime scene in which two bodies are charred beyond recognition; the licence plate on your official car.*

Li read it over a couple of times. He had no idea what any of it meant, or why he was going to be shown these things. Pan looked up from her computer screen, positioned so that she would be looking at Li in profile while he was looking at his monitor. 'All set?' she asked.

'I guess,' Li said. 'Left-hand button for everything on this list, right-hand button for everything else.'

'You got it.' And then it was as if she flicked off a charm switch and became another person. Cool, focused, impersonal. 'At the risk of making you conscious of it, I'm going to ask you to try to blink as seldom as possible when I am showing the images. Alright?'

'Alright.'

'Focus on the screen. The images will appear for only three-tenths of a second, so please concentrate. There will be three seconds between each image, but try to respond with the mouse button immediately. You will see a total of fifty-four images. It will take approximately three minutes. We'll have a rest, and then we'll start again.'

Li found himself inexplicably tense in anticipation of it and had to make himself consciously relax his grip on the mouse. He flicked a glance at the list, afraid he might have forgotten something on it.

'Eyes on the screen please.'

His eyes jumped back to the screen and the sequence began. It was all so fast it was hard for him to think consciously about any of the images he saw. The red car with the missing fender, the bloody shirt on the drive at the crime scene, a Swiss army knife, an apartment block that meant nothing to him. It seemed like a long three minutes. He saw one of the pictures of the crime scene that Pan's graduate had shown them, and the close-up of the man with the back of his head missing. He saw a grey Nissan car that he did not recognise, the statue of Mao from his home town, the murder weapon he had handled only half an hour earlier. There were images of an axe, a licence plate he did not know, a dress with blood on it, the bizarrely familiar pink and white of the police apartment block where he lived in Zhengyi Road.

And then it was over, and Pan was smiling at him, the charm switch flicked back to the on position. 'Just relax, Li Yan,' she said, suddenly informal again, familiar. He allowed himself to blink, and sat back in his chair. The concentration the test had required of him had left him feeling fatigued. And, as if reading his mind, she said, 'It's tiring, isn't it?'

He nodded. 'Are you going to tell me now how it works?'

'Not yet. We're not finished. I'm going to show you the same pictures again, although not in the same order. The computer will randomise them. But I need you to treat them in exactly the same way. Left-hand button for the *targets*, right-hand for everything else. Okay, you ready?'

In fact, they ran through the images another twice before she finally turned on her sweetest smile and told him it was all over. She came back around the desk and removed his headset. 'How long will it take you to figure out whether I was one of those briefed on the crime or not?' he asked.

'I know already.' This quite matter-of-factly.

He was intrigued. 'So, tell me.'

Her smile turned secretive. 'Not yet. I'm saving that for the finale.' She lifted his list of *targets* and slipped it back into his folder. 'But I will tell you exactly what it is I just put you through. And why.' She adopted her sitting position on the edge of the desk again, her legs stretched out in front of her, arms folded. 'It's just a demonstration program,' she said, 'but basically it consists of me showing you fifty-four images. Nine of these are what we call *probes*. That is to say, they relate specifically to the crime that three of you were briefed on. Images that you would recognise instantly if you were one of those three. Another nine of the fifty-four were the *targets* that I gave you a list of. Each *target* corresponds to one of the *probes*. For example, your apartment block would correspond to the private dwelling house where the murder took place. You recognise your apartment block, and if you are one of those briefed, you recognise the murder house. Your brain emits the same recognition signal, the same MERMER.'

'What about the other thirty-six?'

'*Irrelevants.* That's what we call them, because that's what they are. Irrelevant. Although again, a number of them will correspond to the *probes.* So that you see your apartment block, the murder house, and some other apartment block that means nothing to you.'

The logic of it began to drop into place for Li. 'Okay, I get it,' he said. 'You use my apartment block as the benchmark. The thing you know is familiar to me. If you get the same reading from the murder house, you know I've been briefed. But if the murder house and the *irrelevant* apartment block give the same reading, which is different from my apartment, you know I haven't.'

She half nodded, half shrugged. 'I guess that comes somewhere close to it. I would probably have said that the determination of guilt or innocence consists of comparing the *probe* responses to the *target* responses, which contain a MERMER, and to the *irrelevant* responses, which do not.'

Li let the implications tumble around in his mind. 'That's extraordinary,' he said finally. 'If it works.'

'Oh, it works.'

'You would know beyond doubt that a guilty suspect had knowledge of a crime scene that only the culprit could possess. And you could instantly rule out an innocent suspect if you could demonstrate that they had no recognition of specific elements of the crime or the crime scene.'

'Which has been done,' Pan said. 'In the States. Where Doctor Farwell demonstrated to an appeal court that a man who had served twenty-two years of a prison sentence for murder had no details of the crime scene stored in his brain, while the details of his alibi were. And that evidence was ruled admissible by the judge.' She laughed to herself. 'Unlike poor old Bill Hart's dinosaur technology. I can't think of a single court anywhere that accepts the polygraph test as evidence.'

'You don't think much of the polygraph, then?'

'I don't. In a conventional polygraph test, emotion-driven physiological responses to relevant questions about the situation under investigation are compared to responses to control questions which are invasive and personal and not relevant to the issue at hand. Their only purpose is to emotionally and psychologically disturb the subject. So even if the subject is innocent, and truthful, he is subjected to a highly invasive and stressful ordeal. I don't think you could say that about the MERMER test, do you?'

Li had to agree. 'Not at all.'

'The trouble with the polygraph, Section Chief, is that it's not science. It's artful and disturbing psychological manipulation.'

Li blew air through pursed lips. 'You and Margaret would get on like a house on fire.'

Pan inclined her head. 'Margaret ...' She repeated the name. 'Campbell?' Li nodded. 'She's quite a character, I hear. I'd like to meet her.'

'If you can make it tonight you will.' He stood up, his height restoring the mantle of dominance she had taken from him and worn herself during the test. But she didn't seem to mind. The warmth in her eyes as they met his was unmistakable, and the twinkle in them suggested she was flirting.

'I will do my very best to be there,' she said. She stretched out a hand to shake his, and held it as she spoke. 'It's been a real pleasure, Section Chief.'

### III

Margaret watched as a mother lifted her child into the shiny brass seat of the rickshaw. The little girl was perhaps three years old, drowned by a quilted red jacket, a sparkling red band keeping her long, black hair out of her face. Thousands of backsides had polished the seat to a brilliant shining gold. The rest of the life-sized statue was tarnished and dull, including the rickshaw man with his shaved pate and his long pigtail. A camera flashed in the afternoon sunshine. A few yards away a middle-aged man swept his hair self-consciously to one side as he posed for his wife's camera with a couple of brass musicians. A man with a suit and an umbrella stood beside a brass barber shaving the head of an eternally acquiescent client.

A half-empty open-sided blue tourist bus crawled past, the tour guide barking the history of Wangfujing Street through a speaker system that filled the air. *The name Wangfujing derives from a fifteenth-century well* . . . No one was listening.

Beijing's best-known shopping street had changed almost beyond recognition since Margaret had first kept an appointment there with Li Yan outside the Foreign Language Bookstore more than five years before. Vast new shopping complexes in pink marble had risen from the rubble of the old. Giant TV screens played episodes of a popular soap opera. Crowds of affluent Chinese, the new bourgeoisie, roamed the pedestrian precincts viewing luxury goods behind plate-glass windows, anxious to spend their new-found wealth. On the corner of Wangfujing and Donganmen, outside the bookshop, an old man wearing a cloth cap and dark blue cotton jacket pedalled up on his tricycle with a steaming urn to warm the young security men on traffic duty with mugs of hot green tea. They gathered around him like children, with their red armbands, laughing and giggling and poking each other while traffic at the junction ground to a halt.

Margaret smiled. While so much about China had changed in just five years, the character of the Chinese had not. There was something irresistibly likeable about them – unless you happened to be trying to renew your visa. The thought clouded her afternoon with memories of that morning's debacle. She tipped Li Jon's buggy on to its back wheels and bumped it up the two steps to the open doors of the bookstore, brushing aside the heavy strips of clear plastic that kept in the heat.

An overhead heater blasted them with hot air, and Margaret turned off to their right where she knew they kept the stands of English language fiction and non-fiction books. Rows of shelving between grey marble pillars delivered books on every aspect of foreign language and culture to an increasingly literate population, hungry to feed a new-found appetite for learning about the world beyond the Middle Kingdom. People spoke here in hushed and reverent tones, in direct contrast with the cacophony in the street outside.

Margaret found what she was looking for on the middle shelf of the back wall. There were two English-language originals of Thomas Dowman's *The Murders of Jack the Ripper* sitting side by side. She lifted one and found an assistant who wrote her out a slip in exchange for the book. She spotted a manned cash desk on the far side of the shop and took her slip there to pay for the book, before returning with her receipt to collect it from the assistant. It was tiresome, but it was the Chinese way, and you just got used to it. And it was also, she supposed, one way of keeping the unemployment figures down.

Outside, the blue bus was making its return trip, the tour guide's nasal hollering still an assault on the ears. *Before the liberation in 1949, Wangfujing was known as Morrison Street* . . . And still no one was listening. A fresh bunch of people was posing with the brass statues. Margaret pushed Li Jon's buggy to the junction, where the security men had returned to traffic duty, and flagged a taxi, fumbling in her pocket for the address Chi Lyang had written down for her after lunch.

*

The Jade Fingers Blind Massage Club was on the twenty-fifth floor of a new shopping mall in Chaoyang District, off the east Third Ring Road, just south of the Lufthansa Centre. Lyang was waiting for her in the reception room. 'It's all fixed,' she said and nodded to one of two Chinese girls behind the desk who came to relieve Margaret of Li Jon and the buggy. Margaret looked anxiously as the girl wheeled her son away through swing doors. 'Relax,' Lyang said. 'Let go. That's what this place is for. Some time out from life. Enjoy it.'

Margaret said, 'I haven't had time out from life since I don't know when.'

'Then you're long overdue.'

The other girl from Reception led them down a long, narrow corridor. Openings without doors led off into massage rooms every few metres. There was thick, soft carpet underfoot, and a hush suffused the place, broken only by the odd murmur of distant voices. Some of the rooms were empty. In others women swaddled in towels lay on massage tables, groaning while girls in white overalls worked strong fingers into soft flesh.

'Don't worry, it's women-only,' Lyang said, catching Margaret's expression.

Margaret said, 'Why is it called the *blind* massage club?'

'Because all the masseuses are blind,' Lyang said.

Margaret laughed. 'Ask a silly question.'

Lyang said, 'It's a good job for a blind person, based solely on touch. Something I'm more than happy to support. And imagine, a blind masseuse has nothing to distract her. Her entire focus is on you, and the whole landscape of your body beneath her fingers.'

'I thought we were having a foot massage.'

'Today, yes. But some other time you must try the whole body massage. It leaves you feeling fantastic for the rest of the day.'

They turned into a room with two reclining armchairs, a footstool in front of each and a low table between them. The girl from Reception invited them to sit, and they arranged themselves comfortably in the chairs and removed their shoes and socks. A few moments later both receptionists returned with small wooden barrels lined with plastic and filled with hot, aromatic water. Scented herbs floated on the surface, their fragrance rising with the steam. A barrel was placed in front of each chair and Lyang and Margaret slipped their feet into the water. It was so hot Margaret almost had to withdraw her feet immediately, but the burning quickly subsided and she started to relax.

Lyang said, 'They'll leave us now to steep for about twenty minutes.'

Another girl brought in cups of jasmine tea and Margaret took a sip and allowed herself to unwind. A wave of fatigue washed over her and she closed her eyes, remembering the cry of the baby which had wakened her at five that morning. For the next hour and a half her over-sensitised inner alarm system could take a break. Without opening her eyes she said, 'So what was it about Bill Hart that made him worth giving up your job for?'

'Oh, I didn't give it up for *him*. I gave it up for me.'

A slight frown creased Margaret's brow. 'How do you mean?'

'I fell in love,' Lyang said simply. 'What's a girl gonna do? It was him or my job.'

'And you didn't resent that?'

'Well, sure. But it wasn't Bill I resented. It was the god-damned stupid rule we have about cops not marrying foreigners. And, anyway, I didn't do anything he didn't. He gave up a well-paid job in the States to come and work in China for about a tenth of the money. That makes me feel good. It means he must love me, too.'

'Didn't you want to go and live in the States?'

'Not really. This is my home. And besides, Bill wanted to come and live here. He still can't get over the idea of a civil-isation that's five thousand years old.'

'Well, of course, he comes from a country where the most exciting thing we've produced in two hundred years is the burger.'

Lyang laughed. 'You sound just like him. His favourite gag just now is, what happens if you leave an American and a cup of yoghurt alone in a room for a week?' She paused waiting for a response.

Margaret obliged. 'And that would be?'

'The yoghurt develops its own culture.' Which brought a smile to Margaret's lips. And Lyang added, almost apologetic-ally, 'I only tell it because he does.'

Margaret grinned, opening her eyes and tilting her head to look at her. 'As long as you don't tell it to Li Yan. I like giving him a hard time about China, and I hate giving him ammunition for return fire.' She paused. 'So what do you do all day every day?'

'I still work.'

Margaret was taken aback. 'Doing what?'

'At the Academy. It's just part time, but I work mornings as Bill's assistant. I know you don't think very much of the polygraph . . .'

Margaret broke in, 'I'd be lying if I told you otherwise.'

Lyang said, 'And we'd know if you were.' They both laughed. Then she said, 'The truth is, Bill's more of a scientist than a practitioner. The Academy is employing him to develop something based on the polygraph which is more suited to the Chinese. He was responsible for persuading Lynn Pan to come to China to work on the Chinese version of MERMER.' She hesitated and glanced over at Margaret. 'You don't work at all?'

'I give the occasional lecture at the Public Security University.'

'But no pathology?'

Margaret shook her head. 'The Ministry is not particularly keen on Americans conducting autopsies on Chinese crime victims. I think they think it reflects badly on their own pathologists.'

'But Bill said you'd done autopsy work for us before.'

'Special circumstances,' Margaret said. 'And, then, when the baby came, things changed.'

'How?'

'Well, Li Yan and I are not married, for a start.'

'Obviously.'

'But we do live together.'

Lyang sat up, interested. 'Yeah, I was going to ask you about that.'

Margaret waggled a finger at her. 'That's just it, you don't ask. At least, that's the position the Ministry takes. They don't ask, we don't tell, they don't know. Officially. That way we get away with it – as long as we don't marry.'

Lyang whistled softly. 'And Li Yan wouldn't think about giving up his job?'

'I wouldn't ask him,' Margaret said. 'It's a part of him. It would be like asking him to cut off a leg.' She sighed. 'The upshot of it all, though, is that it's no longer politic for him to request permission to use me for autopsies on special cases.' She qualified herself. 'On *any* cases.'

'So you're leading a life of leisure and pleasure as a mother and wife . . . well, almost wife?'

Margaret laughed. 'No, I think the word I think you're looking for is vegetating.'

'So what *do* you do all day?'

'Oh, I stay home and look after our son. Do a bit of housework, a bit of cooking. I never know when Li Yan'll be coming home or when he'll be called out. I don't have any friends in Beijing, so I never go anywhere . . .' She shook her head in something close to despair. 'You know, the kind of domestic bliss every American woman aspires to.' She sat up and turned towards Lyang. It felt good to talk, to get some of this stuff off her chest. It had been a long time since there had been anyone other than Li to whom she could unburden herself. 'It's like I've stopped living, Lyang. Like my whole life's been sucked into my baby, and my only future is to live it vicariously through him.'

'Jesus, Margaret . . .' Lyang had clearly picked up her husband's slang. 'You sound like you need a few bodies to cut up.'

Margaret laughed out loud. 'Yeah,' she said. 'That would probably be good therapy. You've no idea how much I miss the smell of an open intestine, or that slurping sound the brain makes when it plops out of the skull.'

'Hmmm,' Lyang said. 'I can see how you'd miss that.'

The receptionists looked curiously at the two women lying back laughing on their reclining seats when they came in to take away the soak barrels. They returned a few moments later to dry off the two pairs of feet and place them on towels on each of the footrests. Margaret watched curiously as the two blind masseuses were led in to squat on stools at the end of each footrest. Lyang's girl was very young, perhaps only nineteen or twenty. Her eyes were bizarrely pale, almost grey, and seemed fixed beneath beautifully slanted lids. Margaret's masseuse was older, about thirty, and her dark eyes seemed to be constantly on the move, squinting to one side and then back again. Both were slightly built, wearing white cotton overalls, and when Margaret's girl lathered her tiny hands with soft-scented cream and began working on Margaret's feet, Margaret was astonished at the strength in them.

'Of course, you know why Western men like Asian women,' Lyang said, and Margaret could hear the mischief in her voice.

'Why?' she asked, without opening her eyes.

'Because they have such small hands.'

Margaret smiled and frowned at the same time. 'And that's attractive because . . . ?'

'It makes their dicks seem bigger.'

They laughed again, and saw the incomprehension on the faces of their masseuses. A foot massage was supposed to be relaxing, therapeutic, not funny. But Margaret was finding the whole experience therapeutic in other ways. 'I guess that must be why I fell for Li Yan,' she said.

Lyang frowned, knowing there was a gag coming, but not seeing it. 'Why?'

'Because he makes my hands look so small.'

Their raucous laughter was inappropriate, and inordinately loud in the hushed atmosphere of the Jade Fingers Blind Massage Club. Margaret's masseuse found a painful area on the sole of her foot and seemed to dig into it particularly hard with her thumb. Margaret gasped. But there was also an odd pleasure in the pain. She lay back then and succumbed to both the pain and the pleasure as her girl worked her way around her toes, down all the painful bumps in her arch, around the heel and back up the outside edge. She knew what all the muscles were, could picture them as the girl's dextrous fingers sought them out, folded one over the other around the delicate bones of the foot. It was deliciously relaxing.

After a long period of silence, Lyang said to her, 'What have you done about Li Jon?'

'What do you mean?'

'His nationality.'

'Well, he's both, of course. Chinese and American.'

'You've registered him with the Embassy?'

'Sure.' It had been a complex procedure. Chinese and American laws were in conflict over the nationality of a child born to a Chinese-American couple. The Americans, the consul for American Citizen Services at the embassy had told Margaret, defined a child born to one American anywhere in the world as a US citizen at birth. The Chinese used the same legal premise for their citizens abroad, but allowed mixed citizenship couples, legally resident in China, to pick a citizenship for their kid after birth. Margaret had wanted to register Li Jon with the US embassy. Li was anxious for his son to remain Chinese. They had almost fallen out over it. In the end Margaret had persuaded Li that the Chinese were never going to deny his son nationality as long as they were there in China. But she wanted Li Jon properly registered as a US citizen so that there would never be a problem about them taking him to the US if they ever decided to go there. So she had gone to the embassy and had an interview with a sympathetic consul who set in motion a series of background checks on both Li and Margaret before finally issuing Li Jon with a Consular Report of Birth Abroad – which would effectively act as his passport for the first five years and make him officially a US citizen.

'You got one of those Consular Report things?' Lyang asked.

'That's right.'

'Yeah, Bill insisted we did that for Ling, too. So she's a fully fledged stars and stripes citizen. It stuck in my craw a little to have to register her as a *foreigner* with the local police. It was expensive, too.' A thought struck her. 'Hey, how did you do that when you two aren't . . . you know, married? Not even officially living together.'

'We didn't,' Margaret said. 'It was going to be too complicated. Officially, I still live in an apartment provided by the University of Public Security. That comes under the Western Beijing Police district. In reality, Li Yan and I share his police apartment in the Central Beijing Police district. We were just never going to be able to explain it.'

'The endless complications of life in China,' Lyang said. 'You know, you and Li Yan should come over some night for a meal. We've got a lot in common, we four.'

'I'd like that,' Margaret said. 'It would be nice to get out for a change. Where do you live?'

'Ah,' Lyang said. 'That was Bill's only stipulation – that if we were going to live in China, it wasn't going to be in some dilapidated apartment where the Government controls the heating. His first wife died in a road accident, and he had been rattling around on his own in their big town house in Boston. So when we got married he sold it, and we bought one of those fabulous new modern apartments near the Central Business District. You know, the ones built for foreigners. We're in a complex called Music Home International. It's silly, really, but the two apartment blocks have got like huge grand piano lids on their roofs.' She seemed a little embarrassed. 'You can't miss them. But there's a health club with a pool and tennis courts, and there's a beautifully landscaped private garden which is going to be just great for Ling in the summer.'

Margaret felt a twinge of jealousy. Not that any of these things amounted to a lifestyle she aspired to, but they sounded a great deal more appealing than Li's spartan police apartment with its tiny rooms and irregular heating. And the thought returned her to a reality from which she had escaped all too briefly into a world of laughter and freedom from maternal responsibility. She had forgotten what it was like to have a life of your own, and she wasn't sure that a friendship with Lyang would be a good thing. It could be very unsettling.

## IV

Li sat with Procurator Meng, Deputy Commissioner Cao, Deputy Minister Wei Peng and Director General Yan Bo in a stilted silence in the reception room where they had first gathered. They had come in one by one from their MERMER tests flushed and fatigued and oddly self-conscious. Conversation had been desultory, and none of them had talked about the test. They were all, with the exception of Li, smoking. In exasperation, he had eventually gone to the window to draw the blinds and open it. He stood now gazing west, beyond Yuyuantan Park where he had sometimes played chess with his uncle, towards the distinctive minaret-shaped TV tower catching the mid-afternoon sun. It felt like they had been there all day. In fact it had been little more than two hours. But Li was growing impatient now, anxious to get back to his investigation.

He turned as the door behind him opened and Commissioner Zhu, the last of them to be tested, breezed in from the computer room. He was actually smiling and, like the others before him, faintly flushed. 'Charming woman,' he said, adjusting his frameless spectacles on the bridge of his nose.

'Quit dreaming, Commissioner,' his deputy said. Cao was draped languidly on his chair watching his boss with knowing eyes, smoke seeping from the corners of his mouth. 'It's your backing she's after, not your body.' And Li realised that she had probably been doing a number on them all, each of them convinced that her warmth and touch and eye contact meant that they had struck some special chord with her. Li smiled to himself. Whatever it was she had, or did, it worked. And as he glanced around the other faces in the room, he knew that the same thought was also going through their minds.

The door opened and Professor Pan came in briskly, clutching a sheaf of papers. The moment she entered the room, Li knew that something was wrong. Her whole demeanour had altered unmistakably. There was a droop in her shoulders, her face seemed pale suddenly, and drawn. She was still smiling, but the smile was fixed and false, and she seemed reluctant to make eye contact with any of them. 'Gentlemen, I am so sorry to keep you,' she said. Her eyes flickered briefly around the room, and Li saw something strange in them. Something like confusion. All the confidence in them had vanished, and yet she was working hard at maintaining the facade. He wondered if something had gone terribly wrong with the tests. If she was going to fail to identify the three 'criminals'. But then she said, 'The tests are quite conclusive. Commissioner Zhu, Procurator Meng, Section Chief Li. I think my findings would be sufficient to convict you all of murder in a court of law.'

There was a spontaneous burst of applause, and Li looked around his fellow guinea-pigs. If any of them was aware of the change in Miss Pan it did not show.

'Congratulations, Professor,' Procurator General Meng said. 'I think we are all very impressed.'

And Li wondered for a moment if it was all just some kind of sophisticated parlour trick. If it was, it was a very good one. 'How do we know you weren't aware all along which of us was briefed?' he asked.

She swung wounded eyes on him, and he saw the hurt in them. But before she had a chance to speak, Deputy Cao said, 'Don't be ridiculous, Li. If the thing didn't work, she knows we'd find out soon enough.' And although she said nothing, Pan held Li's eyes for longer than she had to, and he saw something else in them. Something confounding. Something like fear and a plea for help.

'I think,' the Deputy Minister said, 'I can speak for everyone here when I say that I believe you can count on our backing for your project.' He looked around, as if defying anyone to contradict him.

Pan tore her eyes away from Li's and forced the smile back to her lips. 'That's very gratifying, Deputy Minister Wei. I'm very grateful to you all for your patience. I know it's been a long afternoon for you.'

'Not at all, Professor,' Commissioner Zhu said. 'I think we've all enjoyed the experience. A welcome break from the routine of the office.'

She nodded, glancing at her watch. 'Well, I don't want to keep you any longer, gentlemen. Thank you so much for coming.' She made a tiny bow, and turned and hurried out of the room. Li saw the smile wiping itself from her face as she disappeared through the door.

'Well, how did it go?' Bill Hart pressed him eagerly as they went down the stairs together.

'Oh, I think she'll get her funding okay,' Li said.

Hart grinned. 'I never doubted it. What did you think?'

Li had to acknowledge, 'I was very impressed. If MERMER is as reliable as that in the field, then it could revolutionise criminal investigation.'

'Of course, it has to be used very carefully,' Hart said. 'I mean, think about it. You're the investigating officer. You make a detailed examination of the crime scene, so now you carry the same information in your brain as the killer. Can we always be sure we'll know which is which, who is who?'

Li nodded. 'A fair point. And I suppose an investigating officer would have to be very careful that he didn't accidentally provide a suspect with information that might read like guilty knowledge in a MERMER test.'

'Absolutely,' Hart said. 'If this thing really is going to work in the field, then the rules of engagement are going to have to be very tightly defined, and applied. Otherwise it could be open to abuse.'

'Like corrupt officers deliberately contaminating a suspect's mind with information from a crime scene so that it will show up on a MERMER?'

Hart smiled knowingly. 'Not that an officer in the People's Republic would dream of doing such a thing.'

'Nor any in the United States,' said Li.

'God forbid.' Hart threw up his hands in mock horror, and they shared a grin. Then Hart's smile faded. 'I guess if Lynn gets her funding, then there's a good chance mine will get cancelled.'

'Why?'

'Shit, Li Yan, Margaret was right. Compared with something like MERMER the polygraph's a dinosaur. And in untrained hands it's just about useless. She put her finger on it when she said it's the operator who's the real lie detector. And it takes a lot of training and a lot of experience to be good at it.' He sighed. 'Your bosses at the Ministry are less than convinced by it. I think they see it as not much more than a very expensive psychological rubber hose with which to beat a suspect.' He laughed. 'Hell, a real rubber hose is a lot cheaper and probably just as effective.'

'And just as inadmissible in court as a polygraph,' Li said. 'So what'll happen if your funding gets cancelled?'

'I'm going to have to go back to the States to look for work.'

'And would Lyang be happy to do that?'

Hart pulled a face. 'I haven't told her yet, Li Yan. I figure there's no point in worrying about it until it happens.' He paused. 'But, no, she wouldn't be happy.'

They came down the final flight of steps into the entrance lobby. Hart shook Li's hand. 'Thanks for coming,' he said. 'And, hey, listen, why don't you bring Margaret round for dinner some night? I get the feeling that she and Lyang might get on pretty well.'

'I'll mention it to her,' Li said.

'Well, what about tonight?'

Li shrugged apologetically. 'I've got an appointment I can't get out of.' There was a hint of embarrassment in his smile.

Hart remembered suddenly. 'Of course, it's your award thing tonight at the Great Hall. I read about that in the paper the other day. You must be very proud.'

Li forced a smile. 'Sure,' he said.

As he pushed out through the swing door Hart called after him, 'Don't forget to ask Margaret about dinner?'

Li waved a hand and was gone, out into the cold afternoon air. He pulled up his coat collar and turned south towards Fuxingmenwai Avenue. A car horn blasting from across the street drew his attention, and he looked round as a large black Ministry limo made a U-turn and drew in at the kerb alongside him. A door opened, and as he leaned down, he saw Commissioner Zhu and Deputy Cao sitting in the back seat. 'Get in, Li,' the Commissioner told him. Li slipped into the front passenger seat beside the uniformed driver. 'Do you have a car with you?' asked the Commissioner. Li shook his head.

'In the name of the sky, Li, you didn't come on your bicycle?' Deputy Cao regarded him with something akin to contempt.

'No, I didn't, Deputy Cao,' Li said.

The Commissioner tapped the driver on the shoulder. 'Section One,' he said. And to Li, 'We'll give you a lift back, and you can brief us on the Beijing Ripper.' Li's surprise must have been evident in his face, because it made the Commissioner smile. A smug smile, Li thought. 'Don't be so shocked, Li. There isn't much goes on in your Section that I don't get to hear about.'

'Why didn't you mention it upstairs?' Deputy Cao asked.

'I didn't think it was appropriate. Not in front of the Deputy Minister and the Procurator General,' Li said.

'So tell us,' the Commissioner said, 'what makes you think these killings are a copycat of the Jack the Ripper murders?'

Li pulled the book from his pocket and handed it into the back of the car. 'Just published in China. A translation from the English original. It details all the killings attributed to the Ripper. The killings here in Beijing are like a carbon copy, even down to the smallest detail.'

'Like?' demanded Deputy Cao.

'Like the contents of her purse being arranged around the feet of victim number three . . . the removal of her uterus and parts of her vagina and bladder. Like the missing left kidney and the womb in victim number four. And dozens of other small details, even down to the number of stab wounds in victim number one.' The Commissioner was still examining the Ripper book. Li went on, 'Then there's the fact that our murderer only kills on the weekends, and that all the victims have been found within the same square mile of the city.'

The Commissioner passed the book to Deputy Cao. 'It *is* him,' he said.

Li frowned. 'It *is* who?'

'Thomas Dowman,' said Deputy Cao. 'The author of the book. We met him when he came to Beijing a couple of years ago.'

'I heard he gave a lecture on the Ripper,' Li said.

'That's right,' said the Commissioner. 'Deputy Cao and I were both there. Almost every senior officer at the Ministry was. A fascinating profile of an unfathomable murderer. Mister Dowman certainly knows his stuff.'

'And so does someone else,' said Li.

The Commissioner leaned forward, grasping the back of Li's seat. 'Let's keep this within the department for the moment, Li. We don't want the press getting wind of it.'

'That's hardly likely,' Li said.

'There are journalists in this city who don't know where to draw the line any more,' Deputy Cao said ominously. 'With the Olympics coming in 2008, the government has been . . .' He hesitated, searching for the right words. '. . . overkeen, shall we say, to show the world what an open society we have become. There are those in the media who are taking advantage.'

'And it's not just a matter of creating public panic,' Commissioner Zhu said. 'That would be bad enough. You only have to look at how press coverage of the Washington sniper last year just about paralysed the US capital.'

'It's a political matter, Li,' Cao said. 'You can imagine the coverage such a story would generate around the world. Not exactly the image of Beijing that the government wants to promote ahead of the Olympics.'

'So let's keep it nice and quiet, Section Chief,' the Commissioner said. He lit a cigarette and blew smoke into the front of the limo. 'I want detailed progress reports on my desk. Daily. I am not going to preside over a police department which permits some lunatic to rerun the Ripper murders from first to last.' He paused. 'Get him, Section Chief Li, before he kills again.' As if Li needed to be told.

# CHAPTER FOUR

## I

The chatter of computer keyboards, like cicadas, filled the air as Li strode along the top floor corridor of Section One. Voices and cigarette smoke drifted out of the open door of the detectives' room. 'Wu! Qian!' he shouted as he stalked past, but didn't wait for a response. At the next door along he turned left into his own office and looked at the piles of paperwork gathering in drifts on his desk. A veritable paper blizzard. Reports from all the detectives working on the case, reports from forensics and pathology on each of the murders. Reports from headquarters on all manner of internal affairs in which he had absolutely no interest. The day's mail, which he had not yet had an opportunity to open, was piled up in a wire tray. He hung his coat on the stand and slumped into his chair, letting his eyes close as it reclined. He could not bear an untidy desk. Somehow it cluttered his mind, fogged his thinking.

'Chief?' Qian's voice from the door made him open his eyes. He sat up. Wu was hovering at Qian's shoulder.

'Qian, the Commissioner has asked for daily progress

reports on the Ripper murders. I want you to take care of them.' He could see Qian's shoulders slump, but it wasn't something he could afford to get bogged down with himself.

'Yes, Chief.'

Wu said, 'I checked out the publication date of the Ripper book. It's been on the shelves here for less than a week, Chief.'

Li reached for the mail and started absently opening envelopes and consigning their contents either to the bin or to the pile on his desk. 'So it wasn't the appearance of the book which sparked off the killings,' he said. 'Given that the first killing was five weeks ago.' He paused to think about it for a moment. 'See if you can track down a telephone number, or even an e-mail address for the author. It might be useful if we could speak to him.'

'Sure, Chief.'

Li screwed up some departmental circular and threw it in the bin. 'And something else.' He fixed them both with a look they knew well. 'Someone in this section is feeding information to headquarters. Specifically the Commissioner's office.'

Qian was shocked. 'What, one of our people, Chief?'

'One of our people, Qian. I don't know who it is. I don't want to know who it is. But it might be worth circulating the thought among the team, that if I ever find out, he can kiss his career goodbye, along with his testicles. I decide what information leaves this building, and what stays within its walls. Is that clear?'

'Crystal, Chief,' Qian said.

Li sliced open the envelope he was holding and pulled out

a handwritten letter. Almost immediately he dropped both on the desk and sat staring at them.

'What is it, Chief?' Wu asked.

'Get someone up here from forensics,' Li said quietly. 'Now!' There was something imperative in his tone, and Wu turned immediately and headed back for the detectives' room and a phone. Qian crossed to his boss's desk.

'What is it?'

'A letter from our killer.'

The single sheet of stationery was folded once – large, untidy characters scrawled in red ink.

Dear Chief,

I am downward on whores and I will not stop the tearing of them until I am caught. Good work the last was. I gave to the lady no time for squealing. I like my work and want to start again. You will hear more of me with my small funny plays. I saved a part of the red substance kept in a bottle from the last work to write with, but it disappeared thick as the adhesive and I cannot employ it. Red ink is good enough, I hope ha ha. Next work that I do I will cut off the ears of the lady to send to the senior police officers just for fun. My knife is so nice and sharp, I want to get to work immediately if I get a chance. Good luck.

    Sincerely yours,

    The Beijing Ripper

    (Don't mind me giving my trade name.)

Apart from the red ink and the strange, stilted language of it, what struck Li most forcibly about the letter was its signature. *The Beijing Ripper.* It was what the Commissioner had called him only half an hour earlier.

'It feels like a translation from another language,' Elvis was saying. He had a photocopy of the Ripper letter in his hands, scowling at its odd phraseology. 'Nobody would write Chinese like this.'

'Unless maybe he was a foreigner,' Qian said, which brought a murmur of speculation from around the table. The meeting room was packed. Every detective on duty was crammed in, every one with a colour photocopy of the letter. This was new. No one in the section could ever remember a murderer sending a letter to the investigating officer. Since such cases did not normally receive widespread, if any, coverage in the media, the murderer would not know who the investigating officers were until they caught him. But in this case, the envelope was addressed to Section Chief Li personally.

Li turned the photocopy over and over in his fingers, considerably disturbed by it. Forensics had been quick to confirm that his were the only fingerprints on the original. It was written on commonplace stationery. The postmark on the envelope was Central Beijing. It had been posted that morning and arrived with the afternoon delivery. It could only have been a matter of hours after his last murder that the killer had written it. It made his killings seem even colder, more calculated – in direct contrast to Pathologist Wang's verdict of frenzy. Of course, they knew now that there was nothing at all frenzied about the murders. They were meticulous replications of another man's madness. But what kind of man was it who could map out his murders with such careful precision, who could cold-bloodedly murder a girl, then set about carving her up according to a one-hundred-and-fifteen-year-old blueprint?

'Is there any significance to the red ink, do you think?' Elvis asked. 'I mean, I know he says it's a substitute for his victim's blood, but . . .'

He left his question hanging. In Chinese culture, red ink in a letter symbolised the end of a relationship. It was one reason why Li had asked for it to be copied in colour, so that if there was significance in the colour of the ink, no one would miss it. But no one in the room had any idea what significance it might have. The end of a relationship with whom? The victim? Did that mean he knew her, or she him?

Li glanced at Wu. He had picked up the Ripper book from the table some minutes earlier, and still had his nose buried in it. 'I hope we're not distracting you from your reading, Wu,' Li said.

Wu looked up. Normally Li would have expected a smart retort. But instead Wu looked wan. Shocked. 'I don't think the red ink has any significance at all,' he told the room. 'Not in any Chinese sense, anyway.' He flattened the book open on the table where he had been reading. 'I think I should read you this.' He stubbed out his cigarette and began: *Dear Boss, I am downward on whores and I will not stop the tearing of them until*

*I am caught. . .* He looked up, sensing that he did not have to read any further. 'Police investigating the Whitechapel murders in London were given the letter by a news agency which received it on the 27th of September, 1888. It's almost exactly the same as the letter you received today, Chief. Except that it's addressed to *Dear Boss*, and signed *Jack the Ripper*. It seems that's where the name first came from.'

Li reached out for the book, and Wu pushed it across the table. He said, 'Seems like they don't reckon it was sent by the killer, though. They figure it was some smart-ass journalist trying to stir up interest in the story.'

Qian said, 'But ours must have come from the killer. I mean, nobody except the police would know about the murders?'

'Whoever he was, he knew my name,' Li said. 'He knew the address of this section.' Which ruled out most of the population of Beijing. Section One was tucked away in an obscure *hutong* in the north-east of the city. An anonymous brick building opposite the All China Federation of Returned Overseas Chinese. It did not advertise itself in any way. Outside of a hardcore criminal element, few people even knew of its existence.

'Hey, come on, Chief.' Elvis was chewing absently on a matchstick, and toying with his redundant sunglasses. 'Most of China knows who you are these days. You've been splashed all over the papers ahead of this award thing tonight. You're a hero.'

Which brought some laughter from around the room. But Li was not amused. He said to Qian, 'Get someone to go through the book and make an abstract of all the salient details. Get that copied and circulating. And since Elvis isn't invited to the ceremony tonight, maybe he could do it.'

'Aw, Chief . . .'

Qian grinned. 'You got it, Chief.'

'And let's get a few more copies of the book itself. Get a dozen. Everyone on the case should read it.'

'Hey,' Wu cut in, 'I just figured out who the killer is. It's the author. He's hoping to turn it into a best-seller by getting the cops to buy up all the copies.'

Which brought a smile even to Li's lips. When the laughter subsided, he said, 'The thing is, if the murderer sticks to his mentor's script, then we should know what his next move is.' He consulted the book again. 'According to the original Ripper's timetable, he didn't strike again for another six weeks, which might just give us a bit of breathing space. That's the good news.' He flipped through a few pages then stopped. 'The bad news is that Jack's next victim was a woman called Mary Jane Kelly, and he cut her up so badly she was hardly recognisable as human.' The silence in the meeting room was very nearly tangible. Li's eyes strayed to the photographs of the dead girls on the wall. Guo Huan had joined them now, a blow-up of one of the photographs from the strip given him by her mother. Her crime scene was set out below her in not so glorious technicolor. There was too much red. 'I don't want another girl up there on the wall,' he said. 'Whatever we do, we've got to stop that from happening.'

# II

The sun was dipping fast in the west now, pink light catching the particles of pollution along the horizon, turning them orange beneath the darkening blue above. Li pulled up on to the sidewalk in front of the main gate of Yuyuantan Park. Red lanterns spun lazily in the dying breeze. A shady character wearing a dark suit and smoking a cigarette cupped in his hand was doing his best to impress a pretty girl leaning against the railings. She was dressed all in white – white coat, white bootees, white handbag clutched demurely in front of her in both hands. Seemingly he was succeeding, because she was staring up at him adoringly, apparently oblivious to the fact that his eyes were constantly on the move, above and beyond her, left and right. He spotted Li's car the moment he parked it by the gate. And he watched suspiciously as Li got out of the driver's side. His eyes flickered towards the registration plate, and Li could see that he recognised the *jing* character followed by *0* as the trademark police registration it was – something only someone with previous experience of the police was likely to know. Li wanted to tell the girl to go home, to have nothing to do with this wide boy. He was bad news. But it was none of Li's business.

He circumnavigated the barrier at the gate of the gardens outside the park. It was here that all the old men came to play cards and chess and chequers and dominoes. In the summer, there was shade from the trees. In the winter there was the warmth of companionship. And it saved them the two *yuan* payable for entry to the park itself. A path overhung by the naked branches of gnarled trees, and lined by bicycles parked three deep, led into the main garden where a statue carved from white stone watched the men in dark clothes huddled around their games. Beyond the trees, the roar of the traffic had become a distant rumble. A woman with short hair and a red jacket sang Peking Opera to the accompaniment of a wizened old man drawing his bow across the two strings of an ancient *erhu*. The evening sky reflected a cold blue off the canal which ran south out of Yuyuan Lake, a body of water which would be frozen solid in under a month, attracting skaters from all over the city. The last golden beams of sunlight warmed a silver-haired old man practising his *tai chi* as he gazed out over the water.

Groups of men were dotted about all over the central concourse, gathered around the benches where the games were being played. Dai Yi was playing chess in the centre of one of the huddles. Li's Uncle Yifu had always called him *Lao* Dai – old Dai – even though he was several months younger. He was a short man, stocky, with a round, smiling face. His head was completely bald and he always wore a black baseball cap with an unusually long peak. He had very round eyes that always smiled, even when the rest of his face bore a grave expression. He was absorbed in his game, as were the spectators – about half a dozen of them. His opponent wore a battered fawn hat with a short brim above a lugubrious face with deep lines chiselled out of folded lava rock. He was rigid with tension, the knuckles on his left hand glowing white as it tightened around his pack of cigarettes. The remains of a cigarette between his lips bled smoke into streaming eyes. But he seemed oblivious. It was obvious to Li as he eased through the group and took in the board, that Lao Dai was one move away from checkmate. The man with the cigarettes was desperately seeking a way out. Finally he slid a wooden disc with a red character, marking it out as his Horse, on a zigzag move and shouted, *'Jiang!'* It was a last act of pure defiance. For Lao Dai 'ate' it with his Cannon and pronounced, *'Jiang si li'* Checkmate. There was a collective sigh as Lao Dai sat back, and the two opponents traded a cursory handshake. The man with the cigarettes threw away the one that was in his mouth and lit another. There was a brief exchange of goodbyes and the gathering began to disperse. The sun was sinking fast now and it was getting colder. Time for something to drink, and something hot to eat.

'Life is no fun any more, Li Yan,' Lao Dai said without looking up, his attention focused on gathering up the discs and putting them in their box along with their embroidered cloth board. Li was surprised that the old man had even seen him arriving. 'It is boring when you win all the time.'

'As boring as it was when you lost all the time to my uncle?'

The old man grinned and looked up at him finally. 'Ah, but when you always lose, you can still look forward to the day when you will win. But when you always win, you can only ever look forward to defeat. It is better to win some, and to lose some. Your uncle always used to say, *ten thousand things find harmony by combining the forces of positive and negative.*' The old man examined his face. 'I see him in you tonight. I have never seen him there before.'

'I wish there was more of him in me,' Li said. 'Then I might know better what to do.'

'Ah, but you are young still. How can you always know what to do? Wisdom only comes with age.'

And Li remembered another of his uncle's sayings. '*The oldest ginger is the best.*'

Lao Dai's smile widened, but was touched by sadness. 'It's hard to believe he's been gone five years. There is not a day goes past that I do not think about him.'

Li nodded. He did not want to get into a discussion about his uncle. The memories that would resurrect would be too painful. 'I came to see if you needed a taxi to take you to the Great Hall tonight.'

The old man waved his hand dismissively. 'No, no, of course not. I will take my bicycle, as always. The day I stop cycling is the day I will die.' He stood up and lifted his precious box of chessmen. 'Walk with me to the subway.' It was too far now for Lao Dai to cycle from his home in the south-east of the city, to the garden outside the park. And the traffic was too dangerous. So he took the subway and the bus, and would be home in just under an hour. It never occurred to him not to come.

They walked past the bristle-headed old man still performing his *tai chi* and on to the path that followed the canal. Lao Dai took small, shuffling steps, and seemed always on the point of overbalancing. The sky above them soared from pale lemon to the deepest, darkest blue. A splinter of moon was visible rising on the far horizon, and the last of the sun, even though they could not see it, glanced its light off countless windows in dozens of high-rises.

'So what troubles you?'

Li said, 'What makes you think I am troubled?'

The old man shook his head. 'To answer a question with a question is evasion. Your uncle could never hide his worries from me either. Which is why he would never meet my eye when we played chess. He would have made a lousy poker player.' Lao Dai stopped and put his hand on Li's arm. 'I could never fill Yifu's footsteps. Nor would I try. But I knew him well, and I know he would want you to come to me if you were in trouble.'

Li was embarrassed and moved at the same time. He wanted to hug the old man, but it was not the Chinese way. Dai and Yifu had served together for many years in the criminal investigation department of the Beijing Municipal Police, Yifu rising to high office before his retirement. Although Dai had not reached the same dizzy heights, he had nevertheless been a Section Chief. He was a good man, clever and principled. Both had been widowers and were inseparable after retirement. Yifu's death had left a huge hole in the old man's life, and with no children to fill the void, Li was the closest thing to family that he had left.

'I am responsible for the murders of young women,' Li said finally.

Lao Dai chuckled. 'You are killing them yourself, I take it?'

'I am failing to catch the man who is,' Li said. 'The longer I take, the more he will kill.'

Lao Dai sighed. 'It is easier to carry an empty vessel than a full one. If you fill your mind with guilt for the actions of another, you will leave no room for the clear thinking you will need to catch him.' He set off again along the path, and Li followed. 'You had better tell me all about it,' he said. And Li did. Everything from the first victim to the last, from the discovery of the Ripper book to the letter from the killer himself. Dai listened without comment. A faraway look glazed his eyes, and concern clouded the smile that usually lit them. 'You have an enemy, Li Yan,' he said at length.

Li was startled. 'What do you mean?'

'This man is not killing these girls only for the pleasure of it. He is constraining himself by following a prescribed course of action. Therefore there is a purpose in it for him beyond the act itself. You must ask yourself what possible purpose he could have. If he does not know these girls or their families what else do all these murders have in common?'

Li thought about it for a moment, and then saw the old man's reasoning. 'The police,' he said.

'More specifically . . .'

'Me?'

'It was you he wrote to, was it not?' He regarded Li with some sympathy. 'By making a hero of you they have made you a target, Li Yan. Where once you were known to only a few, now you are known to all.' And Li remembered Elvis's words at the meeting: *You've been splashed all over the papers ahead of this award thing tonight. You're a hero.* Dai added, 'Their ignorance was your strength, now their knowledge is your weakness. Yifu would have been proud of you tonight, but he would also have opposed this award with all his might.'

'But what possible motive . . . ?'

Old Dai raised a hand to stop him. 'Jealousy, revenge, any one of many twisted things. But you cannot know this, Li Yan. You cannot know who or why, not yet. It is too big a leap. Remember Mao's *Great Leap Forward*, which was in truth a great fall back. Your knowledge is your strength. Take small steps and keep your balance. He who stands on the tips of his toes cannot be steady. He who takes long strides will not maintain the pace.' And Li realised that it was a philosophy Lao Dai applied to his own life, not just in metaphor, but in fact. Dai smiled. 'You know what Yifu would have said?'

Li nodded. 'The answer lies in the detail.'

They had reached the steps of the Muxidi subway. Lao Dai stopped and poked a finger in Li's chest. 'One step at a time, Li Yan. One small step at a time.' And then he patted his arm. 'I will see you tonight. I will be Yifu's eyes and ears. I will be his pride.' And he turned and headed carefully towards the escalator, one small step at a time.

### III

Li Jon was sleeping and Margaret switched on a lamp by her chair. She could no longer read by the dying light of the day, although she had barely noticed it going. She was absorbed in the book. Both fascinated and horrified. All the autopsies she had performed over many years had led her to believe that she had witnessed the fullest extent of man's inhumanity to man, or woman. But as she read Doctor Thomas Bond's medical notes on the post-mortem he had helped perform on the Ripper's most mutilated victim, the unfortunate Mary Jane Kelly, she realised that there was perhaps no limit, and that there would always be horrors worse than she could imagine.

Doctor Bond's notes on what he found at the scene of the crime, and during the subsequent post-mortem, had only been discovered as recently as 1987. Margaret was fascinated by how close, procedurally, his descriptions were to the account she might have made herself more than a century after he had written them.

He laid bare the crime scene in cold, unemotional terms:

The body was lying naked in the middle of the bed, the shoulders flat, but the axis of the body inclined to the left side of the bed. The head was turned on the left cheek. The left arm was close to the body with the forearm flexed at a right angle and lying across the abdomen, the right arm was slightly abducted from the body and rested on the mattress, the elbow bent and the forearm supine with the fingers clenched. The legs were wide apart, the left thigh at right angles to the trunk and the right forming an obtuse angle with the pubes.

The whole surface of the abdomen and thighs was removed and the abdominal cavity emptied of its viscera.

The breasts were cut off, the arms mutilated by several jagged wounds and the face hacked beyond recognition of the features, and the tissues of the neck were severed all round down to the bone. The viscera were found in various parts viz: the uterus and kidneys with one breast under the head, the other breast by the right foot, the liver between the feet, the intestines by the right side and the spleen by the left side of the body.

The flaps removed from the abdomen and thighs were on a table.

The bed clothing at the right corner was saturated with blood, and on the floor beneath was a pool of blood covering about two feet square. The wall by the right side of the bed and in a line with the neck was marked by blood which had struck it in a number of separate splashes.

His post-mortem notes were even more chilling in their detail of the Ripper's bestiality.

The face was gashed in all directions, the nose, cheeks, eyebrows and ears being partly removed. The lips were blanched and cut by several incisions running obliquely down to the chin.

Both breasts were removed by more or less circular incisions, the muscles down to the ribs being attached to the breasts. The intercostals between the 4th, 5th and 6th ribs were cut and the contents of the thorax visible through the openings.

The skin and tissues of the abdomen from the costal arch to the pubes were removed in three large flaps. The right thigh was denuded in front to the bone, the flap of skin including the external organs of generation and part of the right buttock. The left thigh was stripped of skin, fascia and muscles as far as the knee.

The left calf showed a long gash through skin and tissues to the deep muscles and reaching from the knee to five inches above the ankle.

Both arms and forearms had extensive and jagged wounds.

The right thumb showed a small superficial incision about one inch long, with extravasation of blood in the skin, and there were several abrasions on the back of the hand and forearm showing the same condition.

On opening the thorax it was found that the right lung was minimally adherent by old firm adhesions. The lower part of the lung was broken and torn away.

The left lung was intact; it was adherent at the apex and there were a few adhesions over the side. In the substances of the lung were several nodules of consolidation.

The pericardium was open below and the heart absent.

Margaret could visualise it all, and oddly it affected her more than if she had carried out the autopsy herself. Something about the act of exercising your professional expertise removed you, somehow, from the human horror of it all.

The Ripper had taken Mary Jane's heart. It was not found

at the scene of the crime and never recovered. Margaret knew that at least two of the Beijing victims had been missing body parts. She was not sufficiently familiar with any of the cases to make direct comparisons with the victims of Jack the Ripper. But she did know that the Beijing equivalent of the Mary Jane Kelly killing had not yet been committed, and it chilled her to the bone to think that such a fate awaited some poor innocent Chinese girl out there. A living being with hopes and aspirations destined to flounder on the blade of a maniac. Unless Li could stop him. The thought brought home to her just how much pressure he must be under. And with the thought came her frustration that there was nothing she could do to help.

Li turned off Changan Avenue into Zhengyi Road and headed south, the high grey brick wall on his right concealing from public view the compound of the Ministries of State and Public Security, once the home of the British Embassy. Shop windows shone in the dark beneath the trees, uniforms and the paraphernalia of the police exhibited behind plate glass. Batons and baseball caps, tear-gas and truncheons. And books on every subject under the sun, from police procedure to pornography in art. He passed the Shanghainese restaurant where he and Margaret sometimes ate, just a short walk from their apartment, and turned into the compound past the armed officer on sentry duty. He drew up outside the apartment block reserved for senior officers and glanced up to see a light shining from their veranda on the seventh floor.

Inside the main door, he stopped to empty the contents

of his mail box. Bills and circulars. He slipped them into his jacket pocket and walked into the empty elevator. The door slid noisily shut and the metal box rattled its way slowly up seven floors. He tried to empty his mind, as Old Dai had counselled, but found any number of things jostling to fill it again. The murders, the award ceremony and, strangely, Mei Yuan's riddle. He tried to recall it. Something about deaf mutes in a rice paddy. But his concentration was shot, and already it seemed like an eternity since she had told him it that morning. Was it really only that morning he had been called out to the murder of Guo Huan?

The doors of the elevator slid open and he slipped his key in the lock of the apartment. He found Margaret with her legs curled up below her on an armchair, her face buried in a book. The apartment was in darkness, apart from the lamp by her chair. He switched on the overhead light, and she blinked in its sad yellow glare.

'Hi,' she said. And he stooped to kiss her on the cheek, like a husband returning home at the end of a day at the office. And she waiting for him, like some suburban housewife, reading crime stories to fill the hours.

'What are you reading?' he asked.

'Your Jack the Ripper book.'

He frowned. 'In English?'

She laughed. 'In what else? I found it at the Foreign Language Bookstore in Wangfujing.'

He heard the sound of distant alarm bells ringing somewhere in the back of his mind. 'When was it published?'

She flipped through the pages to the front of the book. 'About eighteen months ago.'

'So it's been available here, in English, for some time.'

'Must have been. There were still a couple of copies on the shelf.' She could see that wheels behind his eyes were turning. 'Why? Is there something significant in that?'

'Could be,' Li said. 'The Chinese translation was only published a week ago. So if the killer is using this book as his blueprint he must be an English speaker.'

'Or a foreigner,' Margaret said. And Li recalled Elvis commenting on the Chinese content of the Ripper letter. *Nobody would write Chinese like this.* And Qian's words, *Unless maybe he was a foreigner.* But it was clear that the strange Chinese was just a translation from arcane nineteenth-century English. The killer had lifted the translation from the book. Li's mind froze on that thought. He couldn't have. If he was working from the English original he would have had to make the translation himself. Then how did it come to be an exact match for the translation in the Chinese version of the book? No two translations would be exactly the same. He took out his cellphone and began dialling.

'What is it?' Margaret asked. But all he did was lift a finger to silence her.

'Elvis, it's the Chief. Get on to the Chinese publisher of the Ripper book and find out who translated it. As much background on him as you can.'

'Chief,' Elvis's voice came back at him. 'There's a paragraph on the flyleaf about the translator. And he's a she. Lives in Hong Kong.' A pause. 'You still want me to contact the publisher?'

'No. No,' Li said. 'Forget it.' And he flipped his phone shut. It was inconceivable that the killer was a woman. And Hong Kong was a little far to commute for murder.

Margaret was still watching him. 'Are you going to tell me?' she asked.

He said, 'I received a letter this afternoon from the killer. It was, word for word, the original Jack the Ripper letter. But, of course, it was in Chinese. Character for character the same as the translation in the Chinese version of the Ripper book.'

Margaret immediately saw his problem. 'So you're thinking, if he's been working from the English version, how did he manage to produce the same translation as the Chinese one.'

'Exactly.'

'Well, that's easy.'

'Is it?'

'Sure. He only sent the letter today, right? Or yesterday.' Li nodded. 'So if the Chinese version has been out for a week . . .' She didn't even have to finish.

Li sighed his frustration. 'I'm not even thinking straight any more,' he said. Why had he not seen that for himself? He was blinding himself with guilt and pressure, failing to find the logic in the detail. Old Dai was right. *It is easier to carry an empty vessel than a full one*, he had said. *If you fill your mind with guilt for the actions of another, you will leave no room for the clear thinking you will need to catch him.*

Margaret's voice, laden with sympathy, tumbled softly into his thoughts and startled him. 'Li Yan, you've got to be at the Great Hall in under an hour.'

'Shit!' He looked at his watch. 'I have to shower and change.' He hurried through to the bathroom, divesting himself of clothes as he went. Margaret followed behind picking them up. 'When's Mei Yuan coming?' he called over his shoulder.

'She'll be here any time.'

He stepped into the shower and under a jet of hot steaming water. Margaret stood watching him through the misting glass. He was a fit, powerful man, tall for a Chinese, over six feet, with broad shoulders and narrow hips. He had a swimmer's thighs and calves. The hot water ran in rivulets over firm, toned muscles, and she wanted just to step in beside him and make love to him there and then, with the thought of Mei Yuan due to arrive at any moment, and Li Jon asleep through the wall. A moment snatched. A sense of urgency, like there had once been always in their lovemaking. But she knew the moment would not have been right for him. So she stood, holding his discarded clothes and watching the shape of him blur in the steam as it condensed on the glass.

He called out, eyes shut against the foaming shampoo, 'Are you still there?'

'I'm still here.'

'What did you learn from the book?'

'That nineteenth-century London cops were either incompetent or stupid.'

'How do you mean?'

'Li Yan, they let people sluice away blood and other evidence from crime scenes. Mortuary assistants washed down bodies before the pathologists carried out their autopsies. Vital evidence literally flushed down the drain.' She had been horrified as she read. 'After the night of the double murder, they found some graffiti chalked on the entrance to tenement dwellings, alongside a bloody scrap of skirt from one of the victims. Before they could even photograph it, the Police Commissioner insisted that it be washed off.'

'What!' Li couldn't believe what he was hearing. 'Why?'

'Good question,' Margaret said. 'One I'd have loved to have asked him.'

'But he must have had a good reason.'

'Oh, he gave a reason, but it wasn't a good one. He said he was afraid that the graffiti would spark anti-semitic riots.'

'Why?'

Apparently the Ripper had made some kind of allusion to the Jews, as if a Jew might be responsible for the killings. There was a large immigrant Jewish population in the East End of London at that time, and the Commissioner said he feared that the locals would turn against them.'

'But that's absurd! If it was a real concern, all they had to do was cover it up under police guard until it was properly examined and photographed.'

'You might think that. And I might agree with you. But apparently that never occurred to him. And for a man who ultimately lost his job through his failure to catch the Ripper, destroying what might have been very crucial evidence was a very strange thing to do.'

Li turned off the water and pushed open the shower door.

He stood dripping wet and naked, quite unselfconscious. 'And he was the Police Commissioner?'

'Sir Charles Warren. Commissioner of the Metropolitan Police.' She eyed him lustfully and took hold of him with her free hand, feeling him swelling in her grasp from an immediate rush of blood. 'If we didn't have to be out of here in the next twenty minutes . . .'

He grinned. 'Twenty minutes, huh? I suppose I could always try to speed things up.'

She squeezed him hard, making him flinch. 'I should be so lucky.'

He cupped her face in his hands and kissed her softly, and then parted her lips with his tongue and sought hers. Li Jon started crying in the next room. He dropped his forehead on to her shoulder.

'Shit,' she hissed. And the buzzer sounded at the door. She pushed his clothes into his wet arms and said, 'You'd better get dressed fast. I'll let Mei Yuan in.' As he danced naked through the hall towards their bedroom she shouted after him, 'Oh, and by the way, we're having dinner tomorrow night with the Harts – if you can tear yourself away from the office for once.'

## IV

The Great Hall of the People had played host to some of the fiercest political struggles in modern Chinese history. Built by Mao in the 1950s after the creation of the Republic, it stood along the west side of Tiananmen Square, facing east towards the Museum of Chinese History, and had been witness to the bloody events of 1989 when students demanding democracy were crushed under the wheels of army tanks. An event which had catapulted the Middle Kingdom headlong into such radical change it had produced not democracy, but instead the fastest growing economy in the world.

It was an impressive building, three hundred metres long, its three-storey facade supported by tall marble columns. Along with all the other buildings around the square, it was floodlit. The whole of central Beijing, it seemed, was floodlit, obliterating the stars that shone beyond the light in a clear, black sky overhead.

It took Li and Margaret just fifteen minutes to walk in the cold to the Great Hall from their apartment, along Qianmen Dong Da Jie, and up through Tiananmen from the south end, past Mao's mausoleum. Margaret had queued once to see the great man lying preserved in his coffin beneath a glass dome, and came away convinced that all she had witnessed was a wax effigy.

She held Li's arm, and felt his warmth and strength even through the thickness of his coat. Beneath it he wore his dress uniform, and he cut an impressive figure as he strode across the pavings of the huge square. She was proud of him, even though she knew he was opposed to this award and dreading the ceremony.

There were streams of cars dropping people off on the corner of Renminda Hutong Xilu where they were entering the gardens in front of the hall through turnstile gates. Guests of honour strolled across the vast, paved concourse and stood chatting in groups on the steps beneath the pillars. Margaret felt a small frisson of excitement. The Great Hall of the People was a piece of history and she was about to enter it with the man who would be centre stage in its auditorium. 'How many people are going to be here?' she asked. She had not expected so many cars.

'It will be full,' Li said.

'How many is that?'

'Ten thousand.'

'Ten thousand!' It seemed inconceivable. 'Who are they all?'

'Invited guests,' Li said with a tone, and Margaret felt his tension.

'It must be some size of auditorium.'

'It's on three levels,' he said. 'Sixty metres wide, seventy metres from stage to back, and forty metres high.' Figures that had been dinned into him in primary school. 'And there are no pillars.' The *coup de grâce*. His teacher's eyes had shone with wonder as she told them. Li doubted if she had ever actually seen it for herself – a hick teacher from a primary school in rural Sichuan. He had later seen her beaten to death by Red Guards.

They crossed the concourse, and Li flashed his ID to the guard on duty who immediately saluted and lifted the chain to let them through. On the steps they were greeted by Commissioner Zhu and Deputy Cao, who were standing smoking in the cold night air, accompanied by their respective wives. Zhu glanced at his watch and said, 'You're late.' He made no introductions and ignored Margaret. 'They're waiting for you.' He took Li by the elbow and steered him away up the stairs.

Li called back to Margaret, 'I'll see you after the ceremony.'

She nodded, smiling politely at Cao and the two women. '*Ni hau*,' she said, and made her way up through the pillars to the main entrance, conscious of their silence, and of their eyes on her back.

Inside, she had to put her purse through an airport-style X-ray security machine and walk through a frame that scanned her for . . . she had no idea what. Metal objects, she supposed. Guns or knives. As if she might be intent on attacking the father of her child. Through another doorway, and she was into the main lobby, a huge marbled hall, overlooked by a balcony that ran all the way around it. Stairs led up to it from either end. Tall wooden double doors along the entire length of the central hall, on both levels, led into the auditorium itself. There were already thousands of people thronging the floor, the echo of their voices thundering back at them from a ceiling you could hardly see, enormous chandeliers casting yellow light on a sea of black heads. Margaret felt at once conspicuous, anonymous and lost, aware of her fair hair and blue eyes drawing curious looks. Most of the guests would not have expected to have encountered a *yangguizi* on an occasion like this. She felt a tug on her arm, and turned to find a young Chinese girl grinning up at her.

'Magret,' Xinxin said. Li's niece was nearly ten now and almost up to Margaret's shoulder. Although her English was excellent, she still pronounced Margaret's name the way she had when they had first met and the child had no English at all.

'Xinxin!' Margaret was both pleased and relieved to see her. She stooped to kiss her and give her a hug, and then looked around. 'Where's your mother? And your grandfather?'

By way of reply, Xinxin took her hand – which still felt very small in hers – and said, 'You come with me, Magret. We are invited to reception for guest of honour.' And she glowed with obvious pride and pleasure at the thought that her Uncle Yan was the guest of honour.

The child led the adult confidently through the crowds to the north end of the hall, and up a staircase at the far corner to the pillared balcony above. They hurried then across thick red carpet, past open doors leading to a huge overlit room with chairs set in a circle below a wall displaying a vast aerial photograph of the Forbidden City. 'That Beijing Room,' Xinxin said. 'There is one room for every province in Great Hall. Even one for Taiwan, for when she come back to China.' She grinned as if she understood the politics of it.

Margaret couldn't resist a smile. 'How do you know all this, little one?'

'I come here on tour with school,' she said. 'All school visit Great Hall of People.'

Almost opposite the Beijing Hall, an enormous doorway led to the reception room, already crowded with dignitaries. There were high-ranking police officers and government ministers. Faces Margaret had only ever seen in newspapers or on television screens. She also saw some more familiar faces. Detectives from Li's section. Qian and Wu and a few others whose names she could not recall. Glasses filled with champagne and orange juice were set out on a long table beneath a twenty-foot mural of a Chinese mountainscape illuminated by a rising sun. Most of the guests were drinking champagne.

Li's sister, Xiao Ling, and his father, stood uncomfortably on the edge of the gathering, clutching glasses of orange juice. They did not belong here and they knew it. A retired teacher living in an old folks' home in Sichuan, and a worker on the production line of the Beijing Jeep factory. Li's father had made the trip specially to see his son. There had always been difficulties between them, but his father could not bring himself to miss such a moment. He was staying with his daughter and granddaughter during his visit.

Xiao Ling shook Margaret's hand rather formally. She did not speak English, and she and Margaret had never really hit it off. Neither did Margaret get on with Li's father, who regarded their relationship as 'unfortunate'. He would have preferred that Li had found a Chinese girl to father his son. He, too, shook Margaret's hand. 'I will come tomorrow to see my grandson,' he said. 'With your permission.' As if she might have refused it.

'Of course,' Margaret said.

'In the afternoon,' he added.

'Magret, Magret,' Xinxin clamoured for her attention. 'You want drink?'

'Champagne,' Margaret said quickly. She needed a drink.

Xinxin came back with champagne for Margaret and an orange juice for herself. Margaret took a couple of quick swallows, and felt the bubbles carry the alcohol almost immediately into her bloodstream. She could do with a few of these, she thought.

'Perhaps I might be allowed a glass. It is not often that I have had the chance to drink champagne.' The voice at Margaret's side startled her, and she turned to find Lao Dai standing by her shoulder. He was wearing a thick blue jacket over a knitted jumper, baggy trousers and scuffed leather shoes. A navy blue baseball cap was pulled down over his bald head. She had met him for the first time only after Yifu's death, and they had struck up an immediate rapport. He took her hand warmly in both of his and held it for a moment. 'How are you, Margaret?' His English was almost perfect.

'I am well, Mister Dai,' she said. And she turned to Xinxin. 'Xinxin, could you get a glass of champagne for Mister Dai?' Xinxin skipped off, happy to have an errand to run, and Margaret turned back to the old man. 'And you?'

'Oh, as always,' he said. He shook hands, then, with Xiao Ling and Li's father, and they had a brief exchange in Chinese which, to Margaret's surprise, brought uncharacteristic laughter to their lips.

'What's so funny?' Margaret asked.

'Oh, nothing,' Dai said. 'I told them I shouldn't drink too much champagne or Li Yan would have to arrest me for being drunk in charge of a bicycle.' His eyes twinkled mischievously. Xinxin returned with his champagne and he raised his glass.

'Cheers,' he said, and took a long draught of it, putting the back of his hand to his lips as he then broke wind. One or two faces turned and scowled in their direction. But Lao Dai just lifted his glass and grinned, displaying broken and discoloured teeth, and they turned quickly away again. 'Stuffed shirts,' the old man whispered conspiratorially to Margaret. 'In my day you succeeded on merit. Nowadays it's down to brown-nosing and politics.' He took another quaff of his champagne. 'Li Yan is jade among stones.'

A sprinkling of applause drew their attention, and Margaret craned to see Li Yan being led up a broad staircase to the reception room by the Minister of Public Security, flanked by his deputy and the Commissioner of Police. Trailing behind were Deputy Cao and all the wives. Margaret should have been there amongst them. But she and Li Yan were not married, and she was not Chinese. She would be bad for the image of the poster boy.

The crowd parted, like the Red Sea, to let Li and the entourage through to the champagne. The Minister raised his glass and proposed what Margaret took to be a toast. She heard Li Yan's name, and along with the others she raised her glass and repeated it. The Minister then made a short speech to which everyone listened attentively.

'What's he saying?' Margaret whispered to Dai.

'Oh, he's just talking the usual shit,' said the old man.

Applause marked the end of the speech, and the leading entourage and guests of honour started to make their way through to the auditorium. Lao Dai took Margaret's arm to steady himself, and Xinxin held her hand, and they followed the crowd downstairs and into the first level of the auditorium where nearly four thousand people were already seated. There were another three thousand on the second floor, and more than two thousand on the top.

The stage was vast, each side draped with long red flags. Margaret, Dai and Li's family took seats reserved for honoured guests near the front and found themselves almost on a level with the stage. The lights dimmed and there was a fanfare of martial-sounding music, and a visual presentation began, projected on to a large screen disclosed by a rising curtain. There was a voice-over commentary, images of police officers at work: in offices and cars, catching criminals, giving evidence in court. Some flickering archive footage showed early police officers in green army uniform performing military-style drill outside a police station. The film cut to a modern police station with a well-equipped gymnasium and basketball court, and showed smartly dressed officers in their new black uniforms standing cheering a police football team. Then there was news footage of Li Yan leading a man in handcuffs out of an impressive-looking building. Margaret recognised the man as the former deputy mayor of Beijing whom Li had arrested for fraud and corruption. It had been one of the most high profile cases of the last few years. The deputy mayor had been found guilty and sentenced to death, which would mean a bullet in the back of the head. He was currently awaiting the outcome of an appeal that would reduce his sentence to life imprisonment if successful.

The music soared and swooped, switching from martial to classical and back again. It ended as suddenly as it began and everyone dutifully clapped. A curtain fell, and an officer in uniform walked out to a microphone in centre stage and made a short speech. 'More shit,' Dai whispered to Margaret, and then the Minister of Public Security walked out to thunderous applause. As the applause died away, he took out a sheaf of notes from an inside pocket and embarked on a speech which lasted nearly fifteen minutes. The Chinese were fond of making speeches. Margaret looked at Dai, but he just shook his head. 'You don't even want to know,' he said.

Margaret looked about her and saw TV cameras strategically placed around the hall, recording the entire ceremony. It was probably going out live on one of the China Central TV stations. A phalanx of press and official photographers was clustered around the front of the stage, cameras flashing. Most of the invited guests would be police officers and their families, she thought, or people employed directly or indirectly by the Ministry – a strange brotherhood to which police everywhere seemed to belong.

The Minister finished his speech, to more applause. An elaborate table draped in red silk had appeared from somewhere – Margaret had not seen it brought on – displaying a wooden shield bearing the red, blue and gold crest of the Ministry of Public Security. The police badge. Beijing Police Commissioner Zhu walked on to shake the Minister's hand and take up a position in front of the microphone. His rimless glasses caught and reflected the light, and you could not see his eyes. It made him appear oddly sinister, tall and thin and sightless. He waved a hand towards the shield and began speaking.

Dai whispered, 'He's talking about Li, now.' He listened for a bit and then said, 'He does not much like our young friend.'

'You mean Li?'

Dai nodded. 'He is full of praise. Noisy praise, like a drum with nothing inside it. He says only good things of Li Yan. His tone is honeyed, but there is vinegar on his tongue.'

Margaret glanced around. If Commissioner Zhu's words were having that effect on other members of the audience there was nothing in their faces to show it. The Minister beamed happily at the Commissioner's side, and Margaret wondered if perhaps Lao Dai was reading more into the speech than was intended. And yet she knew that he was a clever man, experienced and perceptive. It gave her cause for disquiet.

Dai said, 'I knew him when he was a rookie cop and I was Section Chief. I didn't trust him then. Look at his face. There is the weasel in it.' And there was, indeed, something weaselly about his face, Margaret thought. He was not the usual pan-faced Chinese. He had a weak, receding jaw, and a forehead that sloped steeply back from his brow. 'He is like a bellows. Empty when at rest, and full of air when set in motion.' Dai chuckled. 'In his case, hot air.'

Zhu finished his speech, and with a flourish stood aside, extending his arm towards the wings to welcome Li on stage. As Li walked briskly to the table to accept his award, he received a standing ovation, almost as if the guests had been briefed. As she herself stood, Margaret wondered if it had been stipulated on their invitation cards. Li took the shield from the Minister, shaking hands with both men. So many cameras flashed the stage was transformed into something like a scene from an old black and white movie, too few frames making the picture flicker and jerk and run too fast. The papers would be full of it tomorrow, and there would be plenty of images to choose from for the hoardings around the city.

Li cleared his throat as he approached the microphone, but spoke in a strong, clear voice.

'Do you want to know what he is saying?' Dai whispered.

Margaret shook her head. She had schooled him in his speech, persuaded him to reduce it from more than ten minutes to a little over three. She knew it by heart. His acceptance of the award not for himself, but on behalf of all his fellow officers. The need for the police in China to move forward, embracing new ideas and new technology to fight the rising wave of crime that was coming with increased prosperity.

His speech was met with yet another standing ovation, and Li walked off with the others as the curtain came down to a loud reprise of the martial music which had kicked off the whole proceeding.

'Well, thank God that's over,' Margaret said. 'Where's the food?'

Old Dai grinned. 'In the Sichuan Room,' he said.

The Sichuan room was at the bottom of a flight of stairs, beyond the empty and forlorn-looking Taiwan Room. It was clad entirely in white marble, pillars, walls and floor, beyond a huge tapestry of a Sichuan forest scene. Tables for a banquet were set out on a pale Chinese carpet. Ten tables, ten to a table. Only special invitees were to be fed in the company of the principal guest of honour. A four-man troupe of Sichuan folk musicians played discreetly at the far end of the room.

Li Yan's family and Lao Dai were escorted to a table near the door. To her surprise, Margaret found herself being seated at the same table as Li, along with the Minister and his deputy, the Commissioner and his deputy, and their wives. She leaned towards him and said in a stage whisper. 'How did you manage this?'

The Minister said in impeccable English, 'He told us that if he couldn't have you at our table, he would take you for a McDonald's instead.' There was no trace of a smile as he spoke, but something in his eyes told Margaret he was not as po-faced as he appeared.

There was a ripple of uneasy laughter around the table.

'Personally, I prefer Tony Roma's,' Margaret said. 'Or the Hard Rock Café – they do good burgers. But I guess I'll just have to make do with this instead.'

No one seemed certain whether she was being funny, or just rude, and her response was met with an uneasy silence. Li looked embarrassed.

'It's a joke,' Margaret said. 'I love Sichuan food.' And she waved a hand in front of her mouth and blew. 'Hot!'

'You like spicy food, then?' Deputy Cao said languidly.

'Sure.'

'Personally, I think Sichuan cuisine lack something in subtlety and sophistication. All that chilli only there to disguise poor quality of meat.'

'What is *your* taste, then, Deputy Cao?' the Minister asked him.

'He likes hotpot,' his wife said. She was a small, wiry woman, with short, bobbed hair the colour of steel. She looked uncomfortable in a black evening gown.

'Ah, yes,' Margaret said. 'Invented by the Mongols, wasn't it? Water boiled up in their helmets over an open fire to cook chunks of mutton hacked off the sheep.'

'So?' Deputy Cao said, a hint of defensiveness in his voice.

The Minister laughed. 'I think Ms Campbell is implying that hotpot is not quite the height of sophisticated eating either.'

Cao shrugged dismissively. 'Well, that is rich coming from American. Not a country exactly famous for its cuisine.' He lit a cigarette.

'Oh, I don't know,' Margaret said breezily. 'There are a hell of a lot more McDonald's around the world than there are hotpot restaurants.'

Even Commissioner Zhu, silent until now, cracked a smile. 'She might have a point there, Cao.' Margaret looked at him carefully, and saw more clearly the weasel in him that Lao Dai had pointed out.

'Only the young in China eat burger,' Cao said. 'With age come wisdom. People eat hotpot for thousands of year. In a hundred year they will still be eating hotpot. I wonder how many McDonald's restaurants there will be.'

'So you don't approve of American culture, then?' Margaret said.

'It is short-lived and worthless,' replied Cao.

'Is that why you smoke American cigarettes?' Margaret nodded towards his pack of Philip Morris lying on the table. 'So your life will be equally short-lived and worthless.'

There was a moment's dangerous silence, before the Minister guffawed. 'I think you've finally met your match, Cao,' he said.

Margaret caught Li's eye, and felt pierced by the cold steel of his silent disapproval. She turned her most charming smile on the Deputy Commissioner and said, 'Actually, I'm only joking, Deputy Cao. I love hotpot, too.' And she turned the same smile back on Li, as if to say, *You see, you can take me places without getting a red face.*

Through all the hubbub of voices in the Sichuan Room, above the sound of crockery as waiters brought food to tables, came the unmistakable warble of a cellphone. Deputy Minister Wei Peng tutted his disapproval. 'Some people have no sense of propriety,' he said. But within half a minute, the individual lacking that sense of propriety revealed himself to be Deputy Section Chief Qian. He was clearly embarrassed to interrupt proceedings at Li's table, but determined nonetheless. His face was drained of colour.

'Please accept my apologies for the interruption, Minister,' he said, and then turned to Li. 'I'm sorry, Chief, there's been another murder.'

Qian's words struck him with the force of a fist in the solar plexus. He almost physically winced. 'There can't have been,' he said.

Qian shrugged. 'Girl found dead. Strangled. Throat cut. Pathologist Wang seems to think it's our man again.'

'But that's not how it's supposed to be . . .' Li had been so sure that the killer would stick to his mentor's script. He felt sick. He had taken his eye off the case, relaxed for just a moment. And a girl had died. He stood up. 'Gentlemen, ladies. I'm sorry, I have to go.'

'Don't be ridiculous, Li,' Commissioner Zhu said sharply. 'You have a whole section of detectives to handle something like this. You can't walk out on your own banquet.' He glanced with some embarrassment towards the Minister. But the Minister remained silent.

Deputy Cao said, 'Oh, let him go. He hasn't learned yet that the art of management is delegation. He thinks he's so good that no one else can do it better. Isn't that right, Li?'

Li calmly folded his napkin and laid it on the table. 'Excuse me,' was all he said, and he headed off through the tables with Qian to where Wu and several others were waiting for them at the door. Animated conversation became suddenly hushed at the sight of the guest of honour leaving the banquet.

'Well,' Margaret said brightly, breaking the tense silence around the table. 'We'd better nominate someone else to toast or we'll *never* get a drink tonight.'

# CHAPTER FIVE

## I

The Gate of Heavenly Peace, and Changan Avenue as far as you could see east and west, was bathed in white and blue and green and pink light. The red tail lights of cars and buses and taxis shimmered off into the distance in long lines of sluggish traffic. Qian wound down the window and clamped a blue-flashing magnetic light on the roof of the Jeep, then dropped down a gear and accelerated across six lanes of vehicles to head west.

'Where are you going?' Li swivelled in surprise in the passenger seat.

'She was found at the Millennium Monument, Chief.' Qian glanced across at him. Wu and Detective Sang sat mute in the back seat.

Li felt something close to relief. 'It can't have been the Ripper, then.' Tagging the Beijing killer as the 'Ripper' had been completely unconscious.

'Why?'

'Because all the other murders have been in the same area

of Jianguomen. Just like Jack the Ripper killed all his victims in the same square mile of London.' He knew it hadn't felt right. 'And today's Monday. He's only ever killed at the weekend. And, anyway, his next victim's not due for another six weeks.'

Wu leaned forward and said, 'Everything else fits, though, Chief. The strangulation, the cutting of the throat . . .' He chewed furiously on his gum. 'And I was really looking forward to that banquet, too.'

They turned off Fuxing Avenue after Sanlihi Road, heading north and then west again, drifting past the floodlit Ministry of Defence building in its restricted military zone, and next to it the Military Museum of the Chinese People's Revolution, the centrepiece of which rose in three tiers to a spire topped by a star in a circle. To their right, Yuyuantan Park lay brooding in darkness, west of the canal where only hours earlier Li and Lao Dai had discussed the murders in the last light of the day. They were less than a mile from the Chinese Academy of Sciences.

A Dali-esque melting clock above the gate to the Millennium Park told them that it was nearly nine-thirty. Towering above it, the Millennium Monument was a huge rotating stone sundial at the top of a broad sweep of steps leading to a circular terrace. The dial was casting its shadows in several conflicting directions, confused by the floodlights now illuminating the crime scene at its base. Its arm was pointing due south, down the length of Yangfangdian Lu to the floodlit spectre of the Beijing West Railway station some two kilometres away. The lights of the multi-storey blocks which lined the avenue, reflected on the two-hundred-and-seventy-metre-long waterway, beneath which five thousand years of Chinese history was carved in bronze plates. It was an impressive vista. And for some poor girl, Li reflected as he pushed through the gate, her last sight on earth. Police and forensics vehicles were pulled into the kerbside at odd angles, and a group of uniformed officers stood stamping and smoking on the causeway just inside the gate. This was not an area dense in housing or nightlife, so only a small crowd of curious spectators had gathered. The uniforms saluted as Li and the other detectives from Section One arrived. There was a young, grey-uniformed security guard amongst them. Beneath a black-peaked cap, he had a fresh face reddened by the icy wind. He wore leather boots and a long grey greatcoat, its black collar pulled up around his cheeks, a red band with yellow characters wound around his left arm. Li stopped and asked him, 'When does this place normally get locked up?'

'By six o'clock, Chief,' the security guard said. 'Or whenever it gets dark. Whichever comes first. We always clear people out when the light starts to go.' He shuffled his feet and slapped leather-clad gloves together to keep his hands warm.

'What time did you close the gates tonight?'

'It was about half past five.'

'Did you check to see if there was anyone still inside?'

'No, Chief. People are always in a big hurry to get out when we start closing up. No one would want to get locked in.'

Li looked at the railing. It was only about a metre high. Easy enough for anyone to get in or out, whether the gate was locked or not. He nodded. 'Where's the body?'

One of the uniforms pointed. 'Right up the top, Chief, behind the arm of the dial.'

'How on earth did anyone find it up there after the place was closed up?'

'It was me, Chief.' It was the young security guard again. His lips were almost blue with the cold. 'We do shifts here. Check round the perimeter once every hour or so.'

'Why?' Li couldn't imagine why anyone would want to guard an empty park.

'There's a lot of valuable stuff in the museum, Chief.'

'Okay. Go on.'

'Well, I checked back here about eight o'clock this evening. That's when I saw the blood.' He waved his hand towards where a section of the concourse and the railing had been taped off. Li walked towards it and the security guard followed, stamping his feet. 'I wasn't sure what it was at first. I thought maybe it was paint. I don't know, some kind of vandalism. But I quickly figured out it was blood.' He fumbled with his gloves to take out and light a cigarette. As an afterthought, he offered one to Li. Li shook his head.

A trail of blood led from the foot of the steps to the railing, where it was smeared all over the chrome. Someone covered in quite a lot of it had clearly clambered over the railing and on to the sidewalk. Li followed the trail with his eyes, but it stopped at the side of the road after four or five metres. Perhaps the killer had got into a car parked there. After all, he could hardly have wandered the streets covered in blood without attracting some attention.

Li said, 'You say you check the perimeter every hour. So you didn't see any blood here at seven?'

There was a moment's hesitation before the security guard said, 'No, Chief.'

Li fixed him with a steady gaze. 'I don't want any bullshit, son. It's important for establishing time of death.' He paused. 'You didn't check the perimeter at seven, did you?'

Li could almost see the blood draining from the boy's face.

'No, Chief.' He shrugged, trying to dismiss his confession as if it were nothing. 'When it's cold like this . . . well, sometimes it's more than an hour.'

Li said, 'I don't care why, I just want the facts. You weren't here between locking up at five-thirty and checking the perimeter at eight, is that right?'

The boy nodded and couldn't meet Li's eye. 'Yes, Chief.'

So the girl had been killed sometime in that two-and-a-half-hour window. 'And you followed the blood up the steps?'

The guard nodded, anxious to make up for his shortcomings. 'Yes, Chief. There's a lot more of it up there. It led me right to her. She's lying at the base of the arm, behind it, about three steps down from the top.'

'You didn't touch her?'

'I did not.' The boy seemed to shudder at the thought. 'You could see her throat had been cut. There was a big pool of blood under her head. I could see in the beam of my flashlight that it was already drying. There's no way she was still alive.'

Li flicked his head at Wu. 'Get a statement off him. Anything he can remember out of the ordinary before he locked up.

Anyone unusual. Just anyone he can remember at all.' He nodded to Qian and Sang and they started the long climb up the steps. Off to their left, lights blazed in the windows of the China Central TV Media Centre, and Li thought that it probably wouldn't be long before they woke up to the fact that there was a murder on their doorstep. If this had been the United States, he knew, the street would already be jammed with TV trucks and satellite dishes and newsmen clamouring for information. He wondered how long it would be before China went that way, too. It was not a prospect he relished, and he had to wonder at the apparently limitless appetite of the media and the public for the gory details of man's capacity for inhumanity to man. Perhaps if they had witnessed some of what he had seen, that appetite might be somewhat diminished.

About two-thirds of the way up, the entrance to the museum was railed off in darkness, and by the time they reached the circle of the dial, immediately below the long, tapering arm that reached into the night sky, all three detectives were puffing for air. What breath they had left was whipped from their mouths by the wind that blew fiercely up here, bitter and cutting. Flights of steps rising past either side of the circle led right to the top, where a one-hundred-and-eighty-degree sweep of chrome railing gave on to an extraordinary view of the city skyline to the north, all the way to the Mountain of Heavenly Longevity and the Yanshan and Taihang mountain ranges. The same TV tower he had looked at catching the sun that afternoon from the windows of the Chinese Academy of

Sciences, was now a silver-lit arrow against the black of the sky.

A cluster of figures was gathered around the base of the sundial arm. Lights on stands rattled and shook in the ferocity of the wind. The tape which marked off the trail of blood all the way up from the causeway below was in danger of blowing away. Frail stands shifted and scraped across the concrete. Forensics men in Tyvek suits, like ghosts, combed the steps for evidence traces. A small group of men crouched around the body. As Li and the others approached, Elvis stood up, his quiff flying about his head, ruined by the wind. They had to shout to make themselves heard above the noise of it.

'Who is she?' Li shouted.

'Don't know, Chief. We haven't moved the body yet. And there doesn't seem to be a purse. The pathologist's still examining her.' His scarf flapped into his mouth and he had to pull it free. 'But it's the same MO. Strangled, but not dead when he cut the throat. Which is why there's so much blood. Left to right, same as always.'

Wang stood up behind Elvis and turned to see Li standing there. 'Ah,' he said. 'The hero's return. I thought you were busy banqueting tonight.'

'I lost my appetite.'

'I'm not surprised. Though this one's not quite as messy.'

'What makes you think it's the same killer?'

'Oh, I don't think there's any doubt, Chief. I read the note you got this afternoon.' He jerked his head over his shoulder towards the body lying behind him. 'He's cut off her ears. Just like he said he would.'

Li was stunned. 'You're kidding.'

Wang shrugged. 'That's all, though. Apart from cutting her throat, he's left the rest of her intact. One thing different – he made a bit of a mess of it this time. Severed both carotids and got blood all over himself. You'd better take a look.'

He moved aside and Li took a step down into the light to look at the body. She was wearing a long, dark coat buttoned up to above the breast. There were calfskin gloves on her hands which lay open at her sides. Her legs were twisted sideways beneath the coat, one lying across the other, and Li could see the bottom of her dark pinstriped trousers above chunky-heeled shoes. The gash in her neck was semicircular and very deep, like a wide, dark smile. Her head was lying at an angle, to the left side, but because the hair was cut so short, the gash on the right side of her head where her ear had been was only too apparent. Li was in shock, and it was several moments before he was able to consciously reason why. He put out a hand and found Qian's arm to steady himself.

'Chief, are you okay?' The concern in his deputy's voice was clear, even although he was having to shout.

She had been so full of life, and charm and charisma. A smile that would have broken most men's hearts. Doe-eyes that looked so deeply into yours you felt almost naked.

'He's broken the pattern in more ways than one,' Li said, but too quietly for Qian to hear.

'What's that?'

Li turned towards him. 'She's no prostitute, Qian.'

Qian was amazed. 'You know her?'

Li nodded. 'I met her this afternoon. She's a professor at the Chinese Academy of Sciences.'

He looked back at her fine features spattered with blood. Open eyes staring into oblivion, lips slightly parted, the delicate line of her jaw tracing a shadow to the bloody hole in the side of her head. Short hair gelled into spikes, and he remembered with a dreadful sense of guilt that last look she had given him. What had seemed, unaccountably, like an appeal for help. To which he had failed to respond.

He turned away, filled with confusion and guilt. Lynn Pan lay dead beneath the Millennium Monument, and he knew that somehow it was his fault.

'Hey, Chief . . .' It was one of the forensic ghosts. He was holding up a clear plastic evidence bag, and had to grab the bottom end of it to stop it flapping about in the wind. 'It's him, okay.' And Li saw, in the bag, the unsmoked end of a brown Russian cheroot.

Li looked at the footprints in the blood, and the trail of it leading away down the steps. The force of it spurting from the severed arteries must have taken the killer by surprise. Maybe he thought she was already dead. He must have been covered in the stuff. It looked, too, as if he had lost his footing, stumbling through the blood pooling around the head. Perhaps removing the ears had been more difficult than he had anticipated. And yet it was all so uncharacteristic of the cold, calculated butchery practised upon the other victims.

Then he had worked to a plan and a pattern, paying homage to his nineteenth-century English hero.

This just didn't fit. The victim was not a prostitute, nor did she correspond to any of the Ripper murders. She had been killed on the other side of town. It was a weekday. The execution had been clumsy, almost slapdash. And yet, there was the note. *The next job I do I shall clip the lady's ears off.* And the telltale Russian cheroot.

Li gazed down on the dead girl's face and ached for her. He remembered her touch, her fingers on his scalp as she adjusted the headset for the MERMER test, her small breasts pressing against her blouse, just inches from his face. The smell of her, sweet and musky. And here she lay, icy cold, all animation gone forever, rigor mortis already setting in.

He couldn't bear it any longer and turned away, climbing the three steps to the chrome rail, the city spreading out below him, thirteen million people going about their lives, unaware that one of the herd lay dead at the foot of this monument to the new millennium. Unaware that some monster lived among them, to all intents and purposes one of them. And how would they know him? For he had no horns, no forked tail. He would look just like them. Perhaps he had a family. A wife, children. And Li remembered thinking that someone knew who he was. That you could not return home after an orgy of killing without taking some of the blood of it with you. Someone knew who that monster was. Someone had looked into his eyes and been privy to their own private view of hell.

The crescent moon had risen higher in the sky now, and in

what little light it cast, Li could see, on the distant horizon, the faint shadow of the mountains across whose contours the Great Wall followed its tortuous route. It might once have kept the marauding hordes from the north at bay, but in this twenty-first century, it had failed to keep out the evil that stalked their streets at night. The wind battered his face, stinging cold and taking his breath away, and it was to the wind he attributed the tears that filled his eyes. He pushed himself away from the rail, wiping his face with the back of his hand and found his deputy standing nearby, watching him. 'I need a drink, Qian,' he said. And they started off down the steps together. Five thousand years of history carved in bronze stretched away below them. How many lives had come and gone in all that time? What did one more, or less, matter?

But it did.

They left Wu and Sang and Elvis at the scene to take statements and put the investigation in motion. Qian drove Li to Sanlitun Lu, more commonly known as Bar Street. It was where Guo Huan's mother had believed her daughter was working as a barmaid. A fifteen-foot plastic beer tankard overflowing with foam stood on the corner of Sanlitun and Gongren Tiyuchang Dong Lu. A bored-looking girl sat behind a window in it selling time on a public phone. They turned north, and the street ahead was ablaze with neon and fairylights. Touts in suits wandered the pavements trying to persuade passers-by that the bar which paid their wages was the best. Qian parked by the kerbside railing about halfway up, and they crossed the road to the Lan

Kwai Fang Bar at number sixty-six. Signs in the window advertised Budweiser, and Carlsberg, *Dedicated to the Art of Making
Beer*. Gnarled trees grew out of the sidewalk alongside picture
windows which gave on to a dark interior of tables draped with
red cloth. Many of the bars and restaurants in Bar Street were
haunted by staff from the embassies at the top end of the street.
A European crowd. French, Belgian, Swiss, Italian, Spanish. But
the Lan Kwai Fang was predominantly Chinese.

Most of the tables were occupied, and there was a babble
of voices and music playing when Li and Qian walked in.
But almost immediately animated conversations dried up and
heads turned in their direction. The music played to silence,
music that didn't stand up to such scrutiny. A cheap pop
singer from Taiwan. Li had forgotten that he and Qian were
both still in their dress uniforms, long coats hanging open to
reveal flashes of silver on black. The two men took off their
caps, as if that would somehow make them less conspicuous,
and slipped on to high stools at the bar. The barman wore
dark slacks with sharp creases and a white shirt open at the
neck, sleeves neatly folded halfway up his forearms. His hair
was beautifully cut and gelled back from his face. He looked
beyond them as several tables emptied, and half a dozen clients slipped out into the night. Then he refocused on the
newcomers and smiled nervously.

'Two beers,' Li said.

'You're joking, right?' The barman seemed perplexed, and
his smile continued to flutter about his lips like a butterfly
on a summer's day.

Li glared at him. 'Do you see me laughing?'

The barman shrugged. 'Cops don't drink in places like this.'

'Where *do* they drink?' Qian asked.

'I don't know. Just not here.' He leaned confidentially across the bar towards them. 'Look, I have no problem serving you guys. It's just . . . you know, you're bad for business.' He nodded towards another couple heading out the door.

Li was running out of patience. 'Sonny, if there are not two beers on the bar within the next thirty seconds you'll find out just how bad for business we could really be.'

'Coming right up, boss,' the barman said, as if the issue had never been in doubt.

Li and Qian took their beers to a recently vacated table by the window, to the barman's further chagrin. Two cops sitting in the window would guarantee no further custom until they left. But he held his peace.

The two detectives drank in silence for some time. Li took a long first pull at his beer, till he felt the alcohol hit his bloodstream, then he nursed his glass on the table in front of him, lost in gloomy thoughts.

'Such a fucking waste!' he said eventually and Qian looked at him carefully.

'She made an impression on you, then, Chief?'

'She was beautiful, Qian. I don't just mean physically. She had something about her. Something inside. It just radiated from her.' He found Qian looking at him quizzically and he smiled wryly. 'Sure, if I hadn't already found the woman I want to spend my life with, I could have fallen for her. Big time.'

And then he saw her blood-splashed profile and the wound where her ear had been removed, and frustration and anger rose in him like bile. *You have an enemy, Li Yan*, Lao Dai had told him, and Li knew that he was right. That somehow, for some reason, all this was about him. He thumped his fist on the table and both their beers jumped. Heads turned towards them. 'I'm going to put a stop to it, Qian. I'm not going to let him do this again.'

Qian nodded reassuringly. 'We'll get him, Chief.'

'What I can't figure,' Li said, 'is how the hell he got her to go up there in the first place. In the dark, after it was closed. I mean, he could never have forced her to do it.'

Qian said, 'Suppose he arranged to meet her there. Suppose she went there before it closed, and then hid up at the top when the lights went out and the guards locked up. He could easily have climbed over the railing when they'd gone.'

'But why? Why would she meet someone in those circumstances?'

Qian shrugged. 'Fear, maybe.'

'Of what? Not of him. She wouldn't have gone there if she'd thought there was anything to fear from him.' But he couldn't rid himself of that look in her eyes the last time he had seen her. He had not understood, then, what it really was. But now he wondered if perhaps she had been afraid, and he had failed to recognise it. But afraid of what?

Qian said, 'He took an enormous risk killing her in the early evening rather than the early hours of the morning. I know it wasn't exactly in full view, but there were security people around. And a goddamned TV station across the road!' He took another mouthful of beer. 'And, of course, it's something else he did differently this time. I mean, what's weird is why he would set out to copy Jack the Ripper and then not.'

Li said, 'Chinese cops have the idea that serial killers never change their MO, probably because we don't get that many here.' He shook his head. 'But it's a mistake. When I was in the States I read up on some of the most famous serial killers from around the world, and a lot of them changed lots of things from murder to murder. From gun to knife, from knife to rope, from rope to hammer. From men to women, or the other way round. And for all sorts of reasons. Some quite deliberately to mislead the police, others just on a whim. Some because it was their MO to change their MO. A serial killer can't be relied on to stick to the script.' And he realised with a shock, that's exactly what he'd been doing – relying on the Beijing Ripper to be faithful to the original. But it wasn't a script. It was history. And you can't rewrite history. So why had the killer done just that?

His cellphone began playing Beethoven in his pocket. He took it out and flipped it open. '*Wei?*'

'It's me, I'm home. How did it go?' Margaret sounded weary.

'Not good,' Li said. 'He's broken his pattern.' He drew a deep breath. 'You remember at lunch today, Bill Hart talked about Lynn Pan, the Chinese-American who's running the MERMER program?'

'Sure.'

'That's who the victim was.'

There was a moment's silent incredulity at the other end of the line, then, 'Jesus Christ,' Margaret whispered. 'You met her this afternoon.'

'Yeah.' Li felt a fleeting pang of guilt at the feelings Pan had aroused in him.

'That must have been tough.'

'It was.'

There was a long silence, and then, 'Is that music I hear?'

'I'm in a bar with Qian, up in Sanlitun.'

'Is there a connection?'

'No, we're having a drink.'

Another silence. Then, 'I had a great time tonight, too,' she said with a tone. 'With your friends from the Ministry. They spoke Chinese all night and left me to my own devices, smiling like an idiot every time one of them looked at me. I've got cramp in my cheek muscles.' In the background Li heard the baby start to cry. Margaret said, 'When will you be home?'

'I've no idea.'

'I'll see you tomorrow, then.' And she hung up.

Li felt rebuked, and resented it. He flipped the phone shut and stuffed it in his pocket. He finished his beer and stood up. 'We'd better go.'

And the barman breathed a sigh of relief as the two cops slipped out into the street. The cold air brought the blood rushing immediately to their cheeks and burned their lungs. Qian said, 'I didn't know she was American.'

It took Li a moment to realise what he meant. 'Your English has improved,' he said.

Qian shrugged. 'I've been taking lessons.'

Li was taken aback and looked at his number two in surprise. 'Why?'

'Seems like English is the language you need to get on these days. The language of the future.'

Li blew a puff of air through his lips. 'Who knows what we'll all be speaking in a hundred years.'

'You and I will be speaking Chinese with our ancestors.'

'You know what I mean.' Li managed a tired smile. 'And you never can tell. If the economy continues growing at the present rate maybe the rest of the world will be speaking Chinese by then.'

They dashed across the road between cars, and when they got into the Jeep Li said, 'So, anyway, what difference does it make?' Qian looked at him quizzically. 'Her being American.'

Qian started the engine. 'There's no way we'll be able to keep it out of the papers, Chief.'

# TUESDAY

# CHAPTER SIX

## I

Her body was slim and firm and beautiful. His hands slipped over the softness of her curves, tracing the line of her hips, gliding across her belly and up to the swelling of her breasts. The nipples pressed hard into his palms. He felt her legs wrap themselves around him, crossing in the small of his back as he slid inside her. Her hair smelled of peaches. 'Help me,' she whispered, and he heard her say, 'I love you.'

'I love you, too,' he said.

'Help me,' she said again.

But he was lost inside her, drifting on a wave of lust, thrusting against it.

'Help me.' It was louder, now, more insistent. Another wave crashed over him. 'Help me!' she screamed, and he opened his eyes. Her smile had slipped from her face. There were black holes where her ears and eyes should have been, and blood ran across her face like vivid red slashes. He screamed and reared up and something struck him hard on the back of his head.

'Chief, are you okay?'

It was Wu, his face a mask of concern. The desk lamp was lying on the floor, the bulb shattered into a thousand pieces. The first yellow sunlight was slanting in the window.

Li blinked and couldn't figure it out. 'What . . . ?'

Wu stooped to pick up the lamp. 'You must have had a nightmare, Chief. The whole section heard you screaming. You sure you're okay?'

'I was asleep?' Li could hardly believe it.

'You dropped off about two, Chief. No one had the heart to wake you.'

'Shit.' Li stood up unsteadily and tried to straighten out the creases in his uniform. He was shaken by his dream. It had left him wrestling with feelings of guilt and horror. He looked at Wu and realised he must have been there all night, too. 'What about you guys?'

'Oh, we all got a few hours at one time or another,' Wu said. There was a bedroom on each floor of the section, three beds to a room. Officers detained beyond their shift could always snatch some sleep if things got bad.

'Where are we at?'

'About ready for a meeting whenever you are, Chief. The autopsy's scheduled for nine.'

Li checked his watch. It was six a.m. 'I need to get changed and showered. Get my brain in gear. Let's wait until after the autopsy before we do the meeting.'

Wu nodded and was in the corridor before Li called after him, 'I never saw the statement you took from the security guard.' Wu had decided to bring him back to Section One, and they had raised all the staff from the museum and the shop who had been on duty at the monument when it closed up for the night, and brought them all in for questioning.

Wu reappeared in the doorway. 'He didn't remember her,' he said. 'I pulled her pic from the computer, but it didn't mean anything to him. Only thing that stuck with him was a car parked at the side of the road when he locked up. About five or six metres south of the gate.'

Li had a mental picture of the bloody tracks beyond the fence coming to an abrupt end at just about that point on the sidewalk. 'Make? Colour? Anyone inside?'

Wu shook his head. 'He was more concerned about hoofing it back to base for a smoke and a warm drink and something to eat. He said it was dark-coloured. A saloon. There might have been someone sitting in it, he wasn't sure.'

Li gasped his frustration.

'We struck it lucky with the girl, though.'

'What girl?'

'From the ticket office. She recognised Pan straight off. Remembered she spoke with a weird accent and was really pretty. Seems she bought a ticket about five-fifteen. Which was unusual, because apparently people don't normally buy tickets that close to closing time. The girl had already cashed up.'

Li saw Pan striding across the causeway, her long coat flapping about her calves, her collar pulled up around her neck. She must have climbed the steps to the top as the sun was dipping behind the mountains. It had been a spectacular sunset the previous night. It must have been something special from up there. Blue mountains against a red sky, lights going on all across the city. Qian was right. She must have hidden there beneath the arm of the dial, waiting for the place to close up, waiting to meet the man who would take her life. But why? He lifted his coat from the stand. 'I'll be back in a couple of hours.'

His bike was where he had left it the previous morning, chained to the railing leading into what had once been the main entrance to the building. The door had not been in use for as long as Li had been there. He cycled out into Dongzhimen Nanxiao Da Jie and headed south with the traffic, past the restaurant on the corner where Mei Yuan plied her trade. The restaurant was shuttered up, and it was too early for Mei Yuan. There were plenty of other bikes on the road, and traffic was already building up towards rush hour. Li cycled at a leisurely rate, buttoned up tight against the cold, and let the city slip by him. His fatigue had been startled out of him by the icy wind. His thoughts, however, were still full of Lynn Pan and his dream of making love to her. But the only image of her he could conjure in his mind was of her body lying cold and dead under the photographer's lights at the Millennium Monument. Throat cut. Ears hacked off. Red blood on yellow stone.

On Jianguomen Da Jie, the cycle lane was choked with morning commuters, all wrapped in hats and scarves and gloves, padded jackets thickening slight Chinese frames, white masks strapped across faces to protect against both the cold and the pollution. With the sun at their backs, the stream of cyclists moved like a river, at the same pace, an odd current carrying someone in a hurry past the main flow.

A girl chatting breezily on her cellphone weaved in and out amongst the more sedate of her fellow bikers. Cycling with the crowd brought an odd sense of belonging, of being a part of the whole. They passed the footbridge at Dongdan, and the vast new Oriental Plaza at Wangfujing. And at the Grand Hotel, Li moved out into the traffic to take his life in his hands and turn left into Zhengyi Road. He had done it a thousand times, and it only ever got harder. In the distance he saw a formation of PLA guards marching across Changan from the Gate of Heavenly Peace, as they did every morning, to raise the Chinese flag in Tiananmen Square.

Most of the leaves in the trees in Zhengyi Road still clung stubbornly to their branches. Those which dropped were swept up daily by women in blue smocks and white masks. But it was too early for the blue smocks, and the leaves which had fallen overnight scraped and rattled across the tarmac in the wind. Li cycled past the entrance to the Ministry compound and turned in at the news-stand at the end of the road to pick up the first editions of the newspapers. The news vendor was wrapped in layers of clothes, a fur hat with earflaps pulled down over her bobbed hair to overlap the collar and scarf at her neck. She wore fingerless gloves and cradled a glass jar of warm green tea. What was visible of her face smiled a greeting at Li.

'How are you today, Mr Li?'

'Very well, Mrs Ma.'

She handed him his usual *People's Daily* and *Beijing Youth Daily*, folded one inside the other, in return for a few coins.

'You're up early today.'

He smiled. 'I haven't been to bed yet.'

'Ahhh,' she said sagely. 'Of course. Another murder.'

He looked at her in astonishment. 'How do you know that?'

She nodded towards the bundle in his hand. 'It's in the paper.'

Li frowned. 'It can't be.' He looked at the *People's Daily*. The front page was covered in the usual CCP propaganda. *Illiteracy rate among adult people slashed*. And, *Yangtze water cleanup ensured*. There was a story about massive new investment in the western provinces, and a photograph of the executive deputy secretary of Tibet answering questions at a press conference. His heart skipped a beat as he saw a photograph of himself receiving his award from the Minister of Public Security. He would not have expected the public organ of the Party to have carried anything on the murders. The *Beijing Youth Daily* was another matter. Independent of the Party, and increasingly bold in its coverage of Chinese internal affairs, it had begun to garner a reputation for running high-risk stories. But even so, Li could not imagine the paper carrying a crime story about which no details had yet been released. Particularly since the latest murder had only been committed the night before. He unfolded its front page and felt as if he had been slapped. *Beijing Ripper Claims Victim No. 5*. The headline ran almost the full length of the left side of the front page in bold red characters. Two strips of sub-heading matched it, side by side, white characters on a red background. *Body discovered at Millennium Monument, throat cut, ears removed*. And, *Four previous victims in*

*Jianguomen found with body parts missing*. Above the story itself, was a photograph of Li pictured at the award ceremony the previous evening. The caption read, *Award-winning Beijing cop, Li Yan, leads investigation*.

'It would make you frightened to go out at night,' the news vendor said. 'He must be insane, this Beijing Ripper, cutting open these poor women and taking out their insides.' Her words dragged Li's eyes from the paper to her face. She must have read the story from start to finish. As, in all probability, would most of the city's population in the hours ahead. It was going to spread panic, and it would certainly be picked up by the foreign media. The political implications were unthinkable. How in the name of the sky, he wondered, had they got hold of this kind of detail?

Margaret was feeding Li Jon in the living room when he got in. She was still in her dressing gown, face smudged and bleary from sleep – or the lack of it. He threw the *Beijing Youth Daily* on to the coffee table in front of her. 'Look!' he said.

She glanced at the paper. 'I see a photograph of you,' she said. 'Is that what I'm supposed to be looking at? Maybe I should cut it out and keep it by the bedside, that way I'd probably see more of you than I do at the moment.'

But Li was in no mood for her sarcasm, and in his agitation, he had forgotten that she would not be able to read the headline. '*Beijing Ripper Claims Victim No. 5.*' He read it for her.

She shrugged. 'So? It's true, isn't it?'

'That's not the point!' His voice was strained by exasperation and anger. 'No one outside of the investigation knows the kind of detail they've printed in there.'

'So someone leaked it.'

Li shook his head. 'It doesn't happen in China.'

'It does now.' Margaret pushed up an eyebrow. 'Welcome to the rest of the world.' She removed the teat from Li Jon's mouth and wiped his lips. 'Good morning, by the way.'

Li threw his hands up in frustration. 'They're going to blame me for this, Margaret.' He cursed under his breath. 'I'm going for a shower.' And he stormed off to the bathroom.

Margaret called after him. 'Your son says good morning, too.'

The slamming of the bathroom door came back in response. After a moment she heard the sound of the shower running, and the shower door banged shut. The phone rang. Usually she did not answer it, because the calls were invariably for Li and the callers spoke only Chinese. But he was in the shower, and in spite of her resentment at being abandoned to play the role of the little wife and doting mother, she did understand the pressure he was under. She lifted the receiver. '*Wei?*' A female voice spoke to her in Chinese. 'I'm sorry, I don't understand,' Margaret said. 'Please hold.'

She hefted Li Jon in her left arm, and took the phone through to the bathroom. Li's uniform and underwear lay crumpled on the floor where he had dropped them. She opened the shower door and immediately felt the hot spray and steam on her face. She saw the shape of Li lathering his head with soap somewhere in the midst of it all and thrust the phone towards him. 'Here,' she said. 'A call for you.'

He fumbled to turn off the water, stinging shampoo running into his eyes as he reached for the phone. 'Shit, Margaret, could it not have waited?'

'I've no idea,' she said, and she slammed the door shut behind her.

Li winced, and stood dripping in the cubicle, clutching the phone to his wet head. The cold of the apartment was already making itself felt as the water cooled, and he started to shiver. '*Wei?*'

It was the secretary from the Commissioner's office at police headquarters. The Commissioner wanted to see him without delay. Li closed his eyes and took a deep breath to calm himself. The storm was about to break. And it was going to break right over his head.

By the time he was dressed and ready to go, Margaret had steamed some lotus paste buns and made green tea. He appeared in the kitchen doorway looking harassed, wearing his long, heavy coat. But he had changed into freshly pressed slacks and a white shirt. Margaret thought he looked stunning, and she always loved the smell of him when he came out of the shower. But he never seemed to be around long enough these days for her to enjoy him.

'I've got to go,' he said. 'Commissioner Zhu is going to cut me up into little pieces and feed me to the fish.'

'Then you should have some breakfast before you go. To fatten you up for the fish.'

'No time. I'll call later.' And he was gone.

She shouted after him, 'Are you remembering we're going

out for dinner tonight?' But the door was already closing behind him. She shut her eyes to try to calm herself, and to prepare herself for the emptiness of the day ahead – before remembering that Li's father had said he would drop by in the afternoon to see his grandson. Perhaps, she reflected, the day would have been better left empty. She felt her blood pressure start to rise once more.

The phone rang again, startling her this time. She swithered about whether to answer it, but if it was important there was still time to call down to Li from the balcony. And, besides, what else did she have to do with her time? She picked up the receiver. '*Wei?*'

A man's voice spoke in a clipped American accent. 'May I speak with Doctor Campbell?'

It seemed so odd to have someone addressing her as Doctor Campbell, not only in her own language, but in a comfortingly East-coast American accent. 'This is she,' she replied.

## II

Police headquarters was a short walk from Li's apartment. The main entrance was two streets down on Qianmen Dong Da Jie, along from the EMS Central Post Office, but Li always entered from Jiaominxiang Lane. The old, arched entrance to the rear compound, opposite the Supreme Court, had been demolished to make way for a new building, clad in marble and designed along classical European lines to blend in with the redbrick one-time CID headquarters on the east side, and the former Citibank on the west. The old Citibank building was now a police museum, and beyond it the new entrance was watched over by two armed PLA guards flanking the gate.

The trees that overhung the lane were still thick with leaves, and the leaves were thick with the dust of construction. The roadway was closed to traffic, and workmen crowded the sidewalks, wheeling barrows and shovelling sand into cement mixers. The Supreme Court had been stripped back to its bones and was being given a new face. Ministry apartment blocks beyond were draped in green netting, behind which yet more workmen put in twenty-four-hour shifts in this relentless process of rebuilding and remodelling the new China.

Li walked briskly through the gates into the rear compound, the sound of pneumatic drills hammering in his ears, drowning the sound of the beating of his heart which, until then, was all he had been able to hear.

The Commissioner's office was on the fifth floor, and Li stood uncomfortably in the elevator with half a dozen other people who, he was sure, could hear his heart beating, too. No pneumatic drills here to drown it out. But if they did, they gave no indication of it. He stepped out into a carpeted corridor and followed it along to the large reception area outside the Commissioner's office. A poster-sized photograph of the face of an armed policewoman, her gun pointing to the ceiling and pressed against her cheek, dominated one wall. The rest of the room was dominated by the Commissioner's secretary, a formidable woman in her fifties who, Li had often surmised, probably bought her clothes mail-order from an outsize store in the US. She was not of typical Chinese dimensions. But in a country where a large proportion of domestic crime involved husband battering, she was not untypical of the older Chinese woman. For all his height and rank, Li always found her intimidating. She was, after all, only a secretary. But like many secretaries, she took her status and power from her boss. And since her boss was Beijing's top cop, that gave her quite a bit of clout.

She glared at Li. 'You're late.' It was not long after seven, and Li figured she must have been called in early. She certainly looked, and sounded, like a woman who had not had her full complement of sleep.

'I came straight away.'

'He's had to go. Deputy Cao will see you.'

Li breathed an inner sigh of relief. Cao was less likely to be riding his high horse. But if he thought he was in for an easier time, he was mistaken.

Cao turned from the window where he had been staring morosely out at the traffic below, and didn't even give Li time to draw breath. His arms were folded across his chest, and in one hand he held a folded and much thumbed copy of the *Beijing Youth Daily*. He almost threw it on to his desk. 'You've done it this time, Section Chief.'

'That had nothing to do with me, Deputy Cao,' Li said.

'It has everything to do with you, Li!' Cao almost shouted at him. 'It's your case. And it's your face on the front page of the paper. And the Commissioner himself told you only yesterday how important it was that this *didn't* get into the press.'

Li held his peace. There was nothing he could say.

Cao waved his arm theatrically in the air. 'The Minister was apoplectic. That's why it's me giving you the bollocking and not the Commissioner himself. He's been summoned to the Minister's office to furnish him with some persuasive explanation for this . . .' he picked up the paper and then dropped it on the desk again, '. . . this piece of shit.'

'Someone leaked it,' Li said lamely.

'Of course someone leaked it!' Cao roared. 'And it could only have been somebody on the inside. A police officer. Somebody under your command.'

'Or above it,' Li ventured.

Cao wheeled on him and inclined his head dangerously. He lowered his voice, 'If I was you, Li, I wouldn't go suggesting that too loudly around here. It won't win you many friends. And believe me, right now you need all the friends you can get.' He snatched a pack of cigarettes from his desk and lit one. 'Someone in your section has been a naughty boy. I suggest you find out who it is.'

'Maybe it's the same officer who leaks inside information from my office to yours.'

Cao dropped into his chair and regarded Li speculatively. He shook his head slightly. 'You're treading on very thin ice here, Li.' He took a long pull at his cigarette. 'You run a slack ship up there. You may have admirers in high places because of a couple of high profile cases, but those of us in the know understand that police work is not about the handful of glamorous cases that might come your way in the course of a career. It's about the daily slog, cracking every crappy case that gets thrown at you. And that means running a tight ship. Administration, organisation, attention to detail, no matter how dull or how unglamorous. It requires a disciplined approach to the running of your section, it requires your junior officers to respect and, if necessary, to fear you.

'But not you. You like to be one of the boys. You flit around from case to case like some kind of latter-day Sherlock Holmes. You think you can bypass all the usual procedures and solve the crime with nothing more than flair and imagination.' He took an angry puff at his cigarette, perhaps in frustration that all his years as a predecessor of Li's at Section One had led to this dead-end deputy's job. 'Well, it doesn't work like that, Li. We have evolved an approach to criminal investigation that gets results by sheer bloody hard work and attention to detail.' He slapped a hand on top of the *Beijing Youth Daily*. 'And splashing the details of the worst serial killings in this city's history across the front pages of trash like this, is not going to help. So I suggest you batten down the hatches up there and find out who's responsible. Because if you don't, rest assured that I shall. And there *will* be hell to pay!'

## III

The sun was rising now above the tops of all the new apartment blocks along Dongzhimen, fingers of cold yellow light extending themselves west along the grid. The icy wind carried the breath of winter from the frozen northern plains, laden with the promise of subzero temperatures in the weeks ahead.

Li watched Mei Yuan's cold red fingers as they worked nimbly about the hotplate to produce his *jian bing*. Her face, too, was red with the cold, skin dried by the wind. Her eyes watered constantly, as if weeping for the lost summer, or for her lost life. She caught him watching her, and she smiled. Her face lit up, radiant in the morning light, no trace in it of the pain she had endured. She wore her fate with dignity, and always came out smiling.

Li, on the other hand, was sunk in gloom. As if the weight of the world rested on his shoulders. Cao's words had stung him, and he wondered if others saw him as Cao did. Cavalier, glory-seeking, too much one of the boys for his subordinates to fully respect him. There were times he took shortcuts, yes, but he never neglected that mind-numbing, painfully slow process of putting a case together piece by piece by piece. He knew the importance of the detail. His uncle had dinned that into him often enough. But sometimes you could get bogged down in it. Sometimes there was so much detail you couldn't see the bigger picture. Sometimes you just had to trust your instincts and make that leap of faith.

'A *fen* for them,' Mei Yuan said.

'What?'

'Your thoughts.'

'They're not even worth a *fen*, Mei Yuan.'

She slipped his *jian bing* into brown paper and handed it to him. 'I read about the murders in the paper this morning.'

'You and the rest of Beijing,' Li muttered gloomily.

Mei Yuan looked at him perceptively. 'Should we not?'

'No,' Li said emphatically. 'You should not. The story was leaked, and the paper should have known better than to print it.'

'Who leaked it?'

'I have no idea.'

'Then why don't you ask the editor of the paper?'

'Oh, I think he'll be facing that question, and many more, from people much higher up than me, Mei Yuan.'

She nodded mutely. 'They are terrible killings, Li Yan. Do you not think, perhaps, that people have a right to know?'

'Why?' Li asked simply, and he took a bite of his *jian bing*. 'Knowing will not protect them, because they do not know who he is. But it won't stop people being afraid, panicking even. And we will be inundated with cranks claiming to be the Ripper, and with calls from people claiming they know who he is. And we will spend hours and days, maybe weeks, sifting through cranks and crap, wasting valuable time going up blind alleys while the killer remains free to kill again. Our efforts to catch him will be hopelessly diluted.'

'Yes,' Mei Yuan said. 'I can see how that could be.' There was sympathy in her eyes when she smiled at him. 'I do not envy you, Li Yan. Trying to catch this man. First you must try to work out who he is. Like a riddle. Only, if you don't come up with the answer someone will die.'

Li said, 'And you know how bad I am at solving riddles.'

'Maybe because there is no life at stake,' she said. 'For me it is easy, because it is a game. But to catch a killer is not a game. If you fail, he will kill again. For me, the very fear of failure, and the consequences of that, would numb my mind.'

'Join the club,' Li said.

'But you *will* catch him.'

'I have to.' And just focusing on that thought freed Li's mind from the clutter which had filled it that morning. What did it matter who had leaked the story? It was another issue, something to be settled another day. A diversion. And he could not afford be diverted. The genie was out of the bottle. There was no way to put it back in. Perhaps, he thought, Mei Yuan was right. He had trouble solving her riddles because it did not matter whether he solved them or not. But the thought that someone might die if he did not catch a killer concentrated his mind in an entirely different way.

'I don't suppose,' Mei Yuan said, 'you will have had much time to consider my last riddle.'

Li smiled ruefully. 'Mei Yuan, I can't even remember it in detail. Two guys planting rice, wasn't it?' He sighed. 'I'm sorry.'

'If you can't remember in detail there is no point in even thinking about it. I told you, the devil is in the detail.'

There it was again. Detail. The answer to everything was always in the detail. 'I just can't give it the time right now, Mei Yuan. Not with this killer still out there.'

'Sometimes, Li Yan, it is good therapy to take your mind off one problem to work on another. Then when you return to the original it might not seem quite so intractable.'

Li finished his *jian bing* and grinned. Mei Yuan was usually right about most things. 'Okay,' he said. 'Give me it again.'

'Two deaf mutes are planting rice in a paddy field in Hunan, a long way from their village,' she said. 'It takes them an hour to go from one end of the paddy to the other . . .' She went through the whole riddle once more. The fact that the two men had just finished lunch, sharing their food and drink, agreeing to meet and share again when they each finished planting their remaining ten rows. Li listened carefully, and it started coming back to him. When the man with the food had finished his work he couldn't see his friend anywhere, and thinking he had gone back to the village, had eaten the food himself.

'So he wakes up the next morning,' Li cut in, 'and the other guy's shaking him and accusing him of being greedy, leaving him there on his own to go off and eat the food by himself.'

Mei Yuan nodded. 'But the man with the food says he only ate it because the other one went off with the drink and left him. The man with the drink insists he was there all the time! They are both telling the truth.'

Li thought about it. They have just finished lunch and have another ten rows to plant. They are both deaf mutes and can only communicate by sign language. They both claim to still be there when they finish their work, but for some reason they don't see one another. 'They're not blind?' he said.

'If they were blind, how could they communicate by sign language?'

'Of course.' Li felt foolish. But they couldn't hear or speak to each other. If they were both there at the end of the day why didn't they see each other? Why did the man with the food think his friend had already gone? And then it dawned on him, and he felt even more foolish. 'Oh, Mei Yuan, that's not fair.'

'What's not fair?'

'They'd just had lunch, so it must have been about midday. They still had ten rows each to plant. But it took them an hour to get from one end of the paddy to the other, then it was ten o'clock at night when they finished. And it was dark. That's why they couldn't see each other.'

Mei Yuan grinned. 'Simple, really. And, of course, they couldn't call out because they were deaf mutes.'

'But what if there was a full moon that night?'

She shrugged. 'It's the rainy season, Li Yan. The sky is cloudy.'

He gave her a look. 'You always have an answer.'

'Because there always is one.'

A shadow fell across his face as he remembered just how few answers he'd come up with on the Ripper murders. 'Yes,' he said. 'There's always an answer. But we don't always *know* what it is.'

Qian spotted Li passing the open door to the detectives' room and hurried into the corridor after him. He caught up with him in Li's office. Li was surveying the shambles that was his desk. The night before he had lifted most of the piles of paper off it to stack against the wall below the window. This morning they had been replaced by fresh ones.

'Chief.'

He turned at the sound of Qian's voice. 'Unless it's important, Qian, I don't have time. I've got to get across town for the autopsy.' He flicked his head towards the wall. 'Is Wu next door?'

'Chief, the autopsy's been postponed.'

Which stopped Li in his tracks. 'Postponed by whom?'

'An order from headquarters. Just came in a few minutes ago.'

Li scowled. 'What in the name of the sky do they think they are playing at?'

Qian seemed almost afraid to tell him. 'Lynn Pan was an American citizen.'

'So?'

'So the American Embassy have requested that one of their people carry out the autopsy. Or at least assist on it.'

'Well, the answer's no,' Li snapped. 'This is an ongoing murder inquiry. I'm not going to have some goddamned American pathologist who knows nothing of the background to the other murders coming in and fucking up our corpse.'

Qian braced himself. 'I don't know that it matters much what we think, Chief. Apparently the Ministry has already agreed. It's been authorised at the highest level, and the autopsy's been postponed till eleven.'

'The hell it has!' Li snatched the phone and started punching in numbers.

'Chief . . .' There was something in Qian's tone that cut through Li's anger.

'What is it, Qian?'

'There have been other developments. Putting off the autopsy for a couple of hours might not be such a bad idea.'

Li slowly replaced the receiver. 'Tell me.'

'There was a break-in last night at the Chinese Academy of Sciences. Lynn Pan's office was ransacked.'

## IV

The head of security met them in the lobby. He was agitated, an ex-cop who saw the break-in on his turf as a potential one-way ticket to unemployment. He was a tall man, nearly Li's height, and wore a grey uniform with clusters of stars and stripes that meant nothing at all. They just looked impressive. It was still early, and staff and students were only now beginning to show up for the day. He steered Li and Wu along a corridor to his office on the ground floor. 'Look, guys,' he said, appealing to the old boys' network, 'I'd really appreciate it if we can keep this low profile.'

'A woman has been murdered,' Li said sharply. 'It's hard to lower a profile like that. What happened here?'

The security man shrugged his eyebrows. 'That's just it. I've no idea. None of the alarms was tripped. I can't find signs of forced entry anywhere.'

Wu was chewing manically, and swinging the left-hand leg of his shades around the little finger of his right hand. 'So how do you know there's been a break-in?'

'Because somebody jemmied their way into Lynn Pan's

offices and cleaned out the lot. Computers, files, just about everything that wasn't nailed down. A real pro job.'

'Not an inside one?' Li said.

The security man pulled a face. 'I don't think so. If they had keys to turn off alarms and get in and out the building, wouldn't they have had keys for her offices, too?'

Wu said, 'If they were smart enough to break in without leaving a trace why would they have to force an internal door?'

'Because once you're in, you don't have to worry about setting off alarms,' the security man said. 'You've done the smart bit. You're not going to be able to hide the fact that you've ransacked a whole department, so why worry about breaking down a door?'

Li wasn't convinced either way. 'Let's take a look.'

Some of Pan's staff and students were gathered in the corridor outside the department. Most of them had just heard the news of her death and were still in shock. Their babble of hushed chatter died away as Li, Wu and the security man stepped out of the elevator. Li said to the security man, 'I don't want anybody touching anything until forensics have been over the place.'

He recognised some of the faces in the corridor. Lynn Pan's assistant, an older woman, who had brought them all tea the previous day and escorted them to the computer room. The student who had briefed them on the 'crime' for the MERMER test. He nodded acknowledgement as he passed them and the security man showed the detectives the double doors which had been forced at the end of the corridor. The wood was splintered and broken around the lock. Crude but effective. Beyond the doors, the reception room where Li had sat with Commissioner Zhu and Deputy Minister Wei and the others appeared to have been left undisturbed. Li glanced from the window and saw the minaret-like TV tower catching the light, sharp against the blue of the sky. He could scarcely believe it had been only yesterday afternoon he had stood at that very window looking out at the tower. Then, Lynn Pan had still been very much alive, a beautiful, vibrant living being, demonstrating her extraordinary expertise. Why would anyone want to kill her?

A short corridor led off to the computer room where the MERMER demonstration had been carried out, Lynn Pan's office through the wall from it, a couple of lecture rooms, another office occupied by Pan's assistant, and a small staff room.

The computer room had been cleared apart from the two tables on which the computer equipment had stood, and a couple of office chairs on wheels. The cables remained, but all the equipment was gone. They moved through to Pan's private office, and Li recognised her scent lingering there still.

Li said to the security man, 'Get Pan's assistant in here.' And as an afterthought, 'I met her yesterday, but I can't remember her name.'

'Professor Hu,' the security man said.

While they waited for her, Li wandered around the office. The desk top was completely cleared. The drawers had been opened and emptied. There was a lacquered wooden cupboard against the back wall, and a filing cabinet next to it. The doors of the cupboard stood ajar and it, too, was empty. There were pot plants on almost every available surface. One, which had perhaps stood upon the desk, lay smashed and broken on the floor, earth spilling across worn carpet tiles. Framed certificates hung on the walls, a testament to Pan's educational history and professional qualifications. There was a photograph of her, along with another woman, taken at a graduation ceremony. They both wore mortar boards and black and crimson gowns, clutching their certificates, and smiling for the camera. It had clearly been taken several years earlier. Pan was younger-looking, long straight hair hanging down over her shoulders. Her smile had been just as radiant then. In another photograph she was pictured with a young, dark-haired American male. Li read the hand-written caption on it. *With Doctor Lawrence Farwell, June 1999.* She had cut her hair short by then. It suited her.

'She was a pretty beautiful woman, huh?' Wu said, peering at the photograph.

'Yes, she was,' Li said. Her eyes burned out of the picture at him, smiling, giving, reaching out, and he remembered the strange emotion which had clouded them in those last moments he had seen her alive. What he had taken as an appeal for help. If only he had answered that appeal. If only he had held back, spoken to her before he left. If only.

The security man returned with Professor Hu. She had shoulder-length wavy hair shot through with streaks of grey. She was around five-five, tall for a Chinese woman, and painfully thin. She wore a grey business suit with a white blouse and a red scarf tied at her neck like a slash of blood. Li found it disturbing. Her eyes were red and swollen. She had obviously been doing a lot of crying.

'Professor Hu,' Li said, 'I'm sorry to meet you again in these circumstances. I want to catch the people who did this. I want to catch the person who killed Miss Pan. And I'm going to need your help.'

'I don't see . . .'

He put a finger to his lips to silence her. 'You know this place better than any of us, Professor. I want you to walk us through it, room by room, and tell us what's missing.'

She nodded her willingness, and he gave her a pair of latex gloves to slip on, so that she could open filing cabinets and drawers and cupboards without disturbing evidence. Although Li did not expect forensics to find anything. This was a highly professional job. The security man had been right in that, at least.

It took them less than fifteen minutes to go through the department. Every drawer and cupboard that was opened told the same depressing story. Empty. Empty. Empty. Every scrap of stationery, every file, the contents of every drawer. Even the bins were empty. Wu said, 'Looks like they didn't know what they were after, so they just took the lot.'

'Why do you say that?' Li said.

Wu said, 'Hey, Chief, you don't break into a place like this just to empty the bins. They've got garbage men for that.'

According to Professor Hu, both Pan's desktop computer

and her laptop were gone, along with all her disks. She said, 'It's as if the place had been packed up for a removal. All that's left is the furniture.'

'Why?' The word which was finding its way most often to the front of Li's mind, found expression now on his lips. He turned to the professor. 'Can you think of any reason why someone would want to steal your files?'

She shook her head helplessly. 'Not one,' she said. 'The work we were doing here was not unique. It wasn't secret. It wasn't even valuable. Not in financial terms.'

'And can you think of a single reason why anyone would want to kill Miss Pan?'

The Professor drew in her lips to try to prevent the tears welling in her eyes. 'Lynn was the most beautiful, kind and thoughtful human being I ever knew,' she said, controlling her voice with difficulty. 'She was goodness personified. Whoever took that life must have been consumed by pure evil.'

They re-emerged into the reception room just as Fu Qiwei, the senior forensics officer from Pau Jü Hutong, arrived with a team of three scenes of crime officers. These were the same officers who had attended the crime scene at the Millennium Monument the night before. Fu was a shrunken man with small, coal dark eyes, thinning hair dyed black and scraped back across his pate. There was nothing he hadn't seen in a long career. Nothing left that would shock him. He had developed an acerbic sense of humour, a kind of protective shield, like a turtle's shell. But he wasn't smiling today. 'A connection?' he asked Li.

Li inclined his head slightly. 'That's what we're going to find out.' He turned to Wu. 'You'd better hang on here. Start taking statements from staff and students. I'm going to take a look at her apartment.' He was about to leave when he had a thought and turned back. 'Professor?' The professor was standing staring out of the window where Li had stood the previous day. She turned.

'Yes, Section Chief?'

'Can you tell me what time Miss Pan left the office last night?'

'It was a little after five.'

Just time for her to walk to the Millennium Monument and purchase a ticket before it closed. He said, 'We have this notion that she might have been going to meet someone at the monument. I don't suppose you'd have any idea who that might have been?'

Professor Hu raised her eyebrows in surprise. 'Well, of course I do.'

The room was suddenly very quiet, and all eyes were on the dead woman's assistant. 'Who?' Li asked.

'Well, I don't know why you're asking me. You should know better than anyone.'

Li frowned. 'I don't understand.'

'She was meeting you, Section Chief. I took the call from you myself.'

Li was barely aware of the change of focus in the room. All eyes were now on him. He felt like Alice in Wonderland, falling into the rabbit hole and tumbling through darkness. 'And what did I say?' he asked.

The professor looked at him oddly. 'You said you needed to speak to Miss Pan urgently, and I put you through to her. She came out of her office a few minutes later with her coat on. She'd had a meeting scheduled for six last night. She asked me to call round everyone and postpone it. Something important had come up and she had to go and talk to you.'

'I didn't call,' Li said, and the professor looked nonplussed. 'What made you think it was me?'

'Because you –' She stopped to correct herself. 'Because the caller said, *This is Section Chief Li Yan. We met this afternoon. I need to speak to Professor Pan on a matter of some urgency.*'

'Someone who knew you were here yesterday afternoon, Chief,' Wu said. 'That must narrow it down.'

Li thought about it. There were any number of people who might have known he was here. It would be impossible to draw a ring and say only those inside knew. He felt sick. Pan had thought she was meeting him. She had gone to her death trusting in him. The caller must have been very persuasive. But what bizarre circumstance would have led her to accept such a strange rendezvous? He still found it hard to believe that someone had been able to pass themselves off as him. He turned to the professor. 'Was there nothing about the call that struck you as . . . odd? I mean, did this person *sound* like me?'

She shrugged. 'I don't know. I'd only met you for a few minutes yesterday afternoon. I thought it was you because he said he was. I had no reason to doubt it.'

And neither would Pan. Her Chinese was almost native, but it was American. Her experience of China was limited.

Regional variations in accent would mean nothing to her. And once again, the words of Lao Dai came back to him. *You have an enemy, Li Yan.* Not only was this killer sending Li letters, fulfilling a promise to cut off a woman's ears, but now he was passing himself off as Li himself. He had used Li to lure Pan to her death, innocent and trusting like a lamb to the slaughter. Li's shock began turning to anger. He turned to Fu Qiwei. 'Get a team out to Pan's apartment. She wasn't picked at random. She was killed for a reason. Maybe we'll find it there.'

Sunlight filled the stairwell from the windows at the rear of the Academy as Li made his way down to the floor below. He was surprised to find Lyang in Hart's office.

'Didn't Margaret tell you I worked here mornings?' she said.

Li said, 'We haven't had much chance to talk in the last twenty-four hours.'

Lyang nodded gravely. 'I saw the paper this morning. It's awful about poor Lynn. She was just about the nicest person you could ever hope to meet.'

Li said, 'Is Bill around?'

'He's doing a polygraph test this morning,' she said. 'A favour for some of your people. Some guy accused of sexually assaulting his thirteen-year-old daughter. He's agreed to take the test to prove his innocence. I'll take you along if you like.'

As they passed down a corridor on the south wing of the fourth floor, Lyang said, 'Bill wasn't too keen on doing this after we found out about Lynn. He was pretty cut up about it. You know it was Bill who brought her over here?' Li nodded.

'He feels really responsible.' She sighed. 'But he'd promised the people from Section Six. So . . .' Her voice tailed off as she knocked gently on a door and opened it a crack. Two officers from the interrogation unit at Pau Jü Hutong turned in their chairs. 'Alright if we come in?' she whispered. Li knew both the faces and nodded his acknowledgement. They waved him in. The room itself was in darkness, the only light coming through what appeared to be a window into an adjoining room. It took Li a moment to realise it was a two-way mirror.

Two cameras mounted on tripods were recording proceedings in the next room. A middle-aged man sat in a chair beside a desk on which a polygraph machine stood idle, spidery needles hovering motionless above the paper conveyor belt on which they would record his responses to Hart's questions. The man had long hair swept back from his forehead and growing down over his collar. His face was pockmarked from adolescent acne, and a feeble attempt at a moustache clung to his upper lip. He was sitting at right-angles to the table, facing a chair in which Hart sat conducting his pre-test interview. A monitor on the camera side of the mirror showed a full-screen view of the interviewee, his head cut off above the top frame of the picture, but inset in close-up in the lower left-hand quadrant, obliterating Hart from the recording.

The Section Six interrogators motioned Li silently to a seat. One of them was a woman of about fifty with a round, friendly face, whom Li knew to be a formidable and aggressive interrogator. The other was an older man with a face chiselled out of granite, who had an uncanny talent for gaining the trust of the people he questioned. They were the antithesis of the stereotypical good-cop-bad-cop double act.

The woman leaned towards Li and whispered so quietly he could barely hear her. 'He's a smooth operator,' she said of Hart. 'That guy was so nervous when he came in he could hardly speak. Now he's eating out of Hart's hand. Can't hardly get the guy to shut up.'

'He'll get to the test itself in a couple of minutes,' Lyang said.

And they heard Hart's voice across the monitor, soft, soothing, persuasive. His Chinese was almost perfect, his American accent lending it a nearly soporific quality. 'Now, Jiang,' he was saying, 'I'm going to make you a promise right at the start. I'm not going to ask you any questions on the test that I'm not going to ask you right now. There'll be no surprises, no trick questions. I need a yes, or a no.'

Jiang nodded, and you could see the tension in his face. He laid his forearms flat along the arms of his chair and stretched his palms wide. He swallowed a couple of times, and opened and closed his mouth as if unsticking his tongue from the roof of it. Li remembered the rice test that Hart and Lyang had talked about yesterday.

Hart went on, 'I'll begin with what are called known truth questions. They're questions, the answers to which you know are true and I know are true. What they do is create a picture for me.' He paused just for a moment. 'Is your name Jiang?'

'Yes,' Jiang said.

'Are you now in Beijing?'

'Yes.'

'Then I have the questions about why we're here today.' Another brief pause. 'Have you ever put your penis in Shimei's vagina?'

Li was startled by the bluntness of the question.

'No,' Jiang said.

'He damn well did!' the female interrogator hissed. 'He might have been drunk at the time, but he did it alright. And he remembers he did it.'

Hart continued in the same hypnotic tone, 'Do you remember if you did put your penis into Shimei's vagina?'

'No.'

'Are you telling the truth about not putting your penis in Shimei's vagina?'

'Yes.'

He shuffled his papers. 'Then I have those questions we discussed about the past. Do you ever remember doing anything about which you were ashamed?'

'No.'

'Do you ever remember performing an unusual sex act?'

Jiang seemed embarrassed by this question. 'No,' he said. Then added, 'Only with my wife.' And a sad smile flitted briefly across his face.

Lyang whispered, 'She ran off with his sister's husband and left him to bring up the kid on his own.'

Hart pressed on. 'Do you remember ever committing a crime for which you were not caught?'

'No.'

'Then I have a question which just kind of covers the entire test. Do you intend to answer truthfully each question on this test?'

'Yes.'

'Then the last question, just for me. Are you afraid I will ask you a question we have not reviewed?'

'No.'

Hart stood up. 'Okay, that's all there is.' And he began wiring Jiang up for the test itself – two bands of sensors strapped around the chest and midriff to monitor heart rate, a cuff on the left arm to measure blood pressure, and sensors on the tips of two fingers on the right hand to detect perspiration. He talked as he worked. 'Now, for each chart, Jiang, I need you to keep both feet on the ground. No moving. No unnecessary talking. Look straight ahead and close your eyes. Think about the questions, think about the answers and try to answer truthfully.'

When he had finished wiring Jiang to the polygraph, he rounded his desk so that he was looking at the subject in profile. 'Now sometimes,' he said, 'I have people come in who just naturally think, I have to beat this sucker. When they do that, generally they have heard that when they get asked a question they should squeeze their toes or bite their tongue or press down on a tack they've hidden in their shoe. They make a big mistake when they do that, Jiang. The reason for that is that the equipment is so sensitive that if you have a heart murmur I'll see that right there on your chart. And when people try doing these things, all they do is cause those pens to go crazy.' He waved his hand at the needles poised above the chart, ready to go. 'And when I see that, I have to ask why, when I already told them how best for me to see the truth, why are they trying to change what I'm looking at.' He looked at Jiang. 'And what's the only logical reason you can think of?'

Jiang seemed taken aback that Hart was asking him. He shrugged and said awkwardly, 'They're trying to cover something up.'

'They're a liar,' Hart said. 'And that's just the way I call it.' He folded his hands in front of him on the desk and gave Jiang a moment or two to think about it. Then he said, 'Now what I'm going to do, Jiang, is I want to see what your body looks like normally on the chart. So I want you to choose a number between one and seven.'

Jiang gave a strained chuckle. 'Not between one and ten.'

'No. Between one and seven.' Pause. 'What's your number?'

'Five.'

'Okay. Now what I'll do is I'll go through all the numbers between one and seven. Each time I ask did you choose that number, the only answer I want is, no. Even when I ask you the number five. That way I have a number of truthful responses, and I have one deceptive response. It gives me a chance to adjust the instruments for your body.'

Lyang was smiling. 'Believe that, you'll believe anything,' she whispered. But everyone else in the room was mesmerised by the proceedings on the other side of the mirror.

Hart set the polygraph going, needles scraping back and forth across the paper that scrolled by beneath them, and took

Jiang through all the numbers in a random sequence. When he had finished, he switched off the polygraph and tore off the chart. 'Excellent,' he said. 'It always amazes me. It does.' He pushed the chart across the desk towards Jiang. 'It don't take no expert. See this green line?' Jiang followed Hart's finger and nodded. 'See how it changes? See the highest point on the chart? See what's below it?' Li had to admit, Hart was a real showman. Like a magician on a stage.

Jiang craned to see what was written there. 'It's the number five,' he said.

Hart smiled at him. 'So now we know what you know. And you know why the pens reacted so strong. So if I see that when I ask the real questions, we'll be able to get right to the bottom of it.'

Jiang slumped back in his seat, his face a mask of misery. He was beaten, even before he took the test. And he was beaten, because he believed he would be.

Hart reset the polygraph. 'Okay, we'll go straight to the questions one time.'

He got Jiang to sit facing forward, eyes closed, feet flat on the floor, and pumped up the air in his cuff, and then he ran through the questions, just as he had during the pre-test. 'Did you put your penis in Shimei's vagina?'

They did it another two times, the order of the questions changing on each run-through.

When they'd finished the third set, 'That's us,' Hart said. Jiang glanced at him apprehensively, but Hart was giving nothing away. He stepped out from behind the desk to unhook

Jiang from the polygraph, then he collected the charts and said, 'I'll be back in a couple of minutes.' He went out and left Jiang alone. Jiang sat staring into space for a long time, before dropping his face into his hands to stifle his sobs.

The door opened in the observation room and Hart came in. He seemed surprised to see Li. 'Li Yan? What are you doing here?'

Li stood to shake Hart's hand. 'I stopped by to talk to you about Lynn Pan.'

Hart's face clouded. 'I feel like it's all my fault. If I hadn't recommended her for the post . . . Jesus!' He raised his eyes to the ceiling and took a deep breath, trying to control his emotions. 'I'm sorry. It's just so hard to believe she's gone.' He looked at Li. 'Did you . . . ? Were you called to the crime scene?' Li nodded. 'Shit. That must have been tough.'

It was what Margaret had said. And Li wondered if it was really any harder dealing with a murder when it was someone you knew. Of course, you brought a lot of emotional baggage to that circumstance. But he had always found it hard to see the living person in the dead one. It wasn't dealing with the dead that was difficult, it was the loss of the living. In this case, he had hardly known Lynn Pan. And yet the sense of her loss had been powerful. Perhaps because she had been so brim full of life.

Li shrugged. 'Sure. It was hard.' He paused. 'I don't suppose you would have the first idea why anyone would want to kill her?'

Hart shook his head. 'It's inconceivable to me,' he said.

'Or why anyone would want to steal her computers, all her files?'

Hart said, 'I heard there'd been a break-in up there. It's all gone?'

'Everything.'

'Jees . . .' He held up his hands. 'I can't help you. I wish to God I could.'

Li said, 'I might as well tell you, because you'll probably hear it anyway . . .' He glanced at Lyang. 'Apparently she thought she was going to meet me last night at the Millennium Monument.'

Hart's consternation was plain on his face. 'Why would she think that?'

'Because someone phoned up after we'd left yesterday afternoon, saying they were me, and arranging a clandestine meeting.'

'Why? What for?' It was Lyang this time.

'I don't know.'

Hart said, 'Man, that's spooky.'

'What about her private life?' Li said. 'What do you know about that?'

'Not a thing.'

'She came round for dinner a couple of times,' Lyang said.

'Yeah, but all we ever talked about were people we knew back in the States. Work. You know, stuff we had in common.'

'And we never got an invite back to her place.'

'The thing is,' Hart said, 'her private life was just that. Private, wasn't it, Lyang? You know, for such an outgoing girl, she really was a very private person. You got so far with her, and then zap. Down came some kind of shutter. So far and no further. I don't know anything about her relationships, what she did in her spare time. Hell, I don't even know if she lived on her own. It's hard to know if there was anything much at all outside of her work.' He sighed and then glanced through the two-way mirror. 'How's our boy doing?'

'Feeling pretty sorry for himself,' said the female interrogator.

Hart glanced at his watch. 'He's had long enough to stew. Time to go get a confession.' He looked at Li. 'Unless there's anything else you want to ask.'

Li said, 'I can't think of anything right now.'

'We'll be seeing you tonight, anyway,' Lyang said. 'You and Margaret are still coming to dinner, aren't you?'

Li had forgotten all about it. 'Sure,' he said.

Hart squeezed his arm. 'Catch you later.' And he went out still clutching his charts. He hadn't looked at them once.

Li was anxious to be away, but he also wanted to see how Hart's interview with Jiang would turn out. 'Will this take long?' he asked Lyang.

'I shouldn't think so.'

So he sat down again and watched as Hart entered the interview room on the other side of the two-way mirror. Jiang sat upright, almost startled, and you could see his tension in the rigid way he held himself. Hart sat down facing Jiang and put the charts on his knee. He still wasn't consulting them. 'On these tests, Jiang,' he said, those hypnotic tones again, 'I can make one of three decisions. I can say a person's telling the truth. I can say a test's inconclusive, that I just don't know. Or I can say a person's not telling the truth.'

Jiang drew in a deep breath, very focused on Hart and what he was saying. He kept nodding, as if he could gain approval by agreeing.

'Now here's the thing,' Hart said. 'We're not dealing with a criminal case here. You're just an ordinary guy, working hard to raise his family, making his contribution to society. Now, some of the criminals I deal with, that they bring down here from the cells uptown, they don't contribute to anything. They're just kind of leeches on society.' He leaned forward, creating a sense of confidentiality between them. 'When I look at the charts, and from talking with you here today, I know you're no criminal, that's for darn sure. In fact, I'm inclined to think you're kind of a nice guy. And life's dealt you a pretty bum hand.'

Jiang nodded vigorously.

'The thing is, is that as far as what Shimei is saying, it happened. And you're remembering it. But you're having a problem bringing it forward to talk with somebody. To try and understand why. And I can understand the fear and embarrassment for you. That's the biggest thing, isn't it?'

Jiang was nodding miserably now.

'Because you can remember it happened, but if you come right out and tell somebody, how do you handle that picture you have of yourself, because you're not like that normally?'

'I'm not,' Jiang whispered.

'We all have a view of ourselves, Jiang. The way we believe

that the rest of the world looks at us. We call that our ego. And when that is threatened, we have what we call an ego defence mechanism which, to protect that image we have of ourselves, will push things back into our subconscious and lead us to deny that they ever occurred – when, in fact, we ourselves know that, yes, it did happen. But because it is so out of character for us in normal situations, we really don't know how to deal with it.'

Jiang was still nodding his agreement. You could see in him, as clear as day, the desire to confess. To tell this soft-spoken sympathetic American the truth, because after all he had already seen it in the chart.

Hart was still talking. 'And so, we are left in a predicament where we feel so much pressure. It's called anxiety. And our anxiety gets to be so great that our total thinking, our total being, is just taken up with trying to fight it.' He leaned even closer, and put a comforting hand on Jiang's knee. 'The thing is that you know, and I know, that what happened was probably brought on by the booze.'

'Yes . . .' Jiang's voice was a whisper.

'And you were lonely. After all, your wife had left you. How long had it been? Two years? That's a long time for a man to be on his own, Jiang.'

Jiang had tipped his head into his left hand, his palm hiding his eyes, but you could see the tears running down his pock-marked cheeks.

'And that's why you did it, wasn't it, Jiang?'

'Yes.' Almost inaudible.

'I need you to tell me, Jiang, that you did put your penis into Shimei's vagina. And all that anxiety is just going to lift right off your shoulders.'

Again, the bluntness of it seemed shocking, but Li knew that the form of words was important for legal purposes.

'I did it,' Jiang said.

'You put your penis in Shimei's vagina?'

'Yes.'

'All the way?'

'Yes.' And he wept openly now.

Hart patted his knee gently. And he still hadn't looked at the charts.

## V

Lynn Pan's apartment was in a new housing development at the south end of Haidian district, not far from Beijing University. The blocks were only four storeys, and had pitched, red-tiled roofs and white painted walls peppered with tiny balconies at every other window. The compound was gated, and guarded by a grey-uniformed Beijing Security officer. Inside there was parking for vehicles, and covered sheds for bicycles. But there were no bicycles parked there. Li flashed his Public Security ID for the guard to raise the gate and the guard said, 'Your people are already here.'

Li nodded and drove through to park up in front of Pan's block. He was puzzled by the black and white parked outside it. Forensics travelled in unmarked vans.

In the lobby, an elderly woman grinned at him toothlessly from behind a grilled window. 'Second floor,' she said, pointing upwards when he showed her his ID.

On the second-floor landing, the door to Pan's apartment was standing wide open and he could hear voices from inside. As he went in, he saw that the lock on the door had been forced. The apartment was a shambles. The polished wooden floor in the square hall was strewn with colourful Xinjiang rugs. There were four doors off it. One to a bathroom. Beside it, one to a tiny kitchen. The door to the right led to a living–dining room, its window giving on to one of the small balconies and over-looking the car park below. The fourth door led to the back of the apartment and a double bedroom. The contents of drawers and cupboards had been tipped out on to floors. The doors to the wardrobe stood open. There were two uniformed officers in the bedroom. They turned, startled, as Li appeared in the doorway.

'What the hell are you guys doing here?' Li asked.

There was no need to show his ID. They knew immediately who he was. One of them said, 'The caretaker called the station about the break-in half an hour ago. They radioed the car. It only took us about fifteen minutes to get here.'

'A break-in,' Li repeated stupidly.

They looked at him as if he had horns. 'Sure, isn't that why you're here?'

Li said, 'Haven't you seen the morning papers? The lady who lives here was murdered last night?'

'Shit.' The one who had spoken first suddenly viewed the apartment in a new light.

'It was in the papers?' the other one said, incredulously.

'I hope you haven't disturbed anything.'

'No, Chief.'

'You've spoken to the caretaker?' They nodded. 'How come the break-in wasn't reported until this morning?'

'They didn't know about it until this morning,' the first one said. 'It was a neighbour coming down the stairs who noticed the door lying slightly ajar. Then she saw that it had been forced and told the caretaker. She called us.'

'And how did burglars get in and out past the security guard?'

'Beats me, Chief. The guy out there wasn't on duty last night. We'll need to pull in the guy who was on the night shift.'

'You guys won't be doing anything. This crime scene is now part of a murder investigation and under the jurisdiction of Section One. You make out your reports and have them sent to my office.'

'Yes, Chief.' They stood looking at him.

'You can go now,' he said.

'Yes, Chief.' And reluctantly the two officers donned their hats and ducked out past him on to the landing. He heard their footsteps retreating down the stairs and the imprecations muttered under their breath.

When they had gone, Li stood and looked around him in the stillness of the apartment. It was full of her smell and her presence. Her personality was everywhere, in the choice of pictures she had hung on almost every available wall space

– Chinese originals bought at the antiques market; signed prints of narrative pictures by an artist called Vettriano; framed photographs of some picturesque market town in southern France. Li wondered what their significance was. She was there, too, in the brightly coloured curtains on every window, in the dazzling Xinjiang rugs she had bought to cover nearly every square inch of floor, in the black bedcovers printed with white and red Chinese characters that had been ripped from the bed and lay crumpled now on the floor.

Her clothes had been pulled off the wardrobe rail and thrown on the bed. Suits, and jeans, leather jackets, sweat-shirts, blouses. A rack of her shoes had been left undisturbed. Trainers and sandals, a pair of Doc Martens, a sturdy pair of brown hiking boots still caked with mud, plain black shoes with chunky low heels. Two Lynn Pans had been torn from the wardrobe. The work persona, the Lynn Pan who liked to wear masculine suits and plain black shoes – although Li knew from their brief encounter that this persona had never masked her essential femininity. And then there was the private persona, the relaxed, informal Lynn Pan who liked to wear jeans and sweatshirts and training shoes, and who enjoyed walking. Where? In the hills out at Badaling? In the Yanshan mountains? And who did she go walking with? Or was she a loner? Certainly, there was no evidence of anyone else sharing her bedroom.

The kitchen was small, but tidy. Although the thieves had opened every cupboard, they had not disturbed the contents. Shelves were neatly lined with dried and tinned foods. The refrigerator was well-stocked with fresh fruit and vegetables. In the freezer there were chicken breasts and fish, and whole-wheat bread that she must have bought in one of the foreign supermarkets. She liked to eat healthily, and she liked to eat at home.

The bathroom shelves were lined with soaps and shampoos and skin cleansers. There was very little in the way of make-up, either here or in the bedroom, and he remembered how little she had worn the afternoon that he met her. A touch of brown on the eyelids, a hint of blusher on her cheeks, the merest smudge of colour on her lips. She'd had a beautiful complexion and fine bone structure. Make-up would have been superfluous.

A small dining table with two chairs sat by the window in the front room. There were potted plants everywhere: green, leafy spider plants, a yucca tree, a beautiful winter-flowering azalea. The air was filled with their fragrance. Bookshelves lined one complete wall. Books on China and Chinese dialects; rows of cookery books with recipes and cuisines from all over the world; a twenty-six-volume encyclopaedia; Webster's Encyclopaedic Dictionary; a dictionary of quotations; reams of fiction – Steinbeck, Hemingway, Greene, Rushdie, Wolfe, and dozens more that Li had never heard of. Clearly, she had been a reader.

There was a two-seater settee covered in silk throws, and one armchair set to get the best light from the window. Obviously where she sat to read. A TV and video had not been touched, but cables lay around a coffee table beside the armchair, and the table itself seemed oddly bare.

A dresser opposite the window had been ransacked. Much of its content lay strewn across the floor. CDs, photo albums, personal papers. Li could read some of the CD titles without stooping to pick them up. Jean Michel Jarre's *The China Concerts*. A large collection of Bach fugues. Handel's *Water Music*. The Beatles' *Sergeant Pepper's Lonely Hearts Club Band*. On a stereo cabinet beside the dresser, the CD drawer of a neat little Sony stack lay open. There was a CD in it. The second disk of *The China Concerts*. Li took a pair of latex gloves from his coat pocket and slipped them on. He switched on the stereo and the CD drawer slid shut. He pressed play and was immediately assaulted by loud synthesiser music, not much to his taste. He picked up the CD box and looked at the titles. *Orient Express, Magnetic Fields, Laser Harp* . . . The final track was called *Souvenir of China*. He flipped through the previous tracks until he got to it, and suddenly the room was filled with the sound of children's voices. Chinese children. The noise of a camera shutter, the sound of synthesiser strings stepping down through a slow, sad melody. More Chinese voices. The punctuation of a monotonous, steady drumbeat.

Li found himself oddly affected by the music, the hair rising on his neck and across his scalp. It was strangely apposite to his mood, the sense of sadness and desolation in this dead woman's apartment, his memory of her forever stained by the bloody corpse lying at the base of the Millennium Monument.

He sat down and picked out a print-sized photo album from the mess on the floor. It had clear plastic sleeves, two photographs in each. They were mostly pictures of Pan and a friend in backpacks and boots, posing on a hillside some-where, spectacular backdrops behind them. Pan's face was red with the cold, and radiant in its smile. The two girls were clearly on their own, the remote on the camera snapping pic-tures of them together. Both were laughing hysterically. There were more sombre pictures of each of them individually, and several panoramas of the plains of northern China laid out below them. In one, Li could detect the plume of pollution hanging over a distant Beijing.

The other girl seemed strangely familiar. And then Li placed her. She had been in the graduation photograph with Pan on the wall in Pan's office. An old friend from back in the States. A plain girl, with an attractive smile.

He heard a sharp intake of breath, and a muted, throaty exclamation of fear. A woman's voice. He turned his head to find himself looking at the plain girl with the attractive smile. She was standing in the open doorway to the hall, but she wasn't smiling. Her hand went to her mouth. 'Oh, my God, what's happened here? Who are you?'

Li stood up immediately and switched off the stereo. The silence seemed deafening in its absence. 'Didn't the caretaker tell you?'

'She never said a thing.' It was a Californian accent.

'There's been a break-in.'

'I can see that. Who *are* you?'

'Section Chief Li Yan, Criminal Investigation Department of the Beijing Municipal Police.'

'Where's Lynn? Does she know about it, yet?'

Li felt sick. Of course, he realised, an American in Beijing was hardly likely to buy the *Beijing Youth Daily*. He didn't even know if she spoke or read Chinese.

'What's your relationship to Miss Pan?' he asked.

'We're friends. We were at university together. Where is she?' There was a hint of panic, now, in her voice.

Li said, 'I'm sorry to be the one to break it to you, but Miss Pan was murdered last night.'

He had not known what reaction to expect, but the feral howl that escaped the girl's mouth punctured him like a cold, steel blade, nearly bringing tears to his eyes. He quickly crossed to the door and led her to the settee. She slumped into it like a woman falling. A dead weight. But apart from that single howl, not another sound issued from her lips. Big, silent tears rolled down her cheeks, and she clutched her hands in front of her, wringing them so hard her knuckles were turning white. Li sat down beside her and gently prised her hands apart, holding one of them in both of his. 'Can I get you water or something?'

She shook her head. She spotted the photo album Li had been looking at and pulled her hand free of his to pick it up. As she flicked through it, Li could see the pain every image inflicted on her, each one with its own special memory. She snapped it shut again and sat silently shaking. Li allowed her some time to regain control. Finally, she said, without looking at him, 'Of course, you didn't know her.'

Li said, 'I met her yesterday afternoon for the first time. Just a few hours before she was killed.'

The girl turned to look at him. Through her tears she examined his face, and he saw a sad smile in her eyes. 'And, naturally, you fell for her.' Li felt the colour rise on his cheeks. 'It's okay,' she said. 'Everybody does.' She corrected herself. 'Did. Everybody fell for Lynn. I never knew anyone who wasn't madly in love with her after five minutes.'

'Which makes it all the more difficult to understand why someone would want to kill her,' Li said.

'How . . . ?' The girl hardly dared to ask. 'How did it happen?'

Li sighed heavily. 'I don't think . . .'

'I want to know!' the girl insisted.

Li said, 'She was strangled, and had her throat cut.'

'Oh, my God!'

For a moment Li thought the girl was going to be sick. But she controlled herself. He said, 'Do you know if she had any special relationship? I mean, do you know if there was someone she was seeing?'

The girl nodded. She was wringing her hands again and staring at the floor. After a long silence she said in a voice that was almost a whisper, 'Me.'

Li frowned in consternation. 'I don't understand.'

The girl said, 'We were lovers. Ever since we met at university. There hadn't ever been anyone else.'

Li was still struggling to come to terms with what the girl was saying. 'You mean, you and she . . . ? She was . . .'

'A lesbian?' the girl asked the question for him. She shook her head. 'I suppose that's what people would call us. But we were really just two people who loved each other.' She bit her lip hard to stop herself from crying, and Li saw blood on her front teeth. 'When she got the job offer out here, there was no question that I wouldn't come with her. Not that I had the first idea what I would do. In the end I got a job teaching English at a private school near the university.'

Li was stunned. It had never once occurred to him that Pan might have been gay. There had been no hint of it in the way she had flirted with him. But then he remembered how she'd had them all in the palm of her hand the previous day. Every one of the six Ministry officials who had gone for the MERMER test had been smitten by her. *I never knew anyone who wasn't madly in love with her after five minutes*, the girl had said. Did that suggest her killer might have been jealous? There was no indication that he knew any of his previous victims. But if he had known Pan, perhaps fallen for her, and then discovered that she was forever beyond his reach . . . A motive? But then why would he break into her department at the Academy to steal all her files? And what did he hope to find in her apartment? Li was in no doubt that the murder and the break-ins were connected. But none of it made the least sense to him.

He was still trying to come to terms with Pan's sexuality. 'You didn't share the apartment with her,' he said.

For the first time, the girl showed apprehension. 'It's frowned upon here, isn't it? Officially?'

Li understood. 'You've nothing to fear from me,' he said.

'We decided it would be safer if we had separate apartments. At least, that's how Lynn wanted it. She always liked her own space. Somewhere she could retreat to, to be on her own.' The sadness in the girl's face was nearly unbearable. 'Me? I would have wanted to be with her every living minute.'

Li heard the sound of a vehicle drawing up out front. He stood up and went to the window. It was the forensics van from Pau Jü Hutong. Fu Qiwei's second team spilled out into the car park. He turned back into the room. 'That's the forensics people arriving,' he said. 'Before they come in and start taking this place apart, do you think you could have a look around, maybe tell me if anything's missing?'

She took a deep breath and nodded her head.

'Thanks,' he said. 'Try not to touch or disturb anything.' He helped her to her feet and squeezed her hand. 'Take your time. I'll keep them out of here until you're done.'

He went out on to the landing to wait for the forensics guys to come up the stairs and ask them to give her a few minutes. And they stood around in silence, smoking and waiting. It was nearly ten minutes before the girl came out. 'Her computer,' she said. 'She always kept a laptop on the coffee table beside the big armchair. It's gone. And I can't find any of her disks anywhere.'

Li was glad of the cold air in his face and his lungs as he stepped out with the girl into the yellow autumn sunshine. The wind tugged at their clothes and stung their skin.

She said, 'Will you need someone to identify her?'

'Yes.' He thought about Bill Hart, or perhaps Professor Hu. 'But you don't have to worry about that.'

'I'd like to do it,' she said.

Li closed his eyes. He saw the gash in her neck, the gaping

wounds on each side of her head where her ears had been hacked off. 'I don't think that would be a good idea.'

'I want to,' the girl insisted. 'One minute she's there. My whole life. The next she's gone. And I don't even get the chance to say goodbye to her? I want to see her. I want that chance.'

'Okay.' Li nodded. There was no point in trying to dissuade her. He knew that people often needed to see the body. A confirmation of death. As if somehow they can't believe unless they see. It was not a need he shared. He had seen enough bodies in his life to know that they were nothing but empty receptacles, that the person who had once animated them was long gone. And that it was better to remember them as they were. As it was, he knew that this girl's last and lasting image of her lover would be one of horror, one that would taint every other memory she had of her for the rest of her days. And he grieved for them both.

# CHAPTER SEVEN

## I

Li arrived at the pathology centre off the Badaling Expressway shortly before eleven. He pulled in beside a Beijing Jeep from Section One, and saw Wu standing smoking in the doorway, waiting for him.

'Hey, Chief.' Wu pushed his shades back on his forehead, threw away his cigarette and followed him into the lobby and along the corridor to the changing rooms.

Li said, 'Did you turn up anything at the Academy?'

'Not a thing, Chief. I talked to all the students and staff who worked with her. No one had a bad word to say about her.'

*I never knew anyone who wasn't madly in love with her after five minutes.*

'And there just doesn't seem any reason why anyone would want to steal those computers and files,' Wu was saying. 'The computer equipment wasn't even new. You'd only get a handful of *yuan* for that stuff on the black market. And like the security guy said, it was a pro job. Why would they want to steal a lot of old junk?'

Li hung up his coat and slipped a green surgical gown over his shirt. 'When we figure that out, we might know why she was killed.' He pulled a shower cap over his head. 'Someone broke into her apartment and took her laptop.'

Wu was sitting pulling elasticated covers over his shoes. He raised one eyebrow. 'You still think she was killed by the Ripper? I mean, the same guy who killed those other women?'

'I know it doesn't make sense, Wu, but it's hard to call it any other way. How else do we explain the letter promising to cut off the ears of the next victim, and then Pan turning up with her ears removed? And then there's the trademark cutting of the throat. The Russian cheroot.'

He looked at Wu, who could only shrug an acknowledgement. 'I don't know, Chief. There's so many inconsistencies. Maybe . . . maybe the other murders were just a smokescreen – to confuse us, to obscure the real reason for killing Professor Pan. Maybe she's what it's all really about.'

Li stopped to consider the idea. 'It's a hell of an elaborate smokescreen,' he said. 'But it's a thought, Wu. It's a thought.'

He pulled plastic covers over his shoes. Regulations in the new facility. Everyone attending an autopsy had to wear protective clothing. They took cotton masks from the locker and pocketed them for later use. It had been established that bone dust breathed in during the cutting of the skull with an oscillating saw, could carry viral particles, including AIDS. These days no one was taking any chances. Although Li thought it unlikely that a woman involved in a long-term relationship with another woman would have AIDS.

They went back out into the corridor and turned towards the autopsy room at the end. 'So has the American pathologist turned up yet?' Li asked.

'Yeah.'

Li felt anger rising in him again, like mercury in a thermometer. 'It's madness, Wu. Absolutely fucking insane! Where's Wang?'

'In the autopsy suite, Chief. They're doing the autopsy together.'

'Well, that's something at least.' He pushed open the swing doors into the autopsy room. 'I don't suppose he speaks Chinese?'

'I shouldn't think so, Chief.' The two pathologists were standing with their backs to the door, examining photographs taken at the crime scene. Wu said in his halting English, 'You don' speak Chinese, Doctah, do you?'

The pathologists turned, and Margaret smiled beatifically at Li. 'Unfortunately, I don't. Although after all this time, I should really, shouldn't I?' She took pleasure in Li's shock at seeing her there, and even more from his immediate attempt to mask it. 'I heard you weren't too happy that some "goddamned American" was going to screw up your case.'

'Where's Li Jon?' he asked.

Which immediately set her on edge. The little wife and mother wasn't to be trusted with the proper care of their child. 'I parked him under the autopsy table,' she said. 'Next to the drainage bucket.' Li's eyes very nearly flickered towards the table, but he stopped them in time. And Margaret added, with more than a tone, 'Mei Yuan has him. Until this afternoon, that is – when your father's coming to see him.' A pause. 'Is there *any* chance you'll be there?'

'I doubt it,' Li said, his voice stiff with tension.

'I'll tell him you were asking for him, then, shall I?' And she turned back to the photographs. 'So . . . now that we have the domestic arrangements out of the way, I suppose we should really get on with the job in hand.'

The photographs were laid out on a side table, a graphic, vividly coloured record of a woman's murder. On another table her bloodstained clothes had been spread out for examination, carefully cut from the body to avoid damaging it during their removal. The spotlessly clean stainless steel autopsy table lay empty in the middle of the floor beneath lights that would focus on the corpse, and a microphone dangled from an outlet in the ceiling to record the pathologists' every observation.

Through windows in the swing doors at the far end of the room, Li could see the assistants retrieving the body from a two-tier storage facility beyond that could handle up to eighty bodies at any one time. He heard the sound of the drawer sliding open, and the rattle of the gurney as they transferred Lynn Pan's dead weight on to it.

Margaret said, 'I've spent the last hour going through Doctor Wang's autopsy reports with him, so I think I'm pretty much up to speed.'

The double doors banged open and the assistants wheeled in the corpse in its white body bag. They manoeuvred the gurney alongside the autopsy table and carefully unzipped the bag, before transferring the oddly pale body on to the stainless steel. A wooden block with a curved indent was placed below the neck to support the head.

Li was almost afraid to look at the body. He knew it was no longer the Lynn Pan he had met yesterday, but it was hard to separate it from the force of her personality. He made himself turn his head. Naked, she looked tiny, like a little girl, small breasts flattened out against her ribs, her legs slightly apart, feet splayed like a ballet dancer's. In life he'd had the impression of someone much bigger, much stronger. She would have been no match for her killer. Fingers like rods of iron clamped around her delicate neck, choking the breath and the life from her.

Margaret turned from the table. 'My God, she's like a child,' she said. She had not known what to expect, and was taken by surprise. 'What age was she?'

Wang consulted his notes. 'Thirty-three, Doctah.'

Margaret crossed to the table and gazed down upon her flawless face, and saw that she had been very beautiful. 'What a waste.' She glanced up and found Li watching her.

He saw the shock and the empathy in her eyes. Shock because it was difficult not to feel a sense of loss when something so beautiful is destroyed. Empathy because she was almost the same age as Margaret, and it is hard in that circumstance not to feel vulnerable yourself. *I never knew anyone who wasn't madly in love with her after five minutes.* Perhaps even in death Lynn Pan had that effect on people.

Margaret took a deep breath. It was her first autopsy for

some considerable time. She had long ago stopped seeing the victims who had passed across her table as anything more than evidence to be examined in the minutest detail, a receptacle for vital clues that might lead to the capture of their killer. It was harder coming back to it than she had imagined. Defences were down. She had been softened by motherhood and domesticity, she had allowed herself to become human again, in a way that you cannot afford when your job is cutting open other human beings.

Li knew it would be hard for her. He watched as she summoned all her professionalism and began her external examination. There was not much of her to be seen under the shower cap and goggles and mask. Her smock and plastic arm cuffs covered every inch of her white skin, latex gloves and the mesh gauntlet on her non-cutting hand hid the beauty of her long, delicate fingers. It was something in the way she held herself that betrayed her tension. If only to Li.

There were several red-purple bruises on Lynn Pan's arms and legs, where perhaps she had fought briefly against her killer. 'No defence wounds on the hands or forearms,' Margaret said. 'No cuts or slashes, which would suggest she was at least unconscious before he cut her throat.'

Around her neck and jawbone there was similar coloured bruising consistent with having been caused by thumb and fingertips where she had been pinned against the base of the sundial arm and choked. A cluster of three round bruises about one and a half centimetres in diameter on the left side, a larger bruise on the right, probably made by the thumb

– suggesting that the murderer might have been right-handed. Margaret was confident that where the head had been banged up against the foot of the monument, she would find an area of subgaleal haemorrhage when she examined the scalp.

'This guy needs to cut his fingernails,' Margaret said. There were marks on Pan's throat, consistent in relation to the bruising with having been left by the killer's fingernails. Tiny crescent-shaped abrasions between half and one centimetre long, flakes of skin heaped up at their concave side. Margaret cocked her head, frowning slightly. 'Usually someone defending themselves against strangulation would leave vertically orientated scratches near the top of their own neck, at the base or sides of the mandible, as they tried to pry themselves free.'

'She was wearing gloves, Doctah,' Wang said.

'Ahh.' Margaret had missed that in the photographs. She *was* rusty.

The slashing of the throat was ugly and vicious. It began five centimetres below the point where the left earlobe had been severed. It made a jagged crescent around the throat, following the line of the jaw, severing the windpipe, both carotid arteries and the internal jugular, and cutting through all the muscle and soft tissue right down to the vertebrae, marking the intervertebral cartilages. The blood vessels contained clot. Margaret thought that the wound had probably been inflicted by a sharp, pointed, long-bladed knife, about six to seven inches long. And it was her view that from the angle of the cut and the tearing of the skin, the knife had been drawn across the throat from left to right.

She examined the face next, pulling back the eyelids and peering at the eyes. 'There is florid petechial haemorrhaging of the conjunctiva and the face,' she said. 'Tiny burst blood vessels,' she added by way of explanation. 'Caused by the pressure created when the blood draining from the head is cut off, but blood is still pumping into it through the arteries.' She turned the head to the right to examine what remained of the left ear. 'He's been in a hurry with this. It's a very crude amputation. He must have pulled the ear away from the side of the head with his free hand and cut down along the shape of the skull with a single stroke of his knife. The wound is not very accurate.' A part of the ear still remained attached to its stump. On the right side, half the lobe remained clinging stubbornly to the side of the head by the smallest flap of skin.

As she examined the hair and the external scalp, Margaret could smell the faint lingering traces of Lynn Pan's shampoo. A soft, sweet, peachy smell that made her seem altogether too human, too recently alive. She stepped back and nodded to Doctor Wang who drew blood for toxicology from the femoral vein at the top of her right leg.

Li could not look as Wang handed the blood to an assistant and then held open Pan's right eyelid to pierce the eyeball with a syringe and draw off a quantity of clear, vitreous fluid. They would turn her over now and examine the back of her, before replacing her front-side-up and carving her open, cutting through delicate ribs with steel shears, removing the heart and lungs and the rest of the organs, cutting round the top of her skull and removing the brain. A monotonous, routine, dehumanising process that would reduce this once vibrant young woman to a dissevered pile of flesh and bones to be stored in a deep freeze for anything up to five years, depending upon how long it took to catch and execute her killer.

Margaret worked her way through the rest of the autopsy with dispassionate detachment. Like riding a bicycle, you never forgot how. She had simply wobbled a little at the beginning. Everything about Lynn Pan was normal and healthy. Her heart, lungs, liver, both kidneys. She had been a model of fitness and good health

Li stood watching, determinedly unemotional, trying to focus his feelings in a positive way. He closed his eyes as Margaret sliced down the length of the intestine and tried not to let the smell affect him. She had been killed for a reason – a reason that had nothing to do with the other murders, although it appeared she had been killed by the same hand. Her computers and files had all been stolen, from her workplace and her home. She knew, or had in her possession, something . . . information, perhaps, that someone did not wish anyone else to know. So the motive for killing her was different from the others. She did not relate in any way to any of the Jack the Ripper slayings or their Beijing copies. And yet they had so much else in common. The method of killing, the Russian cheroot. And the letter which had promised to cut the ears off the next victim, a promise fulfilled in the killing of Lynn Pan. An incontrovertible link.

'Did we manage to recover saliva from the cheroot found at the Guo Huan crime scene?' he asked Wang.

'English, please,' Margaret said without looking up.

Li repeated the question in English.

'Sure,' Wang said. 'The lab confirm this morning. We have DNA match with other killings.'

'How long will it take to DNA-test the cigar end found by Pan's body?'

'I gave it to lab last night,' Wang said.

And Margaret added, 'I have requested that they fast-track the testing process. We should hear later today.'

Li said, 'What are you going to put in your report to the Americans?'

Margaret said, 'For God's sake, I haven't finished the autopsy yet!'

'But you already know the cause of death.'

She sighed, reluctant to commit herself too early. 'Subject to toxicology, I'll be telling the embassy that she died from rapid blood loss caused by the severing of the main arteries of the neck. She had been strangled and was probably unconscious when her throat was cut.'

'Do you think she was killed by the same person who murdered the others?'

She glanced at Wang. 'What do you think, Doctor? You did the other autopsies.'

Wang pulled a face. 'Inconclusive,' he said. 'She was strangled like others, yes. Throat cut, left to right, like others. Yes. But no other injury. This is not like others. Also, she no prostitute, like others. She no killed in Jianguomen, like others.' He looked at Margaret. 'How 'bout you, Doctah?'

'I agree,' Margaret said. 'As things stand, the evidence is inconclusive.'

'What about the letter?' Li said. 'The ears.'

'Circumstantial,' Margaret said. 'It doesn't *prove* anything. You have to make your own judgement on that one.' She stopped what she was doing and looked at him. 'The unsmoked end of that Russian cheroot is the crucial piece of the jigsaw that we don't yet have. *If* they can recover saliva and we get a DNA match, then I think you'd have to say that it was the same killer. If not . . .' she blew a jet of air through pursed lips, '. . . I'd say you were heading for confusion freefall.'

## II

Li and Wu were stepping out into the car park when Li's cellphone rang. Qian's voice sounded oddly strained. 'Chief, where are you?'

'We've just come out of the autopsy.'

'Can you come straight back here?'

'Sure.'

'And bring Wang?'

'Why?'

'We've got something here he's going to have to check out, Chief. It's not something I really want to tell you about on the phone.'

Li sent Wu back inside to get Wang, and he stood on the steps staring gloomily towards the traffic which sped by on the expressway beyond a vast area of what had once been housing, flattened now for redevelopment. He didn't really want to think about what it was that Qian needed Wang to check out. Everything about this case seemed to be slipping away from him. Margaret's *confusion freefall*. Each time, it seemed, he turned around there was a new development – before he'd even had time to assimilate the last one.

'What's happened?' He turned around to find Margaret, showered and changed, on the steps beside him.

'I don't know. Qian didn't want to talk about it on the phone.' He looked at her, and she seemed suddenly very small and vulnerable, her hair still wet and combed back from her face. She seemed thinner. Perhaps she had lost weight and he simply hadn't noticed. He ran a thumb along the line of her jaw and brushed her cheekbone. Her skin was so pale, dotted with tiny faded freckles across the nose. He remembered how Lynn Pan's lover had described her loss. *One minute she's there. My whole life. The next she's gone.* And he felt how it would be if he ever lost Margaret. The thought struck him like a blow to the solar plexus. It was too easy to take the people you loved for granted, and too late to take it back when they were gone. He knew that Margaret was unhappy, chained to the home and the child, and he simply hadn't been dealing with it. In the wake of Lynn Pan's death, she seemed particularly fragile, and he felt the need to hold her and protect her.

Margaret was taken by surprise when he enveloped her in his arms and squeezed all the breath from her lungs. 'Hey,' she protested, laughing, and pulled herself free. 'Who do you think you are, the Beijing Ripper?'

But he wasn't smiling. He was gazing into the deep, dark blue of her eyes. 'I love you, Margaret,' he said.

And she felt the intensity of it. 'I love you, too,' she said quietly.

'I know things aren't satisfactory right now,' he said. 'I know it. I just . . . I just need to deal with this first. And then we'll sort it.'

She nodded seriously. 'I don't know how we do that.'

'Neither do I. But we've got to try.' He squeezed both her hands. 'I can't promise, but I'll try and make it to see my father this afternoon.'

She smiled ruefully. 'I won't hold my breath.'

They broke apart as her taxi arrived. It was a Mercedes. Li cocked an eyebrow. 'Can we afford this?'

'We don't have to. The good old US of A is picking up the tab.' She kissed him lightly on the lips and jumped into the back seat. The taxi was pulling out of the gate when Wu came down the steps with Pathologist Wang.

It took them forty minutes to get back to Section One through the lunchtime traffic, sitting in long, frustrating periods of gridlock on the Third Ring Road before turning south and picking their way through some of the less congested back streets. The restaurant on the corner of Beixinqiao Santiao was packed when Li parked their Jeep outside it. The sounds of diners, the smells of lunch, of barbecue and wok, filled the air, making Li aware of a hunger gnawing at his stomach. But he had no appetite and no desire to eat. Beyond Section One, Noah's Ark Food Room had fallen under the demolition men's hammer, and behind a hoarding where it had once stood, a giant crane soared into the blue autumn sky, dominating the skyline.

They went in the side entrance and climbed the stairs to the fourth floor. There was an odd, faintly medical smell in the air as they walked along the top corridor. It was cold, and when they turned into the detectives' room they saw why. All the windows stood wide open, and officers were sitting around in their coats and typing with their gloves on. Everyone was smoking. In spite of the cold wind blowing in through the open window, and the smoke that filled the room, the smell was stronger here, and carried more than a hint of something rotten.

Qian was sitting on one of the desks talking on the telephone. He hung up when he saw Li and jumped down. 'In here, Chief.' Watched by everyone else in the room, Li and Wu and Wang followed Qian into his office. The windows here were also wide open. The desk had been cleared, and on it stood a cardboard box the size of a shoebox. It had been wrapped in brown paper and secured with clear, sticky tape. Someone had cut open the wrapping, and the paper was folded away from the box, its lid lying on the table beside it. The air was thick with the smell of alcohol, and a stink like meat which had been left in the refrigerator a month past its sell-by date.

'In the name of the sky, Qian . . .' Li screwed up his eyes and blew air out through his mouth. 'What the hell . . . ?'

'It was addressed to you, Chief. Arrived in this morning's mail. But it was stinking so bad the head of the mail room thought I should open it.' Qian looked slightly green around the gills. 'I wish to hell I hadn't.'

'What is it?' Li and Wu and Pathologist Wang approached the open box with a caution which suggested they thought that something might jump out and bite them. Inside, laid out amongst crumpled paper packing was a smooth, faintly reddish-brown-coloured arc of something organic. It was wrapped in plastic and oozing a clear fluid. The stench was fierce. Wu put a handkerchief to his face and moved back, gagging. Li stood his ground with difficulty as Wang snapped on latex gloves and lifted it out of the box.

'It's a kidney,' he said. 'The left kidney. You can tell because the adrenal gland in the fat that's been left along the top edge is still "tall". The gland on the right kidney gets flattened by the liver. It's been cut in half longitudinally. There's about one inch of the renal artery still attached to it.' He sniffed, long since inured to the aromas of the autopsy. 'Been preserved in alcohol by the smell of it, which is why it feels firm and has lost some of its colour.'

'A human kidney?' Li asked, anticipating Wang's response with a growing sense of horror.

'Oh, yes. I'll need to make the proper comparisons of course, but at an educated guess I'd say this is the kidney that was removed from Guo Huan. The renal artery is normally about three inches long. From memory there was around two inches of it left in the corpse.'

Qian went into the top drawer of his desk and lifted out an A4-sized plastic sleeve. Flattened out inside it was a note that had been folded twice over. He handed it to Li, and then moved away towards the open window for air. Li recognised the scrawl of the large, untidy characters, the distinctive red ink.

> *Chief,*
> *I send you half the kidney I took from one woman. Preserved it for you. The other piece I fried and ate. It was very nice. I may send you the bloody knife that took it out if you only wait a while longer.*
> *Signed,*
> *Catch me when you can.*

Li found the plastic sleeve trembling in his hands. 'And it was addressed to me by name?'

'Yes, Chief.'

Li held out his hand. 'Give me some gloves.' He had used up his supply. Qian took a pair from his desk and handed them over. Li pulled them on and then carefully lifted the box away from the wrapping paper. He turned the paper over and smoothed it out on the desk. The label was hand-written. There were half a dozen stamps on it, franked and postmarked the previous day. The circle of red ink was not perfect, but it was perfectly readable. 12.30 p.m. EMS Central Post Office, Beijing.

Li tried to contain his excitement. 'He's made his first mistake,' he said. 'The parcel was too big to post through a letter box. He must have had to pass it across the counter and get it weighed. So somebody saw him. Somebody saw his face. We've got a witness!'

'Hey, Chief, isn't that your old man?' Wu was chewing like a man possessed. He had now pushed several pieces of gum into his mouth to get rid of the taste left there by the lingering smell of the half-kidney. Wang had once explained to him at an autopsy that the smell registered by your nasal sensors was carried on actual particles released into the air by the thing you were smelling. Which is why a particularly strong smell could also sometimes leave a taste in your mouth. Wu had found the concept disgusting, and was now furiously trying to wash away any unwanted particles by stimulating saliva production with his chewing gum.

Li glanced out of the passenger window as they passed the side entrance to the Ministry compound in Zhengyi Road. His apartment was less than two hundred metres beyond the wall. A taxi was pulled in at the kerbside, and the driver was helping his father out on to the sidewalk.

'Yes,' he said. Mister Li senior was going to visit his grandson. And Li knew that Margaret would not be surprised that Li had failed to turn up. Again. A part of him wanted to ask Wu to stop, so that he could get out and explain. But there was no point. An excuse, even a good one, always sounded like an excuse.

Ironically, the EMS post office was just around the corner at No. 7 Qianmen Da Jie. It was a huge, twelve-storey building that took up half the block. Rows of distinctive green EMS vans were parked out front, in a narrow car park screened from the road by trees. Wu parked right outside the main door, waving aside protests from a security man by pushing a Ministry ID in his face. Li stepped out and saw, in the afternoon sunshine, the row of red flags lining the roof of police headquarters on the next half of the block. Wu lit a cigarette. 'Cheeky bastard. Posting the thing to us from right outside HQ. Like he's thumbing his nose at us. How was it he signed his note? *Catch me when you can*?'

Li said grimly. 'We'll catch him alright.' But in his heart he wondered how many more young women would have to die before they did.

The main hall was busy, queues forming at windows along a counter which ran the length of it. Lights reflected off a marble floor, and voices off marble-faced walls. One counter sold nothing but paper, string, tape and glue, and Li wondered if perhaps their killer had wrapped his parcel in the post office itself. He looked along the counters as if he hoped that maybe the murderer's ghost might still be there, some impression, some presence that he had left behind, even just in the memory of one of tellers.

They made themselves known to security and were taken to the manager's office. Wu nudged Li and nodded towards a copy of the *Beijing Youth Daily* lying on his desk. The manager was a dapper man in a dark suit, with a collar and tie. He looked at them warily through steel-framed spectacles and offered them tea. Li declined. He showed the manager a colour photocopy of the parcel label, with its stamps and postmark.

He said, 'One of your tellers took a parcel with this address across his or her counter at twelve-thirty yesterday. He or she stamped it and franked it and put it in the mail basket.'

'So?'

'So, I believe that teller is the only person we know of who has set eyes on the Beijing Ripper.'

He had calculated that his use of the term would have some effect. And he was not wrong. The manager's eyes opened wide and flickered briefly towards the newspaper lying on his desk. 'He was here?'

'We believe so.'

Li could see the thoughts processing behind the manager's eyes as clearly as if they were windows. 'We have thousands of people in here every day,' he said. 'I think it's unlikely that a teller would remember any one of them in particular.'

Wu was looking at a small black and white television screen mounted high on the wall in the far corner of the office. It showed a view looking down on the main hall of the post office. His jaw froze, mid-chew. 'You guys got closed-circuit TV in here?'

The manager glanced towards the screen, the implications of Wu's question dawning on them all simultaneously. 'We have two cameras,' he said. 'One on each side of the hall.'

'And do you record what they see?' Li asked, hardly daring to believe that they might actually have the killer on video.

'We recycle the tapes every seven days.'

'We only need to go back one,' Wu said, his eyes shining with sudden optimism.

\*

The recording equipment was in the office of the head of security. He removed his grey-peaked cap and scratched his head. 'Sure,' he said in answer to Li's question. 'The tapes are all time-coded, so we can find the time you want pretty fast.'

'Let's do it, then,' Wu said.

The security man rummaged in a cupboard and pulled out a VHS tape and put it in an empty machine. He flicked the play switch and then began fast rewinding from the end of it. It went backwards from seven p.m. Li watched the speeded-up comings and goings, like an old Chaplin movie gone mad, with a growing sense of disappointment. He glanced at the other two monitors displaying live pictures from the main hall. He said to the manager. 'And those are your only two camera positions?'

The manager nodded. 'Yes.'

'They're too high for us to see faces. We're really only getting the tops of heads.'

The managed shrugged. 'They weren't designed to pick out faces, just to give us an overview.'

Li felt fingers of frustration choking back his brief optimism. It would be ironic if they managed to catch their killer on tape, but not be able to see his face.

The time-code on the tape was counting back at high speed. The picture was just a blur. Wu said, 'Stop it at twelve-fifteen. We'll watch it from there.' He shoved another piece of gum in his mouth and lit another cigarette.

The tape ran back a little past twelve-fifteen before the security man could stop it. The picture cleared and they had a view of the hall from the left-hand camera. It was running forward now from twelve-thirteen and fifty-three seconds. Li said, 'Can you cue up the tape from the other camera while we're watching this?' The security man nodded. He found the right tape and set it rewinding in another machine.

The others watched a constant stream of activity on the first monitor. A woman with a pushchair. A bunch of school-girls posting some letters. Businessmen with express mail. Ordinary folk going about their ordinary business. The main floor was busy, at least thirty people moving around it at any one time. Maybe more. The picture definition was not good, as if the camera had viewed proceedings through gauze stretched across its lens. Suddenly, Wu shouted, 'There!' And he stabbed his finger at the screen.

Li leaned in and saw a figure in a long, dark coat with a shoebox parcel under his arm walking through the sunshine that spilled in from the main door. 'Shit!' he muttered under his breath. 'He's wearing a baseball cap. He knows about the cameras.' His face was completely masked by the long peak of the black cap, and plunged into shadow by it. His collar was turned up, and they could not even tell if his hair was long or short. He wore gloves, dark trousers, black shoes. There was not one centimetre of him on view.

Wu was shaking his head. 'He's playing with us, Chief. He knew we would see these tapes. He knew how fucking frus-trated we would be when we had him right there in our sights and still couldn't see him. He's like the invisible fucking man.'

They watched as he stood for some time in the centre of the

concourse, as if deciding which queue to join. Then he walked to a window at the far end, almost immediately below the other camera. Its view of him would be hopelessly distorted, and he was about as far as he could get from the camera whose shot they were watching now. He conducted his business with a teller they could not see. After a brief exchange, the window was lifted and his parcel taken across the counter. He waited until it had been weighed and costed, and then took a wallet from his coat pocket and paid in cash. He never once looked around, his face hidden from view at every moment. He turned and walked briskly to the door and was gone.

Li turned to the manager. 'Find out who that teller was and get them in here now.'

The teller turned out to be a plump, middle-aged woman with an attitude. She had done nothing wrong, and as far as she was concerned, she was going to be as unhelpful as possible. They replayed the tape for her and she watched with a bored expression.

'So what am I supposed to be?' she asked. 'Madam Memory? I don't even look at their faces. It's bad enough that I can smell their breath through the grilles in the window.'

'It was an unusual address,' Wu said.

'I don't look at the addresses. I weigh the parcel, I look at the postcode, I get a price. I stamp it, they pay. They go, then it's who's next.'

'You're not being very helpful, lady,' Wu said.

'I'm not paid to be helpful,' she snapped. 'I'm paid to do a job. I do it. I've done if for years. If anyone's got any complaint about my work, that's another matter.' She looked defiantly around the faces. 'Is anyone complaining about my work?'

Li said very quietly. 'Do you have any idea what was in that parcel?'

'Of course I don't. What's it to me what was in the parcel?'

'Well,' Li said patiently, 'it might help you to understand just how much danger you are in.'

For the first time, there was no quick comeback and she visibly blanched. 'What do you mean?'

'I think it would be helpful if I explained,' Li said, 'that the parcel you took from that gentleman contained the kidney of a woman he hacked to death on Sunday.' Her eyes widened. 'You might even have heard of him. He was in the paper this morning. They're calling him the Beijing Ripper.' There was the smallest intake of breath, and her hand went to her mouth. 'Did you see that story by any chance?' She nodded, unable to speak now. 'Well, you're the only person we know of who has seen him.' Her eyes grew wider still. 'And if we know you've seen him, he knows you've seen him. So I don't really think I'd like to be in your shoes tomorrow when he reads that we have interviewed a witness, a teller at the EMS post office, who took a parcel from him on Monday.'

'You wouldn't put that in the paper!' she gasped.

Li shrugged sympathetically. 'Maybe we won't have to. Maybe we'll catch him by then. But we're going to need some help. We're going to need a description. Anything at all you can remember. Anything.' He paused. 'It could be the most important thing you've ever had to do in your life.'

She asked to see the tape again. Then they played her the second tape, but half of the killer was outside the bottom frame of the picture, and they were looking directly down on top of him. There was not so much as a hair on view.

The teller was babbling nervously now. 'I don't know, I don't know. His face was shaded by that cap. And really, I don't look at them, I don't.'

'Anything you can remember,' Li said again. 'Was he tall, short? Was he clean shaven? Did he wear glasses . . . ?'

'Yes,' the teller broke in eagerly. 'He had glasses. I remember that. Like sunglasses, only not as dark. You know, like they react to the sunlight, but the lenses never go really black.'

'Do you remember what kind of glasses?'

She shook her head.

'Think. Did they have heavy frames? Or were they silver or gold? Steel frames like your boss?'

She glanced at the manager who scowled silently at her. She shook her head. 'No. No, I don't remember. But he was clean shaven. I'm pretty sure about that. I would have noticed if he had whiskers.'

'What about his accent?' Li said. 'Was there anything unusual about his voice?'

He could see the concentration on her face. There was nothing that concentrated the mind so well as fear, and the instinct for self-preservation. But to her own and their frustration, she genuinely could not remember.

Li looked at the monitor. He was right there in front of them. Li could reach out and touch the screen. But they were

no nearer to catching him than before. He was taunting, tor-
turing them, of that Li was certain. He plotted and planned his
every move, anticipating what they would do at every stage
so that he was always one step ahead of them.

'We'll need both those tapes,' Wu said to the head of
security, and the security man punched a button and the picture froze on the screen. Li had a sudden inspiration.

'Take a statement from the teller,' he said to Wu, and turned
to the manager. 'I want you to come down to the floor with me.
And I'll need a tape measure. I want to take a few measurements.'

### III

It had been an awkward half-hour. Both Margaret and Li's
father had paid lip service to the thought that Li might turn
up any at moment. But neither really believed it. The old man
had sat in the apartment with his coat and hat on, a fur hat
with fold-up earmuffs pulled down over thin, grey hair, his
gloves folded neatly on his knees. He had spent all of five minutes half-heartedly bouncing Li Jon on them before becoming
bored with the child and handing him back to Margaret. He
had accepted an offer of tea, taken two sips and then left it
to grow cold on a low table beside the settee.

Margaret knew that he disapproved of her. That he would
have preferred a Chinese girl to have been the mother of his
grandson. Just one more grudge to bear his son. And so she
had made no attempt to engage him in conversation. Neither
of them considered it worth making the effort.

Finally she stood up. 'Normally I take Li Jon out for a walk at this time. In his buggy. You're welcome to join us if you want. Or you can wait here in case Li Yan arrives.' She was determined not to sit on in this atmosphere. To her disappointment he stood up, almost eagerly, clutching his gloves.

'I will come with you.'

A girl carved in pewter played a Chinese zither. Another, chiselled from white marble, sat reading a book in the dappled shade of the trees. There were occasional small squares set off the path through the gardens which separated the two sides of Zhengyi Road. Old men in baseball caps sat smoking on the benches that lined them. An old woman in a quilted purple jacket sat gazing into space, her bobbed hair the colour of brushed steel. Couples strolled arm in arm, mothers with children, school kids with pink jackets and jogpants.

Margaret pushed Li's buggy north at a leisurely rate, wind rustling the leaves overhead. The buggy was blue, punctuated by the odd coloured square, and had small yellow wheels. There was a support for his feet, and a plastic tray in front of him for toys. A hood, folded away now, could extend from back to front if it rained. A bag which hung from the back of the pushbar, and a tray under the seat, held extra clothes and toys and a flask of warm milk if it was needed. This was a walk she had taken often in the last few months. An escape from the apartment, and in the cold autumn air a chance to breathe again after the suffocating heat of the summer. But now she resented the silent presence of Li's father as they headed towards the traffic on Changan Avenue.

'Why do you bother?' she said eventually and turned to look at him.

He kept his eyes straight ahead. He was not a stupid man. He knew what she meant. 'Because he is family,' he said.

'Yes,' Margaret said. 'He's your son. And yet you treat him as if somehow everything bad that's ever happened in your life is his fault.'

'He must bear responsibility for his shortcomings. He has been less than diligent in his filial responsibilities.'

'And maybe you haven't been such a good father.' He flicked her a glance. 'You were so obsessed with the loss of your wife, you forgot that your son had lost his mother. If ever a boy needed his father, it was then. But, no, you couldn't see past yourself, past your own hurt. You couldn't reach out to a kid who was hurting just as badly, maybe worse.'

'What would you know about it?' he said defensively.

'I know what Li has told me. What happened, what he felt. Things he probably hasn't told another living being. Certainly not you. And I know that the Cultural Revolution wasn't his fault. That it wasn't his fault his mother was persecuted for being an intellectual. He didn't invent the Red Guards. He wasn't even old enough to be one.'

'You know nothing of these things. You are an American.'

'I'm an American who has spent most of the last five years in China. I have talked to a lot of people, listened to their stories, read a great many books. In fact,' she added bitterly, 'I haven't had much else to do with my life this last year, raising your grandson. I think I know a little about what the Cultural

Revolution was, what it meant to those who survived it. And those who didn't.'

The old man held his own counsel for several minutes as they reached the top of the road and turned west towards the ramp to the underground walkway. As they passed into the darkness of the tunnel beneath Changan Avenue he said, 'In China we treasure a son, because it is his duty to look after us in our old age. He and his wife, and their children, will look after his parents when they can no longer look after themselves.' His voice echoed back at them off the roof and the walls.

'Yeah,' Margaret said unsympathetically. 'That's why the orphanages are full of little girls, dumped by their parents, abandoned on doorsteps. Great system.'

'I did not invent the One Child Policy,' Li's father said bitterly. 'I only thank God I had a daughter before they thought of it. She, at least, has taken her responsibility to her father seriously.'

Margaret forced herself to remain silent. Xiao Ling, she knew, had been anything but the dutiful daughter.

'But Li Yan? The moment he is old enough, he is off to Beijing to live with his Uncle Yifu and train to be the great policeman. Never a second thought for the family he left behind in Sichuan.'

They emerged into the bright sunlight on the north side of Changan, and a shady path led off towards Tiananmen, the trees that hid it from the road casting their long shadows against the high red wall that bounded the gardens outside the

Forbidden City. Margaret bumped the buggy into Nanheyan Street and swung hard left into the gardens. Anger forced her to break her silence.

'That's what really sticks in your craw, isn't it? That he came to live with his Uncle Yifu. Your brother. Who was more of a father to him than you ever were.' She barely stopped to draw breath. 'And don't give me that crap about how Li Yan was responsible for his uncle's death. We both know that isn't true. Even if he still feels guilty about it. But you never fail to play the guilt card, do you. Never miss a chance to turn the knife in all his emotional wounds. Because you know it works every time. I think you must take pleasure in his pain.'

It was out now. She'd said it all, and there was no taking it back. Before them, the old moat wound its way through the remodelled gardens to a tall, arched bridge in white marble beside a pavilion where water tumbled down over moulded rock. Beyond it, the Gate of Heavenly Peace rose in red-tiled tiers into the sky. It was sheltered here, and barely a ripple broke the surface reflection of the willow trees overhanging the water. People strolled along the paths on both sides of the moat, unhurried, drinking in the peace and quiet of this oasis of tranquillity in the very heart of the city.

Margaret and Li's father walked in silence with the buggy, then, Li Jon fast asleep, head tipped to one side, oblivious of the tension between his mother and his grandfather. Margaret looked at her child. Round, chubby cheeks, rosy in the cold. Slanted eyes shut tight, lids fluttering slightly, rapid eye movement behind them reflecting some dream that she would never know and he would not remember. And it struck her with a sudden jolt, that her son shared her genes with those of his grandfather. These two adults, at loggerheads with each other, had come together over thousands of miles and millions of years in the living, breathing form of this tiny child. She felt immediate regret at the harshness of her words and turned towards Li's father with an apology forming on her lips. But it never came, halted by the shock of seeing the tears that streaked the old man's face.

'I have never meant to cause him pain,' he said, and he turned to meet Margaret's eye. 'He is my son. His mother's child. I love him with all my heart.'

She was filled with confusion and consternation. 'Then why . . . ?'

He raised a hand to stop her question and took out a handkerchief to wipe his face. 'There is not much of me in Li Yan,' he said finally. 'Not that I can find. But he is the image of his mother. I see her in everything about him, in everything he does. In his eyes and his smile, in his long-fingered hands. In his stubbornness and his determination.' He paused to draw breath, and fresh tears rolled down his cheeks. 'He thinks that somehow I blame him for her death.' He shook his head. 'I never did. But when he left, to come to Beijing, it was like losing her all over again. He was everything I had left of her, and he took that away from me.' He blinked hard to stop the tears falling from beneath the tangle of white fuse wire that grew from his brows. He put a hand on the push arm of the buggy to steady himself, and she saw the brown spots of age spattered across the crepe-like skin on the back of it. He seemed shrunken, smaller somehow, drowned by his big brown duffle coat, and clothes that hung so loosely on his tiny frame that they only fitted where they touched.

'Oh, my God,' she whispered, realising for the first time that the pain he had inflicted on his son was only a reflection of the pain he felt himself. But only because he had never expressed it, at least not to Li Yan. Not in that way. 'You have to tell him,' she said. 'You need to talk. Both of you.'

'I have never spoken of these things to a living soul,' he said. He looked at Margaret. 'But, then, neither have I spilled tears in public.' He drew breath. 'The Tao teaches us that agitation within robs one of reflection and clarity of vision. In this state of mind it is impossible to act with presence of mind. So the right thing is to keep still until balance is regained.' He waggled his head sadly. 'I have never stopped to think beyond my own pain. Until now. Never stopped to reflect, and regain my balance.' Something like a smile creased his face. 'Harsh words sometimes carry hard truths, and make one stop to reflect.'

Margaret could not think of a single thing to say. She put a hand over his, and felt the cold in it. 'You should be wearing your gloves,' she said. But he only nodded. They had reached the bridge, and Margaret said, 'Could you lift one end of the buggy? He always wakens when I have to bump him up the steps.'

'Of course.' He wiped his face again, and blew his nose, and stooped to lift the foot of the buggy. And together they carried the child that bound them across the steep arch of this ancient bridge to the other side of the moat.

'You push him,' she said, when they got to the other side. And as they walked in silence together towards the pond where golden carp swam around a copper fountain, she slipped her arm through his.

## IV

Pau Jü Hutong was a maze of ancient Beijing courtyard dwellings, narrow alleys with tin roofs and grey brick walls, tiny shops behind sliding windows, and ancient trees that sprouted gnarled branches to shade the tarmac. Old men on tricycles pedalled up and down its length, school kids in woolly hats carrying well-worn satchels made their way home from school in groups of two and three.

Wu drove carefully between the parked vehicles, past the towering white detention centre where Section Six interrogators grilled criminal suspects, and turned in at the entrance to the Beijing Forensic Science Institute. The guard, huddled over a stove in the gatehouse, recognised them through the window, and the steel gates concertinaed to let them in. There was a police mini-van and a black and white Jeep in the forecourt, and half a dozen other unmarked vehicles. Wu parked up and Li got out clutching the two video tapes from the EMS post office. They climbed the steps, past two dancing red lanterns, and plunged into the building.

The AutoCAD computer was in a darkened room on the second floor. Li had phoned ahead, and so they were expected. A lab assistant shook their hands and took the video tapes, assuring them that the process of digitisation would only take a matter of minutes. 'We require just a few frames in order to be able to lift the stills,' she said. They followed her into the adjoining media room where she put the first tape into a player and started running it through. 'Anywhere about there,' Li said, stabbing his finger at the screen. He wanted the biggest and clearest possible images of the killer. The assistant stopped the tape. Their man had just stepped out of the burned-out patch of sunlight on the floor of the EMS hall. She ran it back a short way, and then punched a button on another machine and set the tape playing again. She let it run for about thirty seconds, then ejected it and put in the second tape. They repeated the process, capturing the best images of the man in the baseball cap, before the assistant flicked switches on all of the machines and one of them spat out a shiny silver disk about twelve centimetres in diameter.

She waggled it at Li. 'Digitised on to DVD. Do you have the measurements?' Li nodded and she picked up an internal phone and told someone called Qin at the other end that they were ready for him.

Qin was a big man in every way, nearly as broad as he was tall. He had cropped black hair and thick eyebrows that fell away in steep curves on either side of his eyes. His gold-framed glasses somehow softened the threat of his physical presence. He had been instrumental in developing the AutoCAD software. As he slipped the DVD into the computer and began capturing matching still images from each camera using the time-codes, he explained, 'Used to be that we needed to take measurements from every side of a crime scene to build an accurate 3-D image. Now we just need one to get the scale for the whole thing.' He examined the pictures of the killer striding across the concourse with his long coat and his baseball cap and the box with the kidney under his arm. 'What measurements did you take?'

Li said, 'The length of the hall, the height of the counter, the width of the windows . . .'

Qin cut him off. 'The width of a window will do.' Li placed the piece of paper with the measurements on the computer table. Qin typed in the width of the window in centimetres. 'Okay, now the computer will do the rest.' He ran the mouse dextrously across its mat and the arrow on the screen dipped and dived. Menus dropped down, options were selected. The screen divided into two halves. The left half showed one of the stills of the killer caught in mid-stride. For the moment the other half was blank. Qin pulled down another menu, highlighted one of its options, and the blank half filled in with an outline 3-D graphic image of the EMS hall, with the kidney man at its centre. By manipulating the options, Qin was able to take them through a three-hundred-and-sixty-degree circle around him. At intervals he hit the print button, and the printer spewed out hard copies.

Li and Wu watched, fascinated, as they took a tour of their murderer. The computer could not show them his face, but it gave them an accurate picture of his build and his shape. He seemed tall, with broad shoulders, but carrying little weight, and was slightly stooped. The shape of his head was obscured by the baseball cap.

'That's amazing, Chief.' Wu's jaw was hanging open. He had never seen this technology in action before and had forgotten to keep chewing.

'Can you give us an idea of his height?' Li asked.

'I can tell you exactly what height he is,' Qin said. 'I can even tell you what size shoes he wears.'

Li found himself clenching his fists. It took them one step nearer to him. One step at a time. He looked at the image on screen with an unblinking intensity. There he was, right in front of them. He thought he was being so clever, and although it was still not enough they knew more about him now than he could ever have imagined.

## V

It was late afternoon by the time he got back to the apartment. He had with him a copy of *The Murders of Jack the Ripper*, and Elvis's digest, which he had not yet had a chance to read. At the detectives' gathering a packed meeting room had discussed developments. The kidney, the video tape from the EMS post office, the AutoCAD analysis of the killer. They had new photographs on the wall now. Pan's murder scene. The bloody corpse cheek by jowl with the photograph of Pan and her lover in their graduation gowns. They discussed Pan's sexuality, her autopsy. When Li distributed the computer printouts with the 3-D graphic of the murderer, a tantalising glimpse of their prey, an unusual hush had fallen over the meeting. But for all the interviews, autopsy reports, photographs, printouts – a veritable paper mountain generated by five murders – they were no nearer to catching him. Before he wound up the meeting, Li asked if anyone wished to confess to briefing the *Beijing Youth Daily* on the Beijing Ripper. Unsurprisingly, no one did.

Margaret was in her usual armchair, reading in the last hour of daylight, her book tilted towards the window. She had fully intended to talk to Li about his father when he got in, but he was earlier than she expected, and she knew by his face that something had happened.

'I'm sorry,' he said, 'about missing my father.' He dropped his coat on the settee and slumped into a chair.

She closed her book. 'What happened?'

He said, 'Yesterday it was a letter. Today it was half a kidney.'

'Jesus! Whose?'

'The girl we found Monday morning. We've still got to DNA match it, but Wang's pretty sure. And there was a note with it. Pretty vile stuff. He claims to have eaten the other half.'

Margaret frowned. 'I thought you had assigned an officer to go through the Ripper book and list all the salient facts.'

'I did. Elvis. I think it took him most of the night to do it.'

'Didn't he tell you that Jack the Ripper sent half a kidney to someone through the post?'

Li shook his head. 'He's on night shift, and his digest only got handed out this afternoon. No one's even had the chance to look at it yet.'

Margaret lifted her copy of the book off the floor and started thumbing through it. 'It was sent to a guy who ran some kind of vigilante group that was patrolling the streets trying to catch the Ripper. Ah, here we are . . .' She folded the book back on itself. 'Lusk, that was his name. Chairman of the Mile End Vigilante Group. And there was a note with that, too.' She read it out. '*From Hell. Mister Lusk, Sor, I send you half the kidney I took from one woman. Preserved it for you. Tother piece I fried and ate, it was very nice. I may send you the bloody knife that took it out if you only wait a while longer. Signed, Catch me when you can, Mishter Lusk.*' She looked up and saw that the colour had drained from Li's face.

'It's almost word for word,' he said. And he closed his eyes and the image of the killer was still there, etched indelibly in his memory. 'I've seen him, Margaret.'

Margaret straightened up in the chair. 'What do you mean?'

And he explained about the video and the AutoCAD imaging software. 'Here . . .' He opened his folder and handed her one of the computer printouts, along with a copy of a still from the video.

She gazed at them, fascinated. 'So close . . .' she said, and had no need to finish. She laid the prints aside and looked at him. He seemed exhausted, pale and tense. 'You need a drink,' she said.

'I do.' She got up and went into the kitchen to get him a beer from the refrigerator, and to mix herself a vodka tonic 'Maybe it's good we're going out for dinner tonight,' she called back through. 'You need a break from all this.'

'I'm not sure how much of a break it'll be,' he said. 'It was

Bill who brought Lynn Pan over here, remember. He feels really lousy about it.'

'Oh, yeah, of course.'

She came back through with the drinks and handed him a cold bottle of beer. He put it to his lips and sucked it down thirstily. She said, 'We've got to talk about your dad.' And she saw his eyes close, hoping that the world would just go away. He really didn't want to hear it. And, almost as if to rescue him, the phone rang. Margaret said, 'It'll be for you.'

He shook his head. 'I don't want to know.'

Reluctantly, Margaret picked up the receiver. '*Wei?*' Li opened one eye to watch her as she listened. She slipped her hand over the mouthpiece and whispered, 'It's Wang.' And into the phone. 'I'll get him for you.' But she didn't move. 'Oh,' she said. 'Okay.' Li saw a frown form itself on her face, a frown that turned into consternation. He opened his other eye.

'What is it?'

She held up a hand to silence him. 'Okay. Okay. I'll tell him.' She hung up and looked at him, but he saw that she was looking some place way beyond him, eyes glazed, their focus somewhere else entirely.

'What!' He sat up, forcing her to switch focus to him.

'He just got the DNA results from the lab. From the cheroot found by Pan's body.' She paused. 'It's different.'

'What do you mean?'

'I mean it's different. Not the same as the DNA they got off all those other cheroots.'

Li found himself tumbling through the confusion freefall

Margaret had predicted that morning if the DNA failed to match. Neither of them had believed then that such an eventuality was likely. 'How's that possible?'

Margaret consciously tried to stretch the horizons of her thinking so that it would not be limited by the obvious. But it was only the obvious that came to mind. 'She must have been killed by somebody else.'

He shook his head. 'But that's *not* possible.'

'Why not?'

'Well, think about it. Someone out there is producing carbon copy killings of the Jack the Ripper murders. Always the same MO. Strangulation, and then the cutting of the throat. Half-smoked Russian cheroot left by the body. We get a letter from him threatening to cut off the ears of the next victim. It's word for word the same as the first of the Jack the Ripper letters. The next victim is Pan. She is strangled, has her throat cut. A Russian cheroot is found by the body. Her ears are cut off. It has to be the same killer.'

'Not necessarily.'

'How do you mean?'

'Think about the things that don't match. The fact that Pan wasn't a prostitute. The fact that she was murdered in another part of the city from all the other victims. The fact that she wasn't mutilated – apart from the cutting off of the ears.'

Li shook his head vigorously, heaving himself out of his chair. 'It doesn't matter. The things that don't match don't matter.'

'Why not?'

'Because only the killer of the first four victims would be able to replicate the things that do match in the fifth.' He opened out both palms and cocked his head, as if challenging her to contradict him. And he waited.

She looked at him speculatively for a moment, then said, 'You're overlooking something.'

'What?'

'The killer is not the only person who knows his MO.'

He stared at her uncomprehendingly. 'Well, who else?'

'Every police officer on the investigation.'

He was about to dismiss the notion out of hand. But something stopped him. A memory that wormed its way to the head of the queue of thoughts fighting for space in his mind. A conversation he'd had with Bill Hart after the MERMER demonstration at the Academy. *Of course, it has to be used very carefully*, Hart had said. *I mean, think about it. You're the investigating officer. You make a detailed examination of the crime scene, so now you carry the same information in your brain as the killer. Can we always be sure we'll know which is which, who is who?* But he couldn't bring himself to believe it. 'You're not seriously suggesting that someone on my team murdered Lynn Pan?'

Margaret shrugged. 'Someone who used the other murders as a convenient cover. Someone who knew enough detail to make it convincing and throw your investigation into confusion. Who else but a cop would have access to that information?'

Thoughts tumbled through Li's brain like balls in a lottery drum. He didn't want to believe it, but he couldn't find a convincing counter argument. If the DNA didn't match, it was the only possible answer. Which meant they were now looking for two killers. And one of them was someone he knew.

In his search for some alternative, his eyes fell upon a pile of envelopes and a small parcel wrapped in brown paper sitting on the table. At first he wasn't even looking at them, they were just a convenient focus for the eye. He was running through all the people on his team, the officers from forensics, the pathology lab, everyone who would have access to the kind of information which would allow them to stage Lynn Pan's killing in such a way that Li would think it was another Ripper murder. And then another ugly little thought sneaked up out of left field and he found himself staring at the parcel on the table and listening to the blood pulsing in his head. 'What the hell's that?' he said.

Margaret looked towards the table. 'Just the mail. I picked it up when I came back from the autopsy.' And then she realised what was in his head. 'Oh, God . . .' It was barely a whisper.

The parcel was about twelve centimetres square, wrapped in brown paper and sealed with sticky tape. Li's name and address was written on it, in what seemed to Li like a familiar hand. But there were no stamps. No postmark. It had been hand-delivered. 'Do we have any gloves in the house?' he said, not taking his eyes off it.

Margaret nodded and ran off to the kitchen. She returned a few moments later with a pair of clear plastic disposable food-handling gloves. She kept a box of them in the cupboard above the food preparation area. Li took them and pulled them on, and very carefully began picking at the sticky tape until he had raised a corner of it. Then he eased it free of the paper, a centimetre at a time until he was able to open one end of the parcel. He slid out a plain, white cardboard box tied with a red ribbon. He undid the ribbon and lifted the lid. Inside, nestled in cotton wool stained with blood that had dried and turned brown, were Lynn Pan's ears. Margaret's gasp was quite involuntary. Li felt nausea turning to anger. Tucked down the side of the box was a folded note. He gently eased it out and open it up. Red ink. And what appeared to be the same, spidery handwriting as before.

*Dear Chief,*
*A couple of ears for you. As promised.*
*Sincerely,*
*Jack.*

# CHAPTER EIGHT

## I

A red flag flapped in the wind outside the white-tiled police station on the corner of Fanggu Lu and Fangxing Lu. As the sun went down, the wind was doing its best to detach stubborn leaves from the scholar trees that lined the street. A couple of bicycle repair men on the corner wore gloves to protect oily fingers from the cold as they worked on the skeleton of an upturned cycle, the last job of the day. Li drove past the sports centre on his left, basketball courts and soccer pitches, a domed stadium with indoor tennis courts. Beyond it, traffic buzzed like flies dying in the autumn cold around the multi-storey Feng Chung shopping centre. At the end of the street he parked and crossed to the apartment block on the corner. A *jian bing* lady was selling pancakes from a stand in the gardens, while a warden swaddled in blue coat and red armband wore a white face mask as she patrolled the perimeter, casting a long shadow across the grass.

At the entrance to Lao Dai's apartment, a couple of tricycle goods carriers were parked under a tin roof, and another

Chinese flag snapped and cracked like a whip in the breeze. Li climbed the couple of steps to the door and went in. A short flight of stairs led to a lobby and the elevator. A stairgate stood ajar at the entrance to the stairwell. Off to the left, a corridor led to a door with a plaque which read, *Veteran Senior Officers Activity Centre*. For some reason it was also labelled in English, *Old Cadres*. Li knocked and walked in. An old man with a very large pair of glasses sat reading the *Beijing Youth Daily* next to a dispenser of bottled water. He looked up at Li, his face expressionless, then he looked at the front page of his paper and then back at Li.

'*Ni hau*,' Li said, and the old man nodded silent acknowledgement.

A big screen television stood on a wooden cabinet next to a tall refrigerator which had seen better days. In an alcove at the far end of the room the last sunshine of the day slanted in through windows on two sides. Two old men sat playing chess among the pot plants. From a room in a corridor leading off, Li heard the sound of men's voices raised in an argument.

The apartment was provided by the Ministry of Public Security for retired senior police officers. Li wondered if he, too, would end up in a place like this one day. He pulled up a chair and sat down at the table with the chess players. For some reason, Old Dai never went to the park on a Tuesday.

'You just cannot keep your face off the front pages of the newspapers these days, can you?' Dai said, without looking up.

'So it seems,' Li replied. He paused. 'Dai, I need your advice.'

Dai's chess partner immediately rose to his feet. He had a

long, lugubrious face, and a cardigan that hung open to reveal an egg-stained shirt. 'No cheating,' he said, and he headed out into the stairwell.

Old Dai grinned. 'As if I needed to.' And then his smile faded. 'You are in trouble?'

Li sighed. 'Maybe.'

Dai returned to his examination of the chessboard. 'You had better tell me.'

'I think the woman killed last night might have been murdered by a police officer.'

Dai lifted his eyes from the chessboard, all thoughts of the game banished from his mind. 'Why do you think this?'

Li told him, and Dai sat listening in silence and gazing pensively from the window. When he had finished, Li added, 'Margaret has taken the ears to the pathology department to confirm that they are Lynn Pan's. Not that I think there is any doubt. A visual match will do for now. A DNA match will seal it for the record.'

'And the handwriting?'

'I have requested a calligrapher to compare the characters on the note that came with the ears, to the characters on the one that came with the kidney. Forensics are comparing the inks.'

'But you don't expect a match?'

'No.'

Dai sat in silence for some time. At length he said, 'The parcel with the ears had no stamp or postmark?'

'It was hand-delivered.'

'So whoever left it in your post-box had access to the Ministry compound.'

'A cop,' Li said flatly.

Dai nodded. But it was not a nod of agreement. Only an acknowledgement. 'I am puzzled,' he said.

'Why? What's puzzling you?'

'If this police officer had knowledge of the previous murders, and wished you to believe that Miss Pan died by the same hand, why would he leave his saliva on the cigar? For he would know, surely, that when you tested the DNA it would not match.' He looked Li in the eye. 'That was careless of him, don't you think?'

## II

Li drove north on the East Third Ring Road. It was dark now and the tail lights of the traffic stretched ahead of him into a hazy distance. The city basked in its own light, buildings illuminated against the black of the night sky, a million windows lit like stars in a firmament. When he went to see Dai he had been certain that he was looking for two killers. Both of them somewhere out there. One of them tangible. Li had seen him, been mocked by him, without ever knowing who he was. The other a phantom, an idea born of an unexpected DNA result and a host of inconsistencies. A policeman, someone he knew. One of his team. But, as usual, Dai had made him question everything. *In my day we had no DNA testing*, he had said. *It is possible to pick up a sesame seed but lose sight of a watermelon.*

But when it came to Pan's murder, no matter how much he wanted not to believe it, he could not question Margaret's logic in pointing the finger of accusation at a cop. It was the only explanation that brought consistency to inconsistency. And if it *was* true, then he was even further from solving this puzzle than he had thought.

And yet, Dai had sown a seed of doubt somewhere in the back of his mind, and it had taken root there and was growing. For an experienced cop to have left DNA traces that would blow apart his subterfuge, seemed unthinkable. But, then again, to make a mistake in the heat of the moment, while committing the presumably unaccustomed act of murder, was not. And, still, the biggest question of all was, *why?*

Li felt his eyes closing as confusion and uncertainty washed over him in a wave of fatigue, and the vehicle in front – a taxi – seemed suddenly no more than inches away. He jammed on his brakes, and the car behind blared its horn. He swerved, almost losing control, then pulled himself back on track, tiredness swept away by a moment of fear and the heart it had left pounding fiercely in his chest. This was crazy!

He had arranged to meet Margaret outside the Harts' apartment block on the edge of the Central Business District. She would take a taxi back from the pathology lab, she had told him. On the way she would drop off Li Jon to spend the night at Mei Yuan's tiny *siheyuan* home on the shores of Qianhai Lake.

A dinner party, an evening of social chit-chat, was the last thing Li felt like. All he wanted to do was sleep, to close his stinging eyes, rest his aching head on a pillow and drift off into some dreamworld where whatever happened, he was always assured of waking up. But it was too late to back out now. And what was it the Americans said: a change is as good as a rest?

He turned off the ring road at Jinsong Bridge and swept from the exit ramp on to Lianguang Road. The Music Home apartments were a blaze of lights, green glass and grey cladding. The shopping mall on the ground floor of the main block was still doing business. Li parked in the street and found Margaret waiting for him outside the entrance lobby. He raised his eyebrows in an unasked question and she nodded. 'They match,' she said. 'We'll get the DNA results tomorrow. But, really, we don't need them.' There was nothing more to be said. She took his arm and they went through glass doors into a huge lobby with inlaid floors and an arched gold ceiling. A security man at the desk asked politely if he could help. They told him who they were and he telephoned the Harts' apartment before letting them through to the gardens.

'Jesus,' Margaret said. 'Lyang said this was Bill's one concession to Western comfort, but this isn't comfort, it's goddamned opulence.'

Contained within the complex of apartment blocks, and the two landmark towers with their grand piano lids, were nine thousand square metres of landscaped garden on the theme of the four seasons. There was a beach around a kidney-shaped pool, paths and walkways through clusters of trees representing everything from summer through fall to winter and spring. There was a stream spanned by tiny bridges at several points along its length, and a garden cafeteria. On the east side, a sports complex contained an indoor swimming pool with tennis courts above it. At each end, ramps led down to an underground car park beneath the gardens. Now, however, as the cold November winds blew down from the north, heralding the arrival of winter, the gardens were sad and empty.

Li felt uncomfortable here. As if he had stepped through the looking glass into another world on the far side. This was not the Beijing he knew. There was nothing Chinese about any of it. This, and places like it, were built for the business community, the three hundred thousand foreigners at the heart of the city's new commercial engine, and the Chinese nouveau riche who bought up all the new apartments and rented for profits of thirty and forty per cent. It was a bubble, double-glazed and insulated from the real world that he knew outside. A world where Chinese people worked hard, died hard and earned little, living and dying in tiny apartments with communal toilets and inadequate heating. A world where prostitutes were being murdered by a maniac living out some twisted fantasy.

They made their way through the gardens to the far side and into the tower on the north-west corner. An elevator sped them soundlessly up to the twenty-third floor and they stepped out into a carpeted hallway. Lyang was waiting for them at the far end, at the open door of the Harts' apartment.

'Hey, guys. Welcome to our humble home.' She grinned and kissed them both on each cheek. In the entrance hall, slippers awaited them on a mat, and they kicked off their shoes to slip them on. The floors were dark polished mahogany. A staircase led off to an upper floor, and they walked through lush Chinese rugs into an open living room whose balcony gave on to a stunning view across the city and the gardens below. Concealed lighting along the perimeter of the ceiling was augmented by Chinese lanterns. Antique cabinets, and bookcases groaning with collectors' items, lined walls that were hung with original scroll paintings by famous Chinese artists. Through open sliding doors leading off an open-plan dining room, they could see into a fitted kitchen which issued smells that were, finally, stimulating Li's digestive juices. There was a cinema ratio plasma TV screen on one wall, and beside a state of the art stereo system playing muted jazz, Bill Hart was pouring cocktails at a drinks cabinet.

'Hey,' he said. 'No arguments. You guys have got to taste my patent Beijing margaritas with crushed ice.'

'No arguments from me,' Margaret said.

He kissed her on both cheeks and handed her a drink and then shook Li's hand. 'Good to see you, Li Yan. You look whacked.'

'You're looking pretty good yourself,' Li said wryly, and accepted his drink from the American.

Margaret waved a hand around the room. 'Obviously, I'm in the wrong business. Witchcraft clearly pays better than medicine.'

Hart laughed. 'I thought it was voodoo.'

'Whatever.'

He passed a drink to Lyang. 'Actually, the money's pretty

crap. Well, here in China anyway.' His smiled faded. 'Lyang probably told you, I inherited the house in Boston when my wife died.' He shrugged as if embarrassed. 'I also picked up a fat insurance cheque that I'd happily have torn in a thousand pieces in return for a chance to turn back the clock. But I couldn't. So I figured, spend it. I never expected to have it, I wouldn't miss it when it was gone.' He let his eyes wander around the room. 'So we live well. And if we ever have to go back to the States . . .' his eyes flickered towards Li and then away again, '. . . we can rent this place out to give ourselves a nice little income.'

'You want to see around?' Lyang said. She was dying to show them.

'Sure,' Margaret said.

Li would happily have sunk into one of the comfortable-looking armchairs arranged around a central coffee table, but good manners dictated that he look enthusiastic, and he nodded and forced a smile of false interest across his face.

They put their drinks on the table, and Lyang led them back out into the entrance hall and up polished stairs that turned back on themselves at a halfway landing, leading up then to a long central hallway. At one end was the guest bedroom, which doubled as a study, at the other the master bedroom and the baby's room. There was also a large storeroom which Lyang said the sales people had told them was a maid's room. No windows, no ventilation. 'Foreign architects,' she said. 'They probably imagined that would be luxury to us poor Chinese.'

They peeked quietly into the baby's room and heard the

slow, rhythmic breathing of a sleeping child. There were expensive Chinese rugs everywhere, thick-piled and soft underfoot, and from somewhere they had managed to acquire a four-poster bed for the master bedroom. The view from here faced north, towards the lights of the China World Trade Center. In the street a long way below, a traditional Beijing restaurant was doing good business.

Li figured Mao must be turning in his mausoleum.

When they got back downstairs, Lyang excused herself and hurried into the kitchen. Li sank gratefully into the armchair that had been beckoning ever since they arrived and took a long drink of his margarita over a salted rim. He felt the alcohol rushing straight to his brain and immediately began to relax. Perhaps this wasn't such a bad idea after all. At least he could escape for a few hours from the horrors of the Beijing Ripper and his victims, and the thought that Lynn Pan had been murdered by someone he knew.

'Any developments on the Lynn Pan killing?' Hart asked.

Li groaned inwardly. He wanted to tell Hart it was none of his damned business, but he knew he couldn't do that. 'Afraid not,' he said quickly, before Margaret could say anything. He flashed her a warning look. From now on he was going to share information on the murder with as few people as possible. That included Bill Hart – and most of Section One.

'It's a crying shame,' Hart said. 'I still feel like shit every time I think about it. I wish I'd never put her name up for that job.'

'You wouldn't think of moving over into MERMER yourself?'

Li said. 'They're going to need someone to take over the project. And if you're going to lose your polygraph funding . . .'

Hart put a finger quickly to his lips and nodded towards the kitchen. 'No,' he said in a quite normal voice that belied the warning he had just given. 'It's not an area in which I have any real expertise. Sure, I understand the principles, I can read the graphs, but the science and the software are a mystery to me.'

Margaret said, 'Li Yan never told me how you two met. It wasn't at a séance, was it?'

'Bill did a polygraph for us a couple of years ago,' Li said. 'A guy who murdered his wife and children and parents in their apartment out in Xuanwu District. We were pretty certain he'd done it, but we just couldn't prove it. I think that must have been when you were back in the States.'

'So what did you do?' Margaret asked Hart. 'Hang him out the window by his feet and threaten to drop him if he didn't confess?'

Hart laughed. 'Didn't have to. And, anyway, he'd volunteered for the polygraph. Figured he was too smart for us and could beat the test and prove his innocence.'

'Isn't there a polygraph expert at the Public Security University who normally does tests for the cops?' Margaret said.

'Yes,' Li said, 'but the good professor is in big demand all over the country. Not always available.'

'So you called in the American witch doctor.'

'Careful,' Hart said. 'I'll start sticking pins in that doll of you I keep upstairs.'

Margaret grinned. 'So what happened?'

Hart said, 'I did one of my little parlour tricks. Got him to pick a number and then lie about it. Then I showed him the result on the chart and that was that.'

'What was what?' Margaret said.

'He didn't even have to take the test,' Li said. 'The guy broke down there and then and confessed.'

'Was that before or after you held him under the water?'

Hart shook his head. 'I'm never going to convince you, am I?'

'Probably not.'

Li said, 'So you think you could beat the number test?'

'I've no idea. But we're never likely to find out, are we?'

'I've got a machine upstairs,' Hart said. 'In the study. It would only take a few minutes.'

'No chance,' Margaret said.

'Go on,' Li said. 'You can't sit there and pour scorn on the man's work and then refuse to let him prove himself.'

'It wouldn't work on me,' Margaret said. 'I'd feel guilty even when I was telling the truth.'

Hart smiled. 'Let me be the one to judge that.' He called through to the kitchen. 'Honey? How long till grub's up?'

'Another ten minutes,' Lyang called back.

'Plenty of time,' Hart said.

There were two desks in the study, each pushed against facing walls. A third wall was floor to ceiling window, and facing it a futon was set against the fourth. There were matching iMac computers on each desk, cosmic screen savers mixing through sequential photographs of deep space: planets and moons, gas clouds, comets and galaxies. There was a solitary lamp on Hart's desk illuminating his private polygraph machine, pens poised to point the finger at whomsoever should dare to prevaricate.

'Nervous?' Hart asked.

'You bet,' Margaret said, and she was beginning to wish she'd just kept her mouth shut.

'Sit down.' Hart pulled a chair on castors out from below his desk and beckoned her into it. He opened a drawer and started to take out the wires and cuffs and bands that he would attach to her before starting his little demonstration.

They heard Lyang on the stairs. 'Don't start without me,' she called, and she ran along the hall and hurried in. 'This I've got to see. Dinner can wait.' She sat down by her desk, bumping against it and causing the screen saver on her computer to vanish. She glanced at the on-screen desktop which it revealed. 'Oh,' she said, surprised. 'I've got mail. I never have mail.' She smiled at Margaret. 'We have broadband internet and no one ever writes to me.' She clicked on the icon of a postage stamp at the foot of her screen. It had a red circle with a white '1' inside it, indicating there was a message. The e-mail browser appeared on the screen, and the message was highlighted in the inbox. Lyang sat for a long time staring at it.

Hart was attaching a blood pressure cuff to Margaret's left arm. He glanced across. 'Who's writing to you, honey?'

In a very small voice, Lyang said, 'A dead woman.'

There was an extraordinary moment when time seemed simply to stand still, and they were frozen motionless by her words. It was a moment that seemed to Li to last a lifetime. He had been gazing out over the city, watching cars and trucks and buses etch lines of coloured light into the night, and even they seemed to come to a halt. He turned finally. 'What do you mean?'

'It's from Lynn Pan,' Lyang whispered, and Li felt all the hairs on his arms and shoulders stand up.

They gathered around her computer. The highlighted e-mail was titled *For Bill*, and was timed and dated at 5.03 p.m. the previous day, less than two hours before her murder.

'Well, open it, for God's sake,' Hart said, and Lyang double-clicked on the highlighted bar. The e-mail opened up full-screen.

From: 'Lynn Pan' <lpan2323@sina.com>
Date: Mon, 12 Nov 2003 17:03:00
To: 'Lyang Hart' <lhart@earthmother.com>
Subject: **For Bill**
Bill,
No time to explain. Couldn't e-mail you at work in case of intercept.
Only have Lyang's home e-mail. Scared something might happen
to me. If so visit my private folder on academy website. User name
'lynn.pan'. Password 'scribble'. If I'm okay when you get this, drop it
in the trash. I'll explain later.
Lynn

There was something disturbing about reading the last words set down by a person who had been murdered so soon afterwards. Someone who had known they were in danger, someone who feared the worst. Lyang turned towards Li. 'Why would she be scared something might happen to her when she thought it was you she was going to meet?'

Li had no idea. 'Maybe she thought she couldn't trust me. Maybe she thought someone would get to her first.'

'But why? What was she scared of?'

Li tipped his head toward the computer. 'Maybe we'll find the answer in the private folder she mentions in the e-mail.' He looked at Hart. 'Do you know what she's talking about?'

Hart nodded. 'Websites are just space on a computer somewhere that's linked to the worldwide web. Usually there are public folders, which anyone on the internet can access, and there are private folders, which only you can access. Private storage space, really. Most educational institutions allocate private folder space to staff and students on their websites.'

'So now that you've got her user name and password you could access her private folder from here?'

'Afraid not. You need special software. An FTP client. I don't have that at home.'

'But you do at the academy?' Hart nodded. 'We'd better go there, then.'

Lyang said, 'What about dinner?'

'I just lost my appetite,' Li said.

And as they headed downstairs to get their coats, Margaret said, 'I guess this means we're never going to find out how good a liar I am.' But no one was listening.

## III

They drove in silence through the canyon of light that was Changan Avenue, floodlit buildings rising like cliffs on either side. Past the Forbidden City where the ancient rulers of China once held court. Past the closed world of Zhongnanhai, where the present rulers of China lived in private villas around a glittering lake. Past the telegraph office, the Ministry of Commerce, the Minzu Palace. To the intersection at Muxidi where they turned off on to Sanlihi Road and into the shady side street where they parked in front of the Chinese Academy of Sciences. There were still lights on in most of the windows, night classes in progress, staff and students working late on research projects and theses.

Hart led them up the steps two at a time, and waved his ID card at the security man in the lobby, although it was hardly necessary. They took the elevator to the fourth floor and followed him down a long corridor to his office. He blinked in the harsh glare of the fluorescent strip lights as they flickered and hummed and spilled their ugly light into every dark corner. He rounded his cluttered desk and sat in front of his computer and switched it on. It whirred and creaked and hissed and started to load its operating system.

He sat back. 'It'll take a minute or two.'

They had barely spoken a word in the twenty minutes it had taken them to drive to the academy. Li felt almost brittle with tension. He had no idea what would be in Lynn Pan's private internet folder, but he knew it would be key. He felt Margaret at his shoulder, and she gave his arm a gentle squeeze.

She said, 'So what do people normally keep in their private web space?'

'Mostly stuff you want to save for your eyes only,' Hart said. 'A lot of people are involved in confidential research. Most of the computers here are on a network. So much computing space is shared, it's difficult to keep things private.'

His desktop screen had loaded now. He pulled down a menu and selected *Connect*, then went into a folder labelled *Applications* and double-clicked on something called *Fetch*. More screens unfolded and Hart opened up a *Dialogue Box* which prompted him to enter an FTP address, a user name and a password. He entered the FTP address for the academy's website, then tapped in *lynn.pan* and *scribble*. Almost immediately they were looking at a screenful of icons representing folders that Pan had stored in her private space. 'Jesus,' Hart said. 'What are we looking for here?'

'There,' Li pointed. It was a folder labelled *MPS Demo, Mon. 10th*. 'Those must be the files from the MERMER demo she gave us yesterday afternoon.'

Hart clicked his mouse on the icon and held it down. The image turned into a silhouette, and he dragged it across the screen, out of the website window, and on to his desktop where he released it. The file immediately began copying from the Academy's computer on to Hart's desktop PC. It took less than a minute, after which he disconnected from the website and double-clicked on the folder he had downloaded. It opened up a window filled with more folders. Twelve in total. Six were labelled *Graphs A, Graphs B, Graphs C*, through to *Graphs F*. The remainder were classified *Pics A* through to *Pics F*.

'What are they?' Margaret asked.

'At a guess,' Hart said, 'I'd say that the *Graphs* folders contain the graphs showing the brainwave activity of each of the Ministry people during their demo test yesterday. And the *Pics* folders probably contain the pictures each of them was shown to stimulate that activity.'

'Who's who?' Li said.

'No idea.' Hart turned to look up at Li. 'She must just have labelled you A through F instead of using names.'

'But we could each be identified by the pictures we were shown,' Li said. 'There was personal stuff among them. I was shown photographs of my apartment building, my home town. I guess everyone else was shown theirs, too.'

'Then you would know which graph belonged to which person,' Margaret said.

'Might take a while,' Hart said. 'You know, getting hold of that kind of information. The students who did the research *might* remember, but I'm guessing their notes were probably among the casualties of that burglary last night.'

'Let's have a look at some of the pics,' Li said, and he leaned in as Hart double-clicked on one of the *Pics* folders.

Its window opened up and Hart cursed. 'Shit!' The folder was empty. He went systematically through the other five. Empty. 'What the hell . . .'

Lyang said, 'Why would she upload six empty folders?'

'Christ knows,' Hart said. 'She was probably in a hurry. Maybe the MERMER software puts the pics somewhere else when it's running a demo and she never retrieved them. I just don't know.'

'Maybe you'd better check the *Graphs* folders,' Margaret suggested.

Hart opened up *Graphs A*. Its window contained three files, small icons representing single sheets of paper with folded corners. There was a design within each icon which seemed to be made up from the letters MRM, and each file was labelled with a title in a coloured strip beneath it. *Graph 1, Graph 2, Graph 3*. 'She must have done three run-throughs,' Hart said.

'She did,' Li confirmed. 'Can you open those up?'

Hart shook his head. 'I don't have the MERMER software.' And to prove his point he double-clicked on a file icon and a message in a box appeared mid-screen. *File cannot be opened because the application software that created it cannot be found.*

'So what use is any of this stuff?' Lyang said. 'We don't have any of the pics. We don't know which graph relates to who . . .'

And Margaret added. 'We don't know how any of it relates to her murder, or even if it does.'

Li was staring grimly at the screen. His disappointment was nearly choking him. 'Open up each of the folders,' he said.

Hart shrugged. 'What's the point? We can't open up any of the files.'

'Humour me.'

Hart started going through each of the folders as Li had

asked. They were all the same. Until he got to *Graphs D*, and his hand froze on the mouse. For instead of the files being labelled *Graph 1*, *Graph 2*, *Graph 3*, they were labelled, *LIAR, LIAR, LIAR.*

# WEDNESDAY

# CHAPTER NINE

## I

It was dark when Li left his apartment. Margaret was still asleep, her first undisturbed night for months. The apartment had seemed strangely empty when they got in the night before, with Li Jon spending the night at Mei Yuan's. It was odd how a presence you took for granted was never more apparent than when it was no longer there. Margaret had fallen asleep almost immediately. Li had drifted once or twice, but for most of the long hours of the night had lain awake staring at the ceiling in the reflected light from the street lamps outside. He knew he was in trouble, and had been playing a mind game his uncle had taught him. Take sequential facts that led to a conclusion and rearrange them in any order. Then look at them again with a fresh eye. It was amazing just how often you could reach a different conclusion. But no matter how many times Li rearranged the events of the last forty-eight hours, the conclusion always remained the same. And it scared him.

As he drove west on Changan, retracing his journey of the previous night, the first splinters of sunlight shot like arrows down the length of the city's east–west artery, blinding him when he glanced in the rear-view mirror. It heralded the break of a day that filled him with dread. It brought no illumination. Merely contrast with the darkness he carried in his heart.

He turned north again at the Muxidi intersection and drove past the academy on his right, and Yuyuantan Park on his left. There was little traffic on the road yet, but even as he looked, the cycle lanes were filling up with huddled figures braving the subzero temperature to cross this city of thirteen million inhabitants to factories and offices on its far-flung outskirts. When he reached the traffic lights at the Yuetan Footbridge, he turned right into Yuetan Nan Jie, and there ahead of him were the rows of pink and white four-storey apartment blocks that housed the most senior police officers in China.

He showed his ID to the guard on duty at the gate and drove into the forecourt car park of the first block. He got out of the car and stretched stiff and tired limbs, breathing in the cold, harsh air, and trying to blink away the grit in his eyes. He pulled his long, black coat tightly around himself and looked up at the picture windows with their views of the parkland below, the open balconies where the privileged could dine in the shady cool of a summer's evening, and knew he would never reach those dizzy heights. Not that he wasn't good enough. He was a better cop than most of the residents of these luxury apartments. But he had a big mouth, which he was about to open again. And this time, even he was frightened of the consequences.

Commissioner Zhu was still in his dressing gown – black

silk embroidered with red and gold dragons – when he opened his door to Li. He had been unable to disguise his surprise when Li announced himself on the intercom. A moment's silence, then a curt, 'You'd better come up.'

He ushered Li into the spacious living room at the front of the apartment. Net curtains as fine as gossamer hung over sliding glass doors that led out on to the balcony. In the distance, above the tops of the autumn trees, you could just see the roof of the Chinese Academy of Sciences. Li could hear the Commissioner's wife in the kitchen, where she had clearly been sent and told to stay. The Commissioner stood with his back to the glass doors, his legs apart, arms folded. Against the light Li could not see his face, only the reflected light from his rimless glasses. Beyond him the sky was a deep orange. 'This had better be good, Li. I'm not accustomed to being dragged from my bed by junior officers.'

Li took a deep breath. 'I believe that one of the six of us who took the MERMER test on Monday afternoon murdered Lynn Pan,' he said.

Zhu remained motionless, and Li could not see in his face what impact his statement had made. The Commissioner said nothing for what seemed like a very long time. Eventually he cleared his throat and said in a quiet voice, 'Which one of us?'

'I don't know.'

'Then what makes you think it was any of us?'

And Li told him. About the DNA mismatch, about how only someone with inside knowledge of the police investigation could have so accurately mimicked the Beijing Ripper. About the caller pretending to be him, luring Pan to a rendezvous with death at the Millennium Monument. About Pan's fears, expressed in her e-mail to Hart, and her private folders on the academy website, with the three graphs marked *Liar, Liar, Liar*.

'But you don't know whose graphs they were?'

'No, Commissioner.'

'And how do you propose to find out?'

'I've asked Bill Hart to gather together all the various pieces of information necessary to make that apparent. Miss Pan's assistant, and the students who took part in the demonstration should be able to provide most of what he needs.'

For the first time, the Commissioner unfolded his arms and leaned forward to take a cigarette from a wooden box on a lacquered table. He lit it and blew smoke towards the ceiling. It hung in the still air of the apartment, backlit by the dawn.

'And supposing you do identify this *liar*. What then? How does that in any way prove that he murdered Lynn Pan?'

'It doesn't. But it would tell us where to look.'

'And his motive?'

'The lie, presumably.'

The Commissioner snorted his derision. 'What sort of a lie told during an innocent demonstration could possibly motivate murder? And anyway, how could he lie? We weren't asked any questions.'

Li nodded. It was one of the many things which had plagued him during all the sleepless hours of the night. How *could* you lie, if you had not been asked any questions and had given no answers? And yet Pan had marked the files *Liar, Liar, Liar*.

Somehow, in some way, one of them had been caught in a falsehood. 'I don't have the answer to that yet, Commissioner.'

For the first time, the Commissioner moved away from the window, and Li saw that his face had turned quite pale. He started circling Li like a hunter stalking his prey, and Li remembered their conversation about the Commissioner's boyhood spent hunting in the forests of the remote Xinjiang Province. 'It seems to me, Section Chief, that you are raising a great many questions to which you do not have any answers. You are indulging in the worst kind of unsubstantiated speculation. It goes against every tenet of Chinese police investigation – tried and tested techniques developed over decades by better men than you. Men like your uncle. I am sure he would be turning in his grave if he could hear this conversation.'

'My uncle always trusted his instincts, Commissioner, and taught me to trust mine.'

'Oh, I see. So your instincts are telling you that the Deputy Minister of Public Security might be a murderer. And presumably, since you have such faith in your instincts, you'll be suggesting that we just lock him up?'

Li felt the serrated edge of the Commissioner's sarcasm cutting into his fragile confidence. But he stood his ground. 'There were six of us at the MERMER test, Commissioner.'

Zhu waved his cigarette in the air. 'Well, that would make you and me suspects, too, I suppose.'

'I wouldn't be here, Commissioner, if I thought it was you.'

'Ah, and that would be your trusty instinct again, Section Chief. Am I supposed to be flattered?'

Li decided not to respond to that one. It might be better to let the Commissioner make the next move. So he stayed silent, gazing through Zhu's net curtains at the sun casting shortening shadows through the park.

'And what is it you expect me to do, exactly?' the Commissioner said finally. He stopped circling, and blew smoke in Li's direction.

'There would be one way of shortcutting the whole process, Commissioner.'

'And that would be?'

'If all six of us were to submit to a DNA test.'

He heard the Commissioner spluttering. 'Are you insane, Li? Do you really think I'm going to go to the Deputy Minister, or the Procurator General, or the Director General of the Political Department, and ask them for samples of blood to eliminate them from a murder inquiry?'

Li said nothing, and the Commissioner began pacing agitatedly by the window, smoke trailing in his wake.

'You're really serious about this, aren't you?'

'Yes, Commissioner.'

Zhu stopped and glared at him. 'Then you're going to have to come up with some pretty damned good evidence, because I'm not going to act on this until you have. It would be suicide, Li. For both of us. Do you understand that?'

'Yes, Commissioner.'

Zhu exhaled deeply. 'We are talking about people in extremely exalted positions here, Li. We're talking about power, and politics, not police work.' He stabbed his cigarette into an ashtray, and Li could see from his concentrated frown that he was thinking furiously. 'I might take one or two informal soundings – over a few heads. Just to see how we should proceed.' He glanced at his junior officer sharply. 'But in the meantime, I don't want you breathing a word of this to anyone else, do you understand? Carry on with your investigation into the Beijing Ripper, but for the moment keep your other suspicions to yourself.'

## II

From somewhere, the academy's administrators had secured desks and chairs and a couple of creaking old computers which Hart had got staff and students in Lynn Pan's old department to set up in the computer room which had been stripped bare by the thieves. Hart had been at the academy since seven, and called them all in early.

Li recognised the student who had briefed them on the murder for the MERMER test. She and a long-haired male student were sitting at one of the computers. Hart was at the other with Professor Hu. He looked up when Li came in, and Li saw the strain in his face. In all likelihood, he had managed as little sleep as Li. Professor Hu had tied her wavy hair back in a pony tail, accentuating the thinness of her face. Today her business suit was black and severe as if she were in mourning. And in truth, Li thought, she probably was.

'Grab a chair, Section Chief,' Hart said. 'We're making progress, but not fast.'

Li drew up a chair and wheeled it in alongside Hart and the professor. There was a graph on the screen which they were scrolling through. 'You managed to open up the files, then?' he said.

Hart said, 'Professor Hu was able to download software from an internet site shared with some MERMER people in the States. Apparently Lynn had made some changes to her version of it, but it's essentially the same. The important thing is, it's allowed us to open up the files so we can look at the graphs.'

'Not that they tell us anything,' Professor Hu said. 'We can't even begin to decipher them without the photographs which elicited the responses that they chart.'

Li still had the Commissioner's words ringing in his ears. *You're going to have to come up with some pretty damned good evidence.* 'They're useless, then?' he said.

'Ah, no. Not quite.' Hart's smile was strained. 'The student who assembled the picture sequences for each of the testees did most of the work on her computer at home. She thinks she's got a copy of the pics on a zip disk. I sent her home to find out.'

Li said, 'I don't suppose she remembered which one of them was "D"?'

Hart shook his head. 'Afraid not. As far as she was concerned they were just pictures which related to people she'd never even met. Nor would meet. Home-town pictures were mostly downloaded off the internet, from a list. Another student went and took pictures of apartments at various addresses he was given. But the work had all been shared out. Nobody had a definitive file.'

'So how do the pictures help us?'

Professor Hu said, 'If we compare the graphs with the pictures, at the very least we should be able to tell if "D" was one of the testees briefed on the murder. Or not.'

Li frowned. 'But Professor Pan told me that the computer randomised the pictures. How do you know what order we saw them in?'

Hart said, 'Apparently first time around the computer takes the pictures and shows them in the order it's given them. Then it randomises for the subsequent sweeps.'

'So we only have to look at the first set of charts for each one to tell who had been briefed on the murder and who hadn't,' the professor said.

'Because those of you briefed on the murder will show a MERMER response to every one of the nine photographs that relate to it,' Hart added.

Li nodded. 'Okay, but how do we identify who "D" is?'

'By tying him to the photographs of his apartment and home town,' Hart said. 'That'll be a job for you guys when we get the pics.' He sighed. 'But figuring out what the lie was . . . well, that's a whole other ballgame.'

Li gave voice to the question which had been niggling at him for hours. The question Zhu had gone to straight off. 'How could he have told a lie when he wasn't asked any questions? I mean MERMER's not a lie detector. What could make Lynn Pan think he was lying?'

Hart shrugged and spread his palms. 'Beats me.' He looked at Professor Hu, but she just made a face and shook her head.

Li said, 'You've got my cellphone number. Keep me in touch with progress.'

Li was eating a *jian bing* from a seller at the Xidan market when his cellphone rang. He had stopped off at Xidan for something to fill the gnawing void that was his stomach. He had barely eaten anything in twenty-four hours, not since his last *jian bing* from Mei Yuan. He also wanted time alone to think, to consider how he was going to handle the investigation. Commissioner Zhu's warning to share his suspicions with no one was weighing heavily on his mind. And he knew he could not investigate without the manpower and resources of Section One. At the same time he was still concerned that someone within the section was feeding information to headquarters, which seriously curtailed the number of officers he was prepared to trust.

*Ode to Joy* interrupted his thoughts. He swopped the *jian bing* to his other hand and dug the phone out of his pocket. '*Wei?*' It was Miss Shen Shuji, secretary to Yan Bo, Director General of the Ministry's Political Department. The Director General, she told him frostily, wished to see him at his earliest convenience. Which was Ministry jargon for *now*.

Li closed his eyes. It was beginning. 'I'll be there as soon as I can,' he said.

'Be sure that you are,' Miss Shen Shuji told him. 'The Director General has a meeting at nine and would like to see you beforehand.' She hung up abruptly. Sometimes the secretaries were worse than their masters. Li slipped the phone into his pocket and checked the time. It was just after eight. Yan Bo was at his desk early. Even allowing for the rush-hour traffic, Li knew he could be there in ten to fifteen minutes, so he took his time finishing his *jian bing*, putting off the moment for as long as possible. Whatever Yan Bo wanted, it was unlikely to be an exchange of pleasantries. One way or another, something of what was going on must have found its way to his office.

Reluctantly, Li threw his *jian bing* wrapper in the bin and stepped back into his car. He had left the engine running to keep it warm. Carefully, he pulled out into the traffic flow, avoiding the bicycles, and drove a hundred metres south to the intersection, where he turned east into West Changan Avenue. The sun was blinding, diffused by the dirt on his windscreen. He flicked on the wash-wipe, and sunlight smeared itself all over his vision before clearing to reveal the queues of traffic backed-up from the flag-unfurling ceremony in Tiananmen Square. By the time he reached the entrance to the Ministry compound on the far side of the square, it was nearly eight-thirty.

He showed his ID to the guard at the gate and drove in to navigate his way through the maze of buildings inside the old British Embassy compound now jointly occupied by the Ministries of State and Public Security. Bizarrely, there were children playing in the road, offspring of some senior mandarin, for whom the oddly cloistered world of the two

Ministries was home. Li drove slowly past them, and envied them their youth and their innocence – both of which they would lose all too soon.

He parked beside a flower bed outside the block which housed the Political Department, and took an elevator up to the fourth floor. Miss Shen Shuji, Li was surprised to discover, was an attractive young woman in her mid-twenties. Attractive, he decided quickly, only for about two seconds. She had blue make-up on her eyes and wore red lipstick, and dressed as if she were just about to head out to a fashion show. There was not the trace of a smile on her face. When he told her who he was, she said, 'Sit,' as if he were a dog, and picked up the phone to report to her boss that Section Chief Li Yan had arrived. When he refused to follow her order and instead wandered around her office looking at the wall-hangings, she glared at him for several moments before returning to the task he had interrupted – painting her fingernails the same colour as her lips. After several long minutes, her phone rang and she said to Li, 'You can go in now.'

Li knocked and entered. Yan Bo's office was a large, blue-carpeted room with wood-panelled walls. Yan Bo seemed very small behind his enormous shiny desk, engulfed by a large, leather reclining chair, and dwarfed by the Chinese flags which hung limply from the wall on either side of his desk. Venetian blinds were lowered and half shut, obscuring the view from his window, but allowing long, thin strips of early yellow light to lie crookedly across the contours of the room.

Yan Bo was scribbling something on a tablet of notepaper

on his desk. He pulled off the top sheet, screwed it up and threw it in the bin, beginning again on a fresh one. He behaved as if he were unaware that Li had entered. With his head bowed in concentration over his note taking, Li could see that his hair was very thin on top and carefully combed to disguise the fact. Li stood in uncomfortable silence waiting for this powerful little man to look up. When, eventually, he finished his scribbling and raised his head, he gave Li a look that verged on contempt.

'What the hell do you think you are trying to do, Li?'

Li was taken aback by the aggressiveness of his tone. 'My job, Director General,' he said.

'Don't get cute with me, sonny!' the Political Director snapped back at him. 'There is no part of your job that entails bringing this Ministry into disrepute.'

'I'm not sure I understand what you mean,' Li said.

Yan Bo slapped his hand on his desk, leaving a damp palm print on its shiny surface. 'Accusing a senior officer of murder is hardly going to do much for the public image of the Ministry.'

So much for Commissioner Zhu's consultation with high officialdom, Li thought. He had gone straight to Yan Bo, neatly passing the buck. Li said, 'With respect, Director General, it would hardly be fair to blame the messenger because you don't like the message.'

'Don't be so damned insolent, Section Chief!' Yan Bo stood up and glared at Li, then perhaps realising that he was still looking up at him, sat down again. 'We have barely recovered from the prosecution of Li Jizhou, or the fourteen other officials who were executed in the wake of his conviction.' Li Jizhou was a former vice-minister of Public Security sentenced to death for his part in a smuggling conspiracy which had brought more than eight billion dollars' worth of illicit goods into China during the nineties. The scandal had shaken the ministry to its core. Corruption was a highly sensitive issue. Murder was unthinkable. 'Goddamnit, man! According to Zhu, I am also on your list of suspects. Is that true?'

Li shifted uncomfortably. 'Everyone who took part in the MERMER demonstration has to be considered a suspect.'

'Including you?'

'I've already ruled myself out, Director General.'

Yan Bo glared at him, suspecting sarcasm, but unable to detect any in Li Yan's inscrutability. 'And do you have any *hard* evidence to back up your suspicions?'

Li braced himself. 'Not yet.'

'Not yet.' Yan Bo repeated. 'Not yet?' He gazed at Li with shining black eyes. 'Not ever,' he said. 'I will not entertain groundless accusations being made about senior officers of this ministry. Not to mention the Deputy Minister himself. You might think, Section Chief, that your high public profile and your awards and commendations make you something special. Let me assure you they do not. You are nobody. As you will come to realise very quickly if you continue with this line of investigation. Do you understand?' Li made no reply. 'Do. You. Understand!' Yan Bo thundered.

'Perfectly,' Li said.

'Good. Then I do not wish to hear another thing about it. Get out of my sight.' He pulled his tablet towards him and starting scribbling furiously, and Li noticed that he was using red ink.

## III

Margaret raised her left leg and felt all the stiff muscles of her buttock tug at her hamstring as she stretched. Slowly she turned through ninety degrees, arms raised level with her shoulders and bent up at the elbow, before bringing her foot down and raising the other leg. She felt the same stretching of the muscles, and was amazed at just how out of condition she was. The cold was stinging her face, and although she wore gloves, her fingers were frozen stiff. Her breath wreathed around her head like the smoke of dragon's fire. The plink-plonk of a traditional Chinese orchestra emanating from a ghetto blaster on the wall lent succour to the illusion.

The previous day's autopsy had taken more out of her than she could have believed. The muscles of her arms and shoulders were stiff and sore from wielding heavy shears to cut through ribs, and from turning the body this way and that in the course of its dissection. Her lower back and the tops of her legs ached from the angle at which she had held herself to cut through dead flesh and remove organs. Even her thrice weekly *tai chi* sessions in Zhongshan Park with Mei Yuan had failed to keep her fit and supple for a professional activity she had always taken for granted.

Of course, the trauma of Li Jon's Caesarian birth, and everything else surrounding it, had taken it out of her. She had never regained the strength and vigour she had possessed before it, and slothful hours spent trapped in an apartment, reading and feeding and changing diapers had contributed to a decline of which she had hardly been aware. Until now. It worried her that these might be the first signs of old age. And then she looked around and found herself smiling. Most of the old women working through their slow-motion *tai chi* routines were more than twice her age. Some of them in their seventies or even eighties. She had allowed life, and events, to steal away her initiative. It was time to take control again.

'You're very quiet this morning.'

Margaret turned to catch Mei Yuan watching her closely. As she always did. Like an old mother hen. 'Stuff on my mind,' she said.

'Li Yan?'

'No. I'm afraid I'm obsessing about myself,' Margaret said. And she felt a sudden pang of guilt. Li had left her to sleep on and gone off to fight dragons on his own. They had both understood the full implications of the files they had uncovered the night before in Lynn Pan's private webspace, but had not discussed it. Li had folded in on himself, as he sometimes did, reluctant to share his deepest worries. She hated it when he was like that with her. She felt shut out, rejected. Once or twice she had surfaced briefly during the night from the deepest of sleeps, to become aware of the shallow, irregular breathing which told her he was still awake. But sleep had always dragged her back down into its warm, comforting oblivion. And when, finally, she had woken, he was gone. The sheets on his side of the bed long since turned cold.

Li Jon, in his buggy, waggled his arms and grinned at her, his tiny nose red with the cold. She saw his father in his eyes and his smile, and wondered where the closeness they had once shared had gone. She felt a tiny stab of fear, like pain, and wondered what kind of future they really had.

'Let me try you with a riddle, then,' Mei Yuan said. 'It may relieve you of the burden of self-examination.'

Margaret glanced at her, wondering for a brief moment if the older woman had somehow been able to read her thoughts. 'Okay,' she said. Something else to occupy her mind might be healthier. It was too easy, always, to focus on the negative.

Mei Yuan said, 'It took Li Yan a whole twenty-four hours to work this one out.'

'Shouldn't take me long, then,' Margaret said, and Mei Yuan grinned.

'But like you, he was a little preoccupied,' she said.

The frost was melting now on the trees as the sun rose through gnarled branches and withered leaves. Beyond the big pavilion with the red-painted pillars, a group of men and women were dancing across ancient paving stones to the rhythm of a Latin American band. And on the other side of a bamboo thicket, Margaret saw sunlight catching the shafts of swords as the daily practitioners of the centuries-old art of *wu shu* sliced through frozen air with ceremonial blades.

'Two deaf mutes are planting rice in a paddy . . .' Mei Yuan began, and she took Margaret through the complexities of the riddle just as she had done with Li two days earlier. Margaret listened as they continued with their exercises, carried along by the slow, measured rhythm of the group. When she had finished, Mei Yuan turned to look expectantly at Margaret.

Margaret was silent for a moment, then shrugged. 'They didn't finish planting till ten at night, maybe later. So it had to be dark. Which is why they couldn't see one another.'

Mei Yuan smiled. 'Too easy.'

Margaret laughed. 'Did it really take Li Yan twenty-four hours to work it out?'

'To be fair, I don't think he'd given it a thought until I asked him again the following morning. But, then, I think Li Yan is better at practical mind games than theoretical ones.'

Like solving murders, Margaret thought, to save lives. It was, essentially, what separated them. She only dealt with the dead. Her achievement was in determining how they had died. Li had an obligation to the living – to catch a killer before he killed again. And now the murder of Lynn Pan, with all its political ramifications, had distracted him from the Ripper murders, making it more likely that the killer would remain free to do his worst. She shook her head to snap herself out of it. There was nothing she could do – until, perhaps, he did kill again. 'I have to go to the visa office today,' she said, 'to collect my passport. But I want to go to the flower market first to see if I can't get some fresh flowers to brighten up the apartment. It seems so dull and stale these days.'

'You need more plants in the apartment,' Mei Yuan said. 'More living, growing things. It is good *feng shui*.'

'Well maybe I'll get some pot plants, then. Will you come with me?'

'As long as I can be back at my corner in time for lunch.'

'We'll be back in plenty of time,' Margaret said, pleased to have the company. 'We'll take a taxi.'

The flower supermarket was close to the You Yi Shopping Centre on the banks of the slow-moving Liangma River on the north-east corner of the city. It stood in the shadow of the Sunflower Tower, and cheek-by-jowl with an Irish pub called Durty Nellie's, which boasted a crude painting of a large-bosomed Irish wench clutching a pint of Guinness. Rows of baby pines in green pots were lined up outside the market, Christmas trees for ex-pats. The Christmas season was starting early in Beijing. Next door was a pot plant centre under an arched blue roof.

Margaret asked Mei Yuan to wait for her outside the centre with Li Jon while she ran into the market to get some cut flowers. They would look at the pot plants afterwards. Up half a dozen steps and through glass doors, the market stretched off in a blaze of colour, hundreds of exotic flowers arranged in thousands of pots, the air heady with myriad scents, and the sharp smell of cut green stems. Although it was warm in here, and humid, the girls were all muffled in winter jackets and scarves, smiling when they saw the curling fair hair and blue eyes, urging Margaret to buy from them. 'Looka, looka,' they urged, waving hands at big yellow daisies and purple-spotted orchids. There were red, white and pink roses, tulips from God knows where, flowers Margaret had never seen before, bizarre-looking blue and grey conical things like something you might find growing on a tropical reef. Fat-petalled extravaganzas, and fine, feathery ones. A bewildering choice. Margaret took her time, wandering the aisles, letting her eyes fall to left and right until something took their fancy. Finally she settled for a large bunch of yellow and white chrysanthemums. They stood out for their plainness amidst all the exotica, and it was that which appealed most to Margaret in the end.

They were, of course, ridiculously cheap, and Margaret was pleased with her purchase, enjoying the fresh smell of summer in this deepest cold of November.

She was pushing the door open to go out, sunlight flooding in through the glass, when she heard the scream. It was a deep scream, almost a wail, and carried something primeval in the fear it conveyed. It went through Margaret like a frozen arrow. She hurried out and stopped on the top step. Mei Yuan was standing out amongst the Christmas trees, arms pressed to her sides, tears streaming down her face. Margaret ran to her, dropping the flowers on the steps. She grabbed Mei Yuan by the shoulders, eyes wide with fear. 'Where's Li Jon?' she shouted. 'Mei Yuan, where's Li Jon?'

Mei Yuan's face was wet with tears and mucus. Her eyes were like saucers. 'He's gone,' she managed to say through deep sobs that wrenched themselves from her chest.

'What do you mean, gone?' Margaret was almost hysterical. She looked all around, searching frantically for his buggy.

'I turned away only for a moment,' Mei Yuan wailed. 'To look at the Christmas trees. When I turned back he was gone.'

## IV

Li stared gloomily from his window at the evergreens shading the brown marble facade of the All China Federation for Returning Overseas Chinese on the far side of the *hutong*. His hands were shoved deep in his pockets, as if he thought he might find something there that would show him a way out of his predicament. But they were as empty as he was devoid of ideas. That a senior law enforcement officer, possibly even a Deputy Minister of Public Security, had murdered Lynn Pan, he had no doubt. But it had been made clear to him by two of those officers that this was a line of investigation he was not to pursue under any circumstances. He had no idea if either of them was the guilty party, but it was perfectly possible. Nothing, it seemed, was impossible any longer – except for Li to continue his investigation. For he could hardly do so without it being apparent to the very people who had instructed him not to. The best he could hope for was that Bill Hart would manage to identify 'D'. And that if he could do that, perhaps they would be able to tell what the lie had been which had so panicked Professor Pan into her unlikely meeting with Li at the Millennium Monument. And her subsequent death at the hands of her *Liar*.

He turned back into his office. But there was still the problem of the Beijing Ripper, the tall man in the long coat and baseball cap captured on the EMS video. He was still out there somewhere, plotting his next killing. Planning to replicate the horrific murder of Mary Jane Kelly in precise and gory detail. He might even have chosen his victim by now. It was possible that he had already seen her personal ad in one of the nightlife magazines, or watched her in the lobby of one of the tourist hotels, or stalked her through silent streets late at night. The thought galvanised him into action.

He picked up the phone from his desk and dialled a three-digit number. 'Qian. I need you in here. And bring Wu.' They were his most senior detectives, men he had worked with over many years. Wu had even saved his life. If he couldn't trust them, then all hope was gone from his world for ever.

It was a couple of minutes before there was a knock at the door and Qian came in, followed by Wu. Both looked apprehensive. Everyone in the section was aware that something was going on, but no one knew what. Li waved them to a chair and said, 'Anyone got a cigarette?'

They looked at him, surprised. It was more than a year since Li had given up smoking. An example to them all, even if none of them had chosen to follow it. Wu tossed a pack across the desk. 'They say it gives you cancer, Chief. And heart disease. And fucks with your circulation. But, hell, why let a few little things like that stop you?'

Li ignored him and took out a cigarette. 'Light?'

Qian struck a match and held it across the desk. Li leaned

over and sucked a mouthful of smoke into his lungs and nearly choked. When he stopped coughing, he found Wu grinning at him. 'Never mind, Chief, stick at it. Death's worth persevering with.' Li went to stub it out in his empty ashtray, but Wu held up a hand to stop him. 'Uh-uh,' he said, and took the cigarette from between his fingers. 'No point in wasting it. Some of us are beyond saving anyway.'

Qian said quietly, 'What's going on, Chief?'

Li seemed to consider what he was going to say for a long time before finally he said, 'I'm going to tell you guys stuff that I don't want to leave this office. Is that understood?' They both nodded, and he added, 'By the same token, this is information that could endanger your careers, maybe even your lives. So if you don't want to hear it, you are free to leave, and this conversation never took place.' He waited, and when neither of them moved, he said, 'When I went to the MERMER demonstration at the Chinese Academy of Sciences on Monday afternoon, there were five other people there from Public Security. There was a Deputy Minister, the Beijing Police Commissioner and his deputy, the head of the political department and the Procurator General.' He paused. 'One of them murdered Lynn Pan.'

Whatever they might have expected to hear, Li doubted if it was that. Neither of them reacted immediately. Then Qian said, 'And you know this . . . how?'

So Li told them, just as he had related it to Commissioner Zhu, from the DNA mismatch to Lynn Pan's *Liar, Liar, Liar* files. Then he sat back and let them think about it. If he was going to be shot down in flames by anyone, he'd rather it was by officers in his own section telling him his theory was full of holes. 'Well?' he said eventually, when neither of them had spoken.

The two detectives exchanged glances. 'Shit, Chief,' Wu said. 'I wish I'd known what you were going to tell us before you told us. I might have taken you up on your offer to bale out.' He grinned. 'Only kidding.' But his smile quickly faded. 'We're in a shitload of trouble, aren't we?'

Li nodded. Qian said, 'And you've been told to back off?'

'All the way.'

'So what are you going to do?'

Li rubbed tired eyes and said, 'Whoever killed her can't afford to have me hanging around running the section for much longer. They've got to figure that sooner or later I'm going to work out who they are. So the way I see it is this: I've got to get him before he gets me.'

A knock at the door made them all jump. 'Later,' Li called out sharply. But the door opened anyway.

It was Sang, looking flushed and apologetic. 'Chief, I'm sorry, but I've got to interrupt. I knew you'd want to hear this.'

'What?'

'Switchboard just got a call from the local cops over at Liangma. Kid in a buggy got snatched from outside the flower market.'

'What the hell's that got to do with us?'

Sang looked as if he'd rather eat glass. 'Chief, it's your kid.'

## V

The two security guards who looked after the car park on the west side of the flower market blew smoke into the freezing air and shook their heads. Neither of them had seen anything, they said. They'd noticed the *yangguizi* arriving in a taxi with the older woman, because you didn't often see people with gold hair and blue eyes. But it had been busy, cars coming and going. One of them had gone into the car park to settle an argument between two drivers fighting over the same space. The other had been warming himself over a small paraffin heater they kept in the hut at the gate.

Li felt something like despair. The police activity had prompted the gathering of a large crowd of curious onlookers. And the local police had not arrived quickly enough to stop potential witnesses from slipping through the net. It was a busy time of the day at the flower market. There had been hundreds of people coming and going. A small fruit and vegetable market outside Durty Nellie's had also been attracting custom. Mei Yuan had left the buggy at the foot of the steps and wandered off through the Christmas trees, wondering if she should buy one as a present for Margaret. When she looked around the buggy was gone.

Li had found it difficult to get a coherent story out of her. Through her tears she had managed to tell him that she had run through the crowds looking for the buggy, and then fearing she'd missed it somehow, turned back to where she'd left it. It was then that fear had taken over, and she had screamed, a part of her hoping that it might be enough to stop people in their tracks, and that the whereabouts of the buggy would become magically apparent. Instead, she had drawn only looks of amazement. People had thought she was a mad woman, and then been startled when a *yangguizi* came running from the market and started shaking her by the shoulders.

When Li arrived at the market, Margaret was in shock, sitting in the back seat of a black and white, eyes red and blurred, clutching a soft toy she kept in her purse for Li Jon. A small, grey mouse that he loved to swing by the tail and let fly in whatever direction it would go. He had controlled an initial urge to be angry at her for losing his son, but her pain was too apparent in her face, and he knew that it was not her fault.

He slipped into the car beside her now and held her for a long time, pressing her head into his chest, feeling the silent sobs that punctuated her breathing, and let his own tears run free. The world outside seemed a distant place, like a film projected on a screen, the sound turned down, muffled so that you could barely hear it. You could touch it, but it wasn't real. You could watch it, but didn't feel part of it. As if they were insulated from it all in a bubble of their own pain.

Li had let Wu take charge of the local cops, organising the corralling and questioning of witnesses, broadcasting a citywide alert on police frequencies, shouting and pointing nicotine-stained fingers, chewing manically on a huge wad of gum. A sharp rapping on the glass made him turn. And from that distant outside world, he saw Wu's grinning face looming at the window. It seemed like something surreal. The door opened.

'Chief, we found him.'

Words Li had not expected to hear. He jumped quickly out of the car, Margaret sliding out behind him, clutching his hand. The crowds parted as a tearful, but smiling, Mei Yuan wheeled Li Jon in his buggy towards the car. Margaret ran and grabbed him up into her arms and held him there as if she intended never to let him out of them again. Her tears now were tears of joy.

Li heard Wu's voice. 'The buggy was parked by a bench down on the river walkway, under those willow trees.' He pointed and Li followed his finger. 'No more than a couple of hundred metres away.' There was a huge, four-sided advertising hoarding rising on a tubular steel construction from among scrubby trees and bushes on a piece of waste ground beside the walkway. Beyond it, just visible through the hanging fronds of the willows, there was a bench at the river's edge where old folk would sit in the summer to escape the city heat.

Someone had pushed the buggy away through the crowds when Mei Yuan's back was turned, past the vegetable market and down on to the river walkway, abandoning it by the bench, obscured by the trees. Li began to have an uneasy feeling.

Wu followed him to the buggy and watched as he crouched down to examine it in detail, going through the pouch that hung from the push bar, and pulling everything out from the tray beneath it. A blanket, a waterproof bag with a bottle of milk, several soft toys.

'That's not Li Jon's.'

Li looked up and saw Margaret, still clutching their son, looking down at him. 'What isn't?'

'That panda.'

Li looked at the panda. He was not familiar with all of Li Jon's toys and would not have known that it was not his. It seemed new, as if it had just come out of its wrapping. He turned it over, and there was a folded sheet of paper pinned to its back. He froze, initial uneasiness turning now to real fear. He held out a hand towards Wu. 'Gloves.'

Wu handed him a pair of latex gloves. Li laid the panda in the buggy and snapped them on, then removed the pin from the note. Carefully he unfolded it, and felt shock, like an electric jolt, when he saw the now familiar characters in red ink.

*Chief,*
*A little gift for baby.*
*Happy hunting,*
*Jack*

He heard the trilling of a cellphone and looked up to see faces pressed all around. Eager faces full of wonder and curiosity. There was an odd silence at the heart of the crowd fighting for a view of this bizarre piece of street theatre. He heard Wu's voice speaking on the phone, and then stood up and shouted at the crowd to move back. A ripple went through them like a wave, as the nearest of them recoiled from his anger. He shouted again, and another ripple created more space. He took his wife and baby in his arms and held them tightly, still clutching the note.

'Chief . . . Chief . . .' Wu's voice was insistent. 'Chief, you gotta go. They want you at headquarters downtown. Commander Hu's office.' Commander Hu Yisheng was the Divisional Head of the Criminal Investigation Department of the Beijing Municipal Police. Li's immediate boss.

Li asked for an evidence bag and dropped the note into it and gave it to Wu. He turned to Margaret and said quietly, 'Go straight home. Take a taxi. Stay there. Don't answer the door to anyone but me.'

She stared at him, fear and confusion in her eyes. 'Li Yan, I've got to pick up my passport from the visa office.'

'Get it another day.'

'No, they said today. They've been real bastards about it. I don't feel secure without it.'

He sighed. 'Well, keep the taxi waiting outside, then go straight back to the apartment.'

'When will I see you?'

'I don't know. I'll be in touch.' And he turned and pushed off through the crowd, and she could see from the way he moved that he was rigid with tension. Li Jon gurgled in her ear and she squeezed him even more tightly, something close to panic rising inside her, forcing an intake of breath interrupted by sobs, like the wheels of a bicycle running over rutted snow.

# VI

CID headquarters was housed in the new grey marble building sandwiched between the old redbrick HQ and the police museum. High, arched windows flanked a romanesque entrance between ornamental pillars. The frontage was still shaded by the dusty trees that lined each side of Jiaominxiang Lane.

Li drove past armed guards into the compound at the rear of police headquarters and stepped out into the midmorning sunshine. His mood was bleak as he mounted the steps to the lobby and climbed up to the top floor.

Commander Hu's new office was dominated by one of those arched windows on the building's facade. It rose from floor to ceiling, divided into Georgian oblongs, and gave on to a view, through the trees, of the Supreme Court – still clad in green construction netting. His mahogany desk was inlaid with green leather, and he sat behind it resplendent in his black uniform with its silver badges and buttons, and the number 000023 above the flap of his left breast pocket – which made him twenty-third in the Ministry pecking order. He was not a tall man, but he had an imposing presence, a full head of grey-streaked hair swept back from an unlined forehead and a handsome face for a man of his years. He did not invite Li to sit, gazing at him instead, from behind his desk, with the look of a man disappointed by the failures of his only son. He shook his head sadly. 'I am glad that Yifu did not live to see this day.'

Li felt a sinking feeling in his stomach.

'I don't know what's going on, Li, but someone up there doesn't like you very much, and you've been giving them all the ammunition they need to shoot you down. I only regret that it has fallen to me to be the one who pulls the trigger.'

'Commander . . .'

Hu raised a hand to stop him. 'I don't want to hear it, Section Chief. I really don't.' He opened a drawer in his desk and reached in to pull out the previous day's copy of the *Beijing Youth Daily*. He dropped it on the desktop, with the headline facing Li. 'The journalist who wrote this has provided a statement implicating you in the leaking of the story.'

Li felt the first pricklings of anger. 'It's a lie.'

Hu regarded him thoughtfully for a long time. 'Actually, I'm inclined to believe you. But that doesn't alter the fact that it's your word against his.'

'And you would take the word of a journalist over that of a senior police officer?'

Hu sighed deeply. 'If that was all it was . . .' He opened a folder on his desk. 'I have copies here of an official complaint registered by a serving police officer in the Beijing East district. In it he claims that you assaulted him in the course of his duties.'

Li frowned, wondering what Hu was talking about. And then he remembered the pushy community cop at the antiques market at Panjiayuan who had dealt so insensitively with the mother of Sunday's ripper victim. *You're lucky I don't break your neck*, Li had told him, and he had a sudden recollection of the officer's hat rolling away across the cobbles. 'That officer was interfering directly with a murder investigation and got physical with one of my detectives.'

'Which one?'

'Detective Wu.'

'Well, we'll talk to Wu in due course, no doubt. Meantime we have several sworn statements from witnesses at Panjiayuan that you physically assaulted the complaining officer, knocking off his hat and threatening him in full public view.' Hu breathed stertorously through his nose. 'Is it true, Li?'

Li sighed. 'He was out of line, Commander.'

'No, Section Chief. You were out of line. If this community cop was overreaching his authority or behaving badly, then there are proper channels for dealing with that. But to assault a fellow police officer in full public view does nothing but bring disrepute on Public Security, and undermine the authority of police officers in the eyes of the masses.' He shut the folder and reached out a hand. 'I'll require your Public Security identity card.'

Li's heart was pounding. 'What for?'

'You're being suspended, Li, until such time as an inquiry into your conduct is held by an investigating group of senior officers.' He paused. 'Your ID.'

Li made no move to give it to him. He said, 'Commander, we're in the middle of a serial murder investigation. Someone out there is killing young women. And he's going to do it again if we don't stop him.'

'You're not a one-man band, Li, even if you think you are.

You have a perfectly capable deputy in the section who can take over.'

'You're being used, Commander. You said it yourself. Someone up there doesn't like me. Have you wondered why?'

'I don't want to hear it.'

'Because he's a murderer, that's why. And he knows if he doesn't get me out of the way I'm going to expose him.'

Commander Hu looked at him with something close to pity in his eyes. 'Now you're just being ridiculous,' he said. 'Give me your ID!' His raised voice heralded the end of his patience.

Li stood for a moment, furious, frustrated. Helpless. Then he reached into his pocket for the well-worn maroon wallet that held his identity card and dropped it on the commander's desk. He turned without a word and walked out of the office.

Li paced slowly back and forth across the compound for a long time, thinking furiously. He had no doubt that the misappropriation of his son, albeit temporarily, had been a warning. He was being threatened and outmanoeuvred at every turn. Either Commissioner Zhu had confided in more than just the Director General of the Political Department, or ... the thought coagulated in Li's head like an embolism ... or the killer was Zhu himself. Or the Director General. He held his hands out and saw that they were shaking. The guard on the gate was looking curiously in his direction, and he quickly thrust them back into his coat pockets. He had no idea what he was going to do. Where he was going to go. He was no longer Section Chief Li Yan. He was a disgraced officer awaiting internal investigation. How quickly the hero had become the villain. He glanced towards the guards at the gate again and knew that once he went out he would not be able to re-enter without his ID. There didn't seem anything else for it but to confront the dragon in his lair.

He let anger fuel his determination as he crossed the compound to the main building and rode up in the elevator to the fifth floor. He strode with long, decisive steps, down the hush of the carpeted corridor which led to the Commissioner's inner sanctum. The armed policewoman with her gun pressed against her cheek stared sternly at him from the poster on the wall of the reception room. Commissioner Zhu's formidable secretary guarded the entrance to his lair. She was a dominating presence.

'I need to see the Commissioner,' he said.

'He's busy.' Her response was intended to be a full stop on their conversation. It was clear she did not expect a reply.

'I'll wait.'

She glared at him. 'You will not. Your section secretary will require to make an appointment.'

It was obvious to Li that she knew perfectly well that he had been suspended and no longer had access to his section.

Li took a step towards the Commissioner's door. 'Is he in there?'

She rose to her feet in order to put her full weight behind her threat. 'If you go in there,' she said, 'I shall have you arrested.'

He glared back at her, but knew that it was pointless to do

anything other than accept that he was beaten. He could do nothing if he gave them the slightest excuse to put him under lock and key. He turned away in disgust, and his eyes fell on something in the trash that stopped him in his tracks. Amidst the screwed up sheets of paper and cellophane wrappings in the bin lay the dark red and gold of an empty pack of Russian cheroots. Icy fingers wrapped themselves around his heart. He looked at her again. 'You shouldn't smoke,' he said to her. 'It's bad for your health.'

She looked at him as if he were insane. 'I don't,' she said.

He nodded. 'I didn't think so.'

# CHAPTER TEN

## I

The visa office was even busier than it had been on Monday, and Margaret had to stand in the back of a long line at the visa issuing desk of the foreign section. She had left the buggy in the taxi, and held Li Jon in her arms. There was no way she was letting him go anywhere out of touching distance. He was fast asleep, his head resting on her shoulder, the rest of him a dead weight in arms that were beginning to ache.

She glanced along the desk and saw the frosty-faced visa cop with the bad complexion. Miss Chicken Feet. She didn't look any better today. She looked up and caught Margaret's eye. It was a moment before she recognised her, but when she did, a slow, humourless smile crept across her face and sent a chill of apprehension arrowing through Margaret's very soul.

Margaret looked quickly away and found thoughts that she did not want to entertain for a second flooding her mind. She moved slowly, inexorably, towards the head of the queue with a growing sense of dread. What if there was a problem? What if they wouldn't give her back her passport? There were others behind her now, and she heard American voices chatting about some business success which had led to the need for an extension. 'It's alright, Beijing,' she heard someone say. 'If you got money. Ten years ago you couldn't get a thing. Now there's nothing you can get Stateside you can't get here. Another ten years and everyone'll be speaking English.'

The person ahead of her slipped their passport in their bag and moved away. Margaret found herself at the head of the queue. Her mouth was dry, and her hand shook a little as she pushed her receipt across the counter at the issuing officer. He took it without looking at her and punched information into his computer. Then he looked up curiously at the woman and baby standing in front of him. 'One moment, please.' He turned and disappeared through a doorway, leaving Margaret to stand for what seemed like an eternity, with Li Jon growing heavier by the second. This was turning into a nightmare. She glanced down the desk and saw that Miss Chicken Feet was watching her. The issuing officer returned to his seat, and to her relief pushed her passport across the counter at her. 'Visa denied,' he said.

'What?'

'You give incorrect address. Misleading to police. Present visa expire Saturday. You must make arrangement to leave country before then.'

The taxi ride back to the apartment passed in a blur of unreality. The city rose up above her, towering over her on all sides, traffic squeezing in from every direction to choke her taxi's progress south on the Third Ring Road. She felt mocked, betrayed, robbed. It seemed inconceivable to her that within three days she would have to leave, possibly never to return. This was her home. It was where she had made her life, conceived and given birth to her child. It was where the man she loved had his home, where he worked. It was his country. How could they forbid her to share it with him? She only thanked God that she'd had the foresight to register Li Jon with the American Embassy to obtain his Consular Report of Birth Abroad. If the worst came to the worst, and she really did have to leave, she would at least be able to take him with her.

But somewhere, deep down, she couldn't believe it would come to that. Li wouldn't let it. He must be able to do something. He was a senior officer of Public Security, he must have some kind of influence he could bring to bear. It just didn't seem possible that she would actually have to go.

By the time her taxi was turning into Zhengyi Road, she had persuaded herself that it would all get sorted out. Li would find some way to fix things. But still, she looked at the street she knew so well with different eyes, for somewhere behind them there lurked still the fear that the life that was so familiar to her now would soon be taken away. It left her feeling empty and sick, and she fought to hold on to the optimism she had been trying so hard to build on the ride home.

The taxi dropped her at the roadside outside the ministry compound, and she wheeled Li Jon in his buggy past the armed guard, towards the pink and white apartment block that she had come to regard as home – for better or worse.

There was a black and white police patrol car parked outside the main entrance. It was not unusual to see police vehicles within the compound, but as she approached it she saw two uniformed officers sitting inside, and Margaret began to feel distinctly apprehensive.

She walked past as if it wasn't there, keeping her eyes fixed ahead of her, and turned into the path leading to the main door of the block. She heard car doors opening behind her and then slamming shut. A voice called, 'Mizz Cambo.' She was almost at the steps, and wanted just to run up them and disappear inside, shutting the door behind her, closing out the world. She just knew that this was something she didn't want to hear. She stopped and turned.

'Yes?'

The two officers approached her, faces impassive, unsmiling. 'Mizz Magret Cambo?'

'I just said I was, didn't I?'

'You come with us.' The officer put out a hand and fingers like steel closed around her upper arm.

Margaret pulled herself free indignantly. 'What for?'

'You undah arrest, lady. Fail to give change of address to PSB.'

'Oh, don't be ridiculous!' Margaret's words made her feel braver than she felt. 'Do you know who the father of my child is?'

'Formah Section Chief Li Yan.'

'Former . . .' Margaret's voice tailed away, and she felt her world falling in around her.

'Chief Li disgraced officah. He put cult of personality above duty to country.' It sounded like a mantra that had been put out in a memo. 'You come with us.' And he took her arm again. This time she did not resist. There seemed no point. Powerful currents had her in their grip and were sweeping her away on an uncertain tide. This must be what drowning felt like, she thought. As you were dragged down through the water you knew there was no way back, and you released the breath you had been so desperately holding, succumbing to the water that rushed to replace it in your lungs, slipping into the state of unconsciousness that cradled you before death.

## II

Li had spent most of the last hour just driving aimlessly through the city, letting the traffic flow carry him where it would. He had driven a couple of times around Tiananmen Square, then turned north up Nanchang Street, flanked on one side by the Forbidden City and Zhongnanhai on the other. Trees on either sidewalk grew across it to intermesh and create a tunnel shading it from the late season sunshine. People were going about their everyday lives, cycling to and from work, shopping, walking, chatting idly on corners or on benches, playing chess, flying kites. It seemed wrong, somehow, that their world kept turning as it always did, while his had turned to dust under his feet. His inertia, his inability to decide his next move, was building a frustration in him that was threatening to explode. He beeped his horn fiercely at a cyclist who turned out of the Xihuamen intersection and Li accelerated past him into Beichang Street. There was nowhere else for him to go but Section One. Even if he was impotent to do anything, to be in any way pro-active, Qian and Wu were not. They were still actively involved in both the Ripper case and the Lynn Pan murder. They could still make a difference. He had to talk to them.

Another fifteen minutes found him on Dongzhimen, heading east, past all the red lanterns hanging from the trees, past street vendors steaming huge trays of dumplings in preparation for the lunch trade that was already starting to gather pace. Men and women in suits streamed out of office blocks and shops and into restaurants, wrapped in warm coats against the cold of the wind, wearing sunglasses to protect them from the blinding autumn sun. Li saw Mei Yuan on her corner as he turned into Hepinglidong Street. He remembered her wet face and red eyes and her distress while Li Jon was still missing. In their own distress, both he and Margaret had not fully appreciated the hell that Mei Yuan must have gone through, believing it all to be her fault. He could see that her eyes were still swollen and red as she served a queue of customers. She did not see him as he turned north, and then west into Beixinqiao Santiao to park in the street outside section headquarters.

He had already reached the top floor and was striding towards his office when the duty officer caught up with him. 'Chief,' he called twice, before Li stopped and turned.

The duty officer was a man in his fifties, in charge of security, administration and firearms. 'Yes, Tao?' Li said, although in his heart he knew what was coming.

Tao was red-faced and embarrassed, breathless from having run up the stairs after Li. 'I'm sorry, Chief Li,' he said, and he genuinely was. 'But I'm afraid I can no longer allow you access to the building.'

He took a half-step back, almost as if he was anticipating an explosion. Li was angry, and frustrated, but he knew that Tao was only doing his job. He said, 'I just need to get some stuff from the office.'

Tao seemed almost ashamed. 'Afraid I can't let you do that, Chief. You can't touch anything in here. And I'm afraid I'm instructed to ask you to return any files or documents that you may have taken home with you.'

'In the name of the sky, Tao, I've got personal stuff in there.' He jerked his thumb towards his office, and became aware for the first time that a group of detectives was gathered in the doorway to the detectives' room. He saw a grim-faced Wu amongst them.

'I'm sorry, Chief.' Tao cleared his throat and held out his hand, 'And I'm afraid I have to ask you for the keys to your car.'

Li stared at him. They really were stripping him of everything. No office, no car, no job. No way to fight back. He put his hand in his pocket and took out his car keys and slapped them into Tao's outstretched palm.

'And your tag.'

It was a small, electronic identifier about the size of a cigarette lighter that was read by an infrared security scan as you came in the main door. Li dug it out of his breast pocket and handed it to Tao. Now it was just humiliating. He glanced at the watching detectives. But none of them said a word. He brushed past Tao and headed back towards the stairs. 'I really am sorry, Chief,' he heard Tao calling after him before his footsteps echoing on the stairs drowned out everything else.

In the street outside, he just kept walking, blinking hard to stop the tears from filling his eyes. He was oblivious to everything around him, blinded by anger and fear and impotence, and an acute sense of loss. It was extraordinary how easy it had been to render him powerless. And completely harmless.

In Hepinglidong Street, Chinese flags whipped in the wind outside a barber's shop opposite a huge construction clad entirely in green netting and bamboo scaffolding. A worker with a red hard hat stood on the top of it, a green flag raised in one hand, a red one poised in the other, as a huge steel girder was lifted slowly up the outside of the building by a crane that dominated the sky above it. Its shadow followed at a discreet distance. As far as you could see, looking north, blocks of flats wrapped in green net were in various stages of construction. Li passed the entrance to a crumbling old *siheyuan* courtyard where rusting bicycles nestled under buckled corrugated roofing. There was a tree in the centre of the courtyard, and beyond it you could just see, through its leaves, the windows of Section One.

Someone tugged at his arm. 'Chief.' He looked around and saw Wu struggling to keep up with him.

Li did not break stride. 'What is it, Wu?'

'They told us we weren't to talk to you, Chief.'

'So why are you disobeying orders?'

'You know I never liked taking orders, Chief.' Li heard his grin, and the open-mouthed chewing of his gum. 'Except from you, of course.'

A blue and white wall had been built around the gap site left by the demolition of what had once been a covered food market. Li missed the old Beijing. It had all been comfortingly familiar. Now he felt like a stranger, displaced in an alien city.

'Chief, I can't keep up with you.'

Li stopped and looked at Wu who staggered to a halt and stood gasping for air.

'I had to run to catch you up,' he said by way of explanation.

'Maybe you should give up smoking,' Li said.

'What, and miss the fun of coughing my lungs up every morning?' They stood just looking at each other for a moment. When Wu's smile faded he looked faintly embarrassed. 'We all know you didn't sell that story to the *Youth Daily*, Chief.'

'You know about that?' Li was taken aback.

'Someone's doing a pretty good job of character assassination, Chief.' Then he winked. 'A few of the boys are going to have a quiet word with that journalist. And as for that shit community cop, I've already called CID to tell them it was the other way around. That guy assaulted me.' He paused. 'The boys are going to have a word with him, too.'

Li shook his head. 'I don't want anyone getting into trouble.'

'You're the one that's in trouble, Chief.'

Li said, 'Wu, I'm not your chief any more.'

Wu's jaw kept grinding away steadily on his gum. 'Yeah, you are. Qian's taken over as acting Chief, but everyone knows it's just temporary. He's staying in his old office. And no one's getting to touch a damned thing in yours until you're back.'

Li felt unaccountably moved, and had to blink back the tears he felt pricking his eyes. He looked away towards Dongzhimen so that Wu wouldn't see them. 'I appreciate it,' he said. He pushed his hands deep in his coat pockets and felt awkward. He looked at the ground. 'So what's happening?'

Wu's face clouded. 'Something you need to know, Chief.' He hesitated and Li looked up, frowning.

'What is it?'

'They've arrested Margaret.'

Li couldn't believe it. 'What?'

'It's really stupid,' Wu said. 'Everyone knows she's been living with you for the last year. But officially she's still supposed to be in that apartment across town at the University of Public Security.'

Li looked towards the heavens. 'In the name of the sky, Wu, they allocated that apartment to someone else more than six months ago.'

Wu shrugged. 'The thing is, officially she never informed her local PSB office. So technically she's in breach of regulations.'

'Which everyone knew about. From the tea boy to the god-damned minister!'

'I guess it's just another club to beat you with, Chief.'

Li saw a taxi in the line of traffic crawling past. He waved it down. 'Where's she being held?'

'Yuetan police station. That's the headquarters for the Western District. It's where she's still registered.'

Li opened the door of the taxi, but paused and turned back. 'Thanks, Wu,' he said.

'Hey, Chief,' Wu said, 'I'll be expecting a big promotion when you get back in the hotseat.'

Li sat in the back of the taxi watching the city drift past him without seeing it. Someone was trying to dismantle his life, piece by piece by piece. And they were succeeding. He had no job, no car. The life of his child had been threatened, and his lover had been arrested. He felt like a man falling down a mountain, hitting off the rocks, unable to get a hand or a foothold to stop the fall and start the long climb back. He just kept falling. And every time he looked up another rock would smash him in the face. His cellphone trilled. He took it out of his coat pocket and pressed the handset symbol. '*Wei?*'

'Li Yan?'

He knew immediately that it was his father. And he knew that something must be wrong, for his father never phoned him. 'What is it, Dad?' It felt odd to call him *Dad*. He never usually addressed him as anything, and *Father* seemed absurdly formal. But the telephone seemed to require some form of address. He heard a child crying in the background. 'What's happened?'

His father seemed disorientated, his voice shaky and

uncertain. 'I'm going to miss my train back to Sichuan,' he said. 'Your sister did not come home for lunch. I thought maybe she and Xinxin were eating out somewhere and had forgotten to tell me. So I was fixing something to eat for myself when the school phoned.'

'What school?'

'Xinxin's school.' He sounded indignant. 'What other school would it be?'

'What did they say, Dad?' Li contained his impatience.

'They said that Xiao Ling never came to pick up Xinxin. She always picks up Xinxin at lunchtime. They thought maybe something was wrong.'

'Dad, just tell me what happened.'

'I went to the school myself. In a taxi. And when I got back here with Xinxin I telephoned Xiao Ling's work. The neighbour across the landing gave me the number.' Li bit his tongue. Details he did not need to know. 'When I phoned, they said she had been arrested.'

For what seemed like a lifetime, Li could not even seem to draw a breath. When finally he did, all he could say was, 'What?'

'The police raided the Jeep factory this morning and searched all the staff lockers. In Xiao Ling's locker they found cocaine.' The incredulity in the old man's voice found an echo in Li's brain.

'That's not possible.'

'She's a good girl, Li Yan. She would not use stuff like that.'

'Dad, she couldn't *afford* stuff like that,' Li said. Yet another piece of his life being taken apart. Another demonstration of the power his unknown enemy had over him. Another rock in the face. It was not just Li who was being targeted. It was his whole family. He wanted to punch the roof of the taxi, kick the seat in front of him. He wanted to yell and hit out. But instead he held it all inside himself, seething, dangerous.

'Dad, just stay there with Xinxin. Don't answer the door to anyone except me.'

He heard the fear in his father's voice. 'Li Yan, what is happening?'

'Just sit tight, Dad. I'll be there as soon as I can. But it's going to be a while.'

### III

Yuetan police station was on the corner of Yuetan Nan Jie and Yuetan Xie Jie, a block from the park. It was a modern six-storey building with a glass centrepiece on its front facade that rose through five storeys. A Chinese flag flapped in the wind above the red, gold and blue Public Security emblem.

Li climbed the steps and pushed through glass doors into a shining marble lobby. A uniformed policewoman sat at a desk with a telephone switchboard. She looked up with clear recognition in her face as she saw Li approaching. 'I need to talk to the Chief of Police,' he said.

She fumbled nervously with the switchboard and called through to the Chief's office to pass on his request. She listened, and her face coloured slightly. Then she hung up and said, 'Sorry, the Chief's not available.'

Li clenched and unclenched his jaw. 'What floor is his office on?'

She seemed nonplussed. 'The fifth. But he can't see you.'

'We'll see about that.' Li looked around for the stairs but didn't see any. Through double doors was a public office where officials sat behind glass windows administering household and individual registrations. It was where, legally, Margaret should have notified her change of address. Li headed off in the other direction, down a long corridor.

'You can't enter the building without a pass,' he heard the policewoman calling after him. And the sound of her heels clacking on the tiled floor followed in his wake.

He turned a corner and found himself looking through windows into an indoor basketball court spanned by an arched glass roof. He recognised it from the promotional video they had shown at the Great Hall of the People. A recreational facility for the one hundred and twenty-two police officers based here. Three of them, in jogsuits and trainers, were bouncing a ball up and down the court, taking it in turns to shoot baskets. Li turned in disgust and started back the way he had come, almost bumping into the pursuing policewoman. 'Where are the stairs?' he growled.

'I'm sorry, Section Chief,' she said. 'You can't go up there.'

Li wheeled around on his heels to face her. 'Are you going to stop me?' She just looked at him. 'So tell me where the stairs are.'

'There's an elevator at the far side of the lobby,' she said meekly.

'Thank you.' Li strode back into the lobby and crossed it to the brushed chrome doors of the elevator. As he stepped inside and turned to press the button for the fifth floor, he saw the policewoman, back at her desk, lifting the phone. The doors slid shut, and the elevator whisked him smoothly up through five floors to a white-painted landing where gold characters on a dark blue mural urged officers to *Try To Be Best*. Corridors ran off left and right. From the right, a small round man in the uniform of a Superintendent, First Class, emerged from an office with a plaque above the door which read *Logistics*. Beyond him, Li saw a large reception room, and a door into the Chief's office. The logistics officer blocked his way.

'The Chief is not on duty today,' he said. Introductions were not necessary. Clearly he had been the recipient of the phone call from the lobby.

'I'll see his deputy, then.' Li looked along the doors that lined the corridor. At least three of them were labelled *Deputy Chief*.

'Not available.'

'One of them's got to be here.' Li pushed past the little man and started opening the doors of the deputies' offices. The first two were empty. The logistics officer trailed along behind him. The third was empty, too.

'I told you, he's not available.'

'He must be in the building. There always has to be someone in charge of the building.' Li glared at the smaller man. 'I'm not leaving until I see him.'

The logistics officer sighed. 'He's in the gym.'

'The gym? Where's that?'

'It's on the top floor. If you'll just wait a minute I'll call him.' The logistics officer turned back towards his office.

'No time,' Li said, and he strode off down the other corridor. There had to be a stairwell. He found it at the south end of the building, and climbed the stairs two at a time. On the landing the same armed policewoman with whom he had become familiar on the wall of Commissioner Zhu's reception room, gazed down at him from a framed poster. He noticed, absurdly, and for the first time, that she was quite attractive, and he wondered if she was really a policewoman, or just a model dressed up for the photoshoot.

The gym occupied the whole of the top floor. A telephone was ringing, unanswered. There were three table-tennis tables, a pool table, a row of comfortable leather armchairs lined up against the end wall. Sunshine streamed in windows all along one side. The walls were lined with photographs of winning police football teams. At the far end was an impressive collection of muscle-building machinery and aerobic exercisers. At first Li thought it was deserted, then the clang of heavy weights from the other side of the gym attracted his attention. The Deputy Chief was dressed in shorts and a singlet, reclined on his back along a low bench beneath a stand supporting a bar with transferable weights on either end. With upstretched arms he was lifting the bar from its cradle, and then lowering to his chest and raising it again in sets of five. Air escaped from his lips in loud bursts, like pneumatic brakes on a truck. The telephone stopped ringing.

Li wandered slowly across the shiny floor of the gym until he was standing almost above the deputy. On the wall was a poster of a golden-haired woman with a man's body wearing a ridiculously tiny bikini top. Opposite was a poster of a young Arnold Schwarzenegger, looking for all the world as if someone had stuck a bicycle pump into some orifice and blown him up. Perhaps it was the Deputy Chief's ambition to look like him. Li glanced down. If it was, he had a long way to go. He had short arms and legs, and a wiry, if muscular, body. He would never be a Schwarzenegger. Li waited until the fifth lift, and then leaned over to stop the Deputy putting the bar back in its cradle. The Deputy gasped, and arms already aching from the lifts started shaking with the strain of holding up the bar. If they gave way, the bar would come down with enough force to crush his chest.

'What the hell do you think you're doing?' he shouted.

Li said quite calmly. 'You're holding my partner and my son, and I want them back.'

'Who the . . . ?' To the Deputy Chief, Li's face was upside down. He tilted his head to one side to get a better look. 'You've been suspended,' he said, and gasped again as the pain in his arms started to become unbearable.

'And you think that gives you the right to fuck with my family?'

'You're through, Li. All washed up.' He groaned. 'I'm going to drop this!'

'You're wrong,' Li said. 'Not about dropping the bar. You probably will. And it'll probably take them days to recover all the bits of rib from your lungs. But you're wrong about me being washed up. Because the charges against me are false. And in a day, or a week, or a month, I will be restored to my rank and position. And when that happens, I'm going to make your life so unpleasant you're going to wish you'd dropped this bar on your head.'

'Okay, okay, okay!' The Deputy Chief almost screamed. The veins on his arms were standing out like ropes, and Li could see the elbows starting to give. He pulled the bar back in line with the cradle and the Deputy let go of it, immediately wheeling around to sit on the edge of the bench, doubled over, flexing his arms and moaning from the pain of it. 'You bastard!'

'Believe it,' Li said.

The Deputy cast him a sideways glance. 'If I had a witness, you'd go down for this.'

'I want Margaret and Li Jon now,' Li said. 'Or I'll drop the fucking bar on your head myself.' He cast his eyes around the gym. 'No witnesses to that, either.'

The Deputy Chief got to his feet, folding his arms across his chest, and massaging aching upper arm muscles with his fingers. 'We could only have held them for forty-eight hours. And after that it doesn't matter. She'll have to leave the country anyway.'

'What?' Li was caught completely off guard.

A slow, bitter smile spread across the Deputy's face. A

small revenge. 'Didn't you know, Section Chief Li? Your little American lover has had her visa refused. She's got to be on a plane home by Saturday.'

By the time the Deputy Chief of the Yuetan police station was back in uniform he had recovered a little of his dignity and composure. He would not attempt to stop Li from taking Margaret and Li Jon away with him, but it was not something he would forget in a hurry. Li had made himself another enemy. He held himself stiffly as he took Li down to the ground floor and through to the control room. Officers sat behind glass at a bank of computer screens and telephones, in constant radio contact with all the patrol cars in the district.

Li looked around. 'Where are the cells?' He had a grim picture in his head of Margaret behind metal grilles in a locksafe door, sitting miserably on a hard bunk bed cradling Li Jon.

'We don't have cells here,' the Deputy Chief said, imagining the picture that Li had in his head, and bristling at it. 'Suspects are detained in interview rooms, monitored by closed-circuit TV. Nobody gets abused in this station.' They passed a glass-walled detention room and the Deputy stopped outside a door marked *Family Room*. 'She's in here. Normally we use this place to mediate in family disputes. Kind of appropriate, don't you think?' He opened the door.

Margaret was sitting at a highly polished, six-sided table reading her copy of the Ripper book, her coat hanging over the back of her chair. Li Jon was asleep in his buggy beside her. She looked up as the door opened and saw Li. She was on her feet and across the room and in his arms almost before he could cross the threshold. 'Oh, God, Li Yan . . .' Her fingers dug into the back of his neck. 'I've been so scared. I knew you'd come and get me, I knew it.' She broke away and looked at him, tears brimming in her eyes. 'They've refused to renew my visa. They say I have to be out the country by Saturday.'

Li nodded grimly. 'I heard.'

'Can't you do anything about it?'

He shook his head, overcome again by a sense of helplessness. 'I don't know. If the worst comes to the worst, you and Li Jon might have to go back to the States. Just for a few days, until I can get things sorted out.'

The Deputy Chief had been listening intently. Li had no idea if he spoke English or not. But now he waggled his finger at them. 'No, no,' he said. 'You cannot take baby out of country.'

Margaret stared at him. 'Of course I can. He has a Consular Report of Birth Abroad from the American Embassy. That's recognised worldwide as his passport. Even by you people.'

But the Deputy Chief just shook his head. 'No. You did not register baby as foreign resident with PSB. It is law. You must register and pay fee. Consular Report no good now. Baby Chinese. Stay here.'

## IV

'I'm not leaving without him!' Margaret was almost hysterical in the back of the taxi. 'You can't look after him. Jesus Christ, Li Yan, you can't even look after yourself. And then if they won't let me back in the country, and they won't let Li Jon out . . .' It didn't bear thinking about. There was a chance she might never see her son again. 'I won't go!' To make things worse, Li Jon started to cry.

Li closed his eyes. His chest felt bruised, as if someone had taken fists to it. But it was just stress, and the hammering of his heart. For one brief moment, in the gym, he felt as if he had stopped falling, that he had found a ledge on which to steady himself before starting the long climb back to the top. But the ledge had given way beneath him and he was plummeting again, back into the abyss. 'They'll forcibly deport you,' he said. 'Physically put you on a plane. And there's nothing I can do to stop that.'

'I'll take him to the US embassy, then,' she said. 'And once I'm in, I'll refuse to leave. Then the Americans will have to do something about it. After all, as far as they're concerned, we're both American citizens.'

'That's crazy,' Li said. 'It could spark off a diplomatic incident. You could be in there for months. And then even if they did get you and Li Jon out of the country, there's no way you'd *ever* get back in.'

'I'm not sure I'd want to.'

Li looked at her, hurt, wondering what that said about them. About their relationship. Li Jon's wailing was filling the car, and the driver glanced unhappily over his shoulder and turned up the radio. Unaccountably, Margaret burst into tears. She hated the image of herself as some feeble, tearful female, but she had reached the end of her tether, and control was finally deserting her. Li put an arm around her shoulder and pulled her to him.

'My God,' she whispered. 'What are we going to do? What are we going to do?'

'I don't know,' he said, and he brushed away the tears from her face. 'I wish I did.'

Margaret tipped her head to look at him. 'They said you'd been suspended.' He nodded. 'What for?'

'I've been accused of selling the Ripper story to the *Beijing Youth Daily*.'

She looked at him askance. 'You're kidding.'

He shrugged. 'I've also been charged with assaulting a police officer.'

'And did you?'

He managed a half-smile. 'Just a little.'

Which also brought a smile to Margaret's face. But it didn't stay there long. 'Someone's got it in for you?'

'Yeah.'

'Who?'

'Whoever murdered Lynn Pan.'

'And you've still no idea who that is?'

He shook his head. 'It's hard to investigate a murder when you have no office, no car, no detectives and no authority.'

They fell into silence then. Margaret's tears had dried up, her moment of self-pity passing. Li Yan was in even more trouble than she was.

They were heading east on Jinsong Lu in the direction of the Beijing Jeep factory. On their right, row after row of drab, run-down seventies apartment blocks were like old acne scars on the face of the new Beijing. Margaret said, 'Where are we going?'

'Xiao Ling's apartment.'

'Why?'

'She's been arrested for possession of cocaine. My father's looking after Xinxin, and I think he's just about at his wits' end.'

They left the taxi idling in the forecourt amongst the dozens of bicycles huddled together there, as if for warmth. A handful of small boys was kicking a ball about through broken glass that littered the pavings. Li still harboured a sense of shame that his sister and niece should live in a place like this. But she did not earn much money, and the company provided the apartment. She could not afford to move anywhere else. Inside, a toothless old concierge sat behind a grilled window and told them that the elevator had broken down. They would have to take the stairs. As they headed for the open stairgate, Margaret heard her pulling phlegm into her mouth from her lungs and spitting it out on the floor. She held Li Jon tightly to her and followed Li up the steps.

'You don't think there's any way Xiao Ling actually did have cocaine in her locker?' she asked.

'Not a chance,' Li said. 'Even if the timing had been different, I wouldn't have believed it. But on the same day Li Jon's buggy goes walkabout? The same day you have your visa turned down and get arrested? The same day I am accused of things I didn't do and get suspended from duty?' He paused for emphasis. 'I don't think so.' He stopped on the next landing to catch his breath. The years of smoking were still taking their toll. 'He's trying to destroy me. My family, my career. Anything he can do to discredit me, neutralise me. Here, let me . . .' He took Li Jon from his mother's arms to take his turn at carrying him. 'It had been my intention to try to get him before he got me. But I wasn't quick enough off the mark. He got there first.'

They carried on up a stairwell that had once been painted cream, but was now the indeterminate colour of sludge, scarred and peeling. Each landing was cluttered with over-spill from the apartments. Bicycles and bins, cardboard boxes and sacks of refuse. The air was bitter with the acrid scent of urine. 'I never had the chance to talk to you about your father,' Margaret said. Li glanced back at her, frowning. 'We had a long talk when he came to see Li Jon yesterday afternoon. There's stuff you both need to talk about.'

'I don't think now's the time, Margaret.'

'Maybe not. But in my head I can hear you saying that every time I mention it. There's never going to be a good time, is there? For either of you. But until you talk, you're never going to get things fixed.'

'I didn't break them.'

'Perhaps you didn't, but you haven't done anything to help pick up the pieces either.'

Li stopped on the next landing and turned. 'I've tried, Margaret. Many times. But I've only ever cut my fingers.' He wheeled away to the door at the far end of the landing, and knocked sharply. They heard running footsteps, and the door flew open to reveal a red-eyed Xinxin. She threw her arms around Li's legs and burst into tears. 'They've taken my mommy,' she cried. 'Uncle Yan, they've taken my mommy.' And she craned her neck back to look up at him. 'You'll get my mommy back, Uncle Yan, won't you?'

'Sure, little one,' Li said, with a confidence he did not feel.

Margaret stepped up to take the baby. 'Your uncle will sort everything out, Xinxin. Don't worry, it's all just a mistake.'

Xinxin transferred her hug to Margaret, clinging to her in something like desperation. 'I want my mommy, Magret. I want my mommy back,' she whimpered.

Li's father appeared in the hall. He seemed to have aged in just twenty-four hours, and looked blanched and shrunken, and very fragile. Li said, 'Get your coat and your hat. Are you all packed?'

He nodded. 'I was ready to leave for the train.' He raised his left wrist, and his watch looked very large on it. He squinted at it. 'I have missed it now.'

Li crouched beside his niece. 'Xinxin, I need you to go and pack some underwear and some clothes. Quickly. You're coming to stay with me and Margaret until we get your mommy back.'

'I'll give her a hand,' Margaret said, and she took Xinxin's hand and they hurried off to her bedroom.

Li and his father stood staring at each other. They were within touching distance, and yet the gap between them was apparently unbridgeable. Li said, 'I'm going to have to take you to a hotel.'

The old man examined the floorboards for a while, then said, 'Can't even find room in your home for your own father.'

Li said, exasperated, 'It's an apartment for one, Dad. With Margaret and the baby and Xinxin, you'd have to sleep on the floor. I'll take you to one of those big international hotels. You'll be safe there, and comfortable.'

'And on my own,' he said. 'Just as well I'm used to it.'

Li sighed. It was an emotional complication he did not need. 'I'll get you booked on a train home tomorrow.'

But the old man shook his head. 'I will not go home until I know that Xiao Ling is safe and that she and Xinxin have been reunited.'

It was well past the lunchtime logjam, though too early for the evening rush hour, but still the traffic in Jianguomenwai Avenue was surprisingly light. A traffic cop with white gloves stood pirouetting at the intersection with Beijingzhan Street, waving through a huddle of cyclists. Away at the bottom end of the street the clock towers of Beijing Railway station caught the dipping sunlight as it swung westwards. On the north-east corner of the intersection, the three great concave arcs of the Beijing International Hotel swept up through twenty-two floors to a revolving restaurant on the top. Their taxi swung around a semicircular drive to pull up at the red carpet of its chrome, glass and marble entrance. It was beyond anything in old Mr Li's experience. Li took the old man's bag and helped him from the taxi.

'I cannot afford a place like this,' he said.

'Not your problem,' Li said. He paid the driver, and they pushed through revolving doors into a lobby the size of a football field, marble floors reflecting every light in a ceiling studded with them. Every surface seemed to reflect light, and more of it spilled through floor-to-ceiling windows lining the entrance, falling in great slabs across huge polished desks where assistant managers in immaculate suits sharpened pencils while awaiting enquiries.

Li's father shuffled after him across acres of floor to an end-lessly curving reception desk. A young receptionist in black uniform and white blouse smiled at them, as she had been trained to do, but could not resist a flickering glance to take in the shabby, shambling figure of the old man.

'It's alright,' Li said. 'Our money's as good as any foreigner's.'

The smile vanished from her face. 'Can I help you?'

'I'd like a single room.'

'For how long?'

'One night.'

'Would that be standard or executive?'

'Standard.'

'Smoking or non?'

Li sighed. 'Non.'

The girl tapped at a computer keyboard below the level of the counter. Then she slipped a registration form across it. 'Fill that in, please. And I'll need a credit card.'

Li gave his father a pen to fill in the form. 'How much is it?' he said.

She cocked an eyebrow, as if surprised that he would ask. 'Eighty-one dollars, US.'

'We'll pay when he checks out.'

'I'll still need your card now. It won't be charged to your account until departure.'

Li took out his wallet and passed her his credit card. She took it from him and disappeared to the far end of the counter to swipe it through the machine. 'Eighty-one dollars?' the old man whispered in awe. 'That's crazy.' It was more than he would have earned in a month while he was still teaching at the university.

'It's the nearest hotel to the station,' Li said. 'Even if I can't pick you up tomorrow, you'll be able to get there on your own.'

'And if you haven't got Xiao Ling back . . . ?'

'She'll be fine, Dad. You'll only need one night here.'

The receptionist walked back along the length of the desk and snapped Li's card on to the counter in front of him. 'No good,' she said smugly, taking clear pleasure in her knock-back.

Li scowled. 'What are you talking about?'

'The transaction has been rejected by your credit card company.'

'That's ridiculous! Try it again.'

'I tried it twice, sir. I'm sorry.' But she wasn't.

Li's father stood, pen poised above the registration card. He had not yet got as far as signing it. Li said, 'Can I use a phone?'

The receptionist shrugged and lifted a telephone on to the counter. Li dialled the number on the back of the card, and when he finally got through to an operator demanded to know why they would not process the transaction.

'Your card has been cancelled,' the operator told him.

'Cancelled?' Li was incredulous. He looked up to find the receptionist watching him. 'That's not possible. Who authorised the cancellation?'

'I'm sorry, I am not at liberty to give out that information. Thank you for your enquiry.' And the operator hung up.

Li stood smouldering, angry and humiliated. If they had somehow been able to cancel his credit card, there was a good chance that his bank account had also been frozen. Which meant he would not be able to access any cash, except for the few hundred *yuan* he carried in his wallet. The receptionist was unable to keep the smirk from her face. Li took the registration card from his father and tore it in half. 'We've changed our minds,' he said. And he took his father's arm and led him back across the marble firmament towards the doors.

The old man was confused. 'I don't understand,' he said. 'What's happening?'

'They're fucking with my life, Dad. They're trying to ruin me and discredit me and grind me into the ground.' He took a deep breath to regain his composure. 'I'll have to find you somewhere else to stay.'

'I know what it's like,' his father said. 'They did it to me, too. All those years ago. When I was "hatted" and paraded for public ridicule.' He pulled on his son's arm and made him stop, and looked up into his eyes with a directness Li had never seen there before. He found empathy in them. 'Don't let them break you, son. Not like they broke me. You have to fight them. I know that now. Your mother died fighting them.

And I lived because I didn't. And I've regretted it every day of my life since.'

Every west-facing twisted, knotted branch of every tree was edged with a golden pink. The faces of the old men, normally washed pale with a winter pallor, glowed in reflection of the dying day. Thoughts of cards and chess were turning to the bicycles stacked three deep along the fence, and the cold ride home in the fading light.

Old Dai did not seem unduly surprised to see Li, but was clearly fazed by the sight of his best friend's brother standing there in the park in his fur hat and baggy duffle coat, clutching a battered overnight bag. He gave the older man a long look, then turned back to the final moves of his game. 'You didn't come to play chess,' he said.

'No,' Li said. 'I need a place for my father to stay overnight.'

Dai nodded without taking his eyes from the board. 'Can your father not talk for himself?'

'Yes, I can,' said Li's father.

Dai raised a hand over the board as if about to make a move, then changed his mind. 'I hear you have been suspended, Li Yan.'

'Word travels fast.'

'A word whispered in the ear can be heard for miles.' Dai moved his horse. '*Jiang si le*,' he said, and his opponent gasped his frustration. He immediately stood up and shook Dai's hand, then nodded to Li and his father and headed off towards the bikes. Dai said, 'My apartment is very small.'

Li said, 'So is mine. And Margaret and the baby and my niece are already there.'

'Where is Xiao Ling?'

'She has been arrested for possession of cocaine.'

Lao Dai's head lifted, and his eyes searched Li's. 'So now they are trying to destroy you.'

'Succeeding, too.'

Dai nodded again. 'Of course,' he said, 'Yifu's brother is welcome in my house.' He paused. 'Is there anything else I can do for you?'

Li said, 'You can tell me what I should do?'

Lao Dai shook his head sadly. 'When the blind lead the blind they will both fall into the water.' He thought for a moment. 'The Tao says, overcome by yielding. Unbend by being upright. Be full by being empty.'

Li's father spoke for the first time, surprising them both. 'Those who know the Tao do not need to speak of it. Those who are ever ready to speak of it, do not know it.'

Li almost smiled, in spite of everything. In other circumstances he might have enjoyed being a fly on the wall in Dai's apartment tonight. The two old men were like oil and water. But his father was not finished. He said, 'A wise person makes his own decisions, a weak one obeys public opinion.' He turned his head to look at his son, and in his face Li saw for the first time in his life the encouragement of a father. And he knew that his father was telling him to put his trust in himself.

Dai was packing away his chess pieces. Li said to him. 'Thank you for taking my father. I won't forget it.'

Dai shrugged, without looking at him. 'Don't worry. I won't let you.'

Li turned awkwardly back to his father, and could not think of anything appropriate to say. And to his father's surprise, as well as his own, he found himself embracing the old man for the first time since he was a boy. Then his father had seemed like a giant. Now he was like a child, and Li was afraid to squeeze him too hard in case he broke.

## V

They were holding Xiao Ling in the detention centre at Pau Jü Hutong, a white multi-storey block next to the forensic science building. It was the home of the Section Six interrogation unit. The light was fading, along with Li's confidence, as his taxi pulled up in the *hutong* outside the centre. He could see fires burning in *siheyuan* courtyards, and smelled the sulphurous smoke of the coal briquets which were the standard fuel of the Beijing household. The *hutong* was busy, cyclists returning home from work, motorists inching their way along its crowded length, schoolkids with satchels chatting together in groups, spilling into the roadway and causing a chorus of bells and horns to sound. Their world kept turning, while Li's had frozen on its axis. It was this constant reminder that while other people's lives continued unaffected, he had become like a ghost moving amongst them, unseen, unable to make a difference, trapped somewhere between heaven and hell.

He had expected implacable faces, a thousand reasons

– legal and bureaucratic – for not being allowed to see his sister. But the duty officer had nodded unhesitatingly and told Li to follow him down to the cells. He could have fifteen minutes, he was told.

Xiao Ling rose to her feet when Li walked into her cell, but the light of hope that burned briefly in her eyes died again when the door slammed shut behind him. They had given her white overalls and black canvas shoes to wear. She had no make-up on her face, and her complexion was pasty white, dark shadows smudging her eyes. She searched his face for some clue, some hope. And found neither.

'Why am I here, Li Yan?' she asked quietly.

'You know why.'

'No.' She shook her head vigorously. 'I know that they found cocaine in my locker, and that's what gave them their excuse. But that's not why I'm here, is it?' Li could not find the words to answer her. So she provided them herself. 'I mean, you don't frame up some nobody worker on the production line of a car plant unless you have a good reason.' She paused. 'Like she's the sister of the top crime cop in Beijing.' A pained expression fell across her face like a shadow as she tried to understand. 'Why, Li Yan? What have you done? What have I done?'

He said, 'Did they search anyone's locker other than yours?'

'They didn't need to. They said they had received a tip-off.'

He nodded. 'I know the answer, but I still have to ask you . . .'

'No!' She cut him off, and he saw the hurt in her eyes. 'Of

course not. Do you think I would waste money on shit like that at the expense of my little girl? I nearly lost her once. I won't do it again.' Her eyes shone in the harsh fluorescent light, and she blinked to squeeze the blur of the tears out of them. 'Where is she?'

'Margaret has taken her to our apartment. Dad is staying with Lao Dai.'

She wiped her wet cheeks with her sleeves, and he saw the resentment in her face. 'You still haven't told me why.' She thrust her chin out defiantly, determined not to let her emotions get the better of her.

'Because I'm close to discovering the identity of a killer high up in Public Security. And he's trying to destroy me before I can get any closer.'

She drew a deep, faltering breath. 'It's always about you, isn't it? You have always put yourself ahead of us. Always.'

'Xiao Ling, that's not true.' Li felt the sting of her accusation more acutely because perhaps there was a grain of truth in it.

'You went off to Beijing to make your career and left me to look after Dad.'

'And you got married and left him to go off and live with some brute farmer.'

'It wasn't my place to stay at home!' Xiao Ling bridled with righteous indignation. 'It was my duty to go and live with the parents of my husband.'

Li bit his tongue. He could have accused her of deserting her daughter for the chance of a son. He could have charged her with running away from her husband, and abandoning her father. He could have denounced her as selfish and deceitful. All of which would have been true. None of which had led her to a cell in the detention centre in Pau Jü Hutong. He swallowed his anger. 'I'm going to try to get you out of here,' he said. 'But it won't be easy. They've suspended me from my job, and they're trying to discredit me.'

She looked at him in disbelief. 'If they can do that to you, then what hope in hell do I have?'

'Not much,' he said, his anger finally getting the better of him. They were as different as two people can be who came from the same womb. They had always fought, and she had always infuriated him. 'But I'm the only fucking hope you've got. So don't fight me, Xiao Ling, don't blame me. Help me!'

She glared at him defiantly before the little girl in her bubbled to the surface and her lower lip quivered. 'Just get me out of here, Li Yan. Just get me out.'

By the time he came back down the ramp into the *hutong*, it was dark. The temperature had dropped, and there was a mist rising from the land. Headlights caught it in their beams, and raked the treelined alley, catching icy cyclists and hunched pedestrians in their frozen light. Li slipped his cellphone from his pocket and flicked through its address list. The battery was low, and the light which illuminated the tiny screen flickered in the dark. He found the number he was looking for and pressed the dial button. He put the phone to his ear and listened to the musical sequence of digital numbers, and then the long, single rings. It was answered on the third, and he asked to speak to Pi Jiahong. The girl asked for his name and told him to hold. After a long wait he heard Pi's voice. 'Hey, Li Yan. Long time.' They were old friends. But his voice did not carry an old friend's warmth. He sounded strained and cautious. They had spent their first two years at the University of Public Security together before Pi dropped out to take a law degree at Beida. Now he was one of the most dynamic of Beijing's new breed of criminal lawyer.

'I need your help, Pi.'

'What?' Pi tried to sound jocular. 'The chief of Section One needs *my* help?'

'I've been suspended, Pi.'

There was a brief silence. Then, 'I heard,' Pi said quietly.

Li wondered why he was not surprised. He remembered Dai, in the park, saying, *A word whispered in the ear can be heard for miles*. 'They've arrested my sister for possession of cocaine. They found it in her locker at work. It was a plant, Pi. They're holding her at Pau Jü. She needs legal representation.'

There was a longer silence at the other end. 'I'm kind of busy right now, Li. A heavy case load.'

'I need someone to bail her out,' Li said.

'I can recommend someone . . .'

'I'm asking you.'

Another long silence. 'Li, I'll be honest with you. I'm hearing stuff about you. I don't know whether it's true or not. Probably isn't. But you know how it is. Shit sticks.' He paused. 'And it rubs off.'

Li felt a band of tension tighten around his forehead. His

throat was dry and swollen. 'I'll bear that in mind, old friend,' he said.

'Aw, come on, Li, don't be like that. . .'

The cellphone battery gave out and cut him off, saving Li the trouble. Li thrust the phone in his pocket, wrapped his coat tightly around himself, and set off north towards the Yong Hegong Lamasery and East Andingmen Avenue, where he could get a taxi. It was a long walk in the cold and the dark. Long enough to reflect upon betrayal and lost friendships, upon tears and hopelessness. Long enough to think about Margaret's deportation, about his son, his family, his own powerlessness to alter this course of events. It was far, far, too long a walk.

It took Li another half-hour to get back to the apartment. Conscious of his dwindling resources, he took the subway from Yong Hegong. Three *yuan* instead of thirty in a taxi. The underground train was jammed to capacity, and Li stood clutching the plastic overhead handle, pressed on all sides by fellow Beijingers on their way home from work, some reading papers or books, others listening to music on their iPods, a young couple holding hands. But he didn't hear them or feel them or smell them. He was isolated and insulated, trapped in a bubble, removed from real life. And it was almost as if he was invisible to them. No one looked at him. No one thought twice about a tall Chinese in a black coat, swaying with the crowd in the Beijing metro. He was just one of more than a billion. What difference could he possibly make? He might as well not exist.

He got off at Wangfujing and walked down to the Grand

Hotel. The subway beneath Changan Avenue was deserted. Several of the lights were not working, and it was dark. He heard a sound behind him and turned quickly. But there was nobody there. Just an echo from the far stairway, and his own feeble shadow on the wall. But, still, it left his heart pounding, and he realised just how far he had fallen that he was scared now of his own shadow.

When he turned into the ministry compound, just past the Chung Fung restaurant, he thought that the guard cast him an odd look. Did they all know? Even down to the lowest ranking guard on night shift? Had he really become such a pariah? Or was he just being paranoid? He glanced up the street towards his apartment block and saw a familiar vehicle parked outside the main entrance. It was a Section One Jeep. A panic gripped him, and he started running. He stopped briefly as he reached the Jeep, but there was no one inside. He ran up the steps and into the lobby. The elevator was there, its door standing open, the floor littered with cigarette ends, the smell of stale cigarette smoking clinging to every porous surface. The ride to the fourth floor took an eternity. He fumbled to get his key in the lock, and when he got into the apartment found Margaret already halfway to the door.

'What is it? What's happened?' he said.

'It's alright,' she said. 'Qian is here. He just arrived.'

Li looked beyond her into the sitting room and saw Qian standing awkwardly by the window. Xinxin was sitting on the floor with baby Li Jon propped between her legs watching television.

'Are you alright?' Margaret said. 'You've been away for ages.'

Li nodded. 'I'm okay. My father's with Lao Dai.' He did not want to get into the whole credit card thing right now. He looked again at Qian and stepped into the room. 'What's happening?' he said.

Qian looked grim. 'William Hart has been found dead in the gardens of his apartment building. Apparently he fell from a window on the twenty-third floor.'

# CHAPTER ELEVEN

## I

Steam rose from sewers through gratings in the road at the China World Trade Center, dispersing in the traffic, lost in their exhaust fumes. Lines of cars moved steadily on to the southbound lanes of the East Third Ring Road, and their tail lights arced off into the night. Li sat numbed in the passenger seat next to Qian.

'You could be in big trouble for this, Qian,' he said.

Qian shrugged. 'I've known you for how long, Chief? Fifteen years? More? I think that qualifies us as old friends. Strictly speaking, I'm off duty right now. So I'm giving an old friend a lift to the apartment of an acquaintance who has been killed.'

Li stared off into the night. He was deeply shocked by the death of Hart. Not just because he was someone he had known and liked, but because he was the last hope for identifying Lynn Pan's killer. Which was no doubt why he was dead. Li felt responsible. He should have warned him. But, then, his day had simply collapsed around him, fallen in with the rest of his world. Hart had been the last thing on his mind.

They turned off at the Jinsong bridge, and Qian was waved through by uniformed officers at the entrance to the Music Home Apartments complex. The gardens which Li and Margaret had walked through just twenty-four hours earlier, were jammed with people. Police and forensic vehicles were pulled up at the north-west tower. The whole area was floodlit, and people from the other apartments and the shopping plaza were pressing up against a cordon of officers determined to keep them back. Li and Qian abandoned the Jeep and pressed through the crowds to be let under the tape by the officer in charge of crowd control. They hurried along the path and through a curve of covered walkway that spanned the stream. Hart had fallen on to an area of white tiled concourse around a rocky pond. There was a lot of blood, stark and red against the white of the tiles. His torso was unnaturally twisted, and his arms and legs lay flung out from it at odd angles. His left forearm and hand were missing. The skull was split open. Li could hardly bring himself to look. Instead, he tilted his head up to see the lights of the apartment twenty-three floors above. It was a hell of a fall. No chance of survival.

He tilted his head down again and found that the eyes of every officer at the scene were on him. His arrival had caused a spontaneous hiatus in the proceedings. The photographer's flash had stopped flashing. Pathologist Wang was crouched over the body, but twisted around so that he could catch a sight of Li. Officers from his own section stood gawping at him. Forensics officers in their white Tyvek suits squatted motionless around the body where they had been searching for the tiniest pieces of evidence.

The only movement came from the head of forensics, Fu Qiwei, who was walking towards him through a scene frozen in time, as if someone had pressed the pause button on a VCR. He was grinning, his black eyes shining. And he held out his hand to shake Li's. 'Hey, Chief,' he said. 'Got some fucking memo today saying you'd been suspended and that I wasn't to *consort* with you. Who uses a fucking word like *consort*?' He scratched his head as if trying to puzzle it out. 'Anyway. Never got the chance to read the goddamned thing. Catch up on it tomorrow. More important things to do right now.' Li nodded and shook his hand firmly.

'Memo? What memo?' Wang said. 'I haven't even had the chance to look at my mail today.'

'Me neither,' Wu said, stepping out of the bunch of detectives. He looked around. 'I guess we've all been too busy, haven't we?' Heads nodded their agreement, and as if the pause button had been pressed again, the crime scene came back to life. Only Hart remained dead.

Qian whispered in Li's ear, 'Everybody's with you, Chief.'

Li did not trust himself to speak for a moment, then he turned to Wu. 'What's the story, Detective?'

Wu said, 'Everything points to an accident, or suicide, Chief. Hart was in the apartment on his own. Window on the balcony's wide open. His wife was out shopping somewhere with the baby and wasn't home yet. It was a neighbour returning from work who heard the scream. Looked up and there was Hart dropping like a stone.'

'The neighbour heard a scream?'

'That's right.'

'Was that before or after he came out the window?'

Wu shook his head. 'He can't tell. He heard the scream before he saw Hart. One thing's for sure, though, he was alive during the fall. The neighbour says his arms were windmilling like crazy.'

Li closed his eyes, and could only imagine what thoughts must have being going through Hart's mind as he fell to his death, knowing its inevitability. Did those few seconds it took to fall seem like a lifetime, or were they over in a flash? He opened his eyes again. 'There's no way it was suicide or an accident, Wu. Hart was working all day trying to decipher Lynn Pan's graphs. Either he found out who the liar was, or he was getting close to it.'

Qian said, 'So if you were here in your capacity as Section Chief, Chief, how would you want things handled?'

Li said, 'I'd have officers take statements from every resident in the complex. Find out who was in the garden coffee shop at the time, what staff were on duty. I'd talk to the security officer in the lobby – how did the killer get in without coming through security? Check for closed-circuit TV. Check the taxi companies in case the killer came by taxi, or got away in one. Someone, somewhere, saw something, whether they know it or not. Maybe a stranger in an elevator, someone behaving oddly. We need forensics to go through the apartment with a fine-toothed comb. My feeling is that the killer is a real pro, so we probably won't find anything. But people make mistakes.'

Wu looked at Qian, who nodded. 'I'll get on with it,' he said.

'Wu.' Li put a hand on his arm to stop him. 'Where's his wife?'

'In the apartment. There's a female officer with her. She's pretty upset.'

'Maybe I should identify the body for the record,' Li said. 'Save her the trauma.'

Wu shrugged. 'She's already done it, Chief. Insisted on seeing him.'

Li nodded and Wu went off to issue instructions to the other detectives. He turned to Qian. 'I'd like Margaret to do the autopsy.'

Qian raised an eyebrow. 'That might be a bit difficult, Chief.'

Li said, 'The Americans are probably going to request that one of their people do it anyway. And if we move fast, do it tonight, then it'll be a fait accompli.'

'Okay,' Qian said. 'I'll set it up.'

'One other thing, Qian,' Li said. 'I don't want my son and my niece left alone in the apartment. Is there any way we can get an officer to stay with them until after the autopsy?'

Qian shook his head. 'Not officially. I'd never get away with it.' He hesitated. 'But like I said, officially I'm off duty. I'll stay with them. No one'll lay a finger on them while I'm there, Chief. You can count on it.'

Li looked into the eyes of the older man and saw in them only devotion and trust. He wanted to hug him, but all he said was, 'I know.'

*

Lyang was like a shadow, insubstantial, almost transparent. She sat in a trance at the dining table where they should have eaten the previous night, her hands in front of her, fingers interlocked. Her eyes were swollen nearly shut. She turned them on Li as he pulled out a chair and sat down opposite her. The female officer got up and moved away. Forensics were through in the living room, examining the balcony in the minutest detail. It was from one of its windows that Hart had fallen. They had already found damage to the sill, and scuff marks on the polished mahogany floor that Hart and Lyang had been so careful to protect with slippers laid out at the door for guests. Nothing else seemed out of place, Chinese rugs and wall hangings, the stereo switched on, but the music on pause. There was a drink sitting on the drinks cabinet. Untouched. It was one of Hart's faux margaritas. The ice was all melted now. He must have mixed it when he came in. Hardly the actions of a man about to throw himself off a balcony. Perhaps he had put on the music, mixed himself a drink, and then there had been a knock at the door. He'd put the music on pause, put down his drink and let in his killer.

Lyang spoke unprompted, softly, her voice hoarse. 'He called me about two hours ago on my cellphone,' she said, and Li found it hard not to feel an overwhelming sense of guilt when he met her eyes, even although there was no hint of accusation in them. 'He said he thought he had cracked the graphs. That's exactly what he said. I didn't know what he meant, but he didn't want to say any more on the phone. He said he would tell me when we met back here. I was at the supermarket with Ling. I finished the shopping and came straight back.' Her voice tailed off and she pressed her lips together, eyes closed, regaining composure. 'I missed him by about fifteen minutes. The police were already here, along with just about every nosy goddamned neighbour in the complex.'

Li reached across the table and put his hand over both of hers. It was fully a minute before she could bring herself to continue. 'I wish . . . I wish I'd been able to see him one last time. You know, just to appreciate him for the lovely man he was. To let him know that I loved him.' She caught her breath, and closed her eyes to stop herself from weeping. 'Last time I saw him was this morning when he left the apartment. You know how it is. You don't pay any attention. You don't expect to not ever see someone again. I can't even remember how he looked, if I said goodbye, if he was smiling, or if I was. All I can remember is . . . is how he was down there.' She tilted her head almost imperceptibly towards the window.

'You don't have to talk right now,' Li said.

'I want to,' she insisted. A sudden flame of anger burned in her eyes. 'I came back up here and cried like I've never cried in my life. I cried so hard it was physically painful.' She put her hand to her chest. 'I can still feel it, like cracked ribs.' She took a deep breath. 'And there comes a point when you just can't cry any more. Not straight off, anyway. And I got to thinking how I could do something positive. Something Bill would have wanted me to do. So I searched the apartment to see what he had brought home with him. There was nothing here. Nothing in his study. Not even his briefcase. And he always had his briefcase with him. So then I phoned the academy, and they said he had taken everything away with him.' She clutched Li's hand with both of hers. 'They killed him, didn't they?' she said. 'They came in here and threw him off the balcony and stole all his stuff. And we'll never know what it was he found. What he meant when he said he'd cracked the graphs.'

And Li knew she was right. That his last chance of iden-tifying Lynn Pan's killer and understanding why she had to die had gone out of the window with Bill Hart. The killer was going to get away with it. Two people dead. Li's career in ruins, his future and his family torn apart. And not one way that Li could think of to strike back.

For the first time, he let the suspicions he had been sup-pressing for most of the day fizz to the forefront of his mind. There was only one person who knew everything Li knew. Only one person he had told. Commissioner Zhu, that morning in the Commissioner's apartment. The Commissioner had subsequently spoken to the Director General of the Political Department, Yan Bo, but how much had he told him? Enough to prompt him to warn Li off. But how much had Yan Bo known about Hart? When the Commissioner had asked Li how he intended to find out who the liar was, he'd told him, *I've asked Bill Hart to gather together all the various pieces of information necessary to make that apparent.* Li felt ill at the thought that those words might have sealed Hart's fate.

And then there was the empty pack of Russian cheroots in the trash in the office of the Commissioner's secretary. The same brand as those found beside the Ripper victims, the same brand that forensics had retrieved from the crime scene at the Millennium Monument. Zhu would have had full access to the files on the Ripper murders. Hadn't the Commissioner himself asked Li for daily reports? He would have known what brand of cheroot had been found at the Ripper crime scenes. Easy enough to buy a pack at any tobacconist's, leave one at the scene of Pan's murder, dispose of the rest. But it was careless of him to throw the empty pack in the trash. Was it a sign of his arrogance, his supreme confidence that he was untouchable? Or did he simply just never envisage a circumstance in which it might have been seen there?

And who else would have had the power to engineer Li's suspension, to take his life apart the way it had been? There wasn't anything about Li he wouldn't know. He had his mole in Li's section, his informant, someone who would keep him in touch with everything going on in that office. Li realised he would probably never even know who that was.

There was something else which had been troubling him. A memory from that afternoon at the academy when he and the Commissioner had been briefed together on the murder for the MERMER test. A picture in Li's head of the ease with which the Commissioner had handled the murder weapon, a large hunting knife serrated at the hilt. *You look like you were born with one of those in your hands*, he had said to him. And the Commissioner had told him about his hunting trips with his father in the forests of Xinjiang Province. *We killed the animals by slitting their throats*, he had said. *My father taught me how to gut a deer in under ten minutes.* He knew how to use a knife. How easy would it have been for him draw a blade across Lynn Pan's throat?

All of which brought him back to the single, most troubling question of all. *Why?*

Lyang's voice dragged him away from his darkest thoughts. 'Li Yan . . .' He looked at her. 'Don't leave me alone. Please. I don't think I could face a night here on my own.'

'Lyang . . .' Li squeezed her hands. 'We need to establish . . . we need to know that Bill was pushed.'

'You mean an autopsy?' She seemed almost matter-of-fact about it. And Li remembered that she had been a cop. She knew the procedure.

He nodded. 'I'm going to ask Margaret to do it.'

And something about that thought made the tears fill her eyes again. It was some moments before she could speak. 'I'm glad,' she said. Then even through her pain and tears she found something to make her smile. A memory of the character that her husband had been. 'He'd have enjoyed the irony.' But the smile was short-lived, and she bit her lip.

'We'll come over here afterwards, with Li Jon and my niece, Xinxin. Spend the night if you want.'

'I'd like that.'

And from the bedroom they heard the sound of baby Ling crying. Tears, perhaps, for the father she would never know.

## II

Li stood on the steps of the pathology department watching the headlights of vehicles probing the mist on the Badaling Expressway. Above it, the sky was inky dark, the stars clearer out here on the fringes of the city, away from the lights and the pollution. He cut a faintly absurd figure in his green smock and shower cap, but he was oblivious of his appearance, even if there had been anyone there to see him. There were only a few vehicles in the car park, one or two lights in windows dotted about the dark frontage of the building. A minimum staff on night shift. He had needed air before he could face the autopsy. There had been too many familiar faces recently staring back at him with dead eyes from the autopsy table. It had been only yesterday morning that Lynn Pan had come under the pathologist's knife. Now Bill Hart. Li remembered the soft, seductive voice teasing the confession from the child abuser. Hart himself had described the polygraph as a psychological rubber hose. But that was not how he had used it. He had found empathy with his subjects, made a connection between them with his simple humanity. He had not deserved to die like this.

Li took a last lungful of ice cold air, and turned back into the building.

Margaret looked up as he came through the door into the autopsy room. Their eyes met briefly in common bond. Pathologist Wang stood on the opposite side of Hart's shattered body. Wu leaned against a wall watching from a distance.

Margaret had performed autopsies before on people she knew. But somehow this was much more distressing. She had hardly known Bill Hart, but something about his sense of humour had chimed with her. And their history, although short, had been so recent. Just twenty-four hours ago he had been wiring her up for a polygraph test she never took. A battle of wits they had never fought. And she remembered with a jolt her wisecrack at lunch that first day they met. He had offered to prove the efficacy of the polygraph by giving her a test, and she had agreed, but only if he would let her give him an autopsy. Everyone around the table had roared with laughter. He had never given her that test, but she was about to perform the autopsy. It seemed now like a sick joke.

She closed her eyes for a moment to drag her professionalism back from the edge of despair. When she opened them again, she took in the broken body that lay on the table in front of her and wiped all memory of Bill Hart from her mind. His head was markedly misshapen, with open comminuted fractures of all the cranial bones, and wide lacerations over the scalp. Multiple blunt force injuries is how she would describe them in her report, but the words were insufficient to describe the devastation.

His teeth were in good repair and, remarkably, undamaged, but the maxilla and mandible bones of the jaw were both fractured. There was blood in his mouth and nostrils, and his lips were blue. She spoke up for the benefit of the microphone recording her external examination.

*The neck has been rendered asymmetrical due to fractures. There are faint and poorly defined areas of ecchymosis about the neck, and there is palpable bony crepitance on rotation of the base of the head.*

'He landed on his head by the looks of it,' she said and glanced up to see the pain in Li's eyes.

*The chest is also markedly misshapen by fractures of all of the ribs and a wide laceration that crosses from the left shoulder area over to the right lower chest, through which there is avulsion of muscle and portions of rib and internal organs.*

Somehow in the fall, there had been a traumatic amputation of the left forearm and hand. The autopsy assistant handed it to Margaret in a plastic bag.

*The recovered distal left upper extremity is received separately in a red plastic bag, and comprises the distal forearm and hand. The medial aspect of the wrist bears abraded laceration, and the third and fourth nailbeds bear subungual haematoma. There is a pink, flaky material with the appearance, possibly, of skin under the left third and fourth fingernails.*

Margaret turned to examine the right hand.

*The nailbeds of the right first and fourth fingers show red-purple subungual haematoma, and the index fingernail is torn.*

'Is there significance in that?' Li asked, detecting her concern.

'It means that he put up a hell of a fight not to get thrown out that window. I think we'll find his attacker's DNA in the skin under his fingernails.' She didn't want to think about his panic in those last moments as he fought desperately to stay alive, and she moved quickly to the legs, only to find more evidence of his struggle. She fought a different battle, to control the emotion in her voice.

*There is a patterned abraded contusion crossing the anterior right thigh. This 3 x 1-½ inch, horizontally oriented area bears vertically oriented striations within the abrasion, and contains what appears to be splinters of wood and varnish.*

Almost identical abrasions were evident on the left thigh, above multiple fractures of the femur, tibia and fibula. She turned to Wang. 'Not sustained in the fall. Do you agree, Doctor?'

Wang nodded. 'Bruising too defined,' he said. 'Dark purple, compared with other bruising, which is not so dark, not so defined.'

'And almost symmetrical. Pretty much consistent with him being forced out of the window,' Margaret said. 'Bracing himself against the sill, but being manhandled over it.'

They moved on to the internal examination, where the injuries were even more horrific. There was not much left of the lungs or the heart, the pleural and pericardial cavities having been lacerated by the multiple fractured rib ends, as had the diaphragm and the peritoneal cavity. The spinal column was completely severed. It was a catalogue of fractures – cranial, facial, spinal, the pelvis, the arms, the legs. Most of the organs had been lacerated or torn apart by the force of the impact.

'There's no doubt, then?' Li said finally.

'You know pathologists never like to commit themselves,' Margaret said. She looked into Bill Hart's clear, open, undamaged eyes, and remembered the life and mischief with which they had once shone. She raised her eyes to meet Li's. 'But if you're asking me, he didn't jump.'

She moved away from the table, pulling down her mask

to suck in air. She had had enough, and was content to let Wang finish up. 'I need to shower,' she said to Li. 'I'll meet you in the lobby.'

She stood under the jets of hot water, letting them run freely over her upturned face and streaming down her body, soaking away a little of the tension that held her in its grip. It was probably the last autopsy she would ever perform in China. She had no idea if she would be on an airplane back to the States on Saturday, or cooped up at the US Embassy with her baby son. Neither scenario was one that she wanted to entertain. Nor could she face the thought of another autopsy back home. If that was where she ended up. She had seen more than enough death to last her a lifetime. Perhaps it was giving birth that had changed her. The creation of life, as opposed to picking over the remains of it. Whatever it was, right now she no longer had the stomach for it.

She let her fingers trace the scar of her Caesarian. It was still hard to believe that by cutting her open they had brought life into the world. Her son. And her thoughts turned to his father. Only now, faced with the prospect of losing him, did she realise how unthinkable it was. However unsatisfactory their life here might have been, at least they had been together. And in the end it was that having, that belonging, which mattered most. She wished she could do more to help him, but other than her job she had no idea what. She was as helpless in the face of his faceless enemy as he was.

She dried herself vigorously with the towel and slipped back into jeans and sweatshirt, pulling on her trainers, and drowning herself in the warmth of a large, quilted anorak. Li was waiting for her in the lobby and took her in his arms in a long, silent hug, cradling her head against his chest. She felt small like that, all wrapped up in him, safe from the world and everything out there that was trying to harm them. But she knew it was an illusion. No one was keeping Li safe from harm.

'Section Chief.' The voice made them break apart, and Li turned to see the head of the pathology lab crossing the lobby towards them, double doors swinging in his wake. Professor Nie Rong was a tall, skinny man, with tiny lozenge-shaped spectacles perched always below the bridge of an unusually long nose. The few strands of hair that remained to him were carefully arranged across his great, bald dome. His white lab coat flapped open as he walked, and Li wondered what the head of the laboratory was doing here at this time of night. He seemed oddly reticent, reluctant to meet Li's eye. He shook hands with Margaret, and then folded his arms across his chest, still clutching a well-thumbed folder in his left hand. Li speculated on whether he might be embarrassed by Li's presence at the facility. He must have heard that he had been suspended. 'I'm sorry,' the professor said. 'There's no easy way to say this . . .'

'If you're going to ask me to leave,' Li said, 'we're just going.'

'No,' the professor said hastily. 'It's not that. I . . . I'm afraid there's been a fuck-up in the lab.' It was so unusual to hear the normally mild-mannered and polite head of pathology use such language that Li was startled. 'I'm sorry,' he said again, this time reverting to English and inclining his head towards Margaret. 'You ask for DNA profile in big hurry yesterday.'

Margaret frowned, flicking the still wet curls from her face. 'You mean the sample from the cigar butt found by Lynn Pan's body?'

He nodded. 'We tell you is different from DNA found at other murders.'

Margaret looked at him, mystified. 'So what's changed?'

'Lab assistant mix up samples. DNA same as other murders.'

Margaret immediately looked at Li. 'Jesus,' she whispered, the implications of what the professor had just told them striking her like a slap in the face. She turned back to him. 'You sure?'

'Sure, I'm sure.'

Li was finding it hard to take on board. 'But if that's true, then Pan's killer is the same person who killed the four prostitutes. The Beijing Ripper.' All the distinctions he had drawn between the Ripper killings and the Pan murder came tumbling down around his head.

Professor Nie moved on quickly, perhaps hoping to distract and deflect from the appalling error committed by his lab. He waved the folder in his hand. 'Also we have positive DNA match between kidney sent to you and victim number four. And comparison of notes? One with kidney, one with ears? Calligraphy expert believe written by same hand. But no matter. We make chemical analysis of red ink. Same in both. Paper same, too. Ve-ery distinctive watermark.'

*

On the steps, Margaret took Li's arm, and noticed that the crescent of moon was almost imperceptibly bigger tonight. 'So,' she said. 'The Beijing Ripper is a cop. Makes sense, I guess.'

A tidal wave of thoughts he had been diverting elsewhere as a result of the DNA test were flooding back into Li's head. The Ripper had known Li's name, and the address of Section One, to be able to send him the half-kidney. Just as Pan's killer had known his home address and had access to the ministry compound. And he recalled Lao Dai's words in the park when he first described to him the nature of the murders. *You have an enemy, Li Yan*, he had said. And in response to Li's incredulity, *This man is not killing these girls only for the pleasure of it. He is constraining himself by following a prescribed course of action. Therefore there is a purpose in it for him beyond the act itself. You must ask yourself what possible purpose he could have. If he does not know these girls or their families what else do all these murders have in common?* The police. That is what Old Dai had said. And Li. Someone with a grudge against him. Jealousy or revenge. What had never occurred to either of them was that the killer himself might also be a policeman. 'Commissioner Zhu,' Li said.

'What?' Margaret looked at him, startled.

'He attended the lecture given in Beijing two years ago by Thomas Dowman, the Jack the Ripper author. He knew all about the original Ripper murders, and he personally asked for daily reports on our progress on the Beijing killings.'

Margaret pulled a face. 'Probably half the ministry went to that lecture.'

'He's an expert with a knife. He told me himself his father

taught him how to gut a deer. They poisoned the animals with salt and then slit their throats.'

Margaret cocked an eyebrow. 'That's a little more convincing,' she conceded. And she recalled Dai's comment on him the night he made the speech at Li's award ceremony. *He does not much like our young friend. He is full of praise. Noisy praise, like a drum with nothing inside it. He says only good things of Li Yan. His tone is honeyed, but there is vinegar on his tongue.*

'He's the only one I told about Hart examining the graphs to try and establish the identity of Lynn Pan's liar,' Li said.

But Margaret was shaking her head. Still none of it really made sense. 'But what was the lie she caught him in? I mean what could she possibly have found out about him in the course of those tests? That he was the Beijing Ripper? How?'

Li's head hurt. He tried to shake it free of confusion. 'I don't know. I just don't know.' In spite of all his schooling in the traditions of Chinese detective work, Li still needed a motive. The killing of all those young prostitutes. *There is a purpose in it for him beyond the act itself*, Dai had said. What purpose? To leave Li drowning in a sea of murders he could not solve? To undermine and discredit him? Did the Commissioner really dislike him so much? Li knew, because Zhu had made it clear, that he did not approve of Li's award, or the use of his image to spearhead the ministry's poster campaign. But it hardly seemed a motive for murder.

And then the image returned to him of the figure in the CCTV video crossing the hall in the EMS post office. A tall figure, like Zhu. Slightly stooped. Like Zhu. He closed his eyes and let the air escape slowly from his lungs through slightly pursed lips. What a fool he had been to trust him.

III

The area around the window in the balcony had been taped off. Lyang had been told not to touch anything in that part of the living room. But forensics were long gone. So, too, the crowds in the gardens below. The management had sent someone out to clean the blood from the paving stones. A woman in a blue overall with bleach and a bucket of hot water. She had been at it for nearly an hour, but the stain was still visible, however faintly. Which would not do at all. Li had no doubt that a team of workmen would be there first thing in the morning to tear up the old pavings and lay new. It would not do to have the blood of one of its residents staining the reputation of the complex, a constant reminder to all the others of the tragedy which had taken place there. It was the kind of thing that could lower the value of property. And no one would want that.

Li moved away from the kitchen window, carrying with him the three glasses of Bill Hart's scotch that he had brought in to dilute with water. It was how Bill said true scotch should always be drunk, Lyang had told them. A little water to release the flavour. No ice. That killed the taste. Lyang was sprawled at one end of the settee, her left leg folded up to her chest, an arm around it to hold it there, a cigarette burning in her free hand. It was her first cigarette, she confessed, since the day they told her she was pregnant. It had seemed so important, for the baby's sake, to give up. Now that she was the only one affected by it, she didn't give a damn. 'Bill would have been horrified,' she said, and then bit her knuckle to stop herself crying.

Li handed her a scotch. It was her third. On an empty stomach. And they were large ones. They were all feeling the effects of fatigue and stress, emotionally drained, physically tired. And the alcohol was providing relief and the promise of oblivion. Except for Li. He felt the whisky burning his stomach, but his head remained painfully clear. It was nearly midnight. An hour ago he could barely keep his eyes open. Now he was beyond tired. He knew he would not sleep tonight.

Margaret was curled up in one of the armchairs. She and Lyang had hugged and cried, and now she, too, was drained. Completely exhausted. Looking back, the events of the day seemed to her like a nightmare. Usually you woke up from a nightmare. Margaret knew that only sleep would provide an escape from this one. Alcohol offered her a route to that escape, and she was only too happy to take it. Xinxin was sharing a bed with Ling, and Li Jon was in Ling's old cot. They had agreed that Margaret would sleep with Lyang, and Li would take the settee. They had talked and talked, at first about Bill and the case, and then about nothing of any consequence at all. Margaret raised her glass. 'I'm for bed when I've finished this.' And she drained it in a single pull. 'Which is now.'

'Me, too,' Lyang said, and she also drained her glass.

Margaret eased herself out of the armchair and waited as Lyang got unsteadily to her feet. They knew she had been drinking before they got there, and although she seemed quite lucid, its physical effects on her were obvious now. She half staggered across the room, and Margaret put an arm around her to guide her towards the stairs. Margaret glanced back at Li. 'Will you be okay?'

He nodded and took a sip at his whisky and listened to their uncertain progress up the stairs. He heard them in the hallway overhead, and then their voices distantly in the master bedroom. After a few minutes there was only silence. Li got up and turned off the lights and stood gazing out over the city. There was a time, not so long ago, when the power supply had been erratic, unpredictable. Demand greater than production. Now there seemed a limitless supply of power to burn. To waste. When he had first arrived here from Sichuan nearly twenty years ago, Beijing had shut down at night. Early. There had been very little to entertain a young man beyond his studies. Now the city never slept, and tonight Li knew he would keep it company.

He took another sip of his whisky and looked around the room in the city's reflected light at all the things Bill Hart and Lyang had chosen to turn an empty apartment into a home. Every picture, every rug, every item of furniture, a decision they had made. With most people there was a story behind nearly everything you found in their home. A personal story, a history of a life together, memories shared. But what did any of it mean when you were gone? When you took those memories with you, and all that was left were their material remains, meaning nothing, except perhaps to the partner with whom the memories were shared, and for whom they now brought only pain.

Li was almost overcome by a sense of melancholy. He felt an intense sadness for Bill and Lyang. For himself, and a life in tatters. For Margaret, and all the unfulfilled dreams that had led her finally to a one-bedroomed police apartment in Beijing, a partner who was never there, a baby who depended upon her and had stolen her independence. A life that was no longer her own.

And he thought of his sister lying awake on a hard bunk in a cell somewhere in the north of the city, shut away from her life, removed from her daughter. And Xinxin, stifling her tears to look after baby Ling and her tiny cousin, taking on a mantle of responsibility she had yet to grow into. Like life itself, there was no way to take back a lost childhood.

He wondered, too, if his father was asleep. In a strange house, with a man who didn't like him much, his dead brother's best friend. And he remembered that unexpected moment between them when they had hugged, Li scared to squeeze too hard in case he crushed him like a bird.

All these things somehow had Li at their centre. Like satellites orbiting a planet, held there by the force of its gravity, dependent upon it for their very existence. It felt like an enormous burden of responsibility. And he was tired and beaten down, and did not know if he could bear it much longer. He took a long, final drink of whisky from his glass and felt the heat of it snaking its way down inside him. He saw Lyang's cigarettes lying on the table and took one out of the packet. He lit it with her lighter and this time resisted the urge to choke on his first drag. By the time he finished it, it was as if he had never given up. He stubbed it out viciously in the ashtray, angry at himself for his weakness, and lay back on the settee, staring up at the shadows lying across the ceiling above him. They were static, unchanging, but even as he watched they seemed to take shape and form. The shadow of a man, the head of an elephant, a face. He closed his eyes to shut them out and saw the tall, stooped computer image of Commissioner Zhu crossing the hall of the EMS post office. An outline image passing through three hundred and sixty degrees, showing everything but the face. How could he ever prove it? How could he put a face to that faceless figure? How would he ever know what lie he'd been caught in?

Li sat up with a start. He had been so certain he would not sleep, he was shocked to realise he had been dreaming. A strange dream full of frantic running down endless corridors, a ferry boat slipping from its berth, gangplank falling away as Li leapt across the gap only to miss the rail and fall. And fall. And wake, heart pounding, a cold sweat beading across his forehead. The fear of the fall, that endless tumbling sensation, is what had woken him. But there was something else, something hidden in an obscure, cobwebbed corner of his mind. Had he dreamed it? He couldn't remember. Like the dream itself, the memory of it was fading even as he tried to recall it.

Perhaps *because* he was trying to recall it. He swung his legs on to the floor and rubbed his face in his hands, trying instead to empty his mind, to free it from the constraints of imperfect memory. *The Tao says be full by being empty*, he heard Dai say. And suddenly the memory of what his subconscious had been trying to tell him, pierced his consciousness like a spear.

'Shit!' he heard himself say, and he was on his feet immediately. He found a light switch at the foot of the stairs and climbed them two at a time, his slippered feet sliding on the polished surface. He padded along to the end of the hall, hesitated a moment, then knocked softly on the door of the master bedroom. He opened it as Margaret sat upright in the bed. Lyang lay face down beside her, dead to the world. 'What is it?' Margaret whispered, alarmed. She had been as certain she would sleep as Li had been that he would not. She glanced at the digital bedside clock. 3.15 a.m. And she had not slept a wink.

'I need to talk to Lyang,' Li said, and he moved into the bedroom and perched on the edge of the bed beside the sleeping widow. He looked down at her face in profile, all muscles relaxed, her mouth slightly open, and heard her deep, slow breathing. And for a moment he almost decided it could wait until morning. But it couldn't, and he shook her gently by the shoulder. It was fully half a minute before he could rouse her.

'What's so urgent that you have to wake her up in the middle of the night, for God's sake?' Margaret whispered.

'Trust me,' Li said. 'It's important.'

Lyang raised herself on to one elbow, blinking away the

sleep in her eyes. Li could almost see the recollection of the previous day's events returning to her, grief welling up inside, the pain of a hangover already tightening its grip around her head. 'What . . . ?' But she was still barely conscious.

Li said, 'Lyang, I need you to wake up. This is really important.'

He saw her make the effort. 'What is it?'

'Lynn Pan had her own private space on the academy website. What about Bill? He must have had his own space, too.'

Lyang was still trying to clear her head. But even through the fuzziness something connected. 'Jesus,' she said, a part of her husband left indelibly in her vocabulary. 'He did.' And as the implications of that sunk in, 'So maybe he put his files in there to keep them safe.'

Li glanced at Margaret and saw the fire of hope light her eyes.

Lyang sat at the computer by the light of the single lamp on Hart's desk. Her white satin night-dress hung loosely from her shoulders. Her hair was a mess, her face smeared and puffy. Margaret stood behind her, looking not much better, eyes burning and gritty. Li had pulled up the chair from Lyang's desk, and sat beside her. 'How can you access Bill's private stuff from here? He had to go to the academy last night to get into Lynn's folder.'

'He brought a copy of the FTP software back with him last night.' Lyang shuffled through the desk drawers to find the CD, then slipped it into the tray that the iMac had spat out to receive it. She double-clicked the icon and loaded the software on to the hard disk. 'Okay.' She squeezed her temples and let out a long breath. 'Jees, I feel like shit. Can someone get me a glass of water?'

'I'll get it,' Margaret said, and she disappeared out into the hall.

Lyang opened up the *Fetch* programme and entered the academy's FTP address into the dialogue box.

'You know his user name and password?' Li asked.

'Sure. It's *bill.hart*.' She tapped it in, then paused at the password, trembling fingers hovering over the keys. Li heard her breathing become shallower and saw tears gathering in the corners of her eyes. 'He changed his password to *Ling* after she was born,' she said, before finally she was able to bring herself to type it in and hit the return key.

Margaret returned from the bathroom with a glass of water and Lyang drank thirstily, emptying it in one draught. They were now looking at a screenful of icons, all of Hart's personal and private files. Lyang pushed the arrow about the screen until it was hovering over a folder labelled *Pan's Files*. She dragged it to the desktop and it copied on to Hart's computer. She double-clicked to open it. Inside there were thirteen folders, and a computer-shaped icon with the MRM motif in blue within it. Twelve of the folders looked like copies of the ones they had found the previous night among Lynn Pan's files. *Graphs A* to *F* and *Pics A* to *F*.

Lyang flashed the arrow around the screen with frightening speed, opening and closing folders. There were three graph files in each of the *Graph* folders, but instead of being empty, the *Pics* folders now contained jpeg images of all the photographs the testees had been shown during the MERMER demonstration.

Li said, 'Bill told me that one of Pan's students thought she still had those on disk at home.'

'Looks like she came up with the goods, then,' Lyang said. 'We can look at all of these.'

Margaret leaned in closer to the screen. 'But you won't be able to see the graphs, will you? Not without the software.'

Lyang's arrow shot across the screen and double-clicked on the MRM icon. 'Looks like Bill thought of everything,' she said. The computer whirred, and images flashed across the screen as the MERMER software loaded up. 'He'd have known he'd need a copy of this to work with the graphs at home.'

'What's this?' Li stabbed a finger at the thirteenth folder. It was labelled *Report*.

Lyang opened it up to reveal a word-processing document. She double-clicked to open it. A document unfolded on the screen. It was headed *Preliminary Findings, MERMER Demo – Bill Hart*. 'Seems he already started to write up what he found,' Lyang said, and her voice cracked on *found*. She put her hand to her mouth to hold back her emotion, and bit hard on her finger. 'Typical Bill,' she said.

Li pulled his chair closer to read the document which Hart had written.

A careful comparison of the first of the three graphs in each folder with the known sequence of photographs shown to each subject has enabled us to identify which of them was briefed on the murder for the purposes of the demonstration. MERMER responses to the 'probe' photographs, all of which related to the murder, were easily identified on the graphs. As a result, we were able to pinpoint A, B and C as the 'murderers', thereby eliminating them from our attempts to identify subject D, whom Professor Pan had labelled a 'Liar'.

Li sat stunned. He knew who had been briefed on the murder, because he was one of them. And the Procurator General and Commissioner Zhu were the others. Which meant that Zhu was not the liar, and therefore almost certainly not the killer.

'That blows a bit of a hole in your theory about the Commissioner,' Margaret said helpfully. 'Who's left?'

Li said, 'His deputy, Cao Xu, the Deputy Minister, and Yan Bo, the Director General of the Political Department.' And he remembered Yan Bo scribbling in red ink on his notepad.

'Jesus,' Margaret said. 'So now we're climbing even higher up the ladder.'

Li turned back to the screen, agitated now. There was more.

Identifying why Professor Pan labelled subject D a 'Liar' has proven more difficult. Apart from a continuity of response to the 'probe' pictures – that is to say, none of them showed a MERMER response – the graphs relating to the 'target' and 'irrelevant' pictures appear to be anomalous.

And that was as much as Hart had written.

'Is that it?' Li said.

Lyang shook her head, scrolling up and down the page. 'There's nothing else. If he knew more than that he's taken it with him.'

'But what does he mean, *anomalous*?' Li said.

'Hang on,' Margaret interrupted. 'You two are way ahead of me here. Would someone like to explain what *targets* and *probes* and *irrelevants* are? It's like another language.'

Lyang turned towards her. 'Three of the six subjects were briefed on a murder, for the purposes of the demo. When it came to the test all six were shown nine photographs relating to that murder – things that only the ones who'd been briefed would recognise. They're called *probes*. They were also shown nine photographs of things that were known to them – their apartment, their dog, their car. And these are called *targets*. The idea being that the brain's response to these things that are known to them will be the same as the response to the *probe* photographs. In the case of the ones who were briefed, that is. And not, in the case of the other three.'

Margaret was nodding. 'Okay, and let me guess. The *irrelevants* are photographs that don't mean anything to any of them, so they have negative responses to compare to the positive ones.'

'You got it,' Lyang said. 'And they get to see thirty-six *irrelevants*.'

'So what did Bill mean by *anomalous*?' Li asked again.

Lyang rubbed her tired and swollen eyes. 'I don't know. It

may be that they were getting a MERMER response from some of the *irrelevants*.'

'You mean recognising pictures of things they weren't expected to?' Margaret said.

'Exactly,' Lyang said. 'It can happen. Sometimes an *irrelevant* is accidentally known to them. Usually they are given a list of things in advance, so that if they might be shown something they recognise it can be changed before the actual test. That wouldn't have been done for the demo.'

Li was shaking his head, baffled. 'So how could Lynn Pan possibly tell from any of these responses that somebody was lying? I mean, lying about what? Lying how? All they were doing was looking at pictures.'

'Wait a minute, wait a minute,' Margaret said suddenly. She looked at Li. 'You remember Mei Yuan's riddle?' He looked at her blankly. 'The one about the two deaf mutes in the paddy field.'

Li blinked in surprise. 'So she tried that one out on you after all.'

But Margaret wasn't listening. Her mind was racing off on lateral plains. 'Each of them thought he was left in that field on his own,' she said. 'And that the other one had sneaked off with the food or the drink to keep it for themselves.'

'You've lost me,' Lyang said, looking from one to the other through a haze of fatigue.

So Margaret told her the riddle, but didn't wait for her to work it out. 'It was dark,' she said. 'That's why they couldn't see one another. They were both there, and neither of them was lying about it. They were both telling the truth, but they just didn't know it.'

'You've lost me now, too,' Li said.

Margaret was searching for a way to unfuzz her mind, to express herself clearly. She waved a hand at the computer. 'This MERMER thing. It can't tell if you're lying, right? Your brain sees something it recognises, it makes an involuntary response. You record it right there on the graph, and it's plain for everyone to see. You see something you don't recognise, you have no response. That's also on the graph. So it's got nothing to do with lying. But it's got everything to do with telling the truth.'

They were both looking at her, concentrating hard, waiting, still not getting it.

'Don't you see? You can't help but tell the truth, because you have no control over how your brain responds. Lynn Pan must have known there were anomalies in the *irrelevants*. But that's neither here nor there. If you have a MERMER response to something you're not supposed to, well that's just a measure of the imperfect conditions in which the test was being conducted. But if you *don't* have a MERMER response to something you should have, then that's weird. That's really off the wall. That doesn't make any sense at all.'

Light began to dawn in Li's eyes. 'It's one of the *targets*,' Li said. 'He didn't recognise something he should have.' Then he frowned. 'What the hell could that be?'

Lyang said, 'Well, we only have to look at nine photographs in relation to the graph to find out.'

She went into the *Graphs D* folder and double-clicked on the first of the graph icons, and the MRM software decoded the document. A window opened up on the computer screen showing a jagged graph line running from left to right. Using the mouse to capture the scroll bar at the bottom of the window enabled Lyang to scroll through the length of the graph. Its peaks and troughs related to a bar running along the top of the screen which held tiny icons of the images being shown at that moment to the testee. Each image was labelled *probe, target,* or *irrelevant.* So it was a simple matter to compare the graph responses to the *target* pictures, while enabling them to ignore the other forty-five.

Li focused all his attention on the graph. The MERMER responses, indicating knowledge or recognition, were represented by distinctive peaks that stood out well above the average flat response. The tiny icons of the photographic images were hard to make out. Li saw a car, but it just looked like any other ministerial car. No doubt Subject D, as Hart had called him, would have recognised its number plate. He saw the pink and white ministerial apartments where he had called on Commissioner Zhu first thing the previous morning. But there was nothing in that to give away the identity of Subject D. All five of the senior officers who had taken part in the demonstration with Li that day would have apartments in those blocks. Only Li, as by far the most junior officer, was allocated an apartment in the ministry compound. There was a picture of a young man in his late teens or early twenties. A son, perhaps. Li did not recognise him. There was a photograph of the exterior of a restaurant. It was not one Li knew. A favourite eatery, perhaps. Another showed the main entrance of Beijing Police Headquarters in East Qianmen Avenue. Any one of them would have recognised that one. Infuriatingly, there was nothing that indicated to Li the identity of Subject D.

Lyang suddenly stopped scrolling. 'There,' she said. And she pointed at the screen, almost triumphantly. She had followed in the footsteps of her dead husband and found what he found. 'No MERMER.' The graph showed a flat response to a picture clearly labelled *target*, where there should have been a MERMER response.

'What is it?' Margaret squinted at the picture, but it was too small to be identifiable.

Lyang double-clicked on the icon and the photograph opened up on top of the graph to reveal an orange sky at sunset, framed by the branches of trees drawing the eyes towards two serrated towers in silhouette rising against gold-edged clouds.

'What's that?' Margaret asked.

Li frowned. 'I've no idea. Looks like a couple of pagodas.'

'It's the Double-pagoda Temple,' Lyang said, taking them by surprise, and they looked at her to see tears making slow tracks down her cheeks. 'Also called the Yongzuo Temple. I only know because when he first came here, Bill did the whole tourist bit. Dragged me round every tower and palace and tourist attraction in Beijing. And then we did trips. Overnights to places like Xian and Taiyuan.' She nodded towards the screen and wiped away the tears with the back of her hand. 'Which is where that is.' She forced a smile. 'It was typical of Bill. He knew more about China than the Chinese. The twin towers of the Double-pagoda Temple is the symbol of Taiyuan. But if you don't come from there you probably don't know that.'

Margaret said, 'Well Subject D certainly didn't.' She shrugged. 'But I don't see the significance of it. Why were they showing it to him in the first place?'

Li slapped his hand on the desk. 'It has to be his home town,' he said. 'It's the only category of the nine *target* pictures that it would fit. They showed all of us pictures of our home towns.'

Margaret ran her hand back through tangled, tousy hair. 'But why wouldn't he recognise his home town? I mean, if those pagodas are the symbol of the place . . .'

Li sat staring into space, his brain working overtime. Finally he said, 'There can only be one reason he didn't recognise it.' He looked at Margaret. 'It's not his home town.'

She frowned. 'You mean they made a mistake?'

'No. I mean he's not who he says he is.'

Margaret threw her hands out in despair. 'And we don't even know who he's supposed to be.'

Li pressed fingers into his temple, screwing up his eyes in concentration, trying to get his mind to focus. 'That doesn't matter,' he said. 'We can find that out easily enough now.' He was thinking back to the MERMER test itself. Lynn Pan had shown Li a list of his *target* pictures. He knew he was going to see a picture of his home town in Sichuan. She must have shown the man who killed her a similar list. And he must have known that he wouldn't recognise the place that was his home town. Even before she showed him it. And there was nothing he could do about that. His brain would respond in a way over which he had no control. It would tell her the truth, and reveal his lie. She must have known instantly that there was something far wrong. And he must have been watching for it, knowing she would see it, and planning how he would get rid of her even before the test was over.

But if he wasn't who he was supposed to be – a high-ranking officer in the Ministry of Public Security – who the hell was he?

He closed his eyes and tried to picture the three men. Deputy Minister Wei Peng, squat, toad-like, arrogant, a stickler for protocol. Deputy Commissioner Cao Xu, tall, languid, unpredictable. Director General Yan Bo, older, shrunken, a man who enjoyed exercising his power. 'In the name of the sky,' he said suddenly. 'It's Cao Xu! It's the Deputy Commissioner.'

He opened his eyes and found Margaret and Lyang staring at him. 'How can you know that?' Lyang asked keenly. She had a vested interest. This was the man who murdered her husband, or had him killed.

'Because the figure in the video, the one caught posting the parcel with the kidney in it at the EMS post office, was tall.' One hundred and seventy-seven point five centimetres, Forensic Officer Qin had been able to ascertain from the

AutoCAD graphic. Five feet, eleven inches. 'And he took a size forty-three shoe. There's no way either the Deputy Minister or the Director General fit that profile. It has to be Cao.'

'How can you prove that?' Lyang said.

'By finding out where he says he was born. If it's Taiyuan, that pretty much clinches it.'

Margaret was having trouble dealing with the concept, and she recognised the truth of what Mei Yuan had said to her that morning. Li's mind worked better on the practical than the abstract. He could solve a real problem better than he could solve a riddle. 'But if he's not the Deputy Commissioner, who is he?'

'Oh, he's the Deputy Commissioner, alright,' Li said. 'He's just not Cao Xu.'

# THURSDAY INTO FRIDAY

# CHAPTER TWELVE

## I

Li stood on the edge of the concourse and looked at the clock on the west tower. It was six minutes past seven, and the eastern sky was yellow beneath the deep blue of the vanishing night. He shivered, more from fatigue than the cold. He was well wrapped up against that, with his long coat and thick red scarf. He wore a pair of soft leather gloves and a dark blue, soft peaked cap. His breath billowed around him in the chill of the early morning breeze. There were hundreds of people criss-crossing the vast paved square in front of Beijing Railway Station, all of them insulated against the winter air that swept into the city from the icy plains of the Gobi desert. The last breath of autumn before winter set in.

Li seemed to be the only person there standing still. A tall, dark figure surrounded by animation. Anonymous creatures hurrying, heads down, to the station or the metro, to the bus stops or taxi stands. They moved around him, like the currents of a river around a boulder, talking on their cellphones, or setting grim faces towards the day ahead. Women with blue overalls and white face masks were already out with their brooms and shovels, clearing away the detritus of the crowd, raising dust to carry grit in the wind into sleepy eyes. Crowds of travellers, dark-skinned peasants up from the country, sat on the steps atop huge piles of tattered luggage, smoking and laughing and watching the early morning world go by.

Li felt a tap on his arm and found Wu standing there, looking as bad as he felt, if not worse. His hair was unkempt and whipping about his head in the wind, his face pallid and puffy. His moustache seemed even more sparse that usual. Li had phoned him shortly after four a.m. to ask him a favour, and heard a woman's voice in the background. Wu had not sounded too pleased to hear from him. But here he was at the crack of dawn, as arranged, clutching a dog-eared folder. He could have had little more sleep than Li. The nicotine on his fingers seemed more pronounced than usual, and Li surmised that he had spent most of the rest of the night with a cigarette in his hand.

'What did you get?' Li said.

'Everything you wanted.'

'And it's him?'

Wu nodded. 'Yep. Born in Taiyuan City in 1948 and raised in an orphanage in the southern suburbs. It's all in there.' He thrust the folder at Li. 'Everything you always wanted to know about Deputy Commissioner Cao Xu but were afraid to ask.'

'Where did you get it?'

Wu grinned. 'Off the internet mostly. The ministry's own website.' And then his smile faded. 'And the police net. His registration records. If anyone cared to check, they'd know I was in there. So you'd better get this guy or I'll be in as much trouble as you.'

'I'll get him,' Li said grimly. He was no longer fighting a phantom, some elusive, faceless enemy. He knew his man. And the playing field had just levelled off.

'Why do you have to go to Taiyuan City?' Wu asked. 'Haven't you got enough already?'

Li shook his head. 'In the normal course of events I would go straight to Commissioner Zhu. But Cao's done such a good job of discrediting me I'm going to need better proof than a handful of graphs. There are still too many questions I don't have the answers to.'

'And you think you'll find them in Taiyuan?'

'I have no idea. But it seems like the best place to start. At the beginning.'

Li was about to turn away towards the ticket hall when Wu put a hand on his arm. 'Something else you should know, Chief.' Li turned back. 'We finally made contact with that guy, Thomas Dowman, the one who wrote the Jack the Ripper book. Apparently he had dinner a couple of times with Deputy Cao and his wife when he was here for that legal exchange a couple of years ago. He says Cao was real pally and kept in touch with him by e-mail.' He stuck a cigarette in his mouth and cupped his hands around it as he lit it. Smoke whipped away from his mouth on the breeze. 'Dowman sent him an advance copy of the Chinese translation of the book eight weeks ago.'

\*

As the train puffed slowly away from the industrial southern fringes of the Chinese capital, a pretty girl in a red jacket checked his ticket and gave him a plastic token in return. Li took a small chrome flask from his satchel and emptied into it a sachet of wiry, dry green tea leaves. He leaned down to take out the big flask from below the table at the window and pour boiling water from it into his own. Then he screwed the top back on the smaller one and set it aside to let it infuse.

There were two other passengers in his soft class compartment. Both looked like businessmen, in dark suits and plain ties. To Li's relief, neither of them seemed anxious to indulge in conversation. One had his face buried in a newspaper, and the other was asleep before they left the city. Li opened Wu's folder and settled down to read all about Deputy Beijing Police Commissioner Cao Xu.

The second in command of the Beijing force had come from humble origins, abandoned by an elderly widowed aunt following the death of his parents in an agricultural accident. He had been two years old then. His aunt had been childless, and he was without family. The authorities had placed him in the care of a state orphanage.

He never graduated from school, being inducted, as many of his generation were, into the ranks of the Red Guards during the Cultural Revolution. Mao's teenage missionaries of ideological madness travelled all over China during those years of chaos and persecution. Cao had been no different from the rest, spending several years in various southern provinces before coming to Beijing to join the cheering throngs in Tiananmen Square where Mao would make regular appearances, urging them to greater efforts in rooting out the enemies of the people. But then Mao, and subsequently the Gang of Four, had passed into history, and China returned from the brink to start reinventing itself. Like everyone else, Cao shrugged off those years and started over. He sat and passed the necessary exams to gain entry into the University of Public Security, where Li himself was later trained. When he graduated, he married Tie Ning, a girl he had met during his Red Guard years. Their first child had died aged three, and then Ning had belatedly given birth to a baby boy, now a student at the Chinese University of Hong Kong.

Li unscrewed the cap of his flask and saw that the tea leaves had absorbed enough water to become fleshy and heavy and sink to the bottom. He took a sip and wondered when the man known as Cao Xu had stepped into those shoes. Sometime between the orphanage and the university, he figured. It had to have been at some point during the anarchy of the Cultural Revolution, when almost every facet of a once civilised society had been broken down, and the bureaucracy which had been the glue holding China together for thousands of years had all but disintegrated. Li turned back to the printouts.

Cao had risen quickly through the ranks in the Criminal Investigation Department, before being assigned as a detective to the Section One serious crime squad. Li was struck, as he read, by how similar their career paths had been, Cao blazing a trail ahead of him. He was more than fifteen years Li's senior, but then Li had been a teenager when he enrolled at the Public

Security University. Cao had been well into his twenties. So Li had followed not too distantly in his wake.

Like Li, Cao had become Deputy Section Chief, before taking over as head of the department. He had achieved striking success in a rapidly changing city. The very nature of crime and criminals in the People's Republic was morphing into something quite different then. As economic change swept in, unemployment grew, and crime festered among the increasingly large floating population of itinerant workers travelling around the country looking for work. Cao had introduced changes in policing, modernising the approach of investigators, leading the section to greater reliance on science and technology. He had been a great administrator, politically aware, and a Party member. It was only ever a matter of time before he climbed higher up the promotion ladder.

When he was appointed Deputy Commissioner, his passage to the very top seemed assured.

Then a case he had cracked nearly ten years earlier came back to haunt him. Li took another sip of tea and laid his folder on the table. He remembered it very well. A young man who had raped and murdered several women was finally arrested. The evidence against him was flimsy, but enough to convince the judges in a very high profile trial that he was guilty. The authorities had made a great public show of the trial at the time, to increase public esteem for the police which they were anxious to portray as a modern and effective force, protecting ordinary citizens from crime and criminals. The investigation had been led by the then Section Chief Cao Xu. The young man was convicted and executed.

Seven years later, a brash new Deputy Chief of Section One led an investigation into a similar spate of killings, tracking down and catching the perpetrator – a mentally subnormal middle-aged man living with his elderly mother in a *siheyuan* in the north of the city. Evidence found in his home, and a subsequent DNA test, revealed that he had also been responsible for the killings seven years earlier. Cao Xu had sent an innocent man to his death. And such had been the change in media coverage of such matters during the intervening years, that it had been impossible to sweep it under the carpet. Cao's shining star had been tarnished and was no longer in the ascendancy. The Deputy Section Chief who had led the investigation which discredited him was Li Yan.

Li turned to the window and watched the featureless agricultural plains of northern China drift past. A small cluster of crumbling brick dwellings on the banks of a murky-looking canal. Stubbly fields lying empty and fallow, the early morning sun casting its long shadows across the land. It had never before occurred to him that Cao Xu might hold that against him. He had not set out to discredit the Deputy Commissioner. Cao Xu's mistake had come to light quite accidentally in the course of another investigation. But, as the authorities had blamed Cao, so he might well have seen Li as the cause of his ills. The full-stop on his progress to the very top. An ambitious man thwarted, like a woman jilted, could be dangerous and vengeful.

Li had had few dealings with him since then, having left the Beijing force soon after to take up a job as criminal liaison with the Chinese embassy in Washington DC. He had been there for more than a year before returning to take up the position of Chief with his old section, and had only been in that job for about eighteen months. He could count on one hand the number of encounters he'd had with Cao in that time. He could not recall any rancour between them. Was it really possible that beneath his relaxed and languid exterior, Cao had been festering quietly, blame feeding on jealousy and revenge to grow into something dark and sinister?

But to horribly butcher innocent women in the pursuit of that revenge seemed distorted out of all proportion. Surely there had to be more to it than that?

Li drank more green tea and topped up his flask. He gazed sightlessly from the window and saw Lynn Pan's open, pretty face, the smile that lit it, the warmth of personality that radiated from her eyes and lips and touch. And then he recalled the pale, blood-streaked face on the autopsy table, the ugly gashes where her ears had been hacked off, the gaping wound across her throat. It had all been some horrible accident of fate. Pure chance that an image of Taiyuan had been chosen for that demo. That a ruthless and bloody killer should have been one of its subjects, and that she should have stumbled upon his lie. Not a lie, but a truth. That he could not recognise a place which was supposed to be his home town. If he had been caught in a deception, it was that his whole life was a lie. And she had died to keep it that way.

A solitary figure on a bicycle cycled slowly along the tow-
path, silhouetted against the rising sun. It was a little girl.
Perhaps seven or eight years old, a school satchel slung across
her back. She flashed across the frame of the carriage window
in a second, an image trapped in the mind. A child. A life. Gone
in a moment, like the lives of all those young women that Cao
had murdered. Like the life of Lynn Pan. And Li remembered
the old saying: the star that shines twice as bright burns half
as long.

## II

Taiyuan lay six hundred and twenty kilometres south-west
of Beijing. It was the provincial capital of Shanxi, in whose
central plain the city nestled on the banks of the Feng river,
surrounded by mountains on all sides. The change in the countryside had been gradual. It was lusher here, more temperate,
and sheltered by the snowy peaks that rose up into the clearest
of blue autumn skies. Every slope had been terraced to grow
crops, the plain irrigated to grow rice, a slightly sweet, delicious snow-white rice.

It was early afternoon when Li arrived in the city. The
station concourse was jammed with travellers, and hawkers
selling everything from maps to tiny toffee apples on sticks.
It was warmer here than it had been in Beijing. The sun felt
soft on his face. He bought a street map of the city from
one of the hawkers, and turned east into Yingze Street, away
from the old south gate of the ancient city wall, and kept

walking. The provincial government administration buildings were somewhere along here before the bridge. He passed a street stall selling the local Yingze beer for three *yuan*, and crossed through Wuyi Square. Yingze Park, opposite the towering Telecom headquarters, was crowded with people enjoying the late fall sunshine, strolling at leisure around the lake where in three or four weeks from now they would probably be skating. The square was lined with hotels and government buildings. The Hubin Grand Hall, the history museum, the Taiyuan Customs House, and the headquarters of the local Public Security Bureau. Li was tempted to make himself known to them. Their help would have saved him a great deal of time. But he was suspended from duty. He no longer had his Public Security ID. He was just another citizen with no special rights or privileges.

The shops all along Yingze Street were doing brisk business, and Li had to bump and jostle his way through the crowds to make progress east. No one else seemed to be in a hurry. The pace of life here was much slower than he was used to in Beijing. He passed the crowded Tianlong shopping mall and the Shanxi Chinese Communist Party headquarters, before reaching the government buildings on the east side of the Yingze bridge. The area had been completely redeveloped, modern buildings rising all around from the rubble of the old. There was a vast open space in front of the main building, much of which was taken up by a car park. He climbed the steps into the main hall.

It took about an hour, being passed from desk to desk,

department to department, before he was finally directed to the citizens' registry office at Taiyuan City Hall on Xingjian Road. Here Li found another formidable group of buildings, older, built in the European style, and fronted by a huge courtyard. This time he tracked down the registry office quite quickly, and found himself opposite an elderly lady with short, silvered hair on the other side of the counter. She was like a throwback from another era, in her blue cotton Mao suit and black slippers encasing tiny feet. But she smiled at him welcomingly enough, and asked what she could do to help. 'Ah, yes,' she said when he told her, 'the Wutaishan Orphanage. It was on the south side of the city, within sight of the Yongzuo Temple.'

'You mean the Double-pagoda Temple?'

'That's right.'

'You said, *was*. Does that mean it's moved?'

'Oh, no,' said the old lady. 'It's still there. What's left of it. The place burned to the ground about thirty years ago. They never rebuilt on the site, and the remains of it are still visible. Although it's pretty much overgrown now.' She tilted her head and looked at him curiously. 'I've had quite a few enquiries about the place over the years. Mainly from people who grew up in it, wondering what happened. Not so many now, though.'

'What did happen?' Li asked.

'No one knows. It just went up in flames one night. They got all the children out safely, but by the time the firefighters got there it was too late to save it. An old building, you see. Mostly built of wood. It was all over in an hour.'

Li said, 'What about the records? All the kids who passed through the orphanage over the years. Presumably you still have that information on file here?'

The old lady shook her head sadly. 'I'm afraid not,' she said. 'In those days all the records were kept at the orphanage itself. Everything was hand-written then. I know, because I was working here all those years ago when the place went up in flames. All our records were hand-written, too. We still have them in the basement. Unfortunately, the records at Wutaishan were destroyed along with everything else. The only thing that burns faster than wood is paper.' She scratched her head. 'A great shame. Generations of kids, their history lost forever. And the orphanage was the only family they ever had.'

Li felt himself slipping into a trough of despair. If the orphanage was gone, its records destroyed, there was no way to prove that Cao Xu was not who he said he was. Clearly he had covered his tracks well.

'What's your interest?' the old lady asked, scrutinising him shrewdly.

Li decided to take a chance. 'I'm a police officer from Beijing,' he said. 'We're investigating the history of someone who grew up in the orphanage.'

The old lady smiled. 'I thought as much,' she said. 'I can always tell a policeman. You're too big to be anything else. And too confident.' She paused to think. 'When did this person leave the orphanage?'

Li shrugged. 'I don't know exactly.'

'Approximately, then.'

'I should think he would have been around sixteen or seventeen. Maybe even eighteen. He was born in 1948, which would mean somewhere between 1967 and 1969.'

The old lady thought for a long time. 'Old Mister Meng would have been there around that time.'

'Mister Meng?' Li asked.

She came out of her reverie. 'Yes. He cleans the hall, and the public record office when it shuts at five. He worked as an odd-job man at the orphanage from the mid-fifties until it burned down in the early seventies. There was some speculation at the time about whether he might have been responsible for the fire. But I don't think so. It was just idle chatter. He's worked as a cleaner for the municipality ever since. Retired now, of course. But still doing an hour a day for the extra cash.' She glanced at her watch. 'If you come back in a couple of hours, you'll be able to talk to him if you want.'

It was a short taxi ride to the south-east corner of Taiyuan City, but the twin towers of the Double-pagoda Temple were visible almost as soon as they left the city centre. The taxi driver was a chatty type, engaging Li in reluctant conversation. Was this his first trip to Taiyuan City? What did he think of it? Where was he from? Did he want to take a detour to the Yongzuo Temple? Li declined the offer, to the driver's obvious disappointment. He began to tell Li its history. 'The towers were built in the Ming dynasty,' he said. 'Under the Emperor Waili. They are fifty-three metres high. Thirteen storeys of brick and stone.'

Li looked at the towers as they circled them on the ring road. They were awe-inspiring this close to, octagonal structures, tapering to a point at the top, aiming straight up to the heavens. It was little wonder that they had been chosen as the visual symbol of the city. In past centuries, when the buildings of the town were no more than one storey high, it must have been possible to see them for miles.

'Are you sure you don't want to stop?' the driver said. 'You can see the tablets of the famous calligraphers, Wang Xizhi, Yan Zhenqing and Su Dongpo.'

'Sounds like something I really shouldn't miss,' Li said. 'Next time.'

The driver shrugged. 'As you like.'

The Wutaishan Orphanage was on the old road heading south out of town towards the great expanse of paddy fields on the Shanxi plain. There were rows of brick-built workers' houses in amongst groves of bamboo and eucalyptus, great bundles of dried corn stalks stacked at the roadside. The original wall still stood around a large area of garden, now overgrown and gone to seed. Rusted wrought-iron gates hung open on buckled hinges. Li asked the driver to wait for him and wandered into the grounds. It had obviously become a dumping ground for overspill refuse from the surrounding houses, filled with the carcasses of long dead cars and bicycles. Amongst the tangling overgrowth, you could still make out the foundations of the original complex of single-storey buildings which had made up the orphanage. The thorns of wild roses caught on Li's trousers as he tramped down the growth and made his way to the heart of the site where the main building had stood. Some charred stumps of wooden uprights could still be found poking through the undergrowth. Blackened bricks scattered around where they had fallen when the walls collapsed. He tried to imagine how it must have been, flames reaching into the night sky, the crackle of burning wood, the screams of the children as they were ushered out into the dark to stand at a safe distance and watch the only home they had known vanish in the smoke.

He kicked an old tin can and sent it rattling across the dried ground, and looked up to see the twin towers of the Double-pagoda Temple dominating the skyline. It would have been impossible to have lived here and not recognise them.

But there was nothing here for Li. Nothing but ghosts and memories. Other people's memories.

The taxi took him back to the city in about twenty minutes, and he killed the next hour sitting in Yingze Park, drinking a three-*yuan* can of beer and watching small boys sailing tiny boats in the wind that ruffled the surface of the lake. He let the world pass him by and tried to think of nothing, to keep his mind empty, free to be full only of things that mattered. But despair kept leaking in.

He made his way back to the public records office and got there a little after five. The woman from the citizens' registry was waiting for him at the top of the steps, wrapped up in a large padded jacket and carrying a deep denim bag. She nodded through glass doors to the large reception hall. 'That's him. I told him you'd be looking for him.'

Li saw a wizened old man in faded blue overalls, with a bucket and mop, cleaning the marble tiles on the vast expanse of floor inside. 'Thank you,' he said, and pushed open the door into the lobby.

As Li approached him, the old man glanced up and then returned his gaze to the sweep of his mop across the shiny surface of the tiles.

'Mister Meng?' Li said.

'You'll be the cop from Beijing,' old Meng said, and Li glanced towards the glass entrance to see the lady from the citizens' registry watching them with unabashed curiosity.

'That's right.'

'I had nothing to do with that fire.' Still the old man did not look up.

'I don't think for a minute that you had,' Li said.

The old man gave him a long, appraising look, decayed stumps of teeth gnawing on a piece of his cheek. 'What do you want, then?'

'The lady from the citizens' registry told me that you worked at the orphanage from the mid-fifties.'

'Nosy old bitch!' old Meng complained. 'None of her bloody business.'

'Did you?' Li asked.

The old man nodded. 'I loved that place,' he said. 'Knew every one of those kids as if they were my own. Poor little bastards. The place was run by women. There was hardly a man about the place. No father figure, only matriarchs. Broke my heart when it burned down.'

Li said hesitantly, 'Would you remember one of the kids from back then? I know it's a long time ago, and all I've got's a name . . .'

'Try me.' Old Meng sloshed water from his bucket on to the floor, and Li smelled the bleach in it.

'Cao Xu.'

The old man stopped in mid wipe and looked at Li, a strange light in his eyes. 'Why do you want to know about little Xu?'

'You remember him, then?'

'Of course I do. He was a great kid. One of the favourites at the orphanage. Everyone loved him. He used to call me *papa*.' Li tried to keep from getting excited. His hopes had been dashed too many times in recent days. 'Always had a twinkle in his eye and a quip on his lips.'

It certainly didn't sound like the Cao Xu that Li knew.

'Have you come to visit him?'

Li was aware of stopping breathing, and it took a conscious effort for him to draw breath again. 'Yes,' he said. 'Do you know where I can find him?'

'Of course.' Old Meng glanced at the big clock on the wall. 'But you'll need to wait until I finish at six. And then I'll take you to him.'

Li had never known an hour to pass so slowly. He sat on a low wall in the courtyard outside the municipal building smoking cigarette after cigarette. More for something to do than anything else, he had crossed the road to a small general store on the corner and bought a pack. Now he was nearly halfway through it, and his mouth felt dry and kippered. It was ten past six and almost dark before the old man pushed open the door of the main building and came down the steps towards him, dwarfed by his big coat and wearing a thermal ski cap. He made Li think of his father, and his heart lurched with the memory of the old man abandoned in Lao Dai's apartment. He must be wondering what had happened to his son.

'You got a car?' old Meng said. Li shook his head. 'We'll need a taxi then.'

The taxi ride took less than fifteen minutes. Li sat in the back, while the old man sat up front with the driver arguing about the best route to take, a constant dialogue. Li watched the city slip by him as darkness fell. It was darker than Beijing. Here there were fewer lights. They did not have as much power to waste. Li had no idea where they were, or where they were going. He heard the name *Taigang* mentioned several times, but it meant nothing to him. And then through the windscreen he saw a huge floodlit tower like a cut-down Washington Monument reaching into the blackness. The taxi drew up on the side of a small square dominated by the stone needle and old Meng climbed stiffly out. Li followed him and looked around. This was no residential area. An area of parkland brooded darkly behind a high fence. The gates to it stood opposite the tower.

'We'd better hurry,' the old man said. 'They'll be closing up shortly.'

Li followed him across the cobbles and through the gates. There seemed to be one long, treelined avenue washed by the light of ornamental street lamps, and small paths led off at right-angles to left and right. 'Where the hell are we?' Li asked.

'Tomb park,' said old Meng. And he pointed ahead to a large, floodlit monument. As they approached it Li saw that it was a memorial tomb to the soldiers who died fighting to liberate Taiyuan from the grip of the Nationalists in 1948. It was inscribed *Niutuozai Soldiers' Tomb*.

Li turned away from the glare of the floodlights and looked around him. And as his eyes grew accustomed to the gloom of the poorly lit pathways that criss-crossed the park, he suddenly realised where he was. 'It's a cemetery,' he said. In the cities no one buried their dead any more. Land was at a premium. Cremation was the only permitted form of disposal.

'This way,' old Meng said. And he headed off to the left down a long pathway strewn with leaves. Small posts with built-in lights every few metres cast feeble illumination across their route. Li could see the mounds on either side, and the stone tablets raised in the memory of the dead. He had seen graves in the countryside, where the peasants still buried their dead on the land. He had attended many cremations. But he had never been in a city cemetery like this before, hundreds, maybe thousands, of bodies interred all around him. He pulled his coat tight to keep out the cold, damp sorrow of the place. Old Meng stopped and took out a small flashlight from a bag slung across his shoulder and flashed its beam from one headstone to another. 'Somewhere around here,' he mumbled. Then, 'Ah, here he is.'

Li's mouth was dry, and he felt the blood pulsing in his

throat, as he knelt down beside a small, plain headstone lying crookedly at one end of a short mound. The municipal authorities clearly made some attempt at keeping the cemetery from falling into total ruin, but still the grass grew up around the tablet, almost obscuring it. He pulled it aside, and by the light of Meng's lamp rubbed away the layer of moss that concealed the inscription.

'Scarlet fever,' Meng said. 'Took him in a matter of days.'

Li took the flashlight from him and peered through its light at the faded characters carved in the stone. It said simply: *Cao Xu. 1948–1962*. He had been only fourteen years old when he died.

# CHAPTER THIRTEEN

## I

There were queues of people up ahead trying to get into the hard class waiting room. A female announcer with a high-pitched nasal voice cut above the gabble in the station to announce the departure of the 19.10 train to Shanghai, followed by information about a delay in the arrival of the 14.45 from Xian. Strings of red electronic characters streamed across information boards. A woman in a white smock was selling hot noodles in polystyrene cartons.

Li checked into the soft class waiting room and glanced at the departure board. As far as he could tell, his train would leave on time. A 7.30 p.m. departure, arriving back in Beijing at 2.30 the following morning. Seven hours! He closed his eyes and took a deep breath. It seemed like an eternity.

The real Cao Xu was dead. Carried away in childhood by scarlet fever. He had the testimony of the old man, and knew from him that there were others who worked at the orphanage back then who were still alive and would remember him, too.

And there must be kids they could track down who would recall the real Cao Xu – and his passing.

But Li was the only person who knew how it all fitted together. The only one who could convincingly discredit the man who had stolen a dead child's identity and lived a lie for more than forty years. That put Li, and everyone close to him, in danger. When he left this morning, his cellphone was dead. He had forgotten to recharge the battery. So Margaret had loaned him hers. He took it out now and dialled the number of the Harts' apartment. Lyang answered. Her voice sounded dull and lifeless.

'Everything alright?' Li asked.

'Sure,' she said. 'You want to speak to Margaret?'

Margaret's voice was full of concern. 'Are you okay?'

'I'm fine.'

'Did you find anything?'

'Yes. I found Cao Xu.'

There was a moment of stunned silence on the other end of the line. 'What do you mean?'

'He died, Margaret. From scarlet fever, aged fourteen. I've seen his grave. The orphanage where he grew up was destroyed by fire in the early seventies, along with all its records. He must have torched the place to cover his tracks.'

There was more silence from Margaret's end. 'But if he didn't come from Taiyuan, how did he even know of this boy's existence to be able to steal his identity? And if he set the place on fire, then he *must* have been there. Why didn't he recognise the twin pagodas?'

Li thought about the overgrown remains of what had once been the Wutaishan Orphanage, almost in the shadow of the twin pagodas. It would have been impossible to have been there without seeing them. And if Cao, or whoever he was, had seen them, then he would have registered a MERMER response during the demonstration. A black cloud descended on his mind, obscuring the clarity he thought he had found here in Taiyuan City. 'I don't know. Either the fire at the orphanage was a quirk of fate, and he just took advantage of it, or . . .' He hardly dared think about it. 'Or someone else set the fire for him.'

'Which means that someone else knows that he's not who he says he is.'

'Or *knew*,' Li said. 'It seems that people don't live very long when they know the truth.'

'Oh, Li Yan.' He heard the fear in Margaret's voice. 'For God's sake be careful.'

'Of course,' he said. 'I'll be back sometime before three.'

He disconnected the phone, and dropped into a soft leather seat to stare up at the electronic arrivals and departures board, seething with a latent fury that had been building in him these last few days, determined that the killing would stop here, that he would get his life back again, and that the man who called himself Cao Xu would be brought, finally, to justice.

But he had no idea how he was going to make it through the next seven hours.

## II

The lights of an airplane tracked their way across the vast expanse of black sky visible through the open curtain. Margaret lay on the bed twisted in her nightshirt. It was warm in the apartment, in spite of the subzero temperatures outside, and she had pushed aside the duvet in an attempt to cool herself. For a second night she could not sleep, too many thoughts crowding an already overcrowded mind. She had tossed and turned restlessly, too hot under the duvet, slightly chilled without it. Again and again she turned everything Li had told her over in her head. But still there was something that did not chime, something that did not quite make sense. And underlying everything, was a dread of what awaited her in just over twenty-four hours. Expulsion from China; the thought that she might be parted from her son; the fear that she might never see him again if she was.

It did not help that Lyang had fallen asleep almost as soon as her head hit the pillow, and was now breathing heavily, turned away from Margaret and lying on her side. She had been poor company all day, morose and monosyllabic. Understandable in the circumstances. But Margaret suspected that she had also been taking some kind of sedative. Her eyes were dead, lacking the life that Margaret had seen in them when they'd first met only four days ago. She was slow in response to anything Margaret said to her, and she did not seem to have eaten anything all day. Margaret had done her best to keep the children amused, but it had been a strain. And now when she wanted to sleep, it was eluding her again.

The red digital display told her it was 1.14 a.m. She closed her eyes, and felt the ache behind them. She tried to empty her mind, and let sleep steal in to carry her off. Instead, she was startled upright by the ringing of a telephone on the bedside table.

Lyang moaned in her sleep and rolled over, but she did not wake up. The phone rang three, four times. Long, single rings. Margaret shook her by the shoulder. 'Lyang, wake up for God's sake!'

Lyang opened bleary eyes. 'What . . .'

'The phone!' Margaret almost shouted at her. She was scared to answer herself in case the caller spoke Chinese.

Lyang glanced over at the clock, but couldn't make out the blurred red figures. 'What time is it?'

'It's a quarter past one.'

'Who the hell's phoning at this time of the morning?' Lyang reached over and lifted the receiver. '*Wei?*' She listened for a moment, frowning, then thrust the phone towards Margaret. 'It's for you.'

Margaret's eyes opened wide in surprise. 'Me?' Her heart was still pounding. Who knew she was here apart from Li? 'Who is it?'

'Someone called Dai. He says you'll know who he is.'

'Dai?' Now she was scared. She grabbed the phone. 'Hello?'

'Magret,' Dai said. 'Am so sorry to phone at this hour of night. I don't wanna scare you, but Li Yan's father, he is not well. His heart, maybe. I have telephone for ambulance, but who know when it arrive. Please come here. You doctah, right? He need help.'

'Jesus . . .' Margaret's thoughts were racing. 'Keep him warm, okay? Get him to lie flat with a blanket over him. Don't let him stop breathing. You know CPR?'

'Sure. It part of police training.'

'Okay, hang on till I get there. How long by taxi?'

'Fifteen minute, maybe. Not long.'

'Okay, give me your address . . .' She searched quickly through the drawer in the bedside cabinet and found a pen and a scrap of paper. She scribbled down the address and hung up.

'What is it?' Lyang asked. She was fully awake now, and watching Margaret, concerned.

'I think Li Yan's father's had a heart attack. I'm going straight over there in case the ambulance doesn't arrive in time. Will you be alright with the kids?'

'Sure I will. They're out of it anyway.' She swung her legs out of the bed. 'Let me call you a taxi. It could be long enough before you pick one up in the street at this time of the morning.'

It was bitterly cold as Margaret stepped from the north-west tower into the garden and hurried along the path by the small stream. She pulled her oversized anorak around herself for warmth. The area of white paving stones indelibly stained with the blood of Bill Hart had been replaced by a gang of workmen first thing the previous morning. The lighting in the garden was muted at this hour. Just enough for Margaret to see by. She crossed the stream and up steps to the entrance lobby on the south side. The night security guard looked up from behind his desk where he was reading some lurid magazine and creating a fog of cigarette smoke all by himself. She scarcely gave him a glance as she ran across the lobby and out through the gate to the street. A taxi stood idling at the kerbside. Margaret climbed into the front seat where she found herself separated from the driver by a metal cage. Through the bars, she slipped him the note in Chinese that Lyang had given her of old Dai's address. The driver snorted and spat a gob of mucus out through the open window on his side of the cab. 'OK,' he said. He rolled up his window, passed her back her note, and the car juddered off into the road.

The streets were almost deserted as the taxi made its way on to the Third Ring Road and headed south. Margaret was aware of the driver glancing at her curiously. It was not often that some blue-eyed, fair-haired foreign devil would get into his cab in the middle of the night and ask to be taken into the heart of a Chinese residential area. He turned west off the ring road at the Huawei Bridge on to Songyu Nan Lu, and drove along its treelined length without passing another vehicle. At the cancer hospital they joined the Second Ring Road for a short distance before turning south on Fangzhuang Lu.

Margaret's initial panic was wearing off, to be replaced, as she sat thinking about it, by a growing unease. How on earth had Dai known where to find her? She supposed it was possible that Li had told him. But he had dropped his father off with Dai even before they knew about Bill Hart's murder. Perhaps he had phoned later to leave a contact number.

She replayed the phone call in her mind. She had only met Dai on a handful of occasions, but been struck each time by just how perfect his command of English was. Tonight he had called her *Magret*. He had dropped his plurals and spoken always in the present tense. And yet his English had still been good. Perhaps under stress it was just not as good as at other times. She glanced nervously at her watch. If she had known how to, she would have told the driver to hurry up. He seemed to be taking the journey at an unusually leisurely rate.

They were in Pufang Lu now, heading west through a forest of tower blocks rising above trees rattling dying leaves in the wind. The driver dropped her on the corner opposite Dai's block and pointed it out. She gave him twenty *yuan*. 'Syeh-syeh,' she said, and as she ran across the road the wind blew her anorak open to let the November wind caress her with its icy fingers. The cold made her eyes water.

She hurried down the path past the shuttered *jian bing* stall and turned up steps through the doorway on to the ground floor landing. It was gloomy in here and smelled of stale cooking and body odour. The elevator was turned off, and the gate on the stairwell was shut. She cursed, looking around for some kind of telephone entry system, but could not see anything. By chance she tried the stairgate and it swung open. Either the last resident to use it had forgotten to lock it, or it was broken. She didn't care. She took the steps two at a time, pausing on the third landing to catch her breath, before running up the next two flights. On the fifth landing she stopped for several moments, leaning against the wall, her breath rasping and abrasive in her lungs. Then she heaved herself off the wall and ran along the doors looking for the number 504.

Of course, it was the last door she came to. There was no bell, and she banged on it hard with the flat of her hand. When there was no response, she banged again. Harder, and called his name. A door further along the hall flew open, and a man's voice shouted imprecations at her. She ignored him and kept banging until, finally, she heard stirring within, the rattling of a chain, and the door opened a crack.

'Mister Dai, Mister Dai, let me in! It's Margaret.'

The door opened wider, and a pale-faced Dai stood blinking in the landing light, dressed in his pyjamas, a worn silk dressing gown hastily pulled around him. He looked both frightened and puzzled. 'Margaret . . . What are you doing here?'

Margaret's panic was returning now. 'You phoned me!' she almost shouted.

'What?' The old man looked at her as if she was mad.

'Oh, my God. Oh, my God.' Margaret was almost incoherent. 'There's nothing wrong with Mister Li, is there?'

Dai was shaking his head. 'Of course there isn't. He's asleep. Or, at least, he was. What in the name . . . ?'

But Margaret pushed past him into the tiny apartment. 'Where's your phone?'

Lao Dai shut the door firmly behind them and led her through to a small, tidy sitting room. 'I will not even ask,' he said, and pointed to the phone on a low table beside the settee.

Margaret fumbled for the piece of paper with Dai's address. Thank God Lyang had had the foresight to write her own telephone number on the back of it in case Margaret needed to call. Margaret dialled it now. The phone rang. Three, four, five times. 'Come on, come on,' Margaret urged through clenched teeth. 'Answer, for God's sake!' But it just kept on ringing. By the time it reached the tenth ring, her insides had turned to jelly. How could she have been so stupid! She hung up and looked at Dai, as if he might provide her with the inspiration for what to do next. But he only looked perplexed, and not a little scared.

Li Yan, she thought. He had her mobile. He'd know what she should do. She picked up the phone and dialled. But almost immediately the messaging service kicked in. Either the phone was switched off or there was no signal. She hung up the phone and knew she had to get back to Lyang's apartment. Li Jon and Xinxin were there. She would never forgive herself if something had happened to them. And yet, why else would someone have lured her away with such an elaborate trick? She felt acid rising in her throat.

'I'm sorry,' she muttered jumping quickly to her feet. 'Mister Dai, you've got to call the police for me. Please. My baby's life is in danger.' And she pushed past old Dai and fled down the hall to the front door and out on to the landing.

'Where?' he called after her. 'Where should they go?'

She stopped, thinking furiously. 'The Music Apartments . . . I can't remember what it's called. There are giant piano lids on the roofs. It's where Bill Hart lived.'

She almost fell twice on the stairs, before staggering past

the stairgate and running out into a wall of freezing cold night air.

Outside, the streets were empty. Not a taxi in sight. She remembered Lyang's words. *It could be long enough before you pick one up in the street at this time of the morning.*

She started running east along Pufang Lu crunching dried leaves underfoot, stumbling on uneven pavings. To the south, beyond the sports complex, the lights of the Feng Chung shopping centre still blazed into the night. Every step brought deeper despair, a sense of complete hopelessness. And helplessness. It would take her an hour, longer, at this rate, and what kind of state would she be in when she got there? The tears came, then, turning almost to ice as they streamed down her cheeks. There were lights burning in the police station on the corner of Fangxing Lu, and Margaret hesitated at the steps leading up between chrome pillars to its glass doors. Through them she could see a large board on the wall of the lobby, photographs of every officer working out of that office. And she knew that not one of them would speak English. What could she say to make them understand? Some tearstained mad foreign woman running in out of the night, jabbering incomprehensibly. They would probably lock her up.

The lights of a car raked across the front of the building, and she swivelled in time to see a taxi turning into Pufang Lu. She almost screamed at it to stop, running into the road waving her hands in the air. She saw the driver's face caught in the light of a street lamp. A moment of indecision in it as he saw the crazed *yangguizi* running across the street. But to

Margaret's relief he pulled up. Legs almost buckling under her, she yanked open the passenger door and dropped into the seat beside him. He looked at her, alarmed.

'Oh, Jesus . . .' she whispered, realising that she had no idea how she was going to tell him where to take her. Lyang had not written down her own address. She tried to stop her brain from spiralling into further panic. Think, think, she told herself. Then, 'Jinsong Bridge,' she said, suddenly remembering the turn off the ring road. The driver stared at her, clearly not understanding. '*Jin Song*,' she said, trying to make the tonal distinction between the syllables, as she had heard the Chinese doing. And what was the word for bridge? '*Jin Song Qiao*.'

The driver nodded. '*Ha*,' he said, and to her relief slipped his taxi into gear. They sped off east and then swung north.

Margaret looked down and saw that her knuckles had turned white, her fingers intertwined in a knot of tension in her lap. She tried to relax, to think positive thoughts, to convince herself that she was blowing this out of all proportion. But she couldn't. The fact that someone had telephoned her, pretending to be Dai, to get her out of the apartment, simply filled her with the most unthinkable dread. She remembered Li telling her that Lynn Pan had been lured to the Millennium Monument by someone on the telephone pretending to be him. That could only have been Cao. And tonight, it could have been no one else.

The journey back to the Music Home Apartments – frustratingly the name came back to her now – seemed interminable, the city floating past her in slow motion as they headed north on the East Third Ring Road. At last she saw the grand piano lids on top of the two towers. 'There,' she shouted at the driver, pointing through the windscreen. 'I want to go there.'

He peered in the direction she was pointing and nodded, indicating first, and then turning off at the Jinsong Bridge into Jinsong Lu. He pulled up outside the main entrance to the complex and Margaret threw a bunch of notes at him. She slammed the door behind her and ran through the gates and into the glare of the entrance lobby with its arched gold ceiling. The desk where the security guard had been sitting when she left was vacant. The lurid magazine he had been reading was lying on top of it. The ashtray was full to overflowing, and beside it lay an open pack of cigarettes, half full. His lighter was lying on the floor. Margaret stooped to pick it up, and she knew that there was something terribly wrong.

Something like a moan came up from her throat, animal-like, involuntary, and she battered through the doors and out into the garden. She ran blindly through the foliage, crossing the artificial stream at the first bridge, and hammering across the pavings to the north-west tower. Past the spot where Bill Hart had fallen from twenty-three floors up. And all she could see were the photographs Pathologist Wang had shown her of the terrible mutilations inflicted on those poor prostitutes by the Beijing Ripper. By Deputy Police Commissioner Cao Xu. In the lobby, she repeatedly pressed the button for the elevator. Gasping for breath, she waited a lifetime for the numbers to descend to the ground floor. And to her complete and utter despair, it had to come all the way down from the twenty-third floor.

# CHAPTER FOURTEEN

## I

In the darkness, something caught a fragment of light, deflecting it towards the door. There was someone there, concealed among the shadows. The creak of a floorboard, and then hot breath in the cold air. A knife arced through a shaft of light that slanted in through the window. No time to avoid it. No room to escape. Li screamed and opened his eyes, breath tearing at his lungs, his face a mask of perspiration. His three travelling companions were staring at him resentfully, all awakened from their slumbers. The thundering in his ears passed with a hiss as the train emerged from a long tunnel back into the starlit night. 'Sorry,' he mumbled, embarrassed, and turned towards the window. The crescent moon lay on its back, like a smile in the sky, amused by his embarrassment.

His dream had left him shaken. He checked the time. It was just after 2.15. They should be back in Beijing in a quarter of an hour. He took out a handkerchief to wipe the coating of fine sweat from his forehead, and fumbled for the cellphone in his pocket. He got it to repeat dial the Harts' apartment. It rang, and rang. And no one was answering. And still Li let it ring, panic starting to seize him now in its debilitating grip.

Margaret heard the phone ringing from the hallway as soon as she left the elevator. She hurried along it to the Harts' apartment, tempering haste with caution now. To her horror, she found that the door was not shut. It lay six inches ajar, a wedge of feeble light from the dimly lit hallway falling into the darkness beyond. Cautiously, Margaret pushed the door open and felt for the light switch inside. She flicked it down, but nothing happened. And fear washed over her like iced water. Still the phone was ringing. She pushed the door wide and waited a moment for her eyes to grow accustomed to the gloom before stepping in and running through to the living room to pick up the phone. But all she got was a dialling tone. Whoever was calling had finally given up. She quickly replaced the receiver and spun around. There was no one there. She could see clearly enough now in the ambient light of the city reflecting on walls and ceilings through the apartment's generous windows.

'Lyang?' she called out. And her own voice seemed deafening in the silence that followed it. Then another voice, like a muffled cry, sounded from somewhere up the stairs, and Margaret found herself shaking, almost uncontrollably.

She started towards the stairs, listening carefully, and almost fell over something soft lying on the floor. She crouched down to pick it up and saw that it was one of Li Jon's cuddly toys that she normally kept in the buggy. Her hand flew to her mouth to stop herself from crying out. She stood up and pressed it to her breast, and realised that she had no means of protecting herself or her child. She threw the soft toy on to the settee and moved quickly into the kitchen. On a work surface by the hob, there was a knife block where Lyang kept all her kitchen knives for food preparation. Margaret drew out the biggest of them. A wooden-handled implement with a blade about eight inches long. The weight of it in her hand gave her the tiniest sense of security. Her own preference for autopsy was a French chef's knife. She knew how to use a blade like this, and would not hesitate to do so if her baby had been harmed in any way.

She moved like a shadow back through the dining room into the hallway at the foot of the stairs and began climbing them very gingerly, one step at a time.

There was an odd smell on the top landing, like the sour stink of the autopsy room, and Margaret saw a trail of something dark on the floor leading to the master bedroom. She knelt down and touched it with the tips of her fingers. It was wet, slightly tacky. She raised her fingers to her nose and immediately knew the smell of blood. For a moment, fear almost robbed her of the strength to stand up straight. And shaking now like the leaves fibrillating among the branches of the autumn trees outside, she inched her way along the hall to the master bedroom in the dead silence of the apartment, trying to avoid stepping on the blood. When she got to the door she tentatively put out her hand and pushed it open wide.

There, on the bed, where Margaret had been so desperately seeking sleep just over an hour ago, was the outline of someone lying on their back, half wrapped in what looked like black sheets. Margaret glanced back along the hall, then stepped into the bedroom, and almost fell as her foot skidded away from her on the blood pooling there. And in that moment she realised that the sheets were not black. They were soaked in blood. She steadied herself and took a step forward and nearly screamed. Lyang was lying naked in the middle of the bed, her shoulders flat, but the axis of her body inclined to the left side. Her head was turned on her left cheek, her left arm close to her body, the forearm flexed at a right angle and lying across her abdomen. Her right arm rested on the mattress, bent at the elbow, her fingers clenched around a wad of blood-drenched sheet. Her legs were wide apart, and the whole surface of her abdomen and thighs had been removed, the abdominal cavity emptied of its viscera. Her breasts had been cut off, one of them carefully placed under her head along with the uterus and kidneys, the other by her right foot. Her liver was placed between her feet, the intestines on her right side, the spleen on her left.

Margaret knew without looking that the flaps of flesh removed from the abdomen and thighs had been placed on the bedside table. Doctor Thomas Bond's description came flooding vividly back to her. Words she had read only two days earlier.

*The breasts were cut off, the arms mutilated by several jagged wounds and the face hacked beyond recognition of the features, and the tissues of the neck were severed all round down to the bone.*

She wheeled away, trying to hold down the vomit rising in her throat. The man was completely insane. He had attempted a full replication of the murder of Mary Jane Kelly, the fifth and most horribly mutilated of Jack the Ripper's victims. Almost like some kind of game, he had carved her up according to his mentor's blueprint, placing pieces of her around the body, just as they had been found one hundred and fifteen years before. It was a feast of savagery such as Margaret had never seen. He must surely have slipped now beyond the realms of this world into some dark abyss where the light of human goodness had never shone. Where only evil resided in its purest, blackest form. And if he had been capable of this, what in the name of God had he done to the children?

## II

They came up a long, steeply sloping ramp from the platforms below. Steam and smoke filled the air, along with the hissing of old steam-driven boilers and the voices of porters shouting up and down the quays, pushing metal-wheeled trolleys piled with great stacks of mail in canvas sacks.

The stream of passengers, newly alighted from the train, moved slowly, as if in a trance, subdued and still half asleep, about to be rudely awakened by the icy blasts that awaited them above. Li pushed through the bodies ahead of him, heedless of the curses that followed in his wake. When he got no reply from Lyang's apartment, he had telephoned and got Wu out of his bed for the second night running.

Uniformed ticket collectors stood at the top of the ramp taking tickets from passengers as they filed out through the gates. Li thrust his ticket at the nearest of them and pushed out into the arrivals hall. Wu was waiting by the door, chewing mechanically, scanning the faces as they appeared at the top of the ramp. He raised an arm to catch Li's eye and called out to him. Li hurried over. Wu looked terrible. 'We've got cars on the way,' he said. 'I've left the motor running in mine.'

Li followed him down the steps into the bitter cold of the night, new arrivals streaming out behind them in search of buses and taxis. Wu's Santana was idling in the middle of the concourse, a blue light flashing on the roof.

He called back over his shoulder. 'You'd better be right about all this, Chief. Or I am in the deepest shit.'

For once in his life, Li hoped earnestly that he was entirely wrong.

It was with a sickening sense of anticipation that Margaret pushed open the door to the children's room. The curtains had been drawn and it was darker in here. But there was still enough light for Margaret to see that the bed that Xinxin had been sharing with baby Ling was empty. And so was the cot.

She spun around and looked down the length of the hallway towards the Harts' study at the far end. The door was pulled to. She had been wrong about the trail of blood leading into the master bedroom. It led from it, all the way to the study door. She started walking slowly towards it, the kitchen knife clutched tightly in her hand. Somehow her fear had gone, to be replaced by a slow burning determination that drove her on, like an automaton, towards the study. He was in there. She knew he was. And so was Li Jon. And Xinxin. With that monster. Chinese wall-hangings that Bill and Lyang had chosen together, stirred slightly in the breeze of her passing, their wooden weights clunking gently against the wall. She hesitated for only a second outside the door before pushing it open.

Her eyes fell immediately on two swaddled bundles propped among the cushions on the settee. No trace of blood, just the gentle sound of breathing. The deep, slow breath of sleep. The sound of life. Miraculously Ling and Li Jon were oblivious to the hell unfolding around them. Unharmed. In her relief, Margaret nearly dropped her knife. She took a step into the room, and a sound off to her right made her turn towards the window. A muffled cry escaped from somewhere behind the hand clamped firmly across Xinxin's mouth. Margaret froze in horror.

Deputy Commissioner Cao Xu had wheeled one of the desk chairs up to the window and was sitting on it, his back to the city below him. Xinxin, still in her little pink nightie, was held firmly between his legs, one hand nearly covering her face, the other holding the edge of a long-bladed knife hard against her throat. Margaret could see the sheer terror in her eyes.

It was something else altogether that she saw in Cao's eyes. There was light in them, but a light like darkness, like smouldering coals. Something not quite human. As a little girl, Margaret had heard Biblical tales of the Angel of Death.

If such a thing existed, then she was staring it in the eye right now. He was smothered in sticky, dark blood. It was all over his hands and face, as if he had gorged himself on poor Lyang. Indulged himself in a banquet of slaughter.

'Let her go!' Margaret said. Her only fear now was for Xinxin.

Cao smiled. He moved his head from left to right and Margaret heard bones cracking in his neck. 'How is poor old Mistah Li?'

'Let her go,' Margaret said again, and she took a step towards him. Xinxin squealed as the blade broke the skin on her neck, and Margaret stopped dead in her tracks.

'Did you recognise her?' Cao asked, relaxing again. Margaret frowned her confusion. 'My Mary Jane,' he added. And she knew that he was talking about Lyang. Except that somewhere in his twisted mind he saw her now only as Mary Jane Kelly. She nodded, and he smiled his pleasure. 'I am good,' he said. 'As good as him.'

'Let her go.' Margaret nearly shouted.

'Of course,' he said. 'We make exchange. Little girl for you. You can be my sixth. My Alice. I don't wanna hurt the little girl. She still have her innocence. Only when she lose innocence do I take life.'

Margaret realised that the best she could hope for was to buy herself some time to try to figure out what to do. She had to get him talking, keep him talking. 'It's all over,' she said. 'Li Yan is on his way. We know who you are.'

He smiled. 'No. Perhaps you know who I am not. But you do not know who I am.'

'Who are you then?'

'I am the man who is going to kill you. And your precious Li Yan cannot stop me. He is a fool. He never would catch me, except for the stupid MERMER test. And that idiot Professor Pan. So sure she could seduce us all.'

'How did you do it?' Margaret asked.

'Do what?'

'Break into the academy. Steal all those computers. Break into her house.'

He shook his head, smiling smugly. 'No, no, no. I do not do those things. I am policeman for thirty year. So maybe I know a few people. So maybe they owe me some favour. You know. *Guanxi*. No question ask.' He pressed the blade harder into Xinxin's throat, and Margaret saw a trickle of blood appear. Xinxin stood rigid and still, like a rabbit caught in the headlamps of a car. 'It feels so nice,' Cao said. 'That fine edge of steel, when it cut through soft flesh.'

Margaret felt her panic returning. But she forced herself to speak with a cold calm that she did not feel. 'If you harm a hair on that child's head, I'll kill you.' And she tightened her grip on her knife.

'You will not have to.' The voice came from behind Margaret and to her right, so startling her that she nearly cried out. She turned to see the slight figure of an older woman standing in the doorway. She seemed bizarrely familiar, but Margaret could not place her. She had shortcut silver hair and wore a heavy black jacket buttoned up above grey cotton trousers gathered at the heel over flat, black shoes. Everything about her seemed small and sinewy. Her face, although remarkably unlined, was stretched too tightly over the skull beneath it.

'Tie Ning!'

The sound of Cao's voice made Margaret turn her head towards him again, and the shock in his face brought to her a realisation of who this woman was. His wife. The quiet lady who had looked so uncomfortable in her black evening dress at Li's award ceremony. Her English was better than her husband's and she spoke it for Margaret's benefit rather than his.

'I have been sitting in my car in Jinsong Lu ever since he came in. Trying to find the courage to follow him. Afraid of what I would find if I did. If only I had not been afraid for so many years, perhaps all those young women would still be alive.'

'You followed me here?' Cao said in Chinese. He sounded incredulous.

'You think I don't know?' she said, still in English. 'Ever since I covered up for you all those years ago, when you raped and murdered that poor girl, I have known I made a mistake. I wanted to believe you when you said it was an accident. I was infatuated. I would have done anything.' She looked at Margaret. 'She was a Red Guard, just like us. She was my friend. But I loved him. They would have shot him. So we ran. We hid in Henan Province, in the country. And I went to Taiyuan City to burn down the orphanage there, to steal him the identity of a boy who died.' She took a deep breath, conjuring up some distant memory. 'I knew him, Cao Xu. A gentle boy. We grew up there together.' She turned her gaze back on her husband. 'I pushed you, I know I pushed you. To more success. To greater power. And all the time I wanted to believe. That it had really been an accident. That it had happened only one time. That with time and distance you would become like the boy whose name you took.' She sighed. 'But each time a girl was murdered and they could not find her killer I wondered. I wondered if there was something inside you that I could never reach, never touch. Something dark and hidden, beyond my understanding. Beyond yours.'

'They . . . they know,' Cao almost whispered. 'They know everything.'

She ignored him and took a step closer. 'I never knew for sure until I found blood on your shirt when that first girl was murdered. But, even then, it wasn't until the third killing that I went into your study and found the book, and the cuttings taken from the personal ads. Prostitutes advertising their services. And then I knew.' Margaret saw her lower lip tremble. 'And still I did nothing.' She turned to Margaret, tears running slowly down the parchment skin of her cheeks. 'I am so ashamed. When I read the story in the paper of those terrible murders . . . I knew I was responsible. And that it had to stop.'

Cao listened to her with a mouth half opened in disbelief. And there was fear in his eyes. Margaret was certain that was what it was. He was afraid of her. She had always been stronger than him, driven him onwards and upwards, forced the agenda. But, in the end, his weakness had been greater than her strength.

Somewhere from the streets below, they heard the sound of police sirens rising into the night, the squealing of tyres.

'Let her go,' Tie Ning said suddenly, and Cao flinched. 'Let. Her. Go!'

He would not meet her eye, but in sheepish acquiescence took his hand from Xinxin's mouth and lowered the knife meekly from her neck. Xinxin emitted a long, mournful wail as she ran across the room into Margaret's arms. Margaret held her tightly for just a few moments then forced her to break her grip. 'Go!' she said to her. 'Get out of here. Now!'

Xinxin was sobbing hysterically. 'You come, too, Magret. You come, too.'

Margaret took her roughly by the shoulders and shook her. 'Go!' she almost screamed at her. 'Take the elevator and don't stop until you are out of the building.' Margaret pushed her towards the door and heard her feet slapping on the wooden floor as she ran wailing along the hallway and down the stairs. Margaret would not leave without the babies.

Tie Ning turned to her. 'You go, too.'

Margaret shook her head. 'We'll wait here together until the police arrive.'

Tie Ning shook her head sadly. 'There will be no police.' She snatched the knife from Margaret's hand and in five short strides had crossed the study to the window. Cao sat frozen in fear and disbelief as she swung it viciously across her body from left to right and his neck opened up in a wide, black smile. Blood spurted from severed arteries and gurgled in his open windpipe. He dropped his knife and his hands went to his neck, scrabbling at the wound as if somehow they could keep the blood in.

Tie Ning stood above him watching, as the life ebbed out of him in moments. Fear of her, fear of death, fear of whatever lay beyond, was clear in his eyes. He slithered from the chair on to the floor, and it ran away on its castors to bump into what had once been Lyang's desk. His blood pooled around him on the polished floor.

She turned, her back to the window, silhouetted against floor-to-ceiling glass giving on to the magnificent panorama of Beijing beyond. And still more sirens sounded in the night. Margaret saw blood running along the blade of the knife as Tie Ning raised it from her side. 'I am sorry,' she said.

## III

There were several police cars in the street out front, officers streaming out and into the main lobby. Wu pulled the wheel of his car sharp left and they cut through a side street at the west end of the complex to turn into the street at the back of the towers, opposite a double-storey red and gold restaurant, deserted now and shrouded in darkness. There were three other police vehicles here already. The rear exit from the north-west tower provided the most direct access.

As Wu pulled up at the kerb, several officers gathering on the sidewalk looked up suddenly, and Li heard one of them swearing. He peered up through the passenger window in time to see what looked like a giant bird swooping down on them from above. He barely had time to register the fact that it was not a bird, but a human being, arms and legs extended, a coat opened out like the wings of an eagle, before it smashed on to the hood of the Santana. The car lurched sickeningly, and blood immediately spattered across the windscreen, obscuring their view. As he jumped out of the passenger side, Li could hear Wu cursing in shock and disbelief. One of the officers shouted, 'It's a woman!' And Li's heart seemed to freeze in his chest. He almost couldn't look. Tiny fragments of glass showered on them like rain.

As he turned, he saw silver hair and wide open staring eyes. Wu was at the other side of the car. 'Shit, Chief,' he said. 'It's Cao Xu's wife.'

A police radio was crackling in the cold night air. One of the officers said, 'They found the security guard. Someone cut his throat.'

Li vaulted up the steps to the exit door from the north-west tower and kicked it until the glass shattered and the door burst inwards. He skidded across the lobby through the broken glass as the doors of the elevator parted to reveal a small child standing there in the light. It took him a moment to realise it was Xinxin. She ran to him, howling, and he swung her up in his arms, holding her so tightly she almost couldn't breath.

'Where's Margaret?' he said.

'She's still upstairs.' She fought to draw breath against the sobs that were stealing it from her. 'Uncle Yan, a man tried to cut my throat . . .'

Li turned to the officers running in behind him. 'Someone get her a medic, fast.' He thrust her into the arms of a young uniformed policeman, and slipped into the lift just before the doors slid shut. He heard her call his name as he punched button number twenty-three, and the lift started its high speed ascent.

Curious residents were up and about now, coming out of their apartments into the hallway on floor twenty-three, wrapped in dressing gowns, scratching their heads. Li shouted at them to get out of the way and ran the length of the hall to the open door of the Harts' apartment. 'Margaret!' He screamed her name into the darkness, and to his intense relief he heard her voice call back from somewhere upstairs.

He strode up the stairway into the top hall and saw the door of the study lying open. Margaret was sitting on the settee cradling the still sleeping Li Jon in her arms. 'Thank God,' he whispered, offering thanks to whatever deity it was that had watched over her, even if it was not one he believed in.

As he came into the room, she laid the baby carefully back among the cushions and let him take her in his arms, enveloping her, absorbing her, so that they were almost one. He glanced across the room and saw Cao lying in his own blood, twisted, half propped against the remains of the window, throat and mouth gaping. The freezing November night blew in through the jagged shards of glass that framed the view to the north. 'What happened?' he said.

'Lyang's dead.' He shut his eyes in despair. 'Cao's wife killed him, then she went through the window.' Margaret looked up at him. 'She was the one who burned down the orphanage. She was the one who knew the real Cao Xu. She was one of the orphans.'

He kissed her forehead. 'It's over, Margaret,' he said. 'It's all over.'

She let him press her head gently into his chest. 'Li Yan,' she said, her voice almost a whisper. 'Who was he? Who was he really?'

Li looked over at the bloody remains of the Deputy Police Commissioner. 'I've no idea,' he said. 'Like Jack the Ripper, we probably never will.' He shook his head. 'Chances are we might only ever know him by the name he gave himself. The Beijing Ripper.'

# ACKNOWLEDGEMENTS

As always, I would like to offer my grateful thanks to those who have given so generously of their time and expertise during my researches for *Chinese Whispers*. In particular, I'd like to express my gratitude to polygraph expert, John J. Palmatier PhD; Lawrence A. Farwell PhD, Director and Chief Scientist, Brain Wave Science Human Brain Research Laboratory Inc. (inventor of MERMER); Steven C. Campman, MD, Medical Examiner, San Diego, California; Dr. Richard H. Ward, Professor of Criminology and Dean of the College of Criminal Justice, Sam Houston State University, Texas; Professor Dai Yisheng, former Director of the Fourth Chinese Institute for the Formulation of Police Policy, Beijing; Professor Yu Hongsheng, General Secretary of the Commission of Legality Literature, Beijing; Professor Yijun Pi, Vice-Director of the Institute of Legal Sociology and Juvenile Delinquency, China University of Political Science and Law; William S. Laidlaw, Consul, American Citizen Services, US Embassy, Beijing; Guo Zheng, Division Chief of Beijing Public Security Bureau, Western Division; Wang Hua Lu, Police Chief, Yuetan Police Station, Beijing; and Professor Chen Jianhua, Police Commissioner,

Beijing Forensic Science Research Centre, Pau Jü Hutong. Extracts from Dr Thomas Bond's autopsy notes on Mary Jane Kelly are reproduced by permission of the Metropolitan Police Authority.

Read on for an exclusive China short story

# THE
# GHOST
# MARRIAGE

# CHAPTER ONE

## I

Sweet though it was, the perfume of the incense could not disguise the odour of putrefying flesh. And the summer heat was not helping.

The cadavers were at the back of the room on a long table, surrounded by bowls of fresh fruit, boiled eggs in bowls of rice, dim sum still warm from the steamer, buns, a bottle of chilled white wine running with condensation.

The guests assembled at the far side of the room, near the door, and the window with a view on to the *siheyuan* courtyard. In the *hutong* beyond, children played unaware of the bizarre marriage taking place behind high walls.

The spirits of the dead man and his fiancée stood before a temporary altar: paper effigies to be burned, along with paper money, a paper car, and paper furniture that stood outside as comforts to be treasured in the afterlife. A gong sounded in the hands of the priest, and with a swirl of his red robe he placed a ring on the left hand of the paper groom. From the back of the observers, Feng Qi watched as the dead boy's mother placed a ring on the paper finger of the bride, and he let his eyes return uneasily to the open coffins behind them and the dead girl, whose face was troublingly familiar.

## II

The No. 1 Kindergarten in Anzhenxili was not far from the No. 3 Ring Road, just north of Tiananmen, and the Forbidden City. As she waited for Li Jon, Margaret gazed from a window across the almost unrecognisable cityscape of post-Olympic Beijing, reflecting on how rapidly much of this city had transformed itself from medieval to ultra-modern in the ten years since she first arrived.

She turned at the sound of children's voices filled with the euphoria of freedom after a long day of educational incarceration. Li Jon wrapped himself around her legs, and she lifted him up into her arms: something she would not be able to do for very much longer. He was growing like bamboo. She brushed dark hair from his eyes and saw only his father in him: fine Chinese features that owed nothing to her fair-haired, blue-eyed Celtic heritage. But he had, she knew, inherited his mother's fiery, querulous spirit, and she took pleasure from his father's frustration that he had not transmitted to his son more of his gentle Chinese fatalism.

'Did you get my iPod, Mommy?' He spoke English with her distinctive American accent. But also Chinese, like a native. Both she and Li spoke to their son in their native tongues, sending him to this bilingual kindergarten where he would learn to be a citizen of the world – bridging the cultural divide that had so often caused misunderstanding and conflict between his parents.

'Sure I did, honey. It's waiting for you back at the apartment.'

He descended from her arms and took her hand, impatient to be home as soon as possible.

But he was forced to temper his excitement by a lady who intercepted them at the front door. She wore blue overalls, and a white cloth cap, a few strands of greasy black hair hanging down from one side of it. Her hands were red and calloused, her flat peasant face rough and weathered, with troubled dark eyes. Margaret had seen her before, washing the floor of the lobby with slow, languid movements of her mop.

'Sorry to trouble you, lady.' She was strangely formal, half bowing, almost deferential. 'They tell me you are wife of Section Chief Li Yan.'

Margaret took satisfaction from exercising her increasing skill in Chinese. 'Then I'm sorry to say they tell you wrong.' The woman's disappointment was almost palpable, and Margaret immediately regretted her abruptness. She added quickly, 'An American woman is not permitted to marry a serving Chinese police officer.' She pulled the child at her side a little closer. 'But Li Jon is our son.'

She saw hope flicker again in the woman's eyes, like the flame of a candle stirring in the wind. The woman reached out a hand to clutch Margaret's arm, and Margaret could feel the desperation in her bony grasp. 'Then I beg you to help me, lady.' She glanced at Li Jon. 'You are a mother. I am a mother too. But my little girl is gone.'

## III

The apartment block where Li shared his life with Margaret lay to the east of Tiananmen Square, just south of East Changan Avenue, in the old British Embassy compound that was now occupied by the Ministries of State and Public Security. It was the same two-bedroomed police apartment he had once occupied with his late uncle. Now he and Margaret and their child lived there, in flagrant disregard of the rules. Only his elevated position as Chief of Section One, Beijing's serious crime squad, had persuaded the authorities to ignore his indiscretion. That, and perhaps the fact that Margaret still occasionally took time off from her lectures in forensic pathology at the University of Public Security to perform key autopsies for the Beijing police.

He pulled the door shut on Li Jon's bedroom and stood listening for a moment. It had taken him some time, and the reading of a favourite bedtime story, to persuade the child to put away his new video iPod and settle down to sleep.

Margaret had placed bowls of rice and a plate of sweet and sour pork on the table in the living room, and they sat down to eat together with bottles of beer as darkness fell on Zhengyi Road. The light of the street lamp outside their first-floor window danced as the breeze blew through the leaves of the locust trees that lined the street. But even with all their windows open, the heat remained oppressive and overpoweringly humid. Li's fresh white shirt was already sticking to him. He wiped the sweat from his forehead with the back of his hand, then ran the palm of it back over his short-cut hair.

'There are seventeen million people in Beijing,' he said. 'Thousands of them go missing every day. They look for work, they don't find it, they move on.'

'She's just seventeen, Li Yan.' Margaret had no idea why she was playing advocate for the cleaning woman at the kinder-garten. Except that the appeal from one mother to another had touched something inside her.

'Teenagers are always disappearing. Runaways mostly. Unless there is evidence of a crime there is nothing much I can do about it.'

'Imagine,' Margaret said, 'that we were talking about Li Jon.'

Li's chopsticks paused, midway to his mouth, and he looked at the woman with whom, in spite of every cultural and lin-guistic obstacle, he had fallen in love. She always knew just what buttons to press. Not that he felt manipulated. It pleased him to think that someone could know him that well, and yet still choose to be with him. Finally he popped the pork into his mouth, masticating thoughtfully.

'Where does she live?'

'Somewhere in the north-west of the city. She wrote down her address.' Margaret pushed a dirty piece of paper across the table. 'Her family came to Beijing from Shaanxi Province about five years ago. A place called Chenjiayuan, on the Loëss Plateau.'

Li nodded. He had heard of the Loëss Plateau, a dense laby-rinth of eroding canyons along the Yellow River. A remote and arid place, where some villages were still unreachable by road. Anyone who could, left. Many of them came to the Chinese capital in search of work, sharing homes at first with friends or relatives who had preceded them, before finding somewhere to stay themselves. Beijing was increasingly dividing into small, distinct communities, tiny ghettos that shared the same rural and provincial heritage.

'Her father recently lost his job. Their only income is what the mother makes cleaning at the kindergarten. The girl's been gone almost a week, Li Yan.'

'I suppose they reported it to Public Security.'

'Of course. But like you said, the city is full of missing people.'

Li sighed. 'And what do you suppose I can do about it, Margaret?'

'You could ask Public Security for a progress report. An enquiry from the great Section Chief Li Yan would surely put a fire up their ass.'

Li raised an eyebrow and regarded her with a mixture of affection and irritation. He was accustomed to her sarcasm by now, of course, but cursed himself for still letting it affect him. He thought for a moment. 'And you conducted this entire conversation in *putonghua*?'

Margaret allowed herself a tiny smile of satisfaction. 'Of course.'

Li nodded his approval. 'Good. After ten years you finally seem to be making some progress with the language.'

Her eyes narrowed.

# CHAPTER TWO

## I

Li gazed from his office window, down through the dusty leaves of the trees into the narrow Beixinqiao Santiao below. Faded gold characters spelled out the name of the All China Federation of Returned Overseas Chinese on brown marble across the street. The air was filled with the roar of traffic on the new boulevard that cut through what had once been a quiet, residential neighbourhood, and air pollution reduced the apartment blocks which had appeared all around to carbonised shadows.

The square, four-floor, flat-roofed building that housed Section One was one of the few left standing in an area redeveloped beyond recognition.

Li blew smoke out through the open window, taking another pull on his cigarette before turning at the sound of his door opening. Detective Wu leaned in and forced a smile. He had not been happy to be sent on a commission to the Missing Persons Bureau, like some messenger boy. He was a homicide detective, and above such things. The only thing that pleased him was the message he had brought back. 'Bureau Chief Chen says if things are quiet in serious crime, he would be happy to pass some of his missing persons over to you.'

Li was not amused. The minimum he expected from an inferior officer like Chen was a little respect. But respect was a rare commodity in the brash new China. 'What did he tell you about the girl?'

Wu shrugged his shoulders, working his chewing gum from one side of his mouth to the other. He had not changed in all the time Li had known him, and the moustache he'd been trying to grow for the last fifteen years was still no thicker now than then. Ubiquitous sunglasses were pushed high up on his forehead. 'Nothing, Chief. Her folks reported her missing about five days ago. They opened a dossier, and since then . . . nothing.'

Li knew that in all probability the dossier had never been opened beyond that first entry. The bureau had neither the time nor the manpower to go chasing every missing teenager. 'Okay, thanks, Wu. Oh . . . and you can tell Bureau Chief Chen that if he ever wants to work in serious crime, he's going to have to improve his success rate and find a few missing persons first.'

Wu smirked ironically and closed the door behind him.

Li sat down and gazed at the paperwork accumulating in piles on his desk. In normal circumstances he would have let the matter drop there. But he knew that Margaret would press to know what action he had taken. He sighed and checked his diary. He had a dental appointment later that afternoon in

Haidian District, not far from where the girl's parents lived. He determined to visit them on his way home.

## II

The girl's family lived in one of those Soviet-style apartment blocks thrown up in the seventies in an attempt to solve Beijing's housing problem. It was one of the few remaining in a derelict quarter of Haidian marked for demolition. The sombre, weathered exterior was disfigured by lines of decrepit air-conditioning units, most of which no longer functioned.

Li chained his bicycle to a crowded stand beneath a rusted metal roof. In these days of dense traffic, bicycle was still the most efficient way to get around. The elevator in the block was broken, and he climbed to the fourth floor up a graffiti-covered stairwell that smelled of stale urine.

The narrow hall of the Jiang family's apartment gave access to the single room in which they lived and slept, a bathroom in which it was nearly impossible to turn around, and a tiny kitchen with a single gas ring, a microwave and a stone sink.

Jiang Ning greeted him at the door. It was her day off work, and she was both startled and overjoyed to see him, grateful nearly to the point of tears. She guided him into the disorderly room shared by mother, father and daughter. A double bed was pushed into one corner, a single bed diagonally opposite. A small TV sat on a wooden cabinet behind a square table covered with an impermeable tablecloth. There was an old, worn divan, a single armchair, and almost no room to move.

An emaciated, dark-skinned man with thinning black hair brushed across a narrow skull sat at the table playing solitaire with a pack of soiled playing cards. He wore grey shorts and a dirty white singlet.

'My husband, Jin,' Ning said, and the man nodded cautiously in Li's direction. 'That's Meilin's bed over there.'

Li looked at the tiny single bed, and the posters taped to the wall above it. Chinese sports stars. Runners. Faces and names that had become familiar in every home during the Games. Medals and ribbons were carefully exhibited in a glass-doored cabinet beside the bed, along with several photographs of a teenage girl smiling at the camera.

Ning followed his eyes. 'That's her,' she said. 'The best daughter a mother could hope for. Not hanging about on street corners, or out at clubs and bars downtown. She's an athlete, Section Chief. A junior champion. One day she will run for China, I know it.'

Li wandered over to look at her victor's medals. Meilin was a middle-distance runner – 800 and 1500 metres. She had won an impressive number of events. He turned to face her parents. 'When did you first become aware she was missing?'

'When I returned from visiting my family in Shaanxi last weekend she was gone,' Ning said.

Li's gaze moved to the girl's father. Jiang Jin shrugged. 'She was in and out over the weekend. I was out a lot myself, and back late Sunday night. She wasn't home yet. But I didn't think much of it. She's been seeing some boy over at Dahuisi. Coming home later and later.' He glanced at his wife. 'She's not the angel her mother thinks she is.' And Li sensed the tension between them. 'Anyway, I went to sleep, and didn't start to worry till I woke up in the morning and she still wasn't here.'

'She'd been gone more than twenty-four hours by the time I got back,' Ning said. 'That's when I reported it to Public Security.'

The name 'Ning' meant 'tranquillity', but there was very little tranquil about the missing girl's mother now. Her hands trembled, and she seemed always on the point of tears.

Li looked at her husband again. 'What is it you do, Mister Jiang?'

'Plays cards!' Ning's voice was heavy with resentment.

But Jiang Jin ignored her. 'I start a new job with the city parks division next week.'

Li nodded. 'Tell me about Meilin's boyfriend.'

### III

Lao Rong lived with his parents in one of the few remaining *hutongs* in Dahuisi, just north of Beijing Zoo, in one of four small houses enclosing a traditional *siheyuan* courtyard. Slate roofs descended toward a locust tree that shaded the paved yard. In among the carcasses of long-dead bicycles, coal briquets were already piled high in preparation for the winter. A white-painted sign on the wall outside gave notice that the property was to be demolished.

A call to Wu from his cellphone had pre-armed Li with the

information that Lao, although just nineteen, already had a criminal record. For theft. The boy was alarmed by Li's visit. A tall, thin lad, with long hair that fell into his eyes, he directed the Section Chief away from the house to a dark corner of the courtyard. 'What do you want? I ain't done nothing wrong.'

'I never said you had. But when you act this nervous it makes me wonder.'

'My father'll kill me if I get in trouble with the police again.'

Li looked around the courtyard, at all the doors and windows that stood open, and wondered how many ears were listening from the dark beyond. 'I wanted to ask you about Jiang Meilin.'

Concern immediately inscribed itself on the young face. 'What's happened to her?'

'I was hoping you might tell me. Her parents reported her missing five days ago. Have you seen her?'

The boy paled visibly. He shook his head. 'Not since Sunday. She came here to the house. My folks like her, but they were out. She stayed quite late and went home about twelve.'

'You didn't think it was strange that she hasn't been in contact since then?'

'Well, yes. Normally she would call me. From a public telephone. She doesn't have a cellphone, so I can't call her. And she wouldn't ever let me go to the house. Said her parents wouldn't like it. Usually I only see her at weekends.'

'So you wouldn't have any idea where she might have gone?'

'No.'

'And she never talked to you about leaving home? Running away, maybe?'

The young man's hesitation was almost imperceptible. 'No, she didn't.'

Li took a fresh business card from his maroon Public Security ID wallet and handed it to the boy, holding it at each corner and facing towards him. Lao Rong looked at Li's name and rank before glancing up, open-mouthed. 'Section Chief?'

'Just call me if you hear from her.'

He was almost at Dahuisi Lu when he heard a woman's voice calling after him. He stopped his bicycle and looked back to see a middle-aged woman in a black skirt and cardigan and pink running shoes hurrying after him. In spite of the heat, she wore a headscarf, as if somehow that might hide her identity. When finally she reached him it took her a moment to catch her breath.

'I couldn't help but overhear your conversation with Lao Rong in the *siheyuan*,' she said. One of the many ears listening in the dark, Li surmised. 'He told you that Meilin went home around midnight.'

'Did she not?'

'It was later, Section Chief.' She glanced over her shoulder, back along the *hutong*. 'He's a bad lot, that boy. Been in trouble with your people a few times.'

'Are you telling me he lied?'

'Not exactly. But it was nearer one o'clock when she left. And in tears.'

Li cocked his head, interested for the first time. 'Do you know why?'

She shook her head. 'I just know they had a big argument. Raised voices. I heard him shouting, her crying. But I don't know what it was about.'

Li pursed his lips thoughtfully.

# CHAPTER THREE

## I

The letter arrived three days after Li asked Wu to circulate a poster of the girl's face – an image reproduced from one of the photographs in Meilin's medals cabinet. He had also asked Wu for background investigations on the girl's family, and the boyfriend. Considering his attachment to a missing-persons case to be something close to demotion, Wu had instigated the checks with bad grace, and ordered teams of uniformed Public Security officers to paste up posters in public places all over Haidian. Now he came into Li's office holding a sheet of paper and a torn envelope. His face was, unusually, bright with excitement.

'We've got a response, Chief.'

Li looked up blankly from his desk.

'Jiang Meilin. The missing girl.' Wu waved the paper and envelope. 'Anonymous letter.'

Li stood up and reached into his pocket. 'And you didn't think to wear gloves?'

Wu's face fell. 'I didn't know what it was until after I'd opened it.'

Li produced a pair of latex gloves and put them on. He took the letter and envelope and placed them carefully on the desk, then leaned over to have a look.

'It was posted yesterday in Haidian,' Wu said, as if trying to compensate for his mistake.

Li examined the postmark, then ran his eyes over the neat calligraphy that the sender had used to address the envelope. 'An educated hand,' he said. His gaze returned to the postmark. 'And this is the post office that serves Beida, if I'm not mistaken. It could be the letter was written by a student, or a professor, at Beijing University.'

Wu said nothing. He knew that this was not a conclusion he would have reached himself. But then, that was probably why he was still a detective, while Li was Section Chief.

'The university recently installed a biometric fingerprint scanner to speed up processing in the canteen. So let's see what prints we can lift off this . . .' Li glanced at Wu. 'Excluding yours, of course. Then do a comparison check with their database.'

Li turned his attention to the letter itself. It was a cryptic note:

*I saw your missing girl at a ghost wedding last week. She was the bride.*

Li looked up, perplexed. 'Ghost wedding?'

Wu nodded. 'That's what I thought. I did some asking around. Apparently it's a tradition that still exists in some remote rural communities. It's bad luck for a young man to die unmarried. So the family buys the corpse of a recently deceased female and they perform some kind of marriage ceremony. A ghost wedding. It seems there's a sociology professor at Tsinghua University who is something of an expert on the subject.'

## II

Tsinghua University was once described by the nearly president of the United States, Al Gore, as the MIT of China. It was an eclectic collection of faculties, from mechanics and technology to law, sociology and medicine. Each faculty was represented by one of the vast stone or marble edifices on each side of a wide, tree-shaded avenue leading to the massive master building at the far end. At this time of year there were almost no students on campus. Only occasional cyclists passed along the boulevard, possibly here for special summer classes. Many of the staff, however, were still at work.

Professor Bao seemed happy for Li to interrupt the monotony of the summer vacation, and used the excuse to stretch his legs and get some air. Two young men in shorts and T-shirts played basketball on a tarmac court as the young policeman and the elderly professor walked by.

'*Minghun*,' said Professor Bao, 'is what it is called among the peoples of the Loëss Plateau. An afterlife marriage. It has its roots in the ancient form of ancestor veneration which maintains that we all continue to exist after death, and that the living are obliged to tend to our needs.'

'Including the arranging of a marriage?'

'Indeed. It is traditional Chinese belief that an unmarried life is incomplete, and some parents fear that an unmarried dead son could be an unhappy one. So they find a bride for him after death.'

'How do they do that?'

'Oh, usually through an informal network of family or friends, they will find parents who have recently lost a single daughter. Those parents will sell the body as a way of finding their daughter a place in the dead man's family line. You see, Section Chief Li, outside of the cities, China is really still a paternal clan culture. A woman does not belong to her parents. She has no place on her father's family tree. She must marry into her husband's ancestral lineage.'

'So money changes hands.'

The white-haired old professor nodded and smiled. 'I know, I know. It is illegal to buy and sell bodies, but it happens.'

'Even in Beijing?'

'Unlikely, I would have thought. Unless you had a community of families from an area of China that practised the *minghun*.'

Which was exactly, Li thought, what he had discovered among the condemned urban slums of Haidian District.

# CHAPTER FOUR

## I

Li and Wu arrived back at Section One at almost exactly the same moment. As Li wheeled his bicycle under the stand at the side entrance, Wu pulled his Beijing Jeep into the kerb and jumped out on to the sidewalk. His sunglasses were down, and he was chewing gum enthusiastically, evidently pleased with himself. 'Got our man, Chief.'

'Which man is that, Wu?'

'Our anonymous letter writer. Did just as you suggested. Lifted fingerprints off the letter. There were four sets. I took copies of all four up to Beida and ran them past the scanner. Bingo. Up pops an ID. Feng Qi. Second-year student. He's working at the university over the summer, and still living at the student residences there.'

Li raised one eyebrow and bowed his head to acknowledge a job well done. 'Better bring him in, then.'

'The uniforms are already on their way, Chief.' Wu grinned happily.

## II

Feng was sitting nervously on his own at the table when Li and Wu came into the interrogation room. Anxious dark eyes jumped in their direction. He sat uncomfortably on the edge of his seat, leaning forwards a little, and wringing his hands together. 'You can't hold me here like this. I have rights.'

Li sat down opposite him. 'You've been reading too much Western detective fiction, son. You have no rights. It is your duty to help us in our investigation and tell us what you know. Failure to do so will only plant in my mind the presumption of your guilt.'

'I have nothing to hide.' He tried to sit up straight and present a defiant face.

'Then why did you write to us anonymously?'

The young man's fear that he had somehow been identified was finally confirmed, and his defiance foundered, along with his posture. He started to wring his hands again. 'I didn't want to get involved.'

'You *are* involved.' Wu pulled up a chair and sat down beside Li. 'Witness to a possible murder.'

Feng Qi paled, and with Wu's words, Li for the first time let himself countenance the thought that Jiang Meilin was actually dead. In his mind he saw her smiling photograph from the medals cabinet, and felt her mother's pain. Margaret's plea for him to look into the disappearance of a teenage girl had turned suddenly from a favour into a murder inquiry. 'Better tell us everything you know, son,' he said.

Feng glanced from one to the other. 'Can I have a cigarette?'

Li nodded to Wu, who reluctantly offered them each a cigarette, then passed his lighter around. Blue smoke rose through the hot, still air into the shaft of light that fell at an angle from the narrow window high in the wall.

Feng said, 'Sheng Wei and I were at university together. I'd known him since we were kids back in Shaanxi. My parents moved to Beijing when I was seven, and I didn't see him again till he appeared one day at my middle school. His family had come to the city, too, and were living in a place just down the street.'

'You were both from the Loëss Plateau?'

'Sure.'

'How many people from the plateau live in that area of Haidian?'

The young man shrugged. 'I've no idea. People have been coming here for a couple of generations now. There must be hundreds, maybe thousands.'

'So tell me about Sheng Wei.'

A cloud, like cataracts, crossed the boy's eyes. 'He was killed in a motorbike accident about ten days ago.' His lips tightened as he drew a deep, trembling breath. 'Wei was so smart. He had a great future. Everything to live for. It was a tragedy.' Feng shook his head. 'I thought I was going to his funeral. It turned out to be his wedding.'

'A *minghun*?'

He nodded. 'Bizarrest thing I ever saw. Paper dummies, all dressed up in traditional wedding costume. The spirits of the dead, to be burned after the ceremony and sent to the afterlife as man and wife. There was a priest and everything. Proxy wedding vows, rings, the lot. Sure, I'd heard about it. But I assumed it was one of those urban myths. Just a story.' He closed his eyes for a moment, trying to control his breathing. 'You've no idea what it was like seeing Wei lying there in his coffin. And that dead girl in the coffin next to his. The minute I saw her I knew it wasn't right.'

'You knew her?' Wu said.

'From school. She was about three years behind me. A pretty girl. Kind of quiet. I heard she was doing well in athletics, that she could be up for a scholarship. I was sure I would have heard something if anything had happened to her.' He looked at Li, an appeal for understanding in his eyes. 'But there she was. Wei had been killed in an accident. I had no reason to think that something similar hadn't happened to her, too.' He paused. 'Until I saw the *Missing* posters.' He closed his eyes again and summoned the courage to ask the question that had been troubling his conscience all this time. 'You don't think they killed her, do you?'

Li's mouth was fixed in a grim line. It was some moments before his lips moved. 'Someone did.'

# CHAPTER FIVE

Lianxiang *hutong* was yet another ancient alley scheduled for demolition. Little by little the authorities were effacing the city's history, the labyrinth of *hutongs* and *siheyuan* that denoted a way of life dating back to the Mongols. Already most of it was gone, replaced by luxury apartments and shopping malls. A new generation of wealthy Chinese was replacing the old Beijingers, and the floating population from all around China which had descended on the city looking for work was being swept away. Where, Li wondered, would they all go? Where would they live? After all, not everyone could be rich – even if Deng Xiaoping had declared it *glorious* to be so.

He pushed his bicycle along the narrow alley, between high stone walls, until he found the gate to the condemned *siheyuan* occupied by the Sheng family. In the dark alley leading to the courtyard beyond, he leaned his bicycle against the wall and squeezed past the detritus of disposable lives. The tree shading the courtyard was decorated with bamboo bird cages, and in the confined space the sound of birdsong was almost deafening. The singing was accompanied by the discordant sounds of a piece from the Peking Opera playing on a radio somewhere in the dark beyond open windows and doors. Heat fibrillated in the thick summer air. A very old lady, dressed entirely in black, sat sleeping in the shade.

'Hello!' Li called out. And after a short time a middle-aged woman in a blue blouse and red cardigan emerged from the south-facing door. She looked at him curiously for a moment, before curiosity gave way to fear as realisation dawned.

'Can I help you?' But she knew what he wanted.

'Yes,' Li said. 'You can tell me where you got the body of the girl you married to your dead son.'

Sheng Nuwa and her husband Dai sat side by side in the semi-dark and comparative cool of an inner room, its window shutters closed, the only light spilling in through an open door. Both faces were ghostly pale as they surrendered to Li's hard gaze. Li wondered if this was, in fact, the room where the *minghun* had been played out. Feng Qi's description of the odour had stayed with him, and he wrinkled his nose at the thought of it.

Sheng Nuwa said, 'We had no idea until we saw the *Missing* posters. She was only delivered to us on the day of the wedding. We thought she had come from the crematorium. That's what the man who brought her said.'

'I'll need his name.'

'We don't know it.' It was the husband who spoke this time, and when Li blew his disbelief through pursed lips, he added quickly, 'They told us they weren't able to get us a body, so we had resigned ourselves to proceeding with just the paper dummy. Then this guy arrives at the last minute.'

'Who did you go to originally to ask for a body?'

Sheng Dai glanced darkly at his wife. Their reluctance to speak was clear.

But Li was losing patience. 'Come on! Spit it out! You're in trouble enough as it is. Don't make it worse.'

The dead boy's mother said, 'We were given a name. A certain Gan Bo. He could find wives, we were told, for the living. It's hard these days for a single man to find himself a woman.'

It was, Li knew, a demographic time bomb for the future of his country. A legacy of the one-child policy, and the traditional preference for boys over girls. With only a hundred women for every 130 men, there was a growing demand for mail-order brides. And a criminal element had appeared to satisfy that demand, trading women for money.

Sheng Nuwa brushed a stray strand of hair from her eyes. 'But we were told that sometimes Gan Bo could supply dead ones, too.'

Li could barely conceal his disgust. 'So you put in an order for one.'

Her eyes dropped away from his. 'We were only trying to do the best for our son.'

'And what did Gan Bo say?'

Sheng Dai said, 'He told us he would see what he could do. But he came back a couple of days later and said he couldn't get one in time. And with the summer heat, we couldn't wait.'

'So then some guy just appeared from nowhere?'

'Yes. On the morning of the *minghun*. He brought the girl

in the back of a van. Said that Gan Bo had been able to find a body for us after all. We'd already acquired a second coffin.'

'And you paid him.'

'Yes.'

'How much?'

'He wanted dollars.'

'How much?'

'Twelve hundred.'

Li clenched his jaw involuntarily. So that was what a young girl's life was worth these days. Twelve hundred dollars. The price of a plasma TV. 'Tell me what the man who brought the body looked like.'

But the dead boy's father just shrugged. 'I didn't pay him much attention. I was kind of in shock. He was just some guy. Forty, maybe. A little older. He didn't stay long.'

Li found himself strangely disappointed that this description, however brief, in no way resembled the tall, skinny boy who had been Meilin's lover. 'And the bodies? I suppose you had them cremated.' All evidence destroyed in the furnace.

'That was the original plan,' Sheng Nuwa said. 'But then a cousin with a little land out near Donghulinmen offered to let us bury them there, and we jumped at the chance.'

# CHAPTER SIX

Li and Margaret drove in silence, south-west out of Beijing on the G109. Meilin's parents sat in the back of the Jeep, Jiang Jin with his arm around his wife. But there was no consoling her. Li had broken the news to them that afternoon, and Jiang Ning had barely stopped crying since. Her eyes were red raw. There was only one final act now to be played out in the life and death of their daughter. And that was the identification of her body.

It was dark by the time they reached the cluster of houses among the trees at the end of a rough dirt track leading from the road. Li parked in a dusty square. These were poor rural houses with thin brick walls and low roofs, huddled around a badly equipped village store. Goats tied to a stand of willow trees raised their heads and baaed into the night. They heard the snuffling of pigs, and smelled them before they saw them.

Li guided the little group up a narrow track between crumbling walls towards a halo of light that broke the darkness ahead. Several Public Security vehicles and a white forensics van were assembled around the entrance to a long, low house beside a rectangular wall that enclosed a hundred square metres of wildly overgrown garden.

They passed through a moongate, and the officer standing guard nodded solemnly. Beyond, they could see where the vegetation had been beaten down and the earth freshly disturbed. The area was enclosed by white canvas stretched between wooden posts, and lit by arc lamps. Four men in white Tyvek suits stood around leaning on the spades they had used to uncover the shallow graves. All chatter ceased as Li led the girl's parents to the graveside. Margaret stayed behind, leaving a respectful distance.

Li nodded to the nearest white suit, and the man stepped down into the hole where two coffins lay side by side. His shadow fell across the first of them as he prised open the top. Li heard Jiang Ning gasp as the decaying corpse of a young man was exposed to the full glare of the lamps. The maggots had already started to eat his face, which had taken on a ghoulish look, the flesh of his eyes, nose, and mouth receding, a ghastly grimace revealing long yellow teeth.

As the second lid was levered free, Jiang Ning howled: a piercing, desolate sound that came from deep in her throat and sent a glacial chill through them all, in spite of the heat.

Meilin's body had not achieved the same degree of decomposition. She had been alive, it seemed, at least until the day before the *minghun*, several days longer than her ghost husband. But there was a strange lividity about her face. It seemed, if anything, slightly more distended than his. But there was no doubting who she was. Her mother turned away, burying her face in her husband's chest to suppress her tears. He put comforting arms around her and closed his eyes.

Li became aware of Margaret at his side and half turned. She was looking down into the dead girl's coffin, and he saw that for once the professional detachment of the pathologist was missing. Moonlight flashed in tear-filled eyes.

'I want to do the autopsy,' she said, her voice barely a whisper.

# CHAPTER SEVEN

The naked body of Jiang Meilin was wheeled into the autopsy room by two assistants, and transferred to a steel autopsy table. The air was chill and suffused with the slightly perfumed odour of decay, like meat that has been left in the refrigerator two weeks past its sell-by date.

Margaret stood at the table preparing for the initial examination. Beneath a long-sleeved cotton gown, she wore green surgeon's pyjamas covered by a plastic apron. Plastic covers protected white tennis shoes, and her long blonde hair was secured beneath a plastic shower cap. Now she pulled on a pair of latex gloves, followed by plastic covers, then a steel-mesh glove over her non-cutting hand, before finally pulling on a further latex pair.

She was being assisted by Pathologist Wang, with whom she had conducted autopsies on many occasions. When she had first arrived in China, young and arrogant, and skilled in the latest Western techniques, he had resented the shadow she cast over him and his department. But such resentments were history now, and they had long ago arrived at something approaching mutual respect. Their working relationship was comfortable, and she enjoyed his irreverent sense of humour.

But even Wang could find nothing amusing to say today. He cast his eyes over the slim teenager and shook his head.

'Pity. Pretty girl.'

Margaret looked at the body on the table before her. Meilin was taller than the average Chinese, much of her height concentrated in the long femurs which had given her the power to run fast. But she did not possess the muscle mass that would have made her a sprinter. Instead her legs were slender and elegant. Margaret began with the feet and worked her way up the body looking for any unusual markings. She found some slight bruising on the forearms, noting them on a body chart she held in a clipboard, but did not consider them significant.

Wang examined her hands. 'No sign of trauma,' he said. 'And no blood or skin beneath the fingernails.' He and Margaret exchanged looks, and he nodded to one of the assistants, who drew blood from the femoral artery with a large syringe. 'What do you think they'll find in toxicology?'

Margaret shrugged. 'These days, who knows? Rohypnol would have had a sedative effect after fifteen to twenty minutes. She obviously didn't put up any kind of a fight.'

They continued the external examination. There was no sign of sexual activity, and no trauma around small, flat breasts with their tiny, dark areolae around the nipples.

Then they came to the neck, where a skin-coloured cosmetic foundation had dried and cracked. Using moistened cotton pads, Margaret carefully washed it away to reveal the bruising that the facial lividity had suggested would almost certainly be there: four circles on the left side of the neck, two of which were close to half an inch in diameter, one larger oval on the right side.

'Her killer left his mark,' Wang said.

Margaret carefully traced the line of the little crescent-shaped abrasions that were associated with the bruising. Tiny flakes of skin were heaped up at the concave side. 'And took a little of her away with him beneath his fingernails.'

They moved up, then, to her face, where blood pressure had mounted in her head and caused petechial haemorrhaging of the tiny blood vessels around the eyes and nose. It was not necessary to stop someone breathing to strangle them. It only required around four-and-a-half pounds of pressure on the jugular to prevent blood draining from the head. Death would have come fast.

Margaret pulled back the eyelids and closed them again. 'Strange.'

'What is?' Wang looked more closely.

'There are circles of paler flesh around the eyes, blanched into the lividity.' Margaret stared at the closed eyes of the dead girl, and could almost have sworn she saw patterns in those pale circles. 'As if coins might have been placed over them to keep them shut.' She turned to Wang. 'Do we have a TMDT kit?'

'We do.' And he nodded to one of the assistants, who disappeared to return two minutes later with a four-ounce spray bottle of test solution, and a short-wave ultraviolet light source with a 4-watt bulb, sometimes known as a Wood's lamp.

Margaret took the bottle, and carefully sprayed the solution

around each eye, and they waited in silence for several minutes until it had dried. 'Lights,' she said. And the assistant
turned out the overhead lights, plunging the autopsy room
into total darkness.

Margaret snapped on the Wood's lamp, and an eerie ultraviolet glow filled the room. She moved the lamp over the
dead girl's eyes. There over each one, marked in dark purple
against the yellow background of the dried solution, were
two perfectly round images with clearly engraved markings.

'Coins,' Wang said. 'You were right. What metal is denoted
by purple?'

Margaret stared thoughtfully at the circular patterns
engraved into the lividity around the eyes. 'Brass or copper,'
she said. 'We'll need to take photographs. And samples.'

# CHAPTER EIGHT

## I

Gan Bo ran a computer-dating agency from an office on the twelfth floor of a new tower block in Sanlihi Lu, overlooking Yuyuantan Park. He didn't appear to employ any staff, except for a bored-looking young secretary who was painting her fingernails when Li arrived. She seemed pleased by the interruption, and made a great show of calling her boss on the intercom to announce Li's arrival, before conducting him into the inner sanctum.

Gan's office was big and empty with an enormous desk placed before a glass wall with a panoramic view over the park below. Li could see the sun reflecting off the lake where he and Margaret often skated with Li Jon when it froze over in winter.

Gan himself was a broad man with the yellowish skin and Han features of a southerner. A thick head of hair was gelled back from an unlined face that Li guessed had seen maybe thirty summers. He wore immaculately pressed black trousers, a plain white Armani shirt, and shiny black Gucci shoes. A

Havana cigar smouldered in an ashtray on his desk, and the room was filled with the rich, toasty smell of it. The desk, too, was almost empty, except for a computer screen and keyboard, a telephone, and a cellphone which lay within easy reach of Gan's grasp.

Gan stood up and waved Li nervously towards the only guest seat in the office. 'What can I do for you, Section Chief?'

Li remained standing. 'You can tell me where you acquired the body of a young girl called Jiang Meilin.'

Gan frowned. 'I have no idea what you're talking about.'

'Of course you do. About ten days ago you were contacted by a man called Sheng Dai who had recently lost his son in a motorcycle accident. He asked if you could provide the body of a young girl to take part in a *minghun*, to ensure their son's happiness in the afterlife.'

Gan eased himself back into his chair and lifted his cigar from the ashtray. He puffed on it thoughtfully. 'Yes, I remember that. But I run a computer-dating agency, Section Chief. A legitimate business finding brides for single men.' His smile was smooth, like silk. 'I don't know where he got the idea I could provide him with a dead one, but I sent him away.'

'Oh?' Li sauntered towards the window, his hands in his pockets. 'That's bizarre, Mister Gan. Because on the day of the funeral someone turned up with the body of a young girl and told the Sheng family that you had found her for them.'

Gan rotated his chair towards Li. He could not conceal the look of puzzlement in his eyes, but feigned nonchalance. 'Nothing to do with me.'

'He took twelve hundred dollars for it. But I guess you never saw a cent of that.'

Something like anger shadowed his face, but there was no trace of it in his voice. 'Twelve hundred dollars, Section Chief? That's a lot of money for some dead meat.'

Li could see the distant figures of barbers cutting the hair of clients at the entrance to the park below. Among the trees beyond, groups of old men gathered around to watch games of chess in progress.

'That "dead meat", Mister Gan, was a living, breathing human being just a few hours before.' He turned around. 'Someone murdered that girl to provide a corpse for a ghost wedding. And I think that someone was you.'

Gan paled. 'That's ridiculous!'

'Do you know how they execute murderers, Mister Gan? They take them into a public stadium and shoot them in the back of the head. It would make a hell of a mess of that expensive designer shirt of yours. All that blood and brain tissue.'

'I run a legitimate business.'

'You trade in human beings.'

'Live ones. I never killed anyone in my life.'

'I think you might have trouble convincing a court of that.'

'In the name of the sky, I didn't kill her!'

'Then who did?'

'I have no idea.'

Li leaned over and removed Gan's cigar from his hand, stubbing it out in the ashtray, then put his own hands on the arms of the desk chair, and placed his face just inches away from Gan's. 'You and I both know that this computer-dating crap is just a front. You procure women for desperate men. God knows how. But no doubt that will come to light as we start taking your little empire apart. I don't know if you murdered Jiang Meilin or not, but there's enough circumstantial evidence, I think, to get a conviction. Especially when we can demonstrate to the court how you really make your living.'

He could smell Gan's fear, even above the stink of rancid cigar smoke on his breath.

'Alright, alright.' Gan raised his hands in submission, and Li stood up slowly. 'It's happened, you know, from time to time, that someone has asked me to procure a body for one of these stupid damned ceremonies. I tell them it's not what I do. But I'm a nice guy, you know? I like to help if I can.'

'How exactly do you *help*?'

Gan drew a long breath. 'I know this guy. A porter at a hospital.'

'Which one?'

'The Beijing Hospital in Chongwenmen.'

Li knew it. It was just north of the Temple of Heaven. 'And?'

'And, well, you know, if there just happens to be a recently deceased person of the right specifications available, then sometimes a deal can be done.'

'How?'

Gan shrugged. 'The porter has a friend at the crematorium.' He paused. 'Who's to say whether or not a coffin has a body in it when it goes into the furnace?' There was a long silence.

Then, 'I swear on the graves of my ancestors, Section Chief, I never killed that girl. And I don't know who did.'

For some reason that Li couldn't quite put his finger on, he believed him. 'But you asked the porter if he could get you a body, right?'

'Yes.'

'And he said he couldn't?'

'That's right.'

'I want his name.'

## II

Huan Da was as defiant as he was stupid. But in a detached sort of way, Li almost admired his unshakeable loyalty. He was going to be a tough nut to crack. Gan had collapsed like a house of cards, but Huan was an altogether different proposition.

The smoke of many cigarettes hung thick in the air of the interrogation room. Years of wheeling cancer patients from the ward to the morgue had not diminished Huan's enthusiasm for smoking. He had consumed nearly half a pack in the hour since Wu had brought him in from the hospital.

Confronted with what Li already knew, Huan quickly realised that there was no point in denying his part in the business of supplying corpses for cash. He had taken Li through the whole sordid procedure. There was, he said, not much demand, perhaps one or two a year. But he made more from the sale of a single corpse than he earned in twelve months as a porter.

An uneducated and stupid farm labourer from Sichuan, he had come to Beijing nearly twenty years ago and found the job at the Beijing Hospital almost immediately. He had been introduced to Gan by a mutual acquaintance nearly three years previously, and had supplied perhaps five bodies in that time. He had not kept count, he said.

Shrugging his shoulders implacably, he had told Li, 'I didn't see the harm in it. After all, they were dead already.'

When a request was received from Gan, Huan would scrutinise mortalities at the hospital for the previous few days. If he couldn't find a match, he had colleagues in other hospitals who were always eager for a percentage and would check their own death lists. If a corpse was found that corresponded to the request, then arrangements were made with a contact at the central crematorium to remove the body before the coffin went to the flames. Sometimes, Huan said, the crematorium worker himself would come up with a suitable match, since he had bodies coming in from all over the city.

But where Gan had shown no scruples about betraying a colleague to save his own skin, Huan remained resolutely silent about the identity of his contact at the crematorium, the only other link in the chain who could have known in detail the requirements of the Sheng family.

'That,' Huan said yet again, 'would be a betrayal of trust.' And he lit another cigarette.

Li breathed his frustration through his teeth and lit a cigarette himself.

The door swung open and the duty officer leaned in. 'Doctor Campbell is here, Chief. I put her in your office.'

Li hastily stubbed out the cigarette before searching for the peppermints he kept in his pocket. He was supposed to have quit smoking months ago. Of course, Margaret would smell the smoke on his clothes, but since almost everyone around him still smoked, that was easily explained.

'You can tell her I'm on my way.'

When the duty officer had gone, he popped a peppermint into his mouth and stood up. He looked down at Huan, who seemed calmly unconcerned. Li leaned over him, supporting himself with fists on the table. 'You said you saw no harm in what you were doing, because the souls you sold were already dead. Well think on this, Huan. That girl wasn't dead. She was alive and well, with her whole life ahead of her. The chances are, the person whose identity you are refusing to reveal is her killer. There is no honour in that.' He walked to the door, and held it open for a moment before turning back. 'Besides which, it makes you an accessory to murder, and just as eligible for execution as he is.'

Huan remained expressionless. He sucked in more smoke and blew it at the ceiling.

Margaret had cleared a space on Li's desk and laid out some photographs, and a preliminary autopsy report. The full report would follow tomorrow. She wrinkled her nose the moment Li entered the room, and sniffed the air. 'Peppermints,' she said. 'I hear they can be almost as addictive as cigarettes.'

He raised an eyebrow in feigned innocence. 'Really?'

Margaret smiled ironically. 'Yes. I believe some people take up smoking to disguise the smell of them.'

Li blushed involuntarily. 'What do you have for me?'

She sighed and indicated the photographs on his desk. 'She was strangled. Sedated first, so she didn't put up a fight. We'll know what he used when the blood tests come back from toxicology.'

Li rounded the desk to look at the photographs – sharp, clear colour prints that left nothing to the imagination. He picked up the picture that showed the bruising on her neck.

'Left by the fingers,' Margaret said. 'Four on that side, a thumb on the other, and several abrasions caused by the fingernails.' She picked up another print. 'The purple colouring around her face is caused by vascular congestion, and the petechial haemorrhaging of tiny blood vessels close to the surface. But . . .' She cleared more space and laid out the final two photographs – one of each eye, taken under the ultraviolet light of the Wood's lamp. 'For some reason her killer placed coins over her eyes, whose weight had the effect of leaving their impression in the purple colouring caused by the congestion. Treated with a chemical spray and photographed under ultraviolet, you can clearly see the markings left by each coin.'

Li lifted one of the pictures and studied it without comment.

'We've recovered traces of the metal they left on her skin. So if you were ever able to obtain the coins, we could match them up.' She canted her head to one side to look at the photograph that Li was still holding. 'Although, I have to say,

I've never seen coins quite like these before. They might not be easy to identify, never mind find.' When he didn't respond, she turned to look at him and saw that he had gone quite pale. 'Are you alright?'

'I know exactly what these are,' he said. 'And I know exactly where to find them.'

An unexpected knock at the door surprised them both. Wu entered, clutching a beige dossier. 'Sorry to disturb you, Chief. But I thought you ought to take a look at this.' He joined them at the desk and laid down the dossier to open it. 'Those background investigations you asked me to do . . .' He flipped over a page, and pointed his finger at a paragraph halfway down the one beneath it. 'Can't be a coincidence, can it?'

Li read in silence.

'What is it?' Margaret's growing ability with the spoken word did not extend to the mystifying number of characters that made up written Chinese.

Li's eyes burned with a dark intensity. 'I know who killed her,' he said. He met her eye. 'And you've just provided me with the means of proving it.'

# CHAPTER NINE

They could hear voices raised in anger as they stood on the fourth-floor landing outside the door of the Jiang family apartment. Li's three sharp raps on the door were followed by a sudden silence. Then footsteps.

The door opened to reveal the flushed face of Meilin's mother, long, greasy hair pulled back from her face. She seemed surprised to see Li and Margaret, the shadows of Wu and other officers behind them. There was a dead quality in her eyes, which had lost their brightness from the moment Li brought her the news of her daughter's death. Her mouth opened, but it was some moments before she spoke. 'What's happened?'

Li said, 'May we come in?'

'Of course.' She held the door open, and Margaret followed Li down the dark, narrow hall to the living room at the end. The other officers remained on the landing.

The faces of Meilin's father, still in his singlet and shorts, and her boyfriend, Lao Rong, were turned expectantly towards the door. Li looked at the boy. 'What are you doing here?'

But it was Jiang Jin who answered. 'He thinks because he knew her for a month and called her his girlfriend, that he has some rights. The right to be at her funeral, the right to question how we treated her. *Our* daughter!'

'You weren't her parents, you were her jailers. She was terrified of you, you know that? Terrified to bring me home with her, terrified of how you would react.' Passion and pain coloured Lao Rong's face.

Jiang Jin's lip curled in contempt. 'Yes, because she knew we wouldn't approve of scum like you. And she was right.'

'That's enough!' Li stepped between them.

Margaret pushed past the small group towards the single bed in the corner. Meilin's bed. Sheets and blankets neatly folded, a pillow untouched since the girl's disappearance. She drew two photographs out of a large manila envelope and laid them side by side on the bed. They were the photographs, taken under ultraviolet light, of the impressions left by the coins on Meilin's eyes. But they weren't coins, she knew that now.

Li opened the door of the medals cabinet where they kept her photograph. It seemed more like an altar now. He scanned the array of medals on the shelves, before selecting two and carefully laying one alongside each of the photographs. It was easy to see, even at a glance, that they were an exact match.

Li turned towards Jiang Jin. 'Seem familiar?'

Sweat began to appear on the man's forehead as he stared with rabbit eyes at the pictures and medals lying on the bed. Suddenly he turned, running past his wife and Lao Rong and vanishing into the darkness of the hall beyond. They heard a struggle and raised voices at the door before Jiang Jin, his arm locked behind his back, was marched back into the room by Wu. He was ghostly pale, and sweat trickled down his face. Defeat already in his eyes. He knew it was over.

His wife turned towards Li, face filled with fear and confusion. 'I don't understand.' They flickered towards the photographs, then back again.

'Your husband killed your daughter, Mrs Jiang. For twelve hundred dollars.'

Her eyes opened wide now, incredulous. She turned them on her husband, and he visibly recoiled under their gaze. 'They said they were going to kill me if I didn't pay up.' A feeble, desperate attempt at justification.

'Who?' Li said.

Anger and hatred fought for dominance on his wife's face. 'You bastard! You killed our daughter to pay off your gambling debts?'

Li's mouth set in a grim line. Now he understood why. He said, 'You couldn't supply a dead girl for the *minghun*, because you had just lost your job at the crematorium. So you turned to a live one. Your own flesh and blood. And did the deal yourself.'

'It was my only way out. She was *my* daughter. I gave her life. Why shouldn't I have the right to take it?' Defiance now.

Before anyone could move, Jiang Ning flew at the man she had married, tiny clenched fists hammering at his face and chest. Mucus frothed around her mouth as she screamed and cursed at him. Li stepped quickly forward to put his arms around her and control her flailing arms. She fought him for several moments, before going suddenly limp, turning to bury her face in his chest. He held her like a child.

Jiang Jin was breathing hard, his face red and stinging from the ferocity of his wife's attack. 'You did nothing but complain all these years that we never had a son!' As if somehow it were all her fault.

She half turned her head towards him. 'That never meant I didn't love our daughter. She was my life. And you've taken both.'

'You shit!' Lao Rong took a step towards him, but a single word from Li stopped him in his tracks.

'Don't.'

The boy looked at him, rage and hurt burning together in his eyes.

'Justice will take its course.'

Wu turned Jiang Jin towards the door.

'Just one question.' Margaret's voice stopped them. 'Why did you put the medals on her eyes?'

Jiang Jin looked at her resentfully. 'I couldn't get them to shut. She kept staring at me, the whole damned night, till I couldn't stand it any longer. Everywhere I went in the room her eyes were following me. In the end, I took the medals from the cabinet to cover them and keep them closed.' He was lost for a moment in the memory of it. 'Didn't do any good though. I knew she was still looking at me. Watching. Wherever she was, her eyes were on me. I could feel them.' A sob caught in his throat. 'I still can.'

\*

Neighbours had gathered in the courtyard of the apartment block to watch with naked curiosity as Jiang Jin was taken away by uniformed public security officers. Li and Margaret stood on the sidewalk with a dejected Lao Rong. Li glanced at him and felt a pang of pity for the boy. 'What did you fight about that night, you and Meilin?'

'I wanted her to run away with me. She wouldn't.'

Margaret said, 'Where would you have gone? How would you have lived?'

'I have an aunt in Datong. And I'd saved money. Enough to get us there, and to live on until I could find work.' He kicked at a loose stone and sent it clattering across the hot tarmac. 'If I'd only known about her father's gambling debt, I could have paid it off myself and she would still be alive.'

Li raised an eyebrow. 'You'd saved that much?' The boy cast him a brief sideways look. 'Where would you have got that kind of money, Rong?'

Now the boy turned dark, sincere eyes on him. 'You don't want to know, Section Chief.'

And Li knew that the boy was right. He didn't.